◆ LAS 国际博雅系列丛书

◆浙江大学外国文学研究丛书

Sentiments and the Rise of Modern Textual Culture

in the British Long Eighteenth Century

情感美学与近代文本文化的兴起

英国漫长的 18 世纪文学文化研究

姜文涛◎著

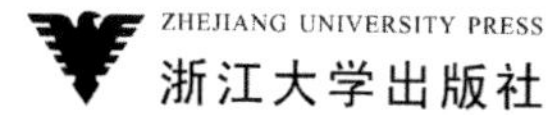

ZHEJIANG UNIVERSITY PRESS
浙江大学出版社

To my family, who are now living in four places of two continents, and to Lu Liu, my sunshine.

Preface

This book investigates a history of representation of emotions in the British long eighteenth century and in the context of a rising textual culture. It does so by tracing the trope of sympathy, which is pervasive in the British eighteenth-century writings such as aesthetic treatises, moral philosophy, and Romantic poetry. Sympathy builds sociality through the communication of feelings and is enacted in the practices of reading, writing and representation, all of which are changing drastically as everyday life is increasingly saturated with textual media. In the process, individual emotions have to be "flattened" (Adam Smith's word) so as to be communicable, while at the same time, literary culture constructs the deep interiority of an emotional self. These developments enable the rise of political economy and psychoanalysis in the nineteenth century. As a historical project, this book is largely organized chronologically. Chapter I outlines a brief etymological history of the inward turn of emotions and sentimentality in the eighteenth-century Britain. Chapter II examines Edmund Burke's aesthetic theory of the sublime. Burke emphasizes the acoustic dimension of words in communicating aesthetic feelings of sympathy. Chapter III analyzes David Hume's moral philosophy of passions. It argues that Hume, by establishing himself as a "man of feeling," attempts to domesticate as individualistic feelings that had been understood as impersonal and contagious. Chapter IV presents the phenomenon of what is called "poetic mediality" in the work of William Wordsworth. Here the oral and acoustic performance of feelings gendered as feminine is poeticized so that scopic desire is generated through the act of reading presented as anthropological speculation. Chapter V explores Adam Smith's moral philosophy of sympathetic sentiment. Smith's definition of a theatrical impartial spectator in a representational economy (in his writings on moral sentiments) makes self analogous to an exchangeable commodity (in his political economy writing) and anticipates the deep (sub)consciousness of interiority in psychoanalytic writings of the late nineteenth century. As an extended comparison and contrast with this Western history, the final chapter turns to examine late imperial Chinese pictorial culture in its imbrication with a "print modern" Chinese Enlightenment discourse of the New Culture Movement, where it argues that the representation of crowds' activities of absorption and theatricality present an emergent form of subjectivity. By traversing divergent genres of writing and different cultural media, this book delineates a genealogy of the emotional self shaped by the material practice of a rising textual culture. It challenges existing versions of more abstract histories of emotion as well as sociological approaches to media studies, both of which present clear and clean histories at the expense of specific and concrete historical practices. Throughout, this book works (1) to explore the rise of visuality through a modern literary medium and how it co-evolves with orality and aurality in representing self; (2) to historicize and thus radicalize the work of writing in the fabrication of interiority; (3) to contribute a comparative approach to historical studies of media and modern literatures.

Acknowledgements

This book comes from my dissertation work conducted at the Department of Comparative Literary and Cultural Studies at the State University of New York at Stony Brook, with potions of it considerably revised. It would not have been possible without the loving support from Professor Ira Livingston (now at Pratt) and Professor Iona Man-Cheong. To me, they are exemplars of what it means to be an intellectual. They are truly the models for me to follow in my intellectual life, and to them, I owe my deepest gratitude. I have benefited enormously from conversations—back then and till now—with Ling Hon Lam (now at Berkeley), which taught me many things on emotion, theatricality and media. My heartfelt thanks also go to Milind Wakankar (now at the Indian Institute of Technology at Delhi), who taught me to read Walter Benjamin and Siegfried Kracauer from standpoints other than the Western, and to Robert Harvey as well, whose meticulous concern and professional spirit are heartily remembered.

My gratitude extends to Clifford Siskin and Mary Poovey, with whom I took two seminars at the English Department of the New York University, and they were germinal for my intellectual thinking upon the British long eighteenth century. So were many things I learned from Kathleen Wilson in the Department of History. Without them, this project would have been much more historically insufficient.

Travels to the University of Glasgow and the Academia Sinica were great helps to my writing. I thank the organizers of the two occasions.

I also thank Don Ihde, Linda Ihde and late Mark Ihde for the time spent in East Setauket.

This book is devoted to my family, now living in four places—Chengdu, Liupanshui, Hangzhou and Madison—of China and the United States. They are the veins of my life. In the last phase of this writing, Lu Liu came into my life, and she has been my sunshine ever since. In the mid-1980s, my uncle Wang Jianfeng—a peasant worker in Beijing and Chengdu for almost three decades now—bought me novels by George Eliot, Charles Dickens, and Standhal from one of the Xinhua Bookstores in Beijing. The literary literacy—one of the themes of this book—that his kindness helped to foster in me is recognized in various venues of my life, intellectual and otherwise.

Table of Contents

Chapter I

Sentiment and Its Inward Turn around the 1740s

I.i. Terminology of Emotion, and Writing as Medium in the Formation of a Metaphysical Selfhood

This current writing takes words like "emotion," "passion," "feeling," "affect," "sensibility," "sympathy," and "sentiment" as interchangeable with each other. This is done intentionally. Historically speaking, "the many names for emotion travel as freely as the emotions themselves" (Pinch 16) and these terms are almost interchangeable in the eighteenth- and nineteenth-century writing. For a perceptual history of the modern selfhood, which is the purpose of this writing, that these terms have in common is much more significant than what differentiates them from each other. Rei Terada in *Feeling in Theory* writes:

> Emotion ... is entangled in the mysteries of consciousness, its history locked inside the classical histories of mind and will ... [and] appears inseparable from expression and subjectivity in the first place, however, its capacity to criticize subjectivity is highly revealing. (Terada 6)[1]

This subtle distinction of "emotion" from other words is significant for this writing, in which emotion and sentiment are more about the

---

[1] For a useful brief discussion on the distinction between "emotion," "feeling," "passion," and "pathos," see Rei Terada, *Feeling in Theory*, pp. 4-5.

configuration of subjectivity in a history of writing as a technology. What remains at stake in this project is more about configuring sensibility in relation to a new mode of inwardness than the difference between different sentiments themselves. In other words, it is about a political economy of emotions in what Clifford Siskin and William Warner recently captures as "a history of mediation" (Siskin and Warner 5) in Western Enlightenment, specifically in the eighteenth century's investment in paper as the medium of circulation and sociality. Marshall McLuhan defines media as "extensions of man" and mediation as "the historically changing sensory and perceptual 'ratios' of human experience" (qtd. in Mitchell and Hansen xii). Following this metaphysical approach to studies of media and mediation, W. J. T. Mitchell and Mark B. N. Hansen recently calls a "techno-anthropological universal sense of media that allow us to range across divides (characteristically triangulated) that are normally left unbroached in media studies: society-technology-aesthetics, empirical-formal-constitutive, social-historical-experiential" (Mitchell and Hansen ix). The contribution of this current writing is to make an investigation upon the inward making of sentimental selfhood in the emergence of textual culture. Issues of sensibility, sentiment, emotion, feeling and affect are examined in their specific relations to a modern print media—what Raymond Williams shorthand as "writing," which, as one of the technological media, is "an ontological condition of humanization—the constitutive operation of exteriorization and invention" (xiii). It is in this historical and theoretical sense that this current writing takes notice of the differences between these terms but do not emphasize them unless it comes under necessary conditions[1].

In what Michel Foucault calls the "Classical age," he defines "natural history" as "nothing more than the nomination of the visible," and during that historical period,

[1] This is a stance similar to that of Rei Terada: "I try to steer a middle course between imposing a single vocabulary on all discussions of texts and giving up on terminological distinctions altogether" (Terada 4).

> what came surreptitiously into being between the age of the theatre [of the Renaissance] and that of the catalogue [of the nineteenth century] was not the desire for knowledge, but a new way of connecting things both to the eye and to discourse. (Foucault 1970: 131-132)

The eighteenth century begins to have a specifically emergent modality of the human body, which "serves as a sort of reservoir for models of visibility, and acts as a spontaneous link between what one can see and what one can say" (135). The knowledge of the human body and psyche is composed in a whole domain of empiricity, at the same time describable and orderable in a totality of representations. In such a historical period, the naturalist Linnaeus defines natural plants as being "a product of number, of form, of proportion, of situation" (qtd. in Foucault 1970: 134). Naming and categorization of natural plants in this way is analogous to the abstract, serialized subject of the market place. In the same epistemological vein, human being also begins to assume a dimension of what Ted Cohen and Paul Guyer calls "impersonal personal" in Kant's aesthetics[1], which is emotively and performatively articulated. This current writing identifies an inward, sensualized, individuated subjectivity coming to a kind of *sensus communis* in the emergence of modern aesthetics[2]. This historical process could be examined in the theoretical light of what Samuel Weber sees in the theatrical "double, or dual, movement" in Martin Heidegger's seminal essay "The Age of the World Picture": "[T]hat of setting things *out in front of* oneself and at the same time bringing things *toward oneself*" (Weber 1996: 78). For Heidegger, "what distinguishes the essence of modernity" (Heidegger 1977: 68) is not merely a priority given to the sense of vision. Instead, it is an "interweaving" of two processes: "[T]hat the world becomes picture and man the subject—which is decisive for the essence of modernity" and that "illuminates the founding process of modern history, a process that, at first sight, seems

---

[1] Ted Cohen and Paul Guyer, Introduction to *Essays in Kant's Aesthetics*, p. 12.

[2] Indeed, this is very Kantian. See Terry Eagleton, *The Ideology of the Aesthetic*, chapter 3.

almost nonsensical" (70). It is a process as follows:

> Whereby the more completely and comprehensively the world, as conquered, stands at man's disposal, and the more objectively the object appears, all the more subjectively (i. e. peremptorily) does the *subiectum* rise up, and all the more inexorably, too, do observations and teachings about the world transform themselves into a doctrine of man, into an anthropology. No wonder that humanism first arises where the world becomes picture. (70)

The increasing grid of subjectivity and inter-subjectivity, sensual, affective and epistemological as well in this "humanism," comes through the eighteenth century with the proliferation of a textual media culture. The technology of modern writing implements an inward as well as outward theatrical turn, a turn influencing what Foucault calls "technologies of self" when modern self co-evolves with commerce, aesthetics and nationalism. This chapter gives a historical context of the discourse of sentiment in the eighteenth century and how it complicates matters like (in)visibility, intelligibility, and forms of exchangeability in "the growing fluidity of social relations[1]" of the century.

Sentimentality is often entangled with the emergence of a modern psychological self. In channeling a circulation of feelings among subjects and objects, brotherhood and otherhood[2], sentiment helps to clarify the liquidity and promiscuity of what is acknowledged as human subjects endowed with increasing inward interiority in the eighteenth century. In that century, sentiments are not yet always lodged within the private, inner lives of individual persons[3]. Rather, they often circulate among persons as somewhat autonomous substances, more as impersonal forces,

---

[1] This phrase is taken from Jean-Christophe Agnew's *Worlds Apart: The Market and the Theatre in Anglo-American Thought, 1550—1750*, p. 59.

[2] A conceptual dichotomy used more in its historical sense by Benjamin Nelson in his *The Idea of Usury: From Tribal Brotherhood to Universal Otherhood*.

[3] Adela Pinch historicizes this inward turn of emotions in the century, which is inspiring for this current writing. See Adela Pinch, *Strange Fits of Passion*.

sometimes contagious, and other times beneficial[1]. Therefore, it comes as no surprise that eighteenth-century accounts of subjectivity, for the concept of which emotion and sentiment occupy an integral part, take subjective events as particularized and observable as phenomenal events. This empirical emphasis upon observation is among what Richard Rorty describes as the rise of epistemology in the seventeenth century. For Rorty, John Locke finds that an analogue of Newton's particle mechanics for "inner space" would somehow be "of great advantage in directing our Thoughts in the search of other Things" and would somehow let us "see, what Objects our Understandings were, or were not fitted to deal with[2]." Regarding this epistemological shift, Mary Poovey observes "that the moral philosopher assumed he could conduct 'experiments' on subjectivity and that the results would simultaneously describe particular events and contribute to systematic knowledge" (Poovey 148) of universal human nature and a philosophy of government[3]. Arguing out of this affective and epistemological reference, this current writing situates an economy of sympathy moving from "(real or supposed) affinity between certain things, by virtue of which they are similarly or correspondingly affected by the same influence, affect or influence each other (esp. in some occult way), or attract or tend toward each other" to that of being more on "relation between two bodily organs or parts such that disorder, or any condition, of the one induces a corresponding condition in the other[4]" in the middle of the eighteenth century. This genealogy of the emotional "technologies of self" is eventually to be individuated and inscribed upon an inward

---

[1] Also see Adela Pinch, *Strange Fits of Passion*, p. 1.

[2] John Locke, *An Essay Concerning Human Understanding*, I, i, 1, and "Epistle to the Reader." For this epistemological turn in the history of modern philosophy as a discipline, see Richard Rorty, *Philosophy and the Mirror of Nature*, chapter 3.

[3] This reminds of what Fredric Jameson argues for a "waning of affect" in our time. See Jameson, *Postmodernism, or, the Logic of Late Capitalism*, p. 10. Especially on pages 15 through 16, when Jameson expresses willingness not "to say that the cultural products of the Postmodern era are utterly devoid of feeling, but rather that such feelings—which it may be better and more accurate, following J.-F. Lyotard, to call 'intensities'—are now free-floating and impersonal and tend to be dominated by a peculiar kind of euphoria."

[4] See *OED* online, under the entry of "sympathy."

"psychosis[1]" in the end of the century. That economy of emotionality and interiority, in turn, pre-mediates the rise of psychoanalysis as a rigorous human science in the end of the nineteenth century as if out of historical necessity[2]. At the same time, like two sides of the same coin, this highly emotionalized individuality requires an exchangeable political economy to maintain a new form of sociality, which includes "the nature of social identity, intentionality, accountability, transparency and reciprocity—the who, what, when, where, and why of exchange" (Agnew 9-10), as historian Jean-Christophe Agnew puts it[3]. This current writing historicizes how *writing* as a communicative technology occupies a very significant position in this shift of interiorizing emotionalism and increasing exchangeability[4]. Whereas voice, as part of the oral culture, makes the members of the audience into a unity, silent reading—as consequential to a proliferating print media culture—makes each reader enter his or her own private inner world. As a result, it shatters the unity of the audience[5]. Modern print media helps to textualize perceptions more into a visual sub-class of representations. Heidegger, Foucault, Hacking and Wellbery take representation as a fundamental category of thought in the eighteenth century[6]. Following this critical literature, this current writing historicizes a new form of self, performance, and subjectivity in mediation as an emergent notion and a

---

[1] Similar to what David E. Wellbery discusses the concept of "soul" in relation to "representations" in the German aesthetic theory by Christian Wolff (1679—1754). See David E. Wellbery, *Lessing's "Laocoon,"* pp. 9-42.

[2] Also see Mary Poovey, *A History of the Modern Fact*, p. 148.

[3] For the argument that the medieval notion of "the individual" is distinct from the modern notion of the "individual subject," see Timothy J. Reiss, *The Discourse of Modernism*, chapter 2; see, generally, chapter 1, on the passage from pre-modern "patterning" to a modern discourse of "analytico-referentiality."

[4] For how writing effects a radically dramatized self in our modern society, see Raymond Williams, *Writing in Society*, pp. 1-10.

[5] See Walter J. Ong, *Orality and Literacy: The Technologizing of the Word,* p. 74.

[6] See Heidegger, "The Age of the World Picture;" Michel Foucault, *The Order of Things,* pp. 46-124; Ian Hacking, *Why Does Language Matter to Philosophy?*, pp. 15-53, 163-170; David E. Wellbery, *Lessing's "Laocoon,"* pp. 9-17. The rise of representation could also be seen as part of the epistemological shift from the seventeenth century, see Richard Rorty, *Philosophy and the Mirror of Nature*, chapter 3.

matrix of practices made possible through modern textual culture. This modern theatricalized selfhood ascends up several layers of artification, partakes of the systems of nature and culture, thereby brings a crucible wherein new social and cultural forms of exchange could be tested and tempered, specifically the marketplace questions of identity, transparency, and accountability. This gives rise to a modern economy of the perceptual and sensorial in what Jonathan Crary historicizes as "the progressive parcelization and division of the body into separate and specific systems and functions" (Crary 1990: 79) in the first half of the nineteenth century.

One example that illustrates the relation between language and emotional subjectivity addressed here comes at hand from a politically feminist history of the British novel. According to Nancy Armstrong, the modern female subject is engendered by the male. In her political history of the novel, the relation between the sentimental affect and the social template for the human is configured in a visual sense. She reads the rape of Pamela by Mr. B in Richardson's novel *Pamela*, which was published almost two decades before Burke and Smith, as a male attempt to penetrate a servant girl's body that "magically transforms that body into one of language and emotion, into a metaphysical object that can be acquired only through her consent and his willingness to adhere to the procedures of modern love" (Armstrong 1987: 6). When Mr. B forcibly takes possession of Pamela's letters, we see the reappearance of erotic desire transferring from Pamela's body to her words:

> Artful slut! Said he—What's this to my question?—Are they [the letters] not *about* you?—If, said I, I must pluck them out of my hiding-place behind the wainscot, won't you see me?—Still more and more artful! Said he—Is this an answer to my question?—I have searched every place above, and in your closet, for them, and cannot find them; so I *will* know where they are. Now, said he, it is my opinion they are about you; and I never undressed a girl in my life; but I will now begin to strip my pretty Pamela. (Richardson 245)

As he proceeds, Pamela capitulates and delivers up what he desires.

Richardson thus displaces the conventionally desirable woman onto a written one, and infuses the new body with erotic appeal. "The pleasure she now offers is the pleasure of the text rather than those forms of pleasure that derive from mastering her body" (6), Armstrong writes. For her, sentimentality (here of love and sexual desire) is textualized into a web of productions, which explains why "at the inception of modern culture, the literate classes in England suddenly developed an unprecedented state for writing for, about, and by women" (Armstrong 1987: 7). In turn, the proliferation of sentiment promoted by "writing for, about, and by women," the "first and foremost" modern individual, is responsible for "the majority of eighteenth-century novels" (7-8). Mr. B. is configured into a reformed novel reader of sentimental novels. He learns to love Pamela not as an "object of desire" but for her "female sentimentality" (117). Thus, a linguistic and emotional text pushed into being through physical violence has generated a specter-like gendered life of its own that started from the emergence of modern mass media, specifically print media of the novel[1]. William Warner states the case more schematically:

> It is at this point that English readers start engaging in the sort of sympathetic identification with and critical judgment of fictional characters that will lie at the center of novel reading from Richardson, Fielding, and Frances Burney through Jane Austen, George Eliot, and Henry James. (Warner 223)[2]

Such spectrality of subjectivity in "mediatic articulation" (to use Samuel Weber's phrase) comes to host female "individuals" as *dividuals*, making female subjectivity as mediated in between the screens of

---

[1] For how the British novel is part of modern mass media, and the rise of the British realism is a gendering process, see William Warner, *Licensing Entertainment: The Elevation of Novel Reading in Britain, 1684—1750.*

[2] Also see William Warner, *Licensing Entertainment: The Elevation of Novel Reading in Britain, 1684—1750*, p. 224, note 21.

writing[1]. Nancy Armstrong argues:

> It was first only women who were defined in terms of their emotional natures. Men generally retained their political identity in writing that developed the qualities of female subjectivity and made subjectivity a female domain. (Armstrong 1987: 4)[2]

Following this point, it is significant to take this first developed female subjectivity as what Samuel Weber defines as the first case where we see a loss of individuality consequential upon modern modes of inscription from modern media such as television, radio, film, and writing:

> As a 'host of spirits,' individuals do not merely cease to exist: they persist, but as dividuals, divided between life and death, spectator and actor, strange and familiar, entering an alien body and soul on the one hand, while on the other remaining sufficiently detached to see themselves taking leave of their selves (rather than of their 'senses'). The individual thus altered is here and there at once, and consequently can be neither exclusively here nor there, neither simply itself or simply other. This impossible 'situation' splits the site itself, rendering it something like a ghost of itself, lacking an authentic place or a proper body. (Weber 2004: 42)

The coming of modern mass media culture, of which writing and literature is their first case, enhances inscriptions between different

---

[1] Weber's interest is more than the technology of reading and writing, also including television, radio and film. His theoretical focus is rather the ways in which modes of inscription are media—the linkage between media "infiltrating" the lines of demarcation by which they are traditionally defined and thereby exposing them as "inscribed in, and as, a network" (Weber 2004: 3). This "mediatic articulation" means that the concatenations of "mediatic articulation" cross the border that is supposed to separate the modern mass media from what has come before, "upsetting" and "dislocating," as Weber says, the commonly held notion of their "radical distinctiveness" (2). Samuel Weber, *Mass Mediauras: Form, Technics, Media.*

[2] This argument has inspired my *media* investigation upon William Wordsworth's "poetic mediality" in this current writing.

media, establishes spaces for crossing boundaries, and thus conflates concatenations of situations engendering spectrality of selfhood. This current writing tries to give a social history of textual media culture, and to suggest how a self-willing discipline and regulation of the spectrality and theatricality of modern selfhood is made possible because of this culture.

Specifically, in this historical period of media transition from an oral and scribal to a print society in Europe[1], a textual economy of feelings, emotions and sensibilities come to occupy a more prominent position. This change remains coterminous if not directly caused by the rise of a textual media culture and the profound changes in modes of visuality that come along with it. Excessive (re)productions of words, images, sounds and the easily wide dissemination of the media system ferment "strange fits of passion"—to use half a line from one of William Wordsworth's "Lucy Poems," which invites anatomies of passions and physiognomies[2]. This current writing situates Adam Smith's political economy of moral sentiments through sympathy as a later part of the textual and literary taming technology[3] to neutralize these "passions" and make them representable. Issues of otherness to lived experience, authenticity and insincerity of selfhood are thus interwoven with "the nature of social identity, intentionality, accountability, transparency and

---

[1] Indeed, the mid-eighteenth century has been well defined as the period in which this media shift happened. See, for instance, Alvin Kernan, *Samuel Johnson and the Impact of Print*, p. 4. For a recent more sociological history of reading, see William St Clair, *The Reading Nation in the Romantic Period.*

[2] As Adela Pinch writes: "Eighteenth- and early nineteenth-century writers seek after the origins and locations of feelings; as they try to pin feelings down, I shall argue, they often discover that one's feelings may not really be one's own" (Pinch 3). We will return to this point later. Robert Southey, a harsh critic of the practice of physiognomy, surveyed the galley slaves "with a physiognomic eye to see if they differed from the rest of the people," once he visited Lisbon. See "Marginal Practices" by Patricia Fara in *The Cambridge History of Science: Eighteenth-Century Science*, p. 495.

[3] Regarding how "literature" was an "engine" of social change, and categorized as "aesthetic" in the second half of the eighteenth century, see Paul Keen, "Preface," in *Revolutions in Romantic Literature: An Anthology of Print Culture, 1780—1832*, p. xvi. For "aesthetic" as a political "distribution of the sensible," see Jacques Rancière, *The Politics of Aesthetics*, pp. 12-19.

reciprocity." This transparent exchangeability remains analogous to properties of commodities in modern society.

I.ii. Etymological History of Sentiment and Its Inward Turn in the Eighteenth Century as a Discourse of Sensibility

An etymological inquiry of the word "sentiment" in the direction to its theatrical relation with textual medium would help to understand how it was an external entity to obtain a somatic existence as a placeholder of modern individual interiority or subjectivity. It remains useful to bear in mind the moment of textual engendering in the history of female subject as illustrated by Nancy Armstrong, a point that will be touched upon regarding aesthetics throughout the current writing. The word "sentiment" and its cognates, the vocabulary of sentience, that is, revolve around the distinction between body, mind, and soul. It "alludes to process (how one senses), power (the capacity or delicacy of the senses), and product (the impressions produced by or the results of thinking and feeling)" (Festa 17), as Lynn Festa writes. In the middle of the eighteenth century, a significant semantic shift occurred to this vocabulary of sentiment. Samuel Johnson's 1755 *Dictionary* defines "sentiment" as "thought, notion, opinion" and rather awkwardly as "the sense considered distinctly from the language or things; a striking sentence in a composition." It is more about the "product" part, extraneous to either the process or the sentient power that brings it into being at the first place. The second entry of Johnson's explicitly states that it is a perception disjoined from words or objects. The lexicographer Johnson does not trouble himself to explain either what makes a sentence striking (and thereby has given the sentence "in a composition" rhetoric power) or what possible affective modes of the subject could originate from the "thought, notion, opinion." Lynn Festa regards Johnsonian "sentiment" as "a portmanteau for discrete and self-contained notions, aloof from the messiness of the senses and even the looseness of language" (19). It is not loaded with any tenuous process or effect of the inward affect. Rather its being "discrete and self-contained" entities ensures a freedom of movements between words, objects and bodies, the historical context of which agrees with Adela Pinch's argument[1]. One can discern a similar property in Johnson's definition of emotion: "disturbance of mind; vehemence of passion, or pleasing or painful." This is more about the intensity of movements and what this does to the mind (not the heart) than any specific affect like envy, irritation, anxiety or paranoia. It stays with the classical etymological origin of the word "emotion," which "stems from the Latin, *e* + *movere*," originally meaning "'to move out,' 'to migrate,' or 'to transport an object[2].'" Thus what Julie Ellison's terminology of "the itinerary of feeling" (1) would almost appear tautological in that historical period. Raymond Williams traces it right when defining "sentiment" as used for "physical feeling" and "both opinion and emotion" from the fourteenth to the seventeenth centuries (Williams 1976: 281). The adjective "physical" appends a descriptive limiter to feeling, opinion and emotion, which are natural, tangible and concrete. The affective or subjective self is still in motion and inter-subjective. Through the eighteenth century sentiment begins to be more closely associated with sensibility, leaning more to the process and power of feelings. Or, to use Williams' words: "a conscious openness to feelings, and also a conscious consumption of feelings" (281). It may not be exaggerating to rephrase it as "a conspicuous consumption of feelings," to appropriate twentieth-century American economist Thorstein Veblen's concept on economics[3]. At least a conspicuous consumption of the "sentimental," at least for some people. Raymond Williams quotes a Lady Bradshaugh in 1749: "[S]entimental, so much in vogue among the polite .... Everything clever and agreeable is comprehended in that word ... a sentimental man ... a sentimental party ... a sentimental walk" (qtd. in Williams 1976: 281).

Indeed, feeling was such a compelling subject central to both

---

[1] See Adela Pinch, *Strange Fits of Passion*.

[2] James R. Averill, "Inner Feelings, Works of the Flesh, the Beast Within, Diseases of the Mind, Driving Force, and Putting On a Show: Six Metaphors of Emotion and Their Theoretical Extensions," in *Metaphors in the History of Psychology*, p. 107.

[3] See Veblen, *The Theory of the Leisure Class*.

aesthetics and social experience that Samuel Johnson regards that attempts "to trace the passions to their sources" constituted "the fashionable study[1]" of his time. In Jeremy Bentham's 1781 *Introduction to the Principles of Morals and Legislation*[2], "sensibility" appears such an important factor to consider that Bentham lists thirty-two categories of causes that will affect different circumstances, hence influence sensibility, and therefore call for specific gradations of penal punishment. On this list there are such items as "moral sensibility," "religious sensibility," "sympathetic sensibility," "sympathetic biases," "antipathetic sensibility," "antipathetic biases," "connexions in the way of sympathy," "connexions in the way of antipathy[3]." Several decades later, the French literary critic Hippolyte Taine detects in the writings of Defoe, Addison, and Steele as the inward and reflective turn in his *Histoire de la littérature anglaise* (1864):

> Two features are common and proper to [these books]. All these novels are character novels. Englishmen, more reflective than others, more inclined to the melancholy pleasure of concentrated attention and inner examination, find around them human medals more vigorously struck, less worn by friction with the world, whose uninjured face is more visible than that of others. (qtd. in Warner 28)

Nevertheless, it is not painted yet as against either Bentham or Taine who feel "too much" or those who "indulge their emotions." The conservative poet Robert Southey's "the sentimental classes, persons of ardent or morbid sensibility" in 1823 (qtd. in Williams 1976: 282) have not come into historical beings yet. This mode of excess in sensibility

---

[1] S. Johnson, "Preface to Shakespeare," cited by Christopher Fox in his *Psychology and Literature in the Eighteenth Century*, p. 1.

[2] *Introduction* was undertaken in the 1770s as part of a plan for huge work. Mary P. Mack says that "Bentham wrote thousands of practice pages between 1769 and 1781. Some of them were incorporated in *The Principles of Morals*, printed in 1780, which was itself only a small fragment of his monumental plan to analyze the entire structure of law" (Mack 130).

[3] See John B. Bender, *Imagining the Penitentiary*, p. 269, note 53.

and its integrated necessity of cleansing have to wait till the coming of a considerable saturation of mass media, including a mature division of labour in the writing technology[1].

The eighteenth-century story is an "Age of Sensibility," to use a label well defined by Northrop Frye several decades ago[2]. The era of sensibility, sometimes, is extended from the end of the seventeenth century into the beginning of the nineteenth[3]. Jerome McGann argues that the term "sensibility" clings to the early decades of the eighteenth century while "sentiment" has attached itself to a second, later phase. McGann wants to keep sensibility "the more primitive of the two," which affiliated with instinct and the body. Sentimentality is elevated to "a sophisticated acquirement, a sympathetic understanding gained through complex acts of conscious attention and reflection" (McGann 1996: 7-8, 63). For Julie Ellison, sensibility as a cultural ethos manifests itself earlier than we think. Its first appearance was probably in the late seventeenth-century civic prestige and mutual friendship practiced by men of equally high social status. With a key historical shift occurring around 1713, it became from then of "transactions between socially equal persons toward scenarios of inequality" (Ellison 6, 9). Ellison does not see any significant difference between sensibility in the first

---

[1] For a similar "cleansing" strategy that occurs in another media—French painting, that is—in the age of Diderot, see Michael Fried, *Absorption and Theatricality*; for how this happens in a media history of the British novel, see William Warner, *Licensing Entertainment: The Elevation of Novel Reading in Britain, 1684—1750*. As a matter of fact, the classes of people with "too much sentimentality" or "ardent or morbid sensibility" seems to be an undefined antagonist, for which Fried designates "theatrical"—what Jon P. Klancher defines as "the stances of both radical rhetoric and mass-cultural display," and "it is worth pointing out that theorists of this *kind* of reader/spectator nearly always fabricate a hybrid antagonist, composedly equally of radical discourse and mass culture" (191). For Klancher, this *kind* of theorists includes Samuel T. Coleridge, see chapter 5 in *The Making of English Reading Audiences, 1790—1832* for his discussion. This tactic is indeed—as Jon P. Klancher points out—throughout media culture, whether literature or otherwise, see Jon P. Klancher, p. 191, note 46. For a Chinese case regarding the historical development of a musical medium *Qin*, see Ronald Egan, "The Controversy over Music and 'Sadness' and Changing Conceptions of the *Qin* in Middle Period China." I thank Professor Ling Hon Lam for this reading.

[2] See Northrop Frye, "Towards Defining an Age of Sensibility."

[3] See Adela Pinch, *Strange Fits of Passion*, pp. 1-16.

half of the century and Adam Smith's "moral sentiment" later on[1]. Janet Todd identifies sentimental literature's heyday as the period from 1740 to 1770. For her, Smith's *Theory of Moral Sentiments* was the "end to a line of British moral philosophy" that admitted "the sentimental aim of trying systematically to link morality and emotion" (27). The discourse of sentiment and sensibility seemed to have passed what Foucault would call a "threshold of epistemologization[2]" in the middle of the eighteenth century. Its cognates, for instance emotion, begin to allude to "specific affect originating from within" (Festa 29). Another critic Amelie Oksenberg Rorty argues that during the period from Descartes to Rousseau, emotions change from "reactions to invasions from something external to the self" into "the very activities of the mind, its own motions ... and along with desires, the beginnings of actions" (qtd. in Festa 19). Similarly, the waywardness and vagrancy of English feelings turns inward, more integrated into the body with its association of the process and the power. The 1783 revision of Chambers's 1728 *Cyclopaedia* explicitly articulates this change:

> [T]he word *sentiment*, in its true and old English sense, signifies a formed opinion, notion, or principle; but of late years, it has been much used by some writers to denote an internal impulse of passion, affection, fancy, or intellect, which is to be considered rather as the cause or occasion of our forming an opinion, than as the real opinion itself. (qtd. in Festa 19)

Sentiment becomes more associated with sensibility in its modern use of *awareness* and the ability to feel[3]. Through the middle of the eighteenth century, its social currency may have been experiencing a

---

[1] See Julie Ellison, *Cato's Tears and the Making of Anglo-American Emotion*. p. 6.

[2] See Michel Foucault, *The Archaeology of Knowledge and the Discourse on Language*, in particular chapter 6, "Science and Knowledge," with its elucidation of several thresholds of emergence of a "discursive formation": the thresholds of positivity, epistemologization, scientificity, and formalization (186-187). For Foucault, these are events whose dispersion is anything but evolutive, which is where his critical archaeological spirit lies.

[3] Also see Raymond Williams, *Keywords*, p. 281.

great change in the economy of its concept, analyses, and demonstrations. In the middle of the century, David Hume defines sympathy as the means by which sentiments were communicated, and "the psychological and emotive transaction which placed them at the heart of social life" (Chandler 2009: 22):

> No quality of human nature is more remarkable, both in itself and its consequences, than that propensity we have to sympathize with others, and to receive by communication their inclinations and sentiments, however different from, or even contrary to our own. (Hume 1978: 316)

By the end of the century, sensibility becomes the capacity to feel and transact sympathy. According to *The Monthly Magazine*, it was "that peculiar structure, or habitude of mind, which disposes a man to be easily moved, and powerfully affected, by surrounding objects and passing events[1]." This discursive phenomenon complicates itself with several realms that seem disparate for decades. G. S. Rousseau suggests this into a list of issues:

> [T]he cults of melancholy, hypochondria as a national institution, the "English Malady," as Cheyne called it, Richardson's novel of sentiment, later on the well-formed and mature "man of feeling," Sterne's bizarre variations and subtle alterations on this theme, the eighteenth century's eventual attack on all forms of sentiment as fake. (Rousseau 151)[2]

The current writing situates the proliferation and inward turn of sentiment and sensibility in a period when literature "moved from a reptilian Classicism, all cold and dry reason, to a mammalian Romanticism, all warm and wet feeling[3]." The transitional period from

---

[1] *The Monthly Magazine*, 1796, 2 (October): 706, quoted in James Chandler, "Sentiment and Sensibility," p. 22.

[2] Also see Samuel H. Monk, *The Sublime*, pp. 45, 49.

[3] See Northrop Frye, "Towards Defining an Age of Sensibility," p. 144.

the rhetorical and scribal culture into a modern textual media culture of the eighteenth century witnessed "the decisive popular fusion of sensibility and taste," and "the emotional susceptibility was allied to aesthetic expression" (Ellison 6). It is not an exaggeration to argue that sensibility constitutes the emergent "science of man"—"human passions" David Hume—from the late seventeenth century through the British Enlightenment and beyond[1].

I.iii. Sentimentality, and Its Relevance with the Rise of Visuality Discourse in the Epistemological Shift

The argument of this section is that the inwardness[2] of feelings, sentiments and sensibility historically co-evolves with a long scopic tradition of vision that exists "in some sense continuous, for instance, from Plato to the present, or from the quattrocento into the late nineteenth century" (Crary 1990: 25-26). The possibility of a discourse of sentimentalization cannot dispense with the rise of visuality. These two issues complement each other, and present themselves respectively in the form of psychoanalytical and social self long existent in Western modernity.

The rise of modern visuality mainly refers to the increasing significance of the visual regime of *camera obscura* from the fifteenth century on, which is often captured as the Cartesian perspectivalism[3]. If modernity has been "dominated by the sense of sight in a way that set it apart from its pre-modern predecessors and possibly its postmodern

---

[1] See G. S. Rousseau, "Nerves, Spirits, and Fibres," in which he defines John Locke's publication of *An Essay Concerning Human Understanding* (1690) as the first to deal with this "science of man", influential to at least three subsequent generations of moral scientists: Mandeville, Shaftesbury, Hume, Adam Smith, La Mettrie, the *philosophes*, and dozens of others. Rousseau's methodology of doing an intellectual history regarding this key problematic is followed in this current writing, however.

[2] For a speculation upon the difference between "inwardness" and "interiority," see Stephen Toulmin's fine essay, "The Inwardness of Mental Life."

[3] See essays collected in *Vision and Visuality*, especially Martin Jay, "Scopic Regimes of Modernity," pp. 3-23.

successor" (Jay 1988: 3), this ocular-centric perceptual mode cannot be achieved without the invention of modern print medium, as works of McLuhan, Ong and Eisenstein convincingly suggest[1]. It makes no historical sense to take the visual mode of *camera obscura*—specifically the invention of linear perspective in the fifteenth century—as a single apparatus. The economy of disciplining and regulating the status of an observer and its tangent forms of subjectivity co-evolves with many other issues of the long period of several centuries. Critical theorist Giorgio Agamben justifies the methodology of *paradigm* that has been reflected in his and Foucault's works on archaeology of knowledge. For him,

> joining Aristotle's observations with those of Kant, that a paradigm entails a movement that goes from singularity to singularity and, without ever leaving singularity, transforms every singular case into an *exemplar* of a general rule that can never be stated a priori. (Agamben 2009b: 22)

The method of *paradigm* for Agamben is not the way Thomas Kuhn used in his historical study of science, and is dated back to Plato and Aristotle by Agamben. This method "is a singular case that is isolated from its context only insofar as, by exhibiting its own singularity, it makes intelligible a new ensemble, whose homogeneity it itself constitutes" (18). Following Agamben's methodology on the relation between paradigm and exemplarity, this section takes the inward turn of sentiment and sensibility along with the predominant model of perception of *camera obscura* in the seventeenth and eighteenth centuries, which was "fundamentally nonreflexive, visual and quantitative," as Donald M. Lowe concludes[2]. It examines how a new stage of organization of subjectivity is reached as effective to the entire

---

[1] See Marshall McLuhan, *Understanding Media: The Extensions of Man*; Walter J. Ong, *The Presence of the Word: Some Prolegomena for Cultural and Religious History*; Elizabeth L. Eisenstein, *The Printing Press as an Agent of Change: Communications and Cultural Transformations in Early Modern Europe*.

[2] See Donald M. Lowe, *History of Bourgeois Perception*, p. 26.

economy of the perceptual, affective and cognitive. David E. Wellbery argues:

> Aesthetics, in its emergence as an independent philosophical discipline in the eighteenth century, is a *representational* theory; that is, the organizing model that lends this theory-type its character depicts the aesthetic field in terms of the category of representation. (Wellbery 1984: 44)

Modern aesthetics and representation are an emergent discursive formation closely related to a shift in perception, mediation of the sensible and epistemology in general, of which the modern mode of visuality forms a part. Foucault writes that "observation" in the last two centuries is "a perceptible knowledge," and it "leaves sight with an almost exclusive privilege, being the sense by which we perceive extent and establish proof, and, in consequence, the means to an analysis *partes extra partes* acceptable to everyone" (Foucault 1970: 132-133). What this observation and practice of visuality valorize are "the appearance of its screened objects: lines, surfaces, forms, reliefs" (133). If visuality is not the exclusive way of organizing knowledge[1], it becomes a significant episteme in talking about what Heidegger categorizes as "the projection of the objectivity of whatever it is" since the Renaissance. Foucault defines this as "a mode that was to be considered as positive, as objective, as that of natural history" (131) in the nineteenth century. This epistemic desire of "tabulation of things" (131) in Western Enlightenment finds its fullest expressions in the pages of the *Encyclopédie*, a way of organizing knowledge made possible by a print media culture. The great project of this thought is an exhaustive ordering of the world characterized by

> discovery of simple elements and their progressive combination; and at their center they form a table on which knowledge is

[1] See Jonathan Crary, *Techniques of the Observer*, chapter 2. Of course, visuality could never be the exclusive epistemological mode. For instance, the tradition of hermeneutics is resolutely tied to aural experience. See Martin Jay, *Downcast Eyes: The Denigration of Vision in Twentieth-Century French Thought*, pp. 105-108.

> displayed contemporary with itself. The center of knowledge in the seventeenth and eighteenth centuries is the table. (Foucault 1970: 74-75)

It is in this sense that the thought of the eighteenth century is, as Foucault says, "through and through a philosophy of the sign," and it formulates a new relation of object and subject. This "tabulation of things" in the visual modality, which is a semi-technology of documentation, provides a site of cultural labor, a body of textual formations that has to be worked through interminably, *ad infinitum*.

It is an epistemology of "imprinting," which as John Locke says, "if it signifies anything, being nothing else, but the making certain Truths to be perceived. For to imprint anything on the Mind without the Mind's perceiving it, seems to me hardly intelligible[1]." In Richard Rorty's words:

> It is as if the *tabula rasa* were perpetually under the gaze of the unblinking Eye of the Mind—nothing, as Descartes said, being nearer to the mind than itself ... it becomes obvious that the imprinting is of less interest than the observation of the imprint—all the knowing gets done, so to speak, by the Eye which observes the imprinted tablet, rather than by the tablet itself. (Rorty 143-144)

Knowledge of self is immediately hinged upon a self observing upon the mediation between the internal and the external. The visual perception directly participates into an epistemological construction of a selfhood. Jonathan Crary points out that perhaps the most famous image of the *camera obscura* is in Locke's *An Essay Concerning Human Understanding* written one decade before the eighteenth century[2]:

> External and internal sensations are the only passages that I can find of knowledge to the understanding. These alone, as far as I can

---

[1] See John Locke, *An Essay Concerning Human Understanding*, I, ii, 5.
[2] See Jonathan Crary, *Techniques of the Observer*, pp. 41-42.

> discover, are the windows by which light is let into this *dark room*. For, methinks, the understanding is not much unlike a closet wholly shut from light, with only some little opening left ... to let in external visible resemblances, or some idea of things without; would the pictures coming into such a dark room but stay there and lie so orderly as to be found upon occasion it would very much resemble the understanding of a man[1].

This becomes a predominant *apparatus* epistemological as well as perceptual through the eighteenth century. A strong sense of introspection is projected as a salient feature in this visualization of the spatial and perceptual operations of the intellect. The significant function of the mind's eye lies in its transparent and decorporealized mediation for an observer isolated, enclosed, and autonomous within the dark confines of the *camera obscura* operation[2]. The eye, as metonymical of the human subject, is prevented from having any capability of self-representation as both subject and object. The positioning of the body is marginalized into an invisible spectral non-existence so that an objective imprinting and representation could ensue. One could identify this as a case of what David Wellbery names as "the principle of transparency" (Wellbery, 1984: 72) in the representational aesthetic theory of the Enlightenment. This transparency economy effaces any possibility of a reflecting self-reflection[3] for the purpose of objective "tabulation of things" before human beings becomes an event in the order of knowledge in the nineteenth century[4]. In the British context under discussion through this writing, it is reflected in the aesthetic disinterestedness as "a major watershed in the history of aesthetics" (Stolnitz 138). This emergence of modern aesthetics is first suggested in the first decade of the eighteenth century by Lord Shaftesbury, which opposes "the desire to possess or

---

[1] John Locke, *An Essay Concerning Human Understanding*, II, xi, 17.

[2] See Jonathan Crary, *Techniques of the Observer*, p. 39.

[3] Also see Jacques Lacan, *The Four Fundamental Concepts of Psycho-Analysis*, p. 81.

[4] Of course, this is a Foucauldian formula, see specifically the last two chapters "Man and His Doubles" and "The Human Sciences" in his *The Order of Things: An Archaeology of the Human Sciences*.

use the object" (Stolnitz 134). It becomes, by the middle of the century, a staple in British thought. Inhibiting any action on behalf of the self, this positions a subject as "a spectator rather than an agent," whose "involvement is controlled and tempered by the detachment of selflessness" (136). Thus, the visual mode of *camera obscura* as an epistemology seems to be a paradigmatic[1] resolution of what Edmund Husserl defines as the major philosophical problem starting from the seventeenth century: "How a philosophizing which seeks its ultimate foundations in the subjective ... can claim an objective 'true' and metaphysically transcendent validity[2]."

It is not far-fetched to read this increasing predominance and prevalence of the *camera obscura* reflecting what Juri M. Lotman's characterization of the Enlightenment as a "battle against the sign[3]." During this battle, language is desacralized, extricated from its place within the ceremonies of religious and absolutist authority, and transformed into a medium of communication and debate among equal subjects. Language and representation become a medium of exchange, that is. At the same time, this also "impels a kind of *askesis*, or withdrawal from the world, in order to regulate and purify one's relation to the manifold contents of the now 'exterior' world" (Crary 1990: 39). Indeed, there exists a historical connection between such an observational empiricist theory of knowledge and what Adela Pinch terms as "emotional extravagance" (3) in the eighteenth century: "extravagance" both in the sense of "that which strays beyond boundaries" and "excessive, lavish, unrestrained emotionality, or sentimentality" (3, 4). This connection leads to the rise of individuality through an epistemological confinement towards its physical and sensory experience, and it is summarized aptly by Nietzsche in *The Will to Power*: "The senses deceive, reason corrects the errors; consequently,

---

[1] "Paradigm" here is taken as meaning what is advocated through Michel Foucault and Giorgio Agamben's archaeological writings. See Agamben (2009), "What Is a Paradigm?."

[2] Edmund Husserl, *The Crisis of European Science and Transcendental Phenomenology*, p. 81. Quoted in Jonathan Crary, *Techniques of the Observer*, p. 41.

[3] Quoted in David E. Wellbery, *Lessing's "Laocoon,"* p. 36.

one concluded, reason is the road to the constant; the least sensual ideas must be closest to the 'true world.'—It is from the senses that most misfortunes come—they are deceivers, deluders, destroyers" (317)[1]. Martin Heidegger calls this "the necessary interplay between subjectivism and objectivism" (66) in the modern anthropology of man. This current writing argues that this paradox of Western modernity could be approached through a critical history of mediation and media study, and it is significant for another emergent media shift.

I.iv. Sympathy as Moral Sentiment, Interiority, and Exchange of Things (and Personae)

It is in this cluster of problems that we situate theories of sentiments in their relations to a history of media. This includes mediation or immediacy in communication, inward and external manifestations of feeling, theatricality of sympathy in structuring a self and a world. What can sympathy, if seen from "the convergence of capitalism and print technology" (Anderson 1991: 46)[2], tell us about the "distribution of the sensible" (to use Jacques Rancière's phrase) and representation of self in this receding episteme of "tabulation of things" (to use Foucault's concept)? How does the capability of sympathy configure into modern human body and intellect? What is the relation between emotional economy and an emergent aesthetics of exchangeability in what Foucault names as "the construction of an empirico-transcendental doublet" of human beings[3]? What theatrical stances—presence or absence—do different forms of humans take at a critical point in the history of global, systematized communication? These epistemological questions are what this writing tries to engage in a historical investigation upon a rising textual media culture.

In the eighteenth century, the writings of the empiricists bring

---

[1] Quoted in Jonathan Crary, *Techniques of the Observer*, p. 40.

[2] Of course, this is Benedict Anderson's central argument regarding the emergence of nationalism in its modern form.

[3] See Michel Foucault, *The Order of Things*, chapter 9, "Man and His Doublets."

feeling "closer to epistemological matters: empiricism allows emotion to be a way of knowing" (Pinch 18-19). Adela Pinch argues that "almost all eighteenth-century thinking about feeling ... concerns the relationship between its epistemological and ontological status, and its social character" (18-19). It differs from the early modern thought of all emotional experience under the heading of "the passions," and "nor only as innate, natural forces tied closely to the body but also as the essence of volition" (18). A reaction towards the Cartesian category of emotion as volition is found in John Locke, who writes in the last decade of the seventeenth century that "*desiring* and *willing* are two distinct *Acts* of the mind; and consequently that the *Will*, which is but the power of *Volition*, is much more distinct from *Desire*" (italicized sic) (250). Adela Pinch identifies a fundamental shift of feelings and emotions, which is separable from the negative pictures of "the passions as fundamentally destructive and in need of restraint" (18) by the seventeenth-century political theorists. Following Pinch's historical argument, this current writing situates this shift in the historical period when "circulation becomes one of the fundamental categories of analysis" (Foucault 1970: 179). David Hume calls "sympathy" "a *communication of sentiments*[1]" (italicized sic), and it suggests more volatile movement of feelings between persons than sensibility. The prevalence of a sympathy trope in the eighteenth century indicates the increasing mobility of feelings among subjects, objects, places, which occurs within a system of signs and a table of identities and differences. It builds affective affinities between circulating commercial markets, credit, public opinions as acting at great distances in the modern system of exchanges. David Hume the moral philosopher captures this social nature of people's ability to feel other people's feelings in this way:

> The minds of all men are similar in their feelings and operations, nor can any one be actuated by any affection, of which all others are not, in some degree, susceptible. As in strings equally wound up, the

[1] David Hume, *A Treatise of Human Nature*, p. 324.

> motion of one communicates itself to the rest; so all the affections readily pass from one person to another, and beget correspondent movements in every human creature. (Hume 1978: 575-576)

In chapter 7, the first volume of his sentimental novel *The Life and Opinions of Tristram Shandy (1759—1767)*, Laurence Sterne describes a village midwife, who, as

> she had all along trusted little to her own efforts, and a great deal to those of dame nature, —had acquired, in her way, no small degree of reputation in the world; —by which word world, need I in this place inform your worship, that I would be understood to mean no more of it, than a small circle described upon the circle of the great world, of four English miles diameter, or thereabouts, of which the cottage where the good old woman lived, is supposed to be the center. (Sterne 10)

The additional proclamation of a provincial English parameter of four miles indicates a world much beyond the local midwife's reputation, whose existence Sterne's readership is obliged to imagine and anticipate. The world is so obviously global that Sterne's message of irony could be easily missed. His French translator hastened in 1776 to add a footnote:

> But do not be fooled: it was not the whole world. She was not known, for example, among the Hottentot and Dutch women of the Cape of Good Hope, who are said to give birth like Mother Nature. The world to her was but a small circle. (qtd. in Festa 1)

Indeed, the eighteenth century is one of striking growth in Britain's world-wide interests. British historian P. J. Marshall writes:

> Both the area and the number of people under British rule increased greatly. Far more ships took out many more British goods to colonial markets and brought back much greater quantities of mostly tropical products. (Marshall 2001: 1)

Of special significance is the Seven Years' War, which formally lasted from 1756 to 1763. The term "British Empire" as a commonly accepted meaning of a collection of territories and peoples ruled by Britain is clearly established in the second half of the century. Sir George McCartney, later as Lord McCartney, an ambassador to China in 1793, wrote in 1773 of "this vast empire on which the sun never sets and whose bounds nature has not yet ascertained" (qtd. in Marshall 2001: 8). Conduits of circulation, not only as an "empire of goods" (qtd. in Marshall 2001: 12) such as tea, silk, sugar, textile, furniture, porcelain, earthenware, but also as that of people, Scots, Irish, blacks, Indians, are formed and woven into a global economy. The British alone transported more than 3.4 million slaves from Africa to the Americas between 1662 and 1807[1]. By 1815, the British Empire embraced one-fifth of the earth's inhabitants[2]. Scale of contact with the world beyond "the four English miles diameter" was greatly increased in all aspects of eighteenth-century life. Abundant fluxes of data from places far away were flowing into and through the metropolis center, often collected as the "imperial archive," to use a phrase from Thomas Richards[3]. Their afterlives are either what would come to be called "science[4]" or "culture[5]" in the modern period. Accordingly, sense of common identity, either a "Britishness" or more precisely an "Englishness" becomes a significant discursive site of contestation for different groups of people and things. Communications in commerce, matters, regions, peoples,

---

[1] See P. J. Marshall, "Introduction," in *The Oxford History of the British Empire*, p. 22.

[2] See Linda Colley, *Britons*, p. 323.

[3] See his book *Imperial Archive: Knowledge and the Fantasy of Empire* (Verso, 1996).

[4] For a brief history upon the historical relation between "science" and "natural history," see Deborah E. Harkness, "A Note about 'Science'," in her *The Jewel House: Elizabethan London and the Scientific Revolution*, pp. xv-xviii. W. G. Ward is given credit for coining a particular collective usage for *science* that remains valiant through modern time, when he wrote in 1867: "We shall ... use the word 'science' in the sense which Englishmen so commonly give to it; as expressing physical and experimental science, to the exclusion of theological and metaphysical." Also see *OED* item b.

[5] For a brief historical survey of the heavily loaded term "culture," see Raymond Williams' definition of the concept in his *Keywords*, pp. 87-93. Also see Terry Eagleton, *The Idea of Culture*.

and thoughts percolates through an economy of empire, which embodies the materialistic and the affective in the accumulation and dissemination of capital. Mechanics of sympathy as happening inter-subjectively or even between objects and subjects helps mediate and regulate the protean empire economy of changes, conflicts, struggles and disparities between the "small circle described upon the circle of the great world." In 1806 the physician Thomas Trotter, in his *A View of the Nervous Temperament*, defines the nervous system to be centered on the "GREAT SYMPATHETIC NERVE ... whose office directs the most important operation in the animal economy and binds together in one great circle of feeling, actions and notions both distant and opposite[1]." The body, as Jonathan Crary convincingly argues, becomes part of the modern system along with society and the economy[2], which requires government and management. Its moral consciousness and physiological productivity begins to function in the mechanism of the state, empire, and modern industrialization[3].

Indeed, as if symptomatic of a need of systematization, the eighteenth century, especially during its middle years, witnesses radical ruptures of constellations between sympathy, sentiment and society. On one hand, we have David Hume saying:

> I am first affrighted and confounded with that forelorn (sic) solitude, in which I am plac'd in my philosophy, and fancy myself some strong uncouth monster, who not being able to mingle and unite in society, has been expell'd all human commerce, and left utterly abandon'd and disconsolate. Fain wou'd I run into the crowd for shelter and warmth; but cannot prevail with myself to

---

[1] Thomas Trotter, "A View of the Nervous Temperament: Being a Practical Enquiry into the Increasing Prevalence, Prevention and Treatment of Those Diseases, 2nd ed. (Newcastle, 1807)," in *Radical Food: The Culture and Politics of Eating and Drinking 1790—1820*, vol. 3, p. 641. Quoted in James Chandler, "Sentiment and Sensibility," p. 24.

[2] See Jonathan Crary, "Modernizing Vision," pp. 29-50.

[3] Also see Jonathan Crary, *Suspensions of Perception: Attention, Spectacle, and Modern Culture*.

> mix with such deformity. (Hume 1978: 264)

Thus David Hume is featured as an evil fanatic and as the lord of a gloomy, gothic castle by James Beattie[1]. Besides this, here we see a "*Frankenstein*-like monster[2]"-philosopher phobic of a self consumed by contemplation and writing, who yearns for a sense of politeness and normality in mingling with "society" and "human commerce." There may exist a prominent self of the division between an atomistic self and a larger scale of the public, the latter of which is materialized in "society" or "exchange between men of the products of nature or art." It is what "human commerce" meant in the eighteenth century[3]. On the other hand, feelings are not lodged within the private, inner lives of individual persons. Adela Pinch argues in her critical investigation upon this period's epistemologies of emotions:

> [T]hey [emotions] rather circulate among persons as somewhat autonomous substances. They frequently seem as impersonal, and contagious, as viruses, visiting the breasts of men and women the way diseases visit the body. (Pinch 1)

In other words, emotions, feelings, and sentiments have a rather exterior and more interchangeable existence in the eighteenth century, and it is internalized as inward psychological activities. A contribution to the *Lady's Magazine* in 1775 reflects this object-like, or *thingness,* property of sentiment and sensibility:

> Sensibility—thou source of human woes—thou aggrandiser of evils! —Had I not been possessed of thee—how calmly might my days have passed! —Yet would I not part with thee for worlds. We will abide together—both pleased and pained with each other. Thou shalt ever have a place in my heart—be the sovereign of my

---

[1] In James Beattie, *An Essay on the Nature and Immutability of Truth*, and allegory (unpublished in his lifetime) "The Castle of Scepticism," see Adela Pinch, *Strange Fits of Passion*, p. 40, note 25.

[2] This phrase is from Adela Pinch, see Pinch, *Strange Fits of Passion*, p. 31.

[3] See *OED* online, under the entry of "commerce."

affections, and the friend of my virtue[1].

Habitation of sensibility suggests either moral superiority or weakness, and is quite selective, excluding what the physician Thomas Trotter names in 1806 as "the untutored and illiterate inhabitants of a forest" (575). For Trotter, two groups of people are notoriously susceptible for such "fine impressions," which, if received by "organ of sensation," "never fail to induce delicacy of feeling, that disposes alike to more acute pain, as to more exquisite pleasure" (Trotter 575). Women are more prone to sensibility because of their physical constitution, which is an argument reiterated by commentators both medical and literary. John Brewer thus generalizes this historical argument:

> Nature has endued the female to constitution with greater delicacy and sensibility than the male, as destined for a different occupation in life ... the female constitution, therefore, [is] furnished by nature with peculiar delicacy and feeling, soft in its muscular fibre, and easily acted upon by stimuli. (575)[2]

Another figure frequently identified as the victim of an excessive sensibility or sentiment is the author or literary man[3]. One Mrs. Donnellan comments to Samuel Richardson:

> The misfortune is, those who are fit to write delicately, must think so; those who can form a distress must be able to feel it; and as the mind and body are so united as to influence one another, the delicacy is communicated, and one too often finds softness and tenderness of mind in a body equally remarkable for

---

[1] *Lady's Magazine*, 1775, 3 (May): 251-255. Quoted in James Chandler, "Sentiment and Sensibility," p. 28.

[2] John Brewer, "Sentiment and Sensibility," p. 26.

[3] See John Brewer, "Sentiment and Sensibility," pp. 26-27.

those qualities[1].

David Hume singles out this anxiety and Robert James labels it as "HYPERCHONDRIACUS MORBUS" in his *Medicinal Dictionary* (1743—1745) for those "*Literati* ... who indulge themselves too much in Study, continual Meditations, and Lucrubrations[2]." Thus, self and sensibility, body and sentiment are woven together, the excessive exemplary cases of which are about to be examined as an English disease. This composition of a selfhood partially through *things* and *mediations with things* accords well with Hume's idea of a Lockean concept of selfhood as a fictional construct. It is an atomized idea of the self through the skepticism expressed in Book I of *A Treatise of Human Nature* (abbr. as *Treatise)*: we lack an impression of a "simple and continu'd self[3]." The Humean skepticism and fright upon the dis-consolation and abandonment of a self itself is indicative of an affective rupture of "soul"—what David Wellbery argues the most important concept in the eighteenth century. It projects itself as not contingent upon orthodoxy Christianity as it was in John Locke and other seventeenth-century philosophers[4].

If the first half of the eighteenth century was "still close to that of scholastic philosophy" (Yeo 241), the second half saw more of "words such as 'Physicks' (and its apparent double, 'Physick'), 'Physiology,' 'Pneumaticks,' 'Pneumatology,' 'Phytology,' 'Somatology,' and 'Aerology'" (242) addressed not only to scholars but also to the reading public. In the historical period when information came of age, and various technologies of knowledge were developed[5], the soul was more associated with "physiology" and "logic." The study of the mind is

---

[1] *The Correspondence of Samuel Richardson*, vol. 4, p. 30. Quoted in John Brewer, "Sentiment and Sensibility," p. 27.

[2] Quoted in John Brewer, "Sentiment and Sensibility," p. 27.

[3] Obviously one can do a biographical reading of Hume's philosophical statement here. For how he changed his name from Home to Hume, and its relevance to his literary construction of a selfhood, see the chapter on David Hume in this writing.

[4] See Roy Porter, *Flesh in the Age of Passion*, p. 370.

[5] See Daniel R. Headrick, *When Information Came of Age*.

transferred from the realm of pneumatology (that is, the traditional doctrine of "incorporeal" substances, concerning God, angels, and so on) to "psychology[1]." David Hartley (1705—1757) significantly writes of a "psychology, or theory of the human mind," locating that endeavor as part of "natural philosophy." According to Chambers' *Cyclopaedia* (1728)—a work hugely influential, since it served as a template for Diderot and d'Alembert's *Encyclopédie*[2], such "psychology," "a Discourse concerning the Soul," constitutes a sub-department *not* of "theology" but rather of "anthropology," the study of man[3]. Indeed, it is one of the beginnings of "the creation of a new body of thinking: the psychologization that is, of identity" (Porter 2005: 371). The formation of modern interiority, as advocated through empiricist natural philosophical writings, is manufactured for a rising consumer society in the eighteenth-century Britain[4]. This "account of subjectivity" helps to "explain desire, propensities, and aversions as being universal to humans as a group" (Poovey 147), which are cultivated by moral philosophers and remain essential to liberal governmentality. Thus, sentiment and sensibility, as sources of either virtue or distress, should be situated at the constellation of social forces such as politeness, good taste, sociality, commerce, and feminization[5] that configure a modern shape of selfhood. In this way, a political economy of feeling and its inwardness and outwardness parameter occupy a very significant position regarding the conceptualization of identity and sociality in

---

[1] See Roy Porter, *Flesh in the Age of Passion*, p. 371.

[2] See Roy Porter, *Flesh in the Age of Passion*, p. 371.

[3] See Roy Porter, *Flesh in the Age of Passion*, p. 371.

[4] See Mary Poovey, *A History of the Modern Fact,* pp. 147-148. For the eighteenth-century Britain as a consumer society, see *The Birth of a Consumer Society: The Commercialization of Eighteenth-Century England* (Eds. by John H. Plumb, Neil McKendrick and John Brewer); *The Consumption of Culture, 1600—1800: Image, Object, Text* (Eds. by Ann Bermingham and John Brewer).

[5] For the relation between feminization, literature and commerce in Eighteenth-Century England, see E.J. Clery, *The Feminization Debate in Eighteenth-Century England: Literature, Commerce and Luxury.*

Western modernity, which witnesses the significance of emotion as part of the rising anthropology of man, the "human sciences," to use Foucault's phrase[1].

[1] The emergence of which, as Foucault writes in a Romantic vein in the last pages of *The Archaeology of Knowledge and Discourse on Language*, suggests the immediate emergent disappearance of human species from the seashore of the world. In *The Order of Things*, Foucault argues that the nineteenth-century "episteme" initially organized the world according to biological models: "… man, his psyche, his group, his society, the language he speaks—all these exist in the Romantic period as living beings" (Foucault 1970: 253-263).

Chapter II

Rhetoric and the Rise of Modern Aesthetics: Emotions in Edmund Burke's Philosophical Inquiry

No man, in his senses, ever thought of applying his eyes to discover what passes in his mind; far less of blaming his eyes for not seeing a thought or idea.

—*Elements of Criticism* (1762), Lord Kames[1]

It is, indeed, difficult to visualize thoughts or ideas through one's eyes, as suggested by the epigraph from *Elements of Criticism*, an influential eighteenth-century aesthetic text by Henry Home (1696—1769), who was also called Lord Kames. What remains of significance, however, is the importance that Lord Kames places upon human "senses" in its possibility to realize and present interior activities, whether these senses are intellectual or not. This visualizing strength of eyes has always been interweaving with epistemological question about self-presence in the mind. Indeed, it is in a visual sense that the word "idea" has its Greek etymology[2]. The objective of this current writing—except the last

[1] *Elements of Criticism*, vol. 1, p. 343.

[2] Voltaire, in his *Philosophical Dictionary*, also wrote: "What is an idea? It is an image that paints itself in my brain .... The most abstract ideas are the consequences of all the objects I've perceived .... I've ideas only because I've images in my head" (Voltaire, *Philosophical Dictionary*, p. 236). The Enlightenment's debt to Descartes's ocular-centric theory of knowledge and its distance from it is readily apparent here, as Martin Jay points out. See Jay, *Downcast Eyes*, pp. 83-84.

chapter, nevertheless, is to situate this visual approach to epistemological issues such as rhetoric, emotion, identity, and language in the eighteenth-century British culture. It was a historical period that witnessed a proliferating print culture, which is a massive shift from an early modern scribal or chirographic culture to a modern typographic culture. The modern print culture is the first of what has made possible Walter Benjamin calls "technological reproducibility[1]." This project is to historicize the theatrical intermediate stage of the visual in between the mind and the thing so as to see how a perceptual change of selfhood is initiated through the formation of a modern printed textual culture. It is concerned with outlining a history of self- or other-presence through vision, and how a modern textual media has made it possible.

Lord Kames addresses this commentary quoted above as a critique towards Scene 8 Act 8 of William Congreve's 1697 tragedy play *The Mourning Bride*:

> Yet I behold her—yet—and now no more.
> Turn your lights inward, Eyes, and view my thought.
> So shall you still behold her—'twill not be.
> O impotence of sight! mechanic sense
> Which to exterior objects ow'st thy faculty,
> Not seeing of election, but necessity.
> Thus do our eyes, as do all common mirrors,
> Successively reflect succeeding images.
> Nor what they would, but must; a star or toad;
> Just as the hand of chance administers! [2]

This reflection upon mental faculty—here as its impotence—of visualizing a presence of either an other or an imagery is from Osmyn after a temporary departure of Osmyn's from Almeria, the speaker's beloved. It is a grandiose emotional moment from the male character,

---

[1] See McLuhan's argument on "the make of typographic man" in his *The Gutenberg Galaxy*. Also see Christopher Bush, *Ideographic Modernism*, p. 67.
[2] Quoted in Henry Home, *Elements of Criticism*, vol. 1, p. 343.

where a yearning to domesticate a female presence of his beloved is expressed. Visuality, containment, and emotionality all percolate with a discursive trope of sympathy with the eyes and with the audience[1]. This probably explains how the successive images in mental faculty reflected in this passage from Congreve's play interests Henry Home. Lord Kames was an active founding member of the Edinburgh Society for the Encouragement of Arts, Sciences, Manufactures, and Agriculture, and the Society for Promoting the Reading and Speaking of the English Language in Scotland, two of the offshoots from the Select Society, to which both David Hume and Adam Smith belonged. As a matter of fact, David Hume was a distant cousin of Home's[2]. The writing of the *Elements of Criticism* was made possible partially because of Hume's suggestion to Lord Kames that criticism could be reduced to a science. During the years 1748—1750, Adam Smith delivered a series of public lectures in Edinburgh, and it was funded by Henry Home. Out of these lectures both Smith's *The Theory of Moral Sentiments* (1759) and *The Wealth of Nations* (1776) were based[3]. Henry Home was conversing with both of them. For instance, in *Elements of Criticism*, he wrote on "ideal presence" achieved from spectating "as distinguished from real presence on the one side, and from reflective remembrance on the other" (Home 2005: 68), an obsession that both Hume and Smith expressed through their work of writing. He also wrote on "sympathy," without which no person could fully understand another, and thus no bonds of society could be secured[4], which is assigned a central role in the theories of both Hume and Smith's. The point of interest is that this impossibility of a visual inward turn towards one's self-presence is extenuating around the middle of the eighteenth century, around which various authors—Home, Hume and Smith included—could be read in the light of a media history

[1] Sympathy, indeed, is an endemic trope in the eighteenth century, which will be elaborated more into details below. See, for instance, Marshall, *The Surprising Effects of Sympathy*. For an analysis of Congreve's, also see Adela Pinch, *Strange Fits of Passion*, pp. 5-6.

[2] At least before he changed the spelling of his family name from "Home" into "Hume." See chapter 3 of this dissertation.

[3] See D. D. Raphael and A. L. Macfie, "Introduction," pp. 1-3.

[4] Henry Home, *Elements of Criticism*, vol. 1, pp. 307-308.

of textual culture. In this historical process, I argue that the rising of a literary modernity occupies a primarily significant role as part of the consequence of a saturating textual culture. I take the concept of "literary modernity" from Paul de Man[1]. Through his reading of Nietzsche's "Of the Use and Misuse of History for Life," de Man writes: "Modernity exists in the form of a desire to wipe out whatever came earlier in the hope of reaching at last a point that could be called a true present, a point of origin that marks a new departure" (Home 1970: 388-389). This denial of history, paradoxically, "discovers itself to be a generative power that not only engenders history, but is part of a generative scheme that extends far back into the past" (390), which is implied in the rise of Western modernity. The activity of modern literature offers a most manifest instance of this very contradiction that Nietzsche discovered at the endpoint of his rebellion against a historically minded culture. It is a culture with its "constitutive affinity with action, with the unmediated, free act that knows no past" (392) on the one hand. On the other hand, it is "not as a single moment of self-denial, but as a plurality of moments that can ... be represented ... as a succession of moments or duration" (398). I situate the ways of representing presence and emotions in a history of this culture, when the modern concept of "literature" as part of modern textual culture was establishing itself in creating a sense of history through the eighteenth century. In this way, I try to radicalize the work of writing in its historical sense as well as in its pertinence to our understanding of modern self.

This history of emotions and representations takes its methodology and terminology from media studies in its critical sense. For instance, the vocabulary of "human sensorium" is from media theorists Marshall McLuhan and Walter J. Ong. It describes the effects of media and ways of mediation upon the ratio of human senses and perceptual proclivities[2].

---

[1] Paul de Man, "Literary History and Literary Modernity."

[2] See for instance, McLuhan "Visual and Acoustic Space" in *The Global Village: Transformations in World Life and Media in the 21st Century*, pp. 35-47, and Ong "The Shifting Sensorium," in *The Varieties of Sensory Experience: A Sourcebook in the Anthropology of the Senses*, pp. 25-30.

McLuhan once wrote on the psychological function of the Western alphabet as follows: "The translating of auditory into visual terms set up an inner life in man which separated himself from the exterior world and, in part, from his own senses, as we know from the study of pre-literate societies" (McLuhan 1962: 284). Alphabetic literacy is instrumental in constructing an inward interiority as a neutral and abstract space: "The interiorization of the technology of the phonetic alphabet translates man from the magical world of the ear to the neutral visual world" (18). This separation of senses brought by the technology of writing promotes the visual over the audile, which is part of the reason—for McLuhan—why a progressive history of Western civilization becomes possible along with the rise of Western possessive individualism: "Only the phonetic alphabet makes a break between eye and ear, between semantic meaning and visual mode; and thus only phonetic writing has the power to translate man from the tribal to the civilized sphere, to give him an eye for an ear" (27). Orality, literacy and visuality are taken in the current writing as they relate to ways of organizing human sensoria and perceptions in media history. In this way, they are what Martin Heidegger calls *techne,* which shares an etymology with "technology," from the Greek root *technikon.* It concerns the work of *enframing* with which Heidegger developed his phenomenological approach: "What is decisive in *techne* does not lie at all in making and manipulating nor in the using of means, but rather in ... revealing[1]." For Heidegger, "the essence of technology lies not in instrumental productions or manipulation of material, but in the process of a special kind of knowing through the *techne*" (Liu 2010: 28), as pointed out by Lydia H. Liu. Epistemological aspiration of knowledge is not a cause or origin of technology as usually presumed. Instead, new technologies present space of revealing and clearing, which enframes the perceptual economy of representation and emotion. The print media, in the current case, realizes and disciplines an organizational ratio of orality, aurality,

---

[1] *The Question Concerning Technology*, p. 58. Also see Lydia H. Liu, *The Freudian Robot: Digital Media and the Future of the Unconscious*, p. 28.

literacy and visuality that affects modern selfhood. It is through this perspective we can delineate a history of textual culture, with an emphasis upon Paul de Manian "literary modernity," through a study on representations, emotions and work of writing.

II.i. Sympathy, Description and Its Sounding Economy

This current writing starts with Edmund Burke's aesthetics of the sublime in the middle of the eighteenth century. I situate his theory at the threshold of the emergence of modern textual mediation or perception, whose maturity and permeation is well reflected in Adam Smith's textual construction of sympathy. Smith's theory of moral sentiments dovetails with sense of transparent exchangeability regarding personhood, human nature and commodity explicated in modern political economy of his later writings. That pre-mediates a potential development of psychoanalysis that appears of historical necessity in the late nineteenth century so as to deal with the existence of the unconscious beyond the exchangeable transparency of selfhood of the political economy writings. Thus, textual culture has obtained a social life of its own, in the history of which there seems to exist a genealogy of genres from aesthetics (Edmund Burke), modern literature (William Wordsworth), moral philosophy (David Hume and Adam Smith) and psychoanalysis in the eighteenth and nineteenth centuries. I take these authors as snapshots of a media history of modern textual culture. All of them participate into this history of modern writing and become parts of the institution of the work of writing. It is of historical contingency that each of them is in a significant position in this social life of the textual culture. I historicize Burke's attitudes toward the function of language in communicating emotions in a tradition of early modern rhetoric, when a proliferating textual cultural media was about to be in its place. Thus it is an attempt to revalorize aesthetic as figuring a problem of textual mediation and its affective economy[1]. Through this I argue that theatricality as the emergence of a new type of aesthetic "interface" provides a site of cultural labor and a body of textual formation during the transition from "the age of flesh[2]" to the age of paper, or to what Samuel Johnson calls an "age of authors[3]." Textual media thus helps manufacture the modern perceptual and emotive with regard to figured conditions of communications made possible through a proliferation of words. Through a critical investigation on sentiment and its relation to language as they are reflected in these authors, I demonstrate how the construct of a specific regime of theatrical selfhood becomes tangent upon the emergent forms of abstraction and exchangeability in a history of textual media. Or, to put it differently, this is a transition from what is formularized by Henry Home as impossible (as quoted in the epigraph) into a phase of applying eyes to psychology—or, psychology as visual as everyday happening. This change of cultural disposition affects the dimensions of different perceptions involved in representation of feelings, and formation of modern individuals in general.

Indeed, sympathy, as one technique of stimulating bodily sentiment and sensation, was a significant element of aesthetics in the middle of the eighteenth century. It involves corporeal engagements and mediation. As practice of sociality, it is registered in the aesthetic theory of the sublime and the beautiful by Edmund Burke, who writes: "We yield to sympathy, what we refuse to description" (Burke 1958: 160). Burke juxtaposes embodied sympathy and disembodied description as complementary with each other. Sympathy comes to rescue of its own accord when "we" cease using the visual "description," and it occupies a higher position of preference in the system of human sensorium. Feelings are not approachable through visual display or representation of

---

[1] For a theological genealogy of "economy" and how it evolves into Hegelian "positivity" and Foucauldian "apparatus," see "What is an Apparatus?" by Giorgio Agamben.

[2] This phrase is appropriated from the book title of *Flesh in the Age of Reason* (Penguin, 2005) by Roy Porter, the historian of medicine.

[3] W. J. Bate, J. M. Bullitt, and L. F. Powell (eds.), *Samuel Johnson: The Idler and Adventurer*, p. 457.

words. Its economy is spiritual, personal, immediate, and less adaptable to communicative mediation. For Burke, the function of language is to communicate and persuade, but on a more local scale: "words" produce "three effects ... in the mind of the hearer. The first is, the *sound*; the second, the *picture*, or representation of the thing signified by the sound; the third is, the *affection* of the soul produced by one or by both of the foregoing" (166). The affective dimension of the mediation comes as that of the auditory and the visual. In this scheme of words, the auditory effects come to be of primary significance, the visual as secondary. As a matter of fact, the pictorial meaning of communication is achieved through the signification from the acoustic. The priority that Burke puts upon the aural-oral aspects of words probably suggests a historical episteme of a scribal or manuscript culture. Indeed, when Burke published his *A Philosophical Enquiry into the Origin of Our Ideas of the Sublime and Beautiful* in 1757, Europe was changing from an oral-scribal to a print society, which ran through the century[1]. The two means of cultural media—the acoustic and the visual, that is—involve different forms or *techne* of consciousness and organization of human sensorium, which has been studied in various disciplines through decades[2]. For instance, the media theorist McLuhan writes: "Manuscripts were meant to be read aloud. Church chantry schools were set up to ensure oral fidelity" (McLuhan 1989: 46). This acoustic regime is an episteme of the pulpit, and it "had ... been coupled with news about local and foreign affairs, real estate transactions, and other mundane matters" (131)[3], as Elizabeth L. Eisenstein argues in her history of the

[1] See Alvin Kernan, *Samuel Johnson and the Impact of Print*, p. 4.

[2] For instance, see the works by Water J. Ong, Marshall McLuhan, Jack Goody, Eric A. Havelock, Régis Debray, Claude Lévi-Strauss, Elizabeth L. Eisenstein, Benedict Anderson and Erich Neumann. The most recent critical essay on this topic with a historical emphasis is "Genesis of the Media Concept" by John Guillory.

[3] For how the periodical newspaper press replaced the pulpit in early modern society as a medium for disseminating news and information, as well as providing psychological reinforcement, also see Elizabeth L. Eisenstein, *The Printing Press as an Agent of Change*, pp. 553-554.

printing press. Burke's aesthetics can be identified more in an episteme[1] of the traditional rhetoric. It remains analogous to the "morning prayer" and the pulpit, which is to be substituted by what Hegel perceives in newspaper reading in the early nineteenth century[2]. The Burkean theory of the sublime and beautiful came into its shape between 1747 and 1756[3], years of changing values and new points of view. His philosophical enquiry was published on 21 April 1757, and the second edition came in 1759, when Adam Smith's theory of moral sentiment was materialized[4]. Following what Foucault elsewhere calls "genealogical[5]," this writing offers an analysis of the bodily economy of sentiments in Burke's aesthetics and a glance into various discourses of sentiments as they remain particularly pertinent with a history of modern textual culture. Through critical inquiries upon the constitution of knowledge,

---

[1] Here I follow Foucault's definition of *episteme* as "a specifically *discursive* apparatus" or "the strategic apparatus which permits of separating out from among all the statements which are possible those that will be acceptable within" (Foucault 1980: 197). As to "apparatus," the definition closest to completion Foucault gives is in an interview from 1977: "What I'm trying to single out with this term is, first and foremost, a thoroughly heterogeneous set consisting of discourses, institutions, architectural forms, regulatory decisions, laws, administrative measures, scientific statements, philosophical, moral, and philanthropic propositions—in short, the said as much as the unsaid. Such are the elements of the apparatus. The apparatus itself is the network that can be established between these elements... I understand by the term 'apparatus' a sort of—shall we say—formation which has as its major function at a given historical moment that of responding to an *urgent need*" (Foucault 1980: 194-195, emphasis original). Also see Giorgio Agamben, "What Is an Apparatus?."

[2] See Susan Buck-Morss, "Hegel and Haiti" in *Critical Inquiry*, p. 844. Also see Benedict Anderson, *Imagined Communities: Reflections on the Origin and Spread of Nationalism*, p. 35.

[3] See Samuel H. Monk, *The Sublime*, p. 87.

[4] See J. T. Boulton, "Introduction" to *A Philosophical Enquiry into the Origin of Our Ideas of the Sublime and Beautiful*, pp. xv-xvi.

[5] As Foucault writes: "I don't believe the problem can be solved by historicizing the subject as posited by the phenomenologists, fabricating a subject that evolves through the course of history. One has to dispense with the constituent subject, to get rid of the subject itself, that's to say, to arrive at an analysis which can account for the constitution of the subject within a historical framework. And this is what I would call genealogy, that is, a form of history which can account for the constitution of knowledge, discourses, domains of objects, etc., without having to make reference to a subject which is either transcendental in relation to a field of events or runs in its empty sameness throughout the course of history" (Foucault 1980: 117).

discourses, domains of objects—such as aesthetics, exchangeability, communication—this current writing traces a genealogical outline of sentiments from perspectives of different textual mediations of perceptions and sentiments.

For Burke, sympathy, as one kind of human "*affections*" (sic), can be accomplished through aesthetic labor, which is reflected through the description with words. However, in Burke's theory work through words does not necessarily breed "sympathy." Concerning the affective function of language as a mimetic medium through description, he remains significantly suspicious, partially from which his political conservatism is derived. As he writes: "It may be observed that very polished language, and such as are praised for their superior clearness and perspicuity, are generally deficient in strength" (Burke 1958: 125). The more detailed linguistic descriptions are, the more insufficiently they would be able to appeal to emotions. This is well observed by J. T. Boulton, who wrote the famous editorial preface to Burke's philosophical enquiry in the 1950s. In Burke's system of language as a technical instrument in social venues of communication, Boulton writes, "the emotive power of language is not proportionate to its image-raising capacity" (Boulton xxvii). Indeed, for Burke, the images once attached to words may fade out, but a residue of the original emotion may become part of the ecology of words, which is charged with an acoustic economy:

> Such words are in reality but mere sounds; but they are sounds, which, being used on particular occasions, wherein we receive some good, or suffer some evil, or see others affected with good or evil; or which we hear applied to other interesting things and events; and being applied in such a variety of cases that we know readily by habit to what things they belong, they produce in the mind, whenever they are afterwards mentioned; effects similar to those of their occasions. The sounds being often used without reference to any particular occasion, and carrying still their first impressions, they at last utterly lose their connection with the particular occasions that gave rise to

> them; yet the sound, without any annexed notion, continues to operate as before. (Burke 1958: 165)

Sound as a medium and oral-aural apparatus, in the process of de-contexutalization, seems to obtain a communicative valence, equivalent to that of floating signifiers in postmodern culture, or what Jean Baudrillard defines as "a hyperreal" in simulation—"the generation by models of a real without origin or reality" (Baudrillard 1). It could leave its original territory and still maintains an operative mechanism. What is of more significance for Burke is that sound serves as the instrument of rhetorical suasion, as he writes:

> Now, as there is a moving tone of voice, an impassioned countenance, an agitated gesture, which affect independently of the things about which they are exerted, so there are words, and certain dispositions of words, which ... touch and move us more than those which far more clearly and distinctly express the subject matter. (Burke 1958: 175)

The "moving tone of voice," "impassioned countenance," and "agitated gesture" of enunciating words are acts more embodied and local, thus the acoustic dimension of words seems to have a life more social than when the postmodern de-territorialized signifiers. Burke's aesthetic theory on the fierce, noble, and almost supra-sensuous appeal of the sublime is more of the acoustic type, though he devotes a good deal of space to his naïve theory of retinal fatigue in producing the visual sublime as Dixon Wecter observes[1]. This is suggested in his extreme sensitivity to sounds—to thunder, roaring cataracts, the crises of wild beasts, artillery, shouting multitudes, drums, tolling bells, and even "low, confused, uncertain sounds" (Burke 1958: 83). What matters is not whether Burke had little or no education in music[2], neither is it about the

[1] See Dixon Wecter, "Burke's Theory concerning Words, Images, and Emotion," p. 179.

[2] His early mentor W. G. Hamilton once remarked, "Burke understands everything but gaming and music," as mentioned by Dixon Wecter, "Burke's Theory concerning Words, Images, and Emotion," p. 179, note 43.

peculiarities of Burke's own sensory equipment[1]. Rather, the economy of sound in his aesthetics as the celebrated sublime suggests a sense of im-mediation and corporeality paradigms of some period in the eighteenth-century West. It is reminiscent of what Foucault defines in his theory of language in its break from the classical episteme:

> ... in the Classical period the expressive function of language was required only at its point of origin, and in order to explain how a sound could represent a thing, [whereas] language in the nineteenth century, throughout its development and even in its most complex forms, was to have an irreducible expressive value, for, if language expresses, it does so not in so far as it is an imitation and duplication of things, but in so far as it manifests and translates the fundamental will of those who speak it. (Foucault 1970: 290)

This shift of the function of language, from that of revealing and disclosing the origin—"its old kinship with *divinatio*" (Foucault 1970: 59) that is—into that of representation and communication, is historically situated in the current writing as imbricate with a rising print culture. The deluge of writing brings forth proliferation of signs, establishes a world more into its visually neutralized form, and creates aesthetic experience of a new audience and a society of readers and writers. The saturating verbal signs in British culture through the long eighteenth century would demand a revaluation of a whole *episteme*, which affects not merely the way objective knowledge is organized and accessed, but also the way how affective knowledge works upon the somatic body. In this way, the "print turn"

---

[1] Dixon Wecter argues that "Burke's stress upon the sublime arising from the sonority of poetry and rhetoric, as well as his theory which disparages clear visualization as an aid to aesthetic emotion, sprang in part from the peculiarities of his own sensory equipment" (180). And at the end of the essay, Wecter quotes observation from Tom Paine: "Mr. Burke has two or three times, in his parliamentary speeches, and in his publications, made use of a jingle of words that convey no ideas" (qtd. in Wecter 1940: 181).

co-evolves with the "affective turn[1]." The transmission of feelings is made possible by the *techne* of a print culture, which enhances the division between the private / domestic and public[2] as reflected in activities of reading and writing. Edmund Burke's aesthetic theory offers a point of departure in this discussion of the role of the perceptual in this affective turn—how and through what means one feels and communicates.

Burke's aesthetic economy of sound and hearing as a mediating sensorium bears relevance to discussions from his contemporaries. For instance, the German philosopher Johann Gottfried Herder (1744—1803) once delivered a speech of "On the Education of Students in Language and Speech" in the context of his secondary school reform, which describes the subject of *Bildung* as organized through the spoken and heard words. His theory reads similar to that of Burke's:

> Youths who have acquired ... unpleasant dialect of merely animal sounds, whether they come from the cities or the country, should make every effort in school to acquire a human, natural speech possessed of character and soul and to rid themselves of their peasant or shrieking back-alley dialects. They should leave off the barking and yelping, the clucking and cawing, the swallowing and dragging together of words and syllables and speak human rather than animal language. Happy is the child, the boy, who from his first years, onward hears understandable, human, lovely sounds that unnoticeably mold his tongue and the sound of his speech.[3]

Constantly hailed as "the founding document of German as a school subject" (Kittler 1992: 37), this shows the self-identified cultural

---

[1] Here I refer to the mode of "sentimentalization" as that of melodramatic excess, which is the theme of Peter Brooks' *The Melodramatic Imagination: Balzac, Henry James, Melodrama, and the Mode of Excess*.

[2] It becomes critical cliché that this process comes along with a rising bourgeoisie. As Louis Althusser writes in *For Marx* in 1969: "It could not be more bluntly put that it was the bourgeoisie itself that invented for the people the popular myth of the melodrama ... serials in the popular press, cheap 'novels'" (p. 139).

[3] Quoted in Friedrich A. Kittler, *Discourse Networks, 1800/1900*, pp. 37-38.

mission for Herder as a German Enlightenment philosopher, the pedagogical function of bildungsroman, that is. If *Bildung* means "the auto-production of a subject that produces or forms itself in the very act of coming to consciousness of itself[1]," this process of phenomenal realization in aesthetics of body comes through purifying acoustic signs of contaminating noises or animalistic sounds. For Herder, "[s]ounds and the sense of hearing provide the ideal means for negotiating and organizing the soul's interior space and its exterior sphere. Sounds are external givens that function as a minimal difference or mark, and they can resonate in the internal space" (von Mücke 170)[2], as Dorothea von Mücke comments. Thus, the acoustic dimension of the aesthetic perception is not peculiar in Burke's philosophical inquiry. It is rather a prevalent discussion. Burke's aesthetic theory upon language suggests this through a strong emotional appeal, which is corporeally embedded rather than mentally represented or visualized. For him, "passion," "emotion," and "affection" are a cluster of lax and apparently interchangeable terms[3], and are more of oratorical effects than of linguistic representations made at a distance. The influence of words through representation upon passions, he claims, "should be but light; yet it is quite otherwise; for we find by experience that eloquence and poetry are as capable, nay indeed much more capable of making deep and lively impressions than other arts, and even than nature itself in very many cases" (Burke 1958: 173). The acoustic eloquence and poetry as locally experienced by an "us" are more communicative. Hence Burke's fascination with the power of rhetoric, which is "an instrument of emotional transport … dominant among the ancients, and the grand style, the purpose of which was to move, … an integral part of their rhetoric" (Monk 1960: 11). Indeed, Burke writes on the sublime in the tradition of critics and theorists

---

[1] Marc Redfield, *Phantom Formations: Aesthetic Ideology and the Bildungsroman*, p. 63.

[2] For an investigation of Herder's establishment of a hierarchy of sensorial perceptions (the hearing, the senses of touch and sight, that is), see von Mücke, *Virtue and the Veil of Illusion*, pp. 170-173.

[3] See Dixon Wecter, "Burke's Theory concerning Words, Images, and Emotion," p. 167, note 2.

preceding him, such as John Dennis, Hildebrand Jacob, and Robert Lowth, whose work "bears witness to the continuation of the rhetorical tradition," and "they would, perhaps, never have studied the question had not the rhetoricians of antiquity and of their own age based much of the persuasive power of their art on the emotions which the great style evokes" (Monk 1960: 84), as Samuel H. Monk's classical study suggests. In sense, this rhetoric tradition even included David Hume[1]. John Ward, a contemporary of Burke's, writes in his *A System of Oratory* that rhetoric

> not only directs to those arguments, which are proper to convince the mind; but also considers the various passions and interests of mankind, with the bias they receive from temper, education, converse, and other circumstances of life; and teaches how to fetch such reasons from each of these, as are of the greatest force in persuasion. (qtd. in Howell 74)

Rhetoric, in the eighteenth century, "was a history of the voice, taught through speech and authenticated by phonocentric values" (Fielding 11)[2]. For Hugh Blair, who was the occupant of the specially created chair of Rhetoric and Belles Lettres at Edinburgh University from 1762 to 1783, language is "the expression of our ideas by certain sounds, which are used as the signs of those ideas," and is communicated by means of the warmth and feeling of the speaker's expression[3]. Burke's appeal to an emotional rhetoric over logic accords well with such a definition and function of rhetoric in its classical tradition[4]. His aesthetics deals with "bodies acting *mechanically* (sic) upon the human mind by the intervention of the senses" (Burke 1958:

---

[1] See Daniel M. Gross's discussion in *The Secret History of Emotion: From Aristotle's Rhetoric to Modern Brain Science*, pp. 113-156. See chapter 3 of the dissertation for a discussion of Hume's economy of emotions through print media.

[2] Penny Fielding, *Writing and Orality*.

[3] Hugh Blair, *Lectures on Rhetoric and Belles Lettres*, p. 98.

[4] For an intellectual-history aspect upon how it was through Addison the essayist that the sublime became an important idea in the philosophy of taste and in an investigation of the pleasures of imagination, not of rhetoric, see Samuel H. Monk, *The Sublime*, pp. 58-60.

112), rather than "the languid and precarious operation of our reason" (107). He considers the emotional effect of words "put together without any rational view," such as *wise, valiant, generous, good,* and *great*—which belong to what he calls "compounded abstract words" (164), when spoken apart from local contexts without "a warm and affecting tone of voice" (166).

II.ii. Rhetoric, History and French Revolution

It is helpful to recall that rhetoric in antiquity assumed the primacy of speech as the substance upon which this art was first and longest practiced. Similar to what Josiah Royce calls Lessing's praise of dynamic poetry as "the verbal motor type[1]," Burke's aesthetic theory is an oral-auditory apparatus of communication. In his historiography of the genesis of modern concept of media, John Guillory argues that "even though rhetoric early on incorporated writing into its practice, the concept of speech retained preeminence in the definition of the art until the demise of formal rhetoric in the curricular reformations of the late nineteenth century" (Guillory 1995: 326). However, Burke's emphasis upon sentiment and emotion makes his theory different from the guidelines given in the rhetorical and belletristic handbooks of the period. For instance, in the notion of clarity. It is a stylistic norm applicable indifferently to speech and writing that language should always be transparent to meaning, and this is a very important Lockean version of words as medium of thought[2]. In this tradition, language is taken as a transparent and neutral instrument to communicate. George Campbell writes in his *The Philosophy of Rhetoric* published in 1776:

> Perspicuity originally and properly implies *transparency* (sic), such as may be ascribed to air, glass, water, or any other medium, through which material objects are viewed. From this original and proper

[1] See Josiah Royce, "Psychological Reasons for Lessing's Attitude toward Descriptive Poetry."

[2] See John Guillory, "Genesis of the Media Concept," p. 338-339.

> sense it hath been metaphorically applied to language, this being, as it were, the medium, through which we perceive the notions and sentiments of a speaker. (qtd. in Guillory 2010: 339)

This is a claim to "establish a post-Lockean stylistic norm" (Guillory 2010: 339). Francis Bacon also captures the psychodynamics of objectivity, clarity and democracy in print in his *The New Organon* published in the previous century. Bacon states: "[T]here is surely nothing in the craft of printing that is not open and almost obvious … which does so much to propagate learning" (114-115). Print, indeed, promotes a rising culture of abstraction with its regulated forum and sentences. It co-exists with the post-Baconian writers' desire to evolve a language in which words would simply be marks of things[1]. What remains at stake for this current writing is Burke's strong sense of emotionalism as a reaction against this technological globalizing tendency in which emotional and historical associations would be non-existent. This tendency is a tradition extending from Bacon to Locke, and it posits "an essential equivalence between linguistic and philosophical standards of clarity, precision, and transparency of thought as the basis of a new empiricist epistemology" (Porter 2005: 17). Robert Stillman has persuasively argued that the rationalist regimes imposed on language within this tradition reflect not only the new ordering of experimental knowledge promoted by the Royal Society, but also a fundamental commitment from its adherents to reinforcing and legitimating the authority of the state. The universal language schemes of Bacon, Wilkins, and others "emerged as rival authority structures designed, in great measure, to contain and control the disorders of words because such disorders threatened chaos in the historical world of things" (Stillman 10). In the aesthetic theory under discussion here, Burke strategically associates these practices of clarity, precision, and

---

[1] See R. Jones, "Science and Language in England of the Mid-Seventeenth Century." Francis Bacon once pointed that Chinese has "direct correspondence between things and words" (Porter 2001: 43). Umberto Eco's *The Search for the Perfect Language* also remains relevant.

transparency of thought through linguistic with the feminine beautiful. Meanwhile, the objects that impress us with their power, obscurity, vastness or infinity, succession and uniformity, or their effect of "painful delight" upon the senses, can be read as a gender issue with the masculine sublime[1]. Acquainted with this rhetorical tradition of language[2], Burke develops a rather different theory upon the relationship of sense-impressions with words and ideas. In his scenario, clarity and perspicuity correlate with the finite and they are less capable of psychological stimulation upon the body:

> But let it be considered that hardly any thing can strike the mind with its greatness which does not make some sort of approach toward infinity; which nothing can do while we are able to perceive its bounds; but to see an object distinctly, and to perceive its bounds, are one and the same thing. A clear idea is, therefore, another name for a little idea. (63)

For Burke the Irish, it is the French who embrace "polished languages," with their "superior clearness and perspicuity," which brings forth ruptures rather than continuity, and thus "deficien[cy] in strength" (Burke 1958: 176).

With a historical hindsight, we may be able to recognize historical precursor to the contemporary revolt against theory in Anglo-American academy in Burke's criticism of the French Revolution in the 1790s. It is not exaggerating to say that when Burke was developing his aesthetic theory in the middle of the eighteenth century, it had already anticipated his attitudes toward the French Revolution elaborated in the 1790s. David Simpson defines this mythological English Franco-phobia "as a central motif in the definition of a nationalism," the pattern of which is

---

[1] For a more elaborated gender reading of Burke's aesthetic division, see W. J. T. Mitchell's "Eye and Ear: Edmund Burke and the Politics of Sensibility" in his *Iconology: Image, Text, Ideology*, pp.116-150.

[2] He makes four direct references to John Locke's *An Essay Concerning Human Understanding*. See Dixon Wecter, "Burke's Theory concerning Words, Images, and Emotion," p. 170.

> based on [English] common sense, on a resistance to generalized thought, and on a declared immersion in the minute complexities of a 'human' nature whose essence is usually identified in an accumulation of mutually incommensurable details rather than in a single, systematized personality. (Simpson 4)

What remains pertinent to the argument is that the British national character—as reflected in Burke's case for the power of English habit and custom—to keep the French contamination away dovetails with a transformation of consciousness and perception brought upon by a diffusion of print technology. In Burke's aesthetic theory, the French pollution is metonymically transferred as an intrusion of the visual and verbal upon the acoustic and interior. The Burkean aesthetics embraces the empathic involvement natural to the oral society and the audile-tactile man, whereas the phonetic alphabet media promotes the rise of the visual component as ways of abstraction and systemization[1]. This visual perception and abstraction is long existent in the historical process of what Martin Heidegger categories as "the world grasped as picture" that started from Renaissance, a process of objectification:

> This objectification of beings is accomplished in a setting-before, a representing [*Vor-stellen*], aimed at bringing each being before it in such a way that the man who calculates can be sure—and that means certain—of the being. Science as research first arrives when, and only when, truth has transformed itself into the certainty of representation. (Heidegger 2002: 66-67.)

In the current writing, this eventually manifests itself in the formalized methods of representation and exchangeability of self in

[1] For the correlation between the visual and the phonetic alphabet, see Marshall McLuhan, *The Gutenberg Galaxy*, p. 39.

everyday life in Adam Smith's political economy of moral sentiments[1]. Strategically, Burke represents the French Revolution as a visual spectacle, which produces a "bewildered English audience." For him, the revolutionary spectacle negates "the laws of Aristotelian dramatic law by failing to resolve the violent struggles in any satisfying symbolic way" (Klancher 103), as pointed out by Jon P. Klancher[2]. He writes in his reflections upon the French Revolution as follows:

> ... [W]hen kings are hurl'd from their thrones by the Supreme Director of this great drama, and become the objects of insult to the base, and of pity to the good, we behold such disasters in the moral, as we should behold a miracle in the physical order of things. We are alarmed into reflexion; our minds (as it has long since been observed) are purified by terror and pity; our weak unthinking pride is humbled, under the dispensations of a mysterious wisdom. — Some tears might be drawn from me, if such a spectacle were exhibited on the stage. I should be truly ashamed of finding in myself that superficial, theatrical sense of painted distress, whilst I could exult over it in real life. With such a perverted mind, I could never venture to shew my face at a tragedy. (Burke 1890: 175)[3].

In other words, the *Reflections* is initiated as a claim to a dramaturgic performance not visualized, not on display, or even not written. The reflexive form, as a text, is made possible by what must remain invisible and unwritten as manifested by the English Constitution

---

[1] J. F. Suter points out that Burke's critique of Rousseau is situated "in the spirit of the British moral tradition, in particular of Shaftesbury and Adam Smith," and Burke "believes that passions can be useful to society if they are suitably educated and tempered by laws and manners" (Suter 52). Indeed, Burke might be arguing in this British tradition of moral philosophy, but there surely exists a large difference between the ways of how passions should be "suitably educated and tempered by laws and manners" in Burke and Smith, the latter of whom is more of a commodity culture, as will be suggested in the Adam Smith chapter of this writing.

[2] Jon P. Klancher, *The Making of English Reading Audiences, 1790—1832*, p. 103.

[3] More on Burke's revolutionary theatre, see Ronald Paulson, *Representations of Revolution*, chapter 2.

that requires a committed silent reading[1]. Thus Burke establishes himself as a writer of Englishness, whose work of writing appears to incarnate precedents, customs, institutions, and habits:

> Society is indeed a contract ... a partnership not only between those who are living, but between those who are living, those who are dead, and those who are to be born. Each contract of each particular state is but a clause in the great primeval contract of eternal society, linking the lower with the higher natures, connecting the visible and invisible world, according to a fixed compact sanctioned by the inviolable oath which holds all physical and all moral natures, each in their appointed place. (Burke 1890: 194-195)

The English "great chain of beings"—to use a phrase from Arthur O. Lovejoy[2], along with all its physical and moral manifestations, is made possible through the primeval oral moment of "the inviolable oath." Natural sympathy is prompted in individuals to good moral action through this moment. An immobile universe of value as inscribed through this apotheosis of the oral moment enables a historical rhetoric[3]. For Burke, there exists a fundamental tendency to preserve the heritage of the past in the history of English law and constitution: "All the reformations we have hitherto made, have proceeded upon the principle of reference to antiquity;" even the Glorious Revolution was "a revolution, not made, but prevented" (qtd. in Suter 68). By insisting that the English constitution is a work of continuity and is justified by its long duration, Burke, indeed, is "attacking the *primacy of the present*, which is characteristic of the philosophy of the Enlightenment" (Suter 58)[4]. It is a calculated historical determinacy, and

---

[1] This point is suggested by Jon P. Klancher in his *The Making of English Reading Audiences, 1790—1832*, pp. 103-108.

[2] This, of course, alludes to his masterpiece work *The Great Chain of Being: A Study of the History of an Idea*. Nevertheless, here it is more than an intellectual history of an idea.

[3] For an excellent rhetoric analysis of this passage, see Jon P. Klancher, *The Making of English Reading Audiences, 1790—1832*, p. 105.

[4] In this sense, Burke is even different from other significant English authors around that historical period, including Hobbes, Locke. See J. F. Suter, "Burke, Hegel, and the French Revolution," p. 58, note 52.

an appeal to temporality as the source of its authority[1], a writing strategy Burke takes to "outauthor" the French revolutionaries as well as the work of writing from French *philosophes*. His written text, as a medium of print, is mediated to this revolutionary moment, which can be represented only *reflectively*[2]. The enlightening rays of light from the French revolutionary practice or work of philosophical writings are described by Burke as a "conquering empire of light and reason" and "a speculative benevolence" (qtd. in Suter 53). The power of intellection and the actions it embodies must be refracted back to a non-visual moment of phonocentrism[3] in Burke's theories and reflections. It cannot be a visual origin of blankness, for he writes: "I cannot conceive how any man can have brought himself to that pitch of presumption, to consider his country as nothing but *carte blanche*, upon which he may scribble whatever he pleases" (qtd. in Suter 53). In this way, the oral and Burke's empirical truth parallel the association of anti-French sentiment and fundamental states of human nature[4]. This economy of sound enacts a superior act of overwriting over the revolutionary act. To address this conservative strategy, Thomas Paine's reply will not only "simplify Burke's terms by inventing an 'intellectual vernacular,' but will wound radical discourse upon a radical critique of such authorship

---

[1] See Jon P. Klancher, *The Making of English Reading Audiences, 1790—1832*, pp. 107-108.

[2] See Jon P. Klancher, *The Making of English Reading Audiences, 1790—1832*, p. 105.

[3] Burke remakes that the best of the French National Assembly were merely "men of theory" (qtd. in Suter 62). For a similar attitude regarding the sense politics in Hegel's response to the French Revolution, see J. F. Suter, "Burke, Hegel, and the French Revolution," in *Hegel's Political Philosophy—Problems and Perspectives*.

[4] Walter Scott, in a sense, embraces this gesture. In the poem "The Bard's Incantation" (written under the threat of invasion in the autumn of 1804), a response to British fears of post-Revolutionary France, "Minstrels and bards of other days" are invited to defend Albion from a Revolutionary "Specter with his Bloody Hand"—The Bard's voice is, "almost literally, the voice of nature as it mingles with the groaning oak, the stormy breeze, and the waves on the lake to proclaim 'the joys of Liberty.' The purity of the voice from an oral past promises concomitant freedom in the form of anti-Jacobin politics" (46), as Penny Fielding points out. See Fielding, *Writing and Orality*.

itself" (Klancher 105)[1]: "A constitution is not a thing in name only, but in fact. It has not an ideal but a real existence; and wherever it cannot be produced in a visible form, there is none" (Paine 71). Orality that is equated with an instinctive and primeval recognition of natural right in Burke's argument has to be exposed as metaphysical and ideal, and thus historically impossible.

"Clearness," "perspicuity" and "clarity," of which Burke holds suspicious in his aesthetic theory, are all visual terms. Burke's attitude towards this visual mediation of ideas and history is suggestive of an antagonism against the objectifying property of language promoted through a proliferating textual culture. Dixon Wecter argues that Burke borrows from Locke's "elaborate system for classifying ideas" in devising his three classes of words, which are taken as "those symbols which have only an arbitrary connection with real objects and which affect us in a different way" (Wecter 1940: 170). Burke defines his *aggregate words* as "simple ideas united by nature to form some determinate composition." *Simple abstracts* are "they that stand for one simple idea of such compositions and no more," and *compounded abstracts* are "the *arbitrary* union of both the others, and of various relations between them, in greater or less degrees of complexity" (Burke 1958: 163-164). These words are able to stir emotion merely by "the sound, without any annexed notion" (165), and their effects "arise in the mind of the hearer" (166). That is how "the power of poetry and eloquence" works, through "raising in it ideas of those things for which custom has appointed them to stand" (163). At places, Burke concedes that words may evoke the full cycle from sound to image-forming and thence to emotion, although here an ellipsis is likely[2]:

> But I am of opinion, that the most general effect even of these words, does not arise from their forming pictures of the several

---

[1] Also see Olivia Smith, *Politics of Language, 1790—1819*, chapter 3. Also see Hazlitt's report of the difference on how Edmund Burke and Thomas Paine writes, in "On the Difference between Writing and Speaking," in *Collected Works of William Hazlitt*, 12: 275.

[2] See Dixon Wecter, "Burke's Theory concerning Words, Images, and Emotion," p. 172.

> things they would represent in the imagination; because on a very diligent examination of my own mind, and getting others to consider theirs, I do not find that once in twenty times any such picture is formed, and when it is, there is most commonly a particular effort of the imagination for that purpose. (Burke 1958: 167)

This antagonism against the visualizing and imaging property of words implies a distrust of an abstract and transparent medium of writing and representation, which, through abstracting and de-territorializing, pulls the mediated communication away from its affective and immediate environment[1]. Burke explains this through a comparison:

> In reality poetry and rhetoric do not succeed in exact description as well as painting does; their business is to affect rather by sympathy than imitation; to display rather the effect of things on the mind of the speaker, or of others, than to present a clear idea of the things themselves. (172)

This conclusion agrees with the traditional distinction, often discussed in the eighteenth century, between spoken words that are conventional signs, and painting that uses natural signs to imitate reality. It even could be dated back to what Aristotle defines as *energeia*: the "actualization of potency, the realization of capacity or capability, the achievement in art and rhetoric of the dynamic and purposive life of nature," not to "the achievement in verbal discourse of a natural quality or of a pictorial quality that is highly natural [*enargeia*]" (qtd. in Bender 1972: 9). Eric Havelock, in his convincing argument on how the beginnings of Greek philosophy are tied in with the restricting of thought brought about by writing (1963), shows the correlation between writing ("verbal discourse") and the visual as perceptual apparatus has existed far from antiquity. The term *idea* meaning "form," is visually

---

[1] This antagonism, as a matter of fact, is also recognizable in Henry Home's theory of criticism quoted in the epigraph of this chapter.

based, and comes from the same root as the Latin *video*, to see. Havelock argues that Plato's entire epistemology is unwittingly a programmed endorsement of writing, which Plato conceives of through analogies with a visible form. It is voiceless, immobile, devoid of all warmth, not interactive but isolated, and abstracted out of the human life-world. Plato does this through rejecting the old oral, mobile, warm, personally interactive life-world of an oral culture, which is represented by the poets that he would not allow in his Republic[1]. The oral culture and its properties could easily be associated with the rhetoric and poetic style in Burke's aesthetic theory. The exploitation of fear and ignorance of rhetoric and thus its "power to seduce"—if we use a phrase from Burke's French contemporary Condorcet (100)[2], is an art of communication based on face-to-face exchange. It is prevalent in Burke's writing, which is charged with emotional persuasion, a rhetoric power assuming the primacy of speech. Both—with Burke—as witnesses of the decline of formal rhetoric and the triumph of print, Condorcet remains more as a prophet, to whom the medium of print, in part creating a new public sphere for its productions, ensures that "all proofs are developed and all doubts discussed" (100) and hence that no tyrannical cause prevails as it did through the old techniques of verbal seduction; whereas Burke appeals to the power of English habit and custom with an emotional rhetoric of persuasion through an acoustic economy of the language.

II.iii. Body Economy of Sentiment and Somatic Aesthetics of Theatricality

Burke's view of language reflects a formula of clarity as impediment to communicating the sublime emotionalism not merely in as *visual* and *written*, an essentially ideographic medium, but also of

---

[1] Also see Water J. Ong, *Orality and Literacy*, pp. 27-28, 79.
[2] Also see John Guillory, "Genesis of the Media Concept," p. 325.

painting, a largely iconological medium[1]:

> ... and even in painting a judicious obscurity in some things contributes to the effect of the picture; because the images in painting are exactly similar to those in nature; and in nature dark, confused, uncertain images have a greater power on the fancy to form the grander passions than those have which are more clear (sic) and determinate. (Burke 1958: 62)

Obscurity, uncertainty, simplicity and infinity are celebrated over clarity and definiteness, the latter of which could be achieved through detailed mimetic descriptions. That "power on the fancy" from "nature dark," a sort of sensation or effect of an object upon the faculty of sensibility is of course Burke's violently emotional sublime, one example of which is the phonocentric moment of "the inviolable oath." It provides an instance of "the sublime that helped to release this flood of emotionalism into the aesthetic theory of the period" (Monk 1960: 61). Immanuel Kant, a contemporary of Burke's, terms that as "matter," and invests it with substance or the permanent in experience, whereas the *formal* and *material* are considered as "secondary" or "superficial" (Caygill 1989: 288-289). This theory of a preexistent virtually unmediated, a mystical sense of oneness, of being within a universal continuum and the hierarchical position that it has over others—such as "means," "form," "media," "technique"—has been a recognizable pattern in the political economy of Western perceptions. Burke, in his writings on aesthetic and politics of revolution, is rather typical of this logocentric metaphysics, which takes a physiological form of *patho-centrism*, as explicitly stated in another passage:

---

[1] I am aware that the use of such terms as "medium" and "technology" might make anachronistic mistakes. Nevertheless, on the other hand, we are all already always anachronistic, since history is a lost myth and historicism is a modernity's mistake we should all avoid. For a historical investigation upon the emergence of the media concept in the late nineteenth century as a response to the proliferation of new technical media, such as the telegraph and phonograph, see John Guillory's essay "Genesis of the Media Concept."

> The truth is all verbal description, merely as naked description, though never so exact, conveys so poor and insufficient an idea of the thing described, that it could scarcely have the smallest effect, if the speaker did not call in to his aid those modes of speech that mark a strong and lively feeling in himself. Then, by the contagion of our passions, we catch a fire already kindled in another, which probably might never have been struck out by the object described. (Burke 1958: 175-176)

This Burkean model of communication requires that the body of both the speaker and the audience be involved with sentimental investments. "[N]aked description[s]" do not convey emotional messages, whether they are "the contagion of our passions" or that "fire." Objects make sense in relation to feeling subjects. The body, and all its sensations, take on communicative implications, which appear to be correlative with orality. This somatic involvement in sign production in conjunction with a theory of media is similar to what Condillac proposes in his *Essai sur l'origine des connaissances humaines* (1746). For Condillac, an infant, who, in the language originating in speech, lacks full control over his bodily motor functions, has to have recourse to the tongue. This most flexible organ complements the language of action: "[T]wo codes develop, supplementing each other and referring to each other at the intersection of the two media, body and voice" (von Mücke 36). It is a theological act to turn this primeval signifying practice into a gestural language so that the social meaning of the human sound can be realized. Condillac produces a moment of tracing a scene of imaginary plenitude in this history of language. He situates a passage in the Old Testament, where the direct force of the spoken word works its tactile, spectacular and theatrical significance upon the body:

> It seems that this mode of speaking was preserved chiefly to instruct the people in regard to matters in which they were most deeply concerned, such as government and religion. Because as it

> acted upon the imagination with greater force, the impression was more durable. Its expression contained even something elevated and noble, which the language of articulated sounds, as yet poor and barren, could not come up to. This mode of speaking the ancients called by the name of *dance*, which is the reason of its being said that David danced before the ark. (qtd. in von Mücke 36)

This *dancing* moment in a history of human perceptual signification, as contextualized in an oral tradition and a culture of spectacle, nevertheless, experiences a division of labor brought about by the advent of the new medium of writing. The new medium separates poetry from music, and thus word from sound. In this way, the modern world is marked by "a language that has come to follow the rules of logic and ... has a full repertoire of artificial signs and thereby the perfect means for analysis" (von Mücke 37). The progress of analytical knowledge and the development of a scientific methodology presents a history into a modern media of language, and Edmund Burke is concerned with the loss of "graphicity[1]" and "tactility" as presented in the primeval moment of this history both in his writing on aesthetics and reflection on the French Revolution.

Terry Eagleton declares modern aesthetics as "born as a discourse of the body" in the mid-eighteenth century (Eagleton 1990: 13), and Samuel H. Monk argues that the chief fault of writers on the sublime during the first half of the eighteenth century is "their habit of over-simplifying the aesthetic experience, of attempting to find the *one* sublime emotion or quality" (Monk 1960: 76). For Burke, this is an aesthetic theory mediated through his medium of writing to advocate a conservative politics of culture and empire. It is emotionally charged with sublime experience that affects the body, and positions the feeling in a rhetoric of history. This theorization accords with materialists in ancient times, for whom matter is a "lyric substance" more akin to

1 See von Mücke, *Virtue and the Veil of Illusion*, p. 37.

comets, meteors, and electrical storms than to some hard, uniform mass.[1] In his *Aesthetica* (1750), Alexander Baumgarten, the German philosopher, formulates "aesthetics" as the "whole region of human perception and sensation, in contrast to the more rarefied domain of conceptual thought." Such a definition predominates before it turns into a discourse about individualized "taste" at the end of the eighteenth century. This historical change of the aesthetic discourse is taken by cultural conservatives like Burke, and it co-evolves with an inward turn of interiority. In Burke's aesthetic formula—as in Condillac's first part of the *Essai*—the body and its aesthetic sentiments are not *separated*, but in a sensual and synesthetic moment of *dancing*, which is more an invention of the primeval out of a writing economy. Writing is usually taken as a means of a transmission of meaning that is designated as particular, secondary, inscribed, and supplementary, the existence of which pre-mediates the primeval moment, either dancing or the Burkean inviolable oath. In other words, the Enlightenment thinkers take a defensive and conservative strategy through making the birth of aesthetics as a body economy with a character of divinity. It is a strategy more indicative of their confrontation with the coming of modern writing[2], which, in a history of modernity, "conform[s] to a law of mechanical economy[3]." If "abstraction"[4] involves "withdrawing," "separation," or "removal," and can be defined in a specifically philosophical sense as "the act or process of separating in thought, of considering a thing independently

[1] See Daniel Tiffany, *Toy Medium: Materialism and Modern Lyric* for a detailed exploration of "poetic substances" and iconologies of matter.

[2] For a case study on Denis Diderot, on how he assumes the role of the universal philosopher and participates in the *Encyclopedié* with a contemplating attitude—a noble defender of humanity, truth, equality, and reason—and how he holds hostility to the partiality of the journalists and the printed media in general (newspapers, periodicals, and newsletters), see Anne Fastrup, "Mediating *le philosophe*: Diderot's Strategic Self-Representations," in *This Is Enlightenment*, pp. 265-283.

[3] Jacques Derrida, "Signature Event Context," in *Limited INC*, p. 4.

[4] See *OED* online, under the entry of "abstraction."

of its associations[1]," Burke's aesthetic theory embraces the totality and immediacy of experience and feeling before being displaced by writing. His French contemporary Diderot centers on the achievements of the blind mathematician Nicholas Saunderson in *Lettre sur les aveugles* (1749), and uses this instance to illustrate the knowledge attainable by the sense of touch alone. Diderot gives a more contemporary definition of "abstraction," with regard to sense of embodiments:

> [A]bstraction merely amounts to the ability to separate in our thoughts the sensible qualities of bodies either from each other or from the body itself, which serves as their material support; error arises if this separation is badly executed or applied; it can be badly executed in metaphysical questions, and it can be badly applied in questions concerned with physics and mathematics. (qtd. in von Mücke, 44-45)[2]

Indeed, the sensory path to knowledge emerged as a problem for the newly reconfigured field of aesthetics. Another example comes from Gotthold Ephraim Lessing (1729—1781), who formulates the media of painting, poetry, theater by adjudicating just how appropriately a given

---

[1] In a way, the history of language and writing outlined by the Enlightenment thinkers is that of separation and gradation, the kind of theoretical foundation for the German comparatist philological studies in the nineteenth century—as identified by Derrida in "Signature Event Context": "Describing the history of the types of writing, their continuous derivation from a common root that is never displaced and which establishes a sort of community of analogical participation among all the species of writing, Condillac concludes (in what is virtually a citation of Warburton, as is most of this chapter): 'Thus, the general history of writing proceeds by simple gradation from the state of painting to that of the letter; for letters are the final steps that are left to be taken after the Chinese marks which, on the one hand, participate in that of letters just as the hieroglyphs participate both in Mexican paintings and Chinese characters. These characters are so close to our writing that an alphabet simply diminishes the inconvenience of their great number and is their succinct abbreviation'" (Derrida 1988: 5).

[2] The great medieval thinker William of Ockham articulated the problem also with considerable sensory acuity: "To abstract is to understand one thing without understanding another at the same time even though in reality the one is not separated from the other, e. g., sometimes the intellect understands the whiteness which is in milk and does not understand the sweetness of milk. Abstraction in this sense can belong even to a sense, for a sense can apprehend one sensible without apprehending another" (qtd. in Jones, 93).

art form targets its particular sense whether it is eyesight, hearing or feeling[1].[2] Negating a possible "abstraction" in the distribution of the sensory qualities of bodies at the first place, Burke maintains that the affective serves as the message and the channel of subjective and saturating communication or continuum. Ruptures between the body, its thoughts, sensations and ideas are politically not justifiable. This address of sensations is from its physiological embryology, part of the science of man starting from Locke's *An Essay Concerning Human Understanding*, as G.S. Rousseau's classical essay argues[3]. If mediation is the manner in which, according to Raymond Williams, the producer becomes alienated from his product[4], the immediacy is an absolute state in which the producer and production becomes unified into one seamless organic unity. It is a myth of an experiential totality for Burke, the loss of which could be attributed to the institution of the artificial signs of a print culture.

Burke's French contemporary Denis Diderot, in his *Lettre sur les sourds et muets* (1751), puts this in a slightly different way:

> Thus, poetic discourse is touched by some spirit that moves and vivifies all of its syllables. What is spirit? Only a few times have I felt its presence, but all I know of it is that it is due to this spirit that things are said and represented simultaneously, that at the same time they are grasped by the understanding, the soul is moved by them, the imagination sees them, and the ears understand them. And this discourse is not merely a concatenation of energetic terms,

---

1 See Caroline Jones, "Senses," p. 93.

2 "The first person to compare painting with poetry was a man of fine feeling who observed that both arts produced a similar effect upon him .... A second observer, in attempting to get at the nature of this pleasure, discovered that both proceed from the same source. Beauty .... A third, who examined the value and distribution of these general rules, observed that some of them are more predominant in painting, others in poetry .... The first was the amateur, the second the philosopher, and the third the critic" (Lessing, *Laocoön: an Essay on the Limits of Painting and Poetry*, p. 3).

3 See G. S. Rousseau, "Nerves, Spirits, and Fibres," pp. 139-140.

4 See Raymond Williams, "From Medium to Social Practice," in his *Marxism and Literature*, pp. 158-164.

> which expose the thought with force and nobility; it is also a tissue of hieroglyphs piled upon each other, that paint the thought. In this sense I could say that all poetry is emblematic. (qtd. in von Mücke 46)

For Diderot, what poeticizes the primeval moment of spirit and origin is all at once oral (said), visual (seen), and acoustic (heard). More significantly, this associated concatenation of perceptions combines with a palimpsest of pictorial writing and representation to communicate this spirit, which is identified as an emblematic property of poetry. Thus, Diderot "gives primacy to the simultaneity of a multiplicity of perceptions that constitute the totality of the soul as a 'moving picture'" (von Mücke 46). Addressing what is defined by Baumgarten as the crucial issue for the new mid-eighteenth-century discipline of aesthetics that engages all the driving springs and motives of the soul[1], Diderot turns his and the painter's gaze inwardly to a "*tableau mouvant*" instead of the exterior material details traced by the painter's brush:

> The paintbrush merely executes over time what the eye of the painter embraces in an instant. Linguistic formulations required decomposition; but to see an object, to find it beautiful, to experience an agreeable sensation, to want to possess it, all this is the state of the soul in one single instant. (qtd. in von Mücke 46)

Dorothea E. von Mücke points out that this is the same project of "establishing and maintaining the soul's unity and the unity of perception" for a "totality of the operations of the soul[2]," whether the objects of their critical negation are linguistic decomposition or imitative description. The overall effect of an aesthetic object and its correlation with the multiple sensorial perceptions it evokes is distinctly and clearly elaborated by this of Burke's contemporaries:

> The state of our soul is one thing, the account we give of it to

---

[1] See von Mücke, *Virtue and the Veil of Illusion*, p. 46, note 25.
[2] See von Mücke, *Virtue and the Veil of Illusion*, p. 46.

> ourselves or others is another thing. On the one hand, there is the total and instantaneous sensation of this state; on the other hand, there is the successive and detailed attention we must give to this state in order to analyze it, to express it, and to understand it. Our soul is a moving picture after which we continuously paint: it takes us quite some time to render it with some degree of fidelity, but it exists in its entirety and all at once: the mind does not proceed step by step like verbal expression. (qtd. in von Mücke 46)

The totality and instantaneity of an immediate perceptual to the world is privileged over the figured actions of communication, either verbal expression or imagistic imitation, both of which set up conditions for "objectivity" and "abstraction" in the sense of personal disengagement or distancing. Actions of communication through writing coordinate with the modern consciousness deeply conditioned by literacy and print, and are entirely different from what Jack Goody and Ian Watt call "direct semantic ratification" (Goody 29) by the real-life situations in which the word is used here and now[1]. Terry Eagleton argues that the distinction that the term "aesthetics" initially enforces in the mid-eighteenth century "between the material and the immaterial: between things and thoughts, sensations and ideas" remains "that which is bound up with our creaturely life as opposed to that which conducts some shadowy existence in the recesses of the mind" (Eagleton 1990: 13). Here in the Burkean scenario, the distinction seems to be a rehearsal of the romantic division between the physical as the organic, living and feeling substance, and the material as the inert, dead, or mechanical[2]. Or, on this point, Immanuel Kant, the German philosopher contemporary with Burke, defines more explicitly in Part I, Book II, of the *Critique of Judgment*: "Beauty is concerned with limited objects, with forms; the sublime is to be found in objects that are limitless, that have no form, though they are always accompanied with a 'super-thought' of totality" (qtd. in Monk 6). Thus, aesthetics could be taken as

[1] Also see Water J. Ong, *Orality and Literacy*, p. 46.
[2] See Arthur O. Lovejoy's classic essay, "On the Discrimination of Romanticisms."

an instance of the body economy of presence, or what Giorgio Agamben calls "apparatus," a concept with its evolution from the Greek *oikonomia* that Agamben extends from that of Michel Foucault:

> [L]iterally anything that has in some way the capacity to capture, orient, determine, intercept, model, control, or secure the gestures, behaviors, opinions, or discourses of living beings. Not only, therefore, prisons, madhouses, the panopticon, schools, confession, factories, disciplines, juridical measures, and so forth (whose connection with power is in a certain sense evident), but also the pen, writing, literature, philosophy, agriculture, cigarettes, navigation, computers, cellular telephones and—why not—language itself, which is perhaps the most ancient of apparatuses—one in which thousands and thousands of years ago a primate inadvertently let himself be captured, probably without realizing the consequences that he was about to face. (Agamben 2009a: 14)

This celebrated somatic aesthetics, as an apparatus of the body and feeling, could be spectacular or theatrical, but its aesthetic preference is primarily that of "immediacy" and "authenticity" in the primeval moment of communicating sentiments before the coming of the modern textual culture.

II.iv. Sentiment, Immediacy, and *Ekphrasis*

Burke assigns this reliance on feeling—"the contagion of our passions," as a means of somatic communication, that is—as the "business" of poetry and rhetoric, which is "to affect rather by sympathy than imitation; to display rather the effect of things on the mind of the *speaker* [*emphasis mine*], or of others, than to present a clear idea of the things themselves" (Burke 1958: 172). This preoccupation with emotions as an aesthetic and epistemological question was widely addressed by theorists in the mid-eighteenth century[1]. Lord Kames states that "by a good tragedy, all the social passions are excited," and passions arise "from that eminent principle of sympathy, which is the cement of human society[2]," for instance. What is specific in Burke's aesthetics is an emphasis upon an auditory and tactile immediacy, suggested by "a fire kindled" by "the contagion of our passions." This somatic presence of bodily sentiment as a medium of communication remains antagonistic to visual mimesis and its consequences in sensorial formation, the latter of which, as argued through this current writing, dovetails with a rising modern textual culture and deserves a very significant position in discussions of Western perceptual modernity[3]. For Burke, poetry and rhetoric are superior to painting, which, as a very *visual* medium, can "succeed in exact description" (Burke 1958: 172) and "imitation" through presenting "a clear idea of the things themselves" to its visual spectators. Poetry and rhetoric are more of oral and acoustic media, and are more accustomed to invoking a sense of immediacy and presence. They address an English audience before the coming of ideas, signs, and styles which establish and cross new cultural and social boundaries. This suggests a cultural moment of the mid-eighteenth-century Britain when a "reading public" in the modern sense is not formed yet. It is not until the late eighteenth century that is ushered in a confusing, unsettled world of reading and writing[4].

David Wellbery elaborates very well the difference between painting and poetry as two different media in his investigation upon Lessing's *Laocoön* (1766):

> The signs of painting are motivated both materially and formally. Their spatial structure corresponds to the spatial structure of the

---

[1] See Samuel H. Monk, *The Sublime*, p. 28. Also see Adela Pinch, *Strange Fits of Passion*, pp. 1-16.

[2] Lord Kames, *Essays on the Principles of Morality and Natural Religion*, pp. 12, 16. Quoted in James Averill, *Wordsworth and the Poetry of Human Suffering*, p. 134.

[3] For a genealogical history of the rise of visuality in the West, see Jonathan Crary, *Techniques of the Observer*.

[4] See Jon P. Klancher, *The Making of English Reading Audiences, 1790—1832*.

> corporeal object represented and the individual signs duplicate the material nature of that object insofar as they are solid, colored and fully determined as material things. The motivation of poetic signs, however, is only formal. The sign vehicles bear no similarity to the action-referent except as regards their successivity. The poem replicates only the form of perception, not its content. Poetry is a natural sign only because its signs present themselves to the reader in the same successive form as would the action itself. Poetry, therefore, maintains the advantages provided by its more advanced stage of semiosis; its individual signs remain arbitrary. The distinguishing feature of poetry is that it recovers for language the form of intuitive presence because the poem as a whole attains to the status of a natural sign. (Wellbery 1984: 236-237)

The difference between these two generic conventions is that between a natural sign from an arbitrary sign. It is distinguished by "the manner in which signifier and signified are related" (von Mücke 14). Dorothea von Mücke suggests as follows: "Whereas for the arbitrary sign the two are merely yoked together by convention, the signifier of a natural sign is informed by the signified" (von Mücke 14). The notion of "the poem as a whole" and poetry as a natural sign immediately raises the issue of textual mediation of perception. It suggests that through poetry, an immediate presence would be presented, and a quasi-immediate access to the "natural" world would be established. It is exactly in the same way that Burke organizes the socializing function of aesthetics into an *immediate* and *affective* economy. Which could be labeled as an "anti-theatrical transparency or immediacy," a pattern of perception not irrelevant to Burke's puritanical background[1]?

A historical investigation into the political connotation of the word "immediacy" and the historical world in which it once worked, would suggest an interesting understanding of further layers of power and control in the history of mediation. In this conception, "immediacy"

[1] For a puritanical tradition of the anti-theatrical prejudice, see Jonas Barish's *The Antitheatrical Prejudice*, especially chapters IV, V and VI.

describes the condition of the relationship of a person who is subject to a power superior to her. Existing primarily in the feudal context of medieval Europe, "immediacy" describes the essentially binding relationship of the tenant to the landlord, or the vassal to the sovereign: "In *Feudal* language, said of the relation between two persons one of whom holds of the other directly, as in *immediate lord, tenant, tenure*"[1]. The understanding of "immediacy" in such a manner fades out of the lexicon in direct correlation to the political diminishment of the feudal "holding" of a person within one's power. Yet this leads to a political economy reading of the human sensorial orientation in general. J. F. Suter argues that Burke

> develops an interesting dialectic between talent and property, between those who have nothing apart from their native gifts and natural ability (lawyers, doctors, traders, writers) and those whose influence in the states comes from inherited wealth (aristocrats, squires, clergymen). (Suter 63)

For Burke, property is a "sluggish, inert, and timid" principle. It must predominate in the state, and must be protected from the "invasions" of that "vigorous and active" principle of ability. Burke thinks that the "solid substance of land" (qtd. in Suter 63) must "counterpoise the superior skill and vigour of the burghers" (Suter 63). Suter argues that "Burke's idea of 'a natural and just order', maintained by a 'chain of subordination' between the landlord, the farmer and the labourer is still that of a predominantly feudal society, based on the 'natural' production of the land" (71). For Baumgarten, aesthetics is the sister of logic, a kind of *ratio inferior* or feminine analogue of reason at the lower level of sensational life. Burke takes this feminine analogue of the sublime as constitutive of the autonomy of culture, and society as an expressive or organic totality. In his aesthetic theory, the intuitive dogmatism of imagination, the priority of local affections and unarguable allegiances, the incontrovertible character of "immediate" experience, all work for a

[1] See *OED* online, under the entry of "intermediate," A1b.

discourse that history is a spontaneous growth impervious to rational analysis[1]. Then, the questions become: What kind of politics of psycho-physiology does this imply? How to reorient this aesthetic and critical speculation on the sublime in the eighteenth-century Britain in relation to a history of feelings in mediation? What is its significance to a(n) (anti-)theatrical construct of selfhood that has been distributed and disseminated in Western affective modernity? These are the questions that I try to address through setting up a triptych of aesthetics (as a psycho-physiology of the intelligible and the sensible), politics (in its relation to aesthetics), and a historical development of the print as a media or *techne* (or more or less, as a technology of self in the Foucauldian sense)[2].

The very possibility of affective dispersal has indeed become a significant aesthetic concern of Burke's. The attitudes of suspicion and hostility he holds of "verbal description" or "naked description" in a rhetoric of affective communications is a reaction against the very notion of *ut pictura poesis* ("as a painting, so also a poem"), the practice of which by the mid-eighteenth century had been established more than a hundred years as a dogma of criticism[3]. This sentiment holds a relation of what W. J. T. Mitchell defines as "institutions of the visible" (visual arts, visual media, practices of display and spectating) and "institutions of the verbal" (literature, language, discourse, practices of speech and writing, audition and reading)[4]. A contemporary of Burke's, Lessing shares this sentiment in his *Laocoön* (1766). It is a sentiment against *ekphrasis*, which is the verbal representation of visual representation[5]. In Lessing's aesthetic polemic, it is "prescribed as a law to all poets"

---

[1] These are the forms, identified by Terry Eagleton, in which the aesthetic becomes a weapon in the hands of political reactionaries, a pattern recognizable through Burke and Coleridge to Matthew Arnold and T. S. Eliot, see Terry Eagleton, *The Ideology of the Aesthetic*, pp. 16, 60.

[2] This follows a methodology of recent media studies, as outlined by W. J. T. Mitchell and Mark Hansen in their "Introduction" to *Critical Terms for Media Studies* (2010).

[3] See Roy Park, "*Ut Pictura Poesis*," p. 155.

[4] See W. J. T. Mitchell, "Word and Image," pp. 49.

[5] See W. J. T. Mitchell, "Ekphrasis and the Other." Also see James Heffernan's article, "Ekphrasis and Representation," and Heffernan's *The Museum of Words*.

that "they should not regard the limitations of painting as beauties in their own art." For poets, to "employ the same artistic machinery" as the painter does would be to "convert a superior being into a doll." It would make as much sense, argues Lessing, "as if a man, with the power and privilege of speech, were to employ the signs which the mutes in a Turkish seraglio had invented to supply the want of a voice" (qtd. in Mitchell 1994: 154-155). W. J. T. Mitchell takes this phobia of Lessing's regarding literary emulation of the visual arts as "not only of muteness or loss of eloquence, but of castration, a threat which is re-echoed in the transformation from 'superior being' to 'doll,' a mere feminine plaything" (Mitchell 1994: 155). Mitchell elaborates this ekphrastic fear of free exchange, transference and reciprocity between visual and verbal art as a phobia of "a dangerous promiscuity" and an attempt to "regulate the borders with firm distinctions between the senses, modes of representation, and the objects proper to each" (155). For Burke under discussion here, it is a defensive stance taken to maintain the pure English sense of custom, manners, tradition and sensibility through the technique of *immediacy* of feelings.

II.v. Print, Communication of Feelings, and Reformulation of Sympathy

If print, in Burke and Condorcet's time, was still an art, "in the special sense of being a highly skilled craft or what was called a mechanical art" (Guillory 2010: 325), the Burkean rein of rhetoric or oratory may be situated into a historical context, in which speech and rhetoric still dominated the most important social venues of communication. It remains arguable whether a rhetorical hermeneutics is adequate to support a history of communication, and whether a communication concept as an explicit challenge to the system of rhetoric emerged in early modernity [1]. Discontent with rhetoric became discernible in the seventeenth century,

[1] See John Guillory, "Genesis of the Media Concept," pp. 327; also see Alan G. Gross and William M. Keith, *Rhetorical Hermeneutics: Invention and Interpretation in the Age of Science*; and Wilbur Samuel Howell, *Eighteenth-Century British Logic and Rhetoric*.

nevertheless. John Guillory argues in his seminal essay that such a discontent "produced the first attempts to advance a different concept for the goal of speech, a concept we now know as communication"[1]. The way Burke configures aesthetics is in the middle of this reorientation of language toward the goal of communication as a pressure of the print medium on the conceptualization of writing. It suggests a changing figuration of what Foucault reformulates notions of state and power as "governmentality" in an early Western modernity as well. Significant to governmentality is the operation of "biopower," or "a power bent on generating forces, making them grow, and ordering them, rather than one dedicated to impeding them, making them submit, or destroying them" (Foucault 1990: 136). Amit S. Rai explains that it is a new permutation of modalities of practices, discourses, sentiments, and disciplines, which is much more than "policing"—"that far-flung apparatus of normalization which tied together as widely disparate phenomena as hygiene boards, and evangelical missions" (Rai 62). This Foucauldian conceptualization of the modern technology of self seems significant to understand the Burkean aesthetics in relation to "persuasion, communication, means, medium, media, mediation, representation," which is a linked set of evolving terms that John Guillory uses to chart the reorientation of language toward the goal of communication in the early modern genesis of the media concept (Guillory 2010: 326). Its historical predecessors include aesthetics in the way Terry Eagleton declares it "born as a discourse of the body" in the eighteenth century, or as "the distribution of the sensible," the way Jacques Rancière takes it[2]. In *The Order of Things*, Foucault outlines the paradigmatic shift from resemblance to representation in the knowledge of Western culture from the end of the sixteenth century. He takes such a shift significant to and simultaneous to the rise of modern Western governmentality, in which sympathy is taken as one of the four essential "forms of

---

[1] Also see Walter J. Ong's book *Ramus, Method, and the Decay of Dialogue: From the Art of Discourse to the Art of Reason.*

[2] See Jacques Rancière, *The Politics of Aesthetic: The Distribution of the Sensible.*

resemblance" at the moment when "resemblance was about to relinquish its relation with knowledge and disappear, in part at least, from the sphere of cognition" (Foucault 1970: 17). For Foucault, sympathy

> excites the things of the world to movement and can draw even the most distant of them together. It is a principle of mobility: it attracts what is heavy to the heaviness of the earth, what is light up towards the weightless ether; it drives the root towards the water, and it makes the great yellow disk of the sunflower turn to follow the curving path of the sun. Moreover, by drawing things towards one another in an exterior and visible movement, it also gives rise to a hidden interior movement—a displacement of qualities that take over from one another in a series of relays .... Sympathy is an instance of the *Same* so strong and so insistent that it will not rest content to be merely one of the forms of likeness; it has the dangerous power of *assimilating*, of rendering things identical to one another, of mingling them, of causing their individuality to disappear—and thus of rendering them foreign to what they were before. Sympathy transforms. It alters, but in the direction of identity, so that if its power were not counter-balanced it would reduce the world to a point, to a homogeneous mass, to the featureless form of the Same: all its parts would hold together and communicate with one another without a break, with no distance between them, like those metal chains held suspended by sympathy to the attraction of a single magnet. (Foucault 1970: 23-24)

Foucault defines this form of resemblance in the early modern Europe through its physics, not its chemistry, nor biology: to excite, to mobilize, to assimilate, and to homogenize. It is a form of knowledge on a science of mechanics and thermodynamics, as Foucault illustrates:

> [F]ire, because it is warm and light, rises up into the air, towards which its flames untiringly strive; but in doing so it loses its dryness (which made it akin to the earth) and so acquires humidity (which

links it to water and air); it disappears therefore into light vapour, into blue smoke, into clouds: it becomes air. (Foucault 1970: 23)

It is descriptive of the classical world, where the world is linked together like a chain through the way the figures of knowledge are organized by articulations of the semantic web of resemblance like *convenientia, aemulatio, analog* and *sympathies*[1]. Their primary concern is similar to what is covered in Book I of Newton's *Principia*, "the two principal cases of attractions," namely, the question of action at a distance. R. W. Home puts it in this way: "[O]scillatory motions brought about by forces varying directly as the distance between two bodies, and motions in conical orbits brought about by forces varying inversely as the square of the distance" (Home 360). It is more of the nonhuman realm of what Wordsworth called "rocks, and stones, and trees,"[2] and all the rest—the earth, the oceans, the atmosphere, the planets, and stars in their courses. In the British context, the science of man—the human realm—"may not have had an influence on the manifold aspects of routine daily life until the mid-eighteenth century" (Rousseau 145), which began to be dealt with in John Locke's *Essay* published in 1690. Decades ago, Northrop Frye [3] famously defines the mid and late eighteenth century as an "Age of Sensibility." Extravagant feelings, emotions, sentiments and epistemologies of them were proliferated by the production of various "sets of physiological texts" (Rousseau 143). It includes the eighteenth-century schools of Scottish morality, English empirical philosophy, and even French ethical thought. Out of such a historical context, Burke's aesthetics of the sublime and the beautiful proposes an approach to the study of man by means of a theory of sensory perception and a theory of knowledge, which directly form his understanding of the physiology and psychology of perception. Instead of taking "beauty, sublimity, taste, imagination, and the picturesque"

---

[1] See Foucault, *The Order of Things*, pp. 17-44.

[2] See Wordsworth, "A slumber did my spirit seal," in *Romanticism: An Anthology*, p. 478.

3 See Northrop Frye "Towards Defining an Age of Sensibility." Also see R. F. Brissenden, *Virtue in Distress: Studies in the Novel of Sentiment from Richardson to Sade*.

merely as "the most important ideas" in eighteenth-century England as Samuel H. Monk's classic study on the sublime did, this current writing outlines a genealogy of the politics of the body in mediation.

It is, therefore, not fortuitous, nor anomalous that sympathy and liberal sentiment emerged in the eighteenth century at precisely the moment that Foucault locates the rise of governmentality. As Amit S. Rai writes:

> [I]ndeed, discipline was enabled by, and security legitimized through sympathy for the other—the poor, the heathen, criminals, delinquents, deviants, prostitutes, slaves, colonial subjects, and the insane were to be sympathized with, and their condition ameliorated. In other words, sympathy was central in making the other proper to the self, and so a way of habituating the self to propriety. (Rai 62)

Mobility of affinity between things is transferred upon that of sensibility, cognate with the proliferation of feelings. It seems that, in the eighteenth century, sympathy, an European concept primarily on "(real or supposed) affinity between certain things, by virtue of which they are similarly or correspondingly affected by the same influence, affect or influence each other (esp. in some occult way), or attract or tend toward each other," becomes more on "relation between two bodily organs or parts such that disorder, or any condition, of the one induces a corresponding condition in the other."[1] For Burke, it

> must be considered as a sort of substitution, by which we are put into the place of another man, and affected in my respects as he is affected; so that this passion may either partake of the nature of those which regard self-preservation, and turning upon pain may be a source of the sublime; or it may turn upon ideas of pleasure; and then, whatever has been said of the social affections, whether they regard society in general, or only some particular modes of it, may

[1] See *OED* online, under the entry of "sympathy."

be applicable here. (Burke 1958: 44)

The physical becomes the social. Affinity changes to substitution. This means affective mediation, one of the three principal links in "the great chain of society" (44), is taken as partaking the nature of self-preservation. These invoke in the mind pain, sickness, death and strong emotions of horror. This source of the sublime is an aesthetic of feelings deployed by Burke to establish some specific form of emotional sociality. Through "this principle chiefly that poetry, painting, and other affecting arts, transfuse their passions from one breast to another," (44) physical objects are connected to mental and psychological states. At one place, he quotes this "curious story of the celebrated physiognomist Campanella" from a "Mr. Spon, in his *Récherches d'Antiquité*":

> This man, it seems, had not only made very accurate observations on human faces, but was very expert in mimicking such as were any way remarkable. When he had a mind to penetrate into the inclinations of those he had to deal with, he composed his face, his gesture, and his whole body, as nearly as he could into the exact similitude of the person he intended to examine; and then carefully observed what turn of mind he seemed to acquire by this change. So that, says my author, he was able to enter into the dispositions and thoughts of people as effectually as if he had been changed into the very men ... Our minds and bodies are so closely and intimately connected, that one is incapable of pain or pleasure without the other. Campanella, of whom we have been speaking, could so abstract his attention from any sufferings of his body, that he was able to endure the rack itself without much pain; and in lesser pains everybody must have observed, that, when we can employ our attention on anything else, the pain has been for a time suspended; on the other hand, if by any means the body is indisposed to perform such gestures, or to be stimulated into such emotions, as any passion usually produces in it, that passion itself can never arise, though its cause should be never so strong in action; though it should be merely mental, and

immediately affecting none of the senses. (Burke 1958: 133)[1]

Contrary to the expressive mode of emotions that internalizes feelings[2] and emphasizes inner feelings as the ultimate motivation for external expressive behavior[3], the dissemination of the Campanella case in that historical period[4] suggests the popularity of the circumstantial mode of emotions: human feelings and emotions[5] not inward yet. The physiological and psychological inward turn of interiority was not in its place until the saturation of textual signs and the literary culture it produced were simultaneously put in the process. This passage on an economy of the exteriority of emotions and how Campanella takes it as a theatrical performance, again confirms that Burke's episteme of writing is situated more of an early modern rhetoric. It is also important to bear in mind that Burke prescribes an ordering of these "affecting arts."

---

[1] For a brief cultural history of English account of Campanella's discoveries and its relation to Bacon, Hobbes, John Bulwer and the arch-enemy of the English stage, William Prynne, see Jean-Christophe Agnew, *Worlds Apart*, pp. 95-96.

[2] And "this process of internalization *fabricates the distinction between interior and exterior life*, offering us a distinction between the psychic and the social that differs significantly from an account of the psychic internalization of norms" (Butler 19), as Judith Butler suggests in *The Psychic Life of Power: Theories in Subjection.*

[3] Which was popular in nineteenth-century psychology (as adopted by Stanislavski's dramaturgical theory)—part of what the writing presented as work, as institution and practice, pre-mediates through the long eighteenth century, as I would argue through the current writing. In the 1920s Soviet Union, the popularity of the Stanislavski system was challenged by Vsevolod Meyerhold, who developed biomechanical acting as an actor's training techniques by synthesizing behaviorist psychology, Taylorist motion economy, and Soviet theories of kinetics to treat the external gestures, movements, and expressions as stimuli to induce certain feelings and emotions—thus emotion is an effect of physical actions to be experienced externally. See Alma Law and Mel Gordon, *Meyerhold, Eisenstein and Biomechanics: Actor Training in Revolutionary Russia*, pp. 33-43. This came to me through an excellent study by Bao Weihong on the application of Meyerhold's theory by Tsai Ming-liang in his films, see Bao Weihong, "Biomechanics of Love: Reinventing the Avant-garde in Tsai Ming-liang's Wayward 'Pornographic Musical.'"

[4] Also see Jean-Christophe Agnew, *Worlds Apart*, pp. 94-95.

[5] I don't invoke a strict distinction between words like *emotion, feeling, passion*, a thorough discussion of which can be found in Thomas Dixon, *From Passions to Emotions: The Creation of a Secular Psychological Category*.

II.vi. Tradition, Class, and Sympathy of the Other

Here is another example. This is from a section entitled "Examples that WORDS may affect without raising IMAGES":

> Here is not one word said of the particulars of her beauty; nothing which can in the least help us to any precise idea of her person; but yet we are much more touched by this manner of mentioning her than by these long and labored descriptions of Helen, whether handed down by tradition, or formed by fancy, which are to be met with in some authors. (Burke 1958: 172)

Parsimony in verbal descriptions is counterbalanced through the very mentioning of Homer in a dismissive gesture. "Tradition" or "fancy" are obtainable through an access to the classical "long and labored descriptions of Helen," the study of which is open only to "such people rather than 'proletarians' who spoke and wrote a type of educated language," as art historian Ernest Gombrich observes (Gombrich 10). Or like Burke himself, who had chances to adore the queen *in person*:

> It is now sixteen or seventeen years since I saw the queen of France, then the dauphiness, at Versailles; and surely never lighted on this orb, which she hardly seemed to touch, a more delightful vision. I saw her just above the horizon, decorating and cheering the elevated sphere she just began to move in, — glittering like the morning-star, full of life, and splendor, and joy. (Burke 1890: 84)

This explains why the "contagion of passions," the transfusion of "passions from one breast to another" "often capable of grafting a delight on wretchedness, misery, and death itself"—which are the sources of the sublime—are either classical or empirical. The beggars in the eighteenth-century London streets, whose activity remained illegal and subject to a wide range of punishments[1], probably would not have an affective and epistemological existence. It is similar to the relational economy of shame in Aristotle's *On Rhetoric*, in which a slave is merely a vehicle of emotion, but not an origin or end[2]. They may be among those sympathized subjects, with whose distresses one obtains a sense of delight:

> [T]here is no spectacle we so eagerly pursue, as that of some uncommon and grievous calamity .... The delight we have in such things, hinders us from shunning scenes of misery; and the pain we feel, prompts us to relieve ourselves in relieving those who suffer. (Burke 1958: 46)

This touches upon an important trope in the eighteenth-century aesthetics, which is the relation of the sublime to the pathetic[3]. It is also significantly reflected in the relation Burke establishes between self-preservation, pain, and the sublime:

> Whatever is fitted in any sort to excite the ideas of pain, and danger, that is to say, whatever is in any sort terrible, or is conversant about terrible objects, or operates in a manner analogous to terror, is a source of the sublime; that is, it is productive of the strongest emotion which the mind is capable of feeling .... When danger or pain presses too near, they are incapable of giving any delight, and are simply terrible; but at certain distances, and with certain modifications, they may be, and they are delightful, as we every day experience. (39-40)

For Burke, pain and danger, sickness and death are ideas that give rise to the strongest passions—of which we are capable—and can be a source of pleasure leading to the sublime. If the keystone of Burke's

---

1 See Nicholas Rogers, "Policing the Poor in Eighteenth-Century London: The Vagrancy Laws and Their Administration."

2 See Daniel M. Gross, *The Secret History of Emotion*, pp. 39-43.

3 See Samuel H. Monk, *The Sublime*, pp. 43-83.

aesthetic is emotion, terror would be the foundation of his theory of the sublime. It is significant to observe that it was Burke

> who converted the early taste for terror into an aesthetic system and who passed it on with great emphasis to the last decades of the century, during which it was used and enjoyed in literature, painting, and the appreciation of natural scenery. (Monk 1960: 87)[1]

This aesthetic theory is not upon complete sympathetic *substitution*. Instead, distance is necessary to ensure an imaginative bridging of it through a sympathetic positioning—the double movement of the gaze of sympathetic power—that repeats and adapts the effective paradox of a sympathetic relation[2]. As Steven Bruhm argues:

> The history of pain ... is in many ways a history of looking; it is a narrative of watching a pained object while occupying a contradictory space both within and outside the object. And within that narrative is a multitude of discourses that mediate the way a culture, or indeed an individual, experiences pain at any given time or place. (Bruhm xx)

It is in this way that Burke, in an instance that has achieved a certain currency lately, exemplifies a morbid celebration of England and Englishness:

> Perhaps it may appear on inquiry that blackness and darkness are in some degree painful by their natural operation, independent of any associations whatsoever. I must observe, that the ideas of darkness and blackness are much the same; and they differ only in this, that blackness is a more confined idea. Mr. Cheselden has given us a very curious story of a boy, who had been born blind, and continued so until he was thirteen or fourteen years old; he was then couched for

---

[1] For instance, see *The Adventures of Ferdinand Count Fathom* by Tobias George Smollett, part 1.

[2] Also see Amit S. Rai, *Rule of Sympathy*, p. 73.

> a cataract, by which operation he received his sight. Among many remarkable particulars that attended his first perceptions and judgments on visual objects, it gave him great uneasiness; and that some time after, upon accidentally seeing a negro woman, he was struck with great horror at the sight. The horror, in this case, can scarcely be supposed to arise from any association. The boy appears by the account to have been particularly observing and sensible for one of his age; and therefore it is probable, if the great uneasiness he felt at the first sight of black had arisen from its connexion with any other disagreeable ideas, he would have observed and mentioned it. (Burke 1958: 144)

Blackness is associated with darkness, which creates an "independent" occasion of distancing and experiencing gothic horror[1]. E. J. Clery finds an interesting instance of the late eighteenth-century gothic horror, which is Horace Walpole's enormous armored hand blocking the passage up the staircase. In that scene, the "dead hand of the past weighing on the present" would be "embodied" in the figures of spirits and supernatural forces, which haunt the living[2]. A parallel case in Burke is that this cataract instance offers such a congenial relation to aesthetic distance and the spectacle through a racially and gendered "other" haunting English perceptions and judgments on visual objects. It is a figurative expression of a English sense of power in (im)possibility of sympathy.

II.vii. Empiricism, Physiological Effect of Sensibility, and Anti-pictorial Narration

In the Preface to the first edition of the *Enquiry*, Burke writes that the confusion in aesthetic ideas could be remedied only by

---

[1] Also see Paul Gilroy, "Cultural Studies and Ethnic Absolutism."

[2] E. J. Clery, "Introduction," in Horace Walpole, *The Castle of Otranto, a Gothic Story*, pp. xxxi-xxxii.

> a diligent examination of our passions in our own breasts; from a careful survey of the properties of things which we find by experience to influence those passions; and from a sober and attentive investigation of the laws of nature, by which those properties are capable of affecting the body, and thus of exciting our passions. (Burke 1958: 1)

Aesthetics is rather an economy of psychological affect and physiology effect for Burke to correct the confusion and ambiguity of discussions of beauty and sublimity, which is the primary reason why the young Burke undertook his investigation of the subject[1]. It is also very empirically based, as J. T. Boulton observes in the stylistic symptoms of Burke's general approach: "I have more than once observed .... From hence I conclude"; "This I know only by conjecture ... but I have since experienced it"; "I have heard some ladies remark" (Boulton xvii). At another place Burke states: "When we go but one step beyond the immediate sensible qualities of things, we go out of our depth" (Burke 1958: 129-130). No wonder Samuel H. Monk would attribute an immense amount of speculation on aesthetic questions in the eighteenth century throughout Europe to "the emphasis which empiricism had placed on sensation" (Monk 1), significant as Burke's *Enquiry* remains as an eighteenth-century archive. David Wellbery argues that by the 1730s the new discipline of aesthetics began to displace the traditional discipline of rhetoric:

> In one and the same movement, art becomes the subject matter of theory and aesthetic experience is transformed into something that takes place between subjects and their representations, without the mediation of inherited bodies of erudition and independently of a locally defined cultural site. (Wellbery 1984: 232)

If we follow this historical argument, Burke's (and British in general) empirical inclination of "the inherited bodies of erudition" and "locally

---

[1] See Samuel H. Monk, *The Sublime*, p. 85.

defined cultural site" requisite for the traditional discipline of rhetoric were to be replaced by a new paradigm of relations between subjects and their representations. That is manifest through the emergence of modern aesthetics. Nevertheless, claimed as "a distinct knowledge of our passions" (Burke 1958: 129), such an esoteric and "classy" communication of affective message is inclined to keep its organization away from exchangeability, suggestive of an obdurate inclination of Burke's conservatism that may possibly lead to a solipsist, private and absorbed myth of aesthetics. This emphases of Burke's upon the local and personal, and his having a stake in "our passions in our own breasts" in an argument on the aesthetics of sympathy reminds, for another time, of its etymology and predominant meaning about to change around mid-century.

In the eighteenth century, this empirical reformulation of passions, specifically sympathy, was rather part of the medicine discourse on "sensibility" in a physiological sense. Physicians began to have concepts of "sensibility" as "the coordinating principle of bodily integrity, providing the basis for the overall integration of the body function" (Ellis 19). Christopher Lawrence argues that, from this framework, sympathy "was no more than the communication of feeling between different bodily organs, manifested by functional disturbance of one organ when another was stimulated" (qtd. in Ellis 19). Steven Bruhm, another critic, draws a similar argument:

> What comes to be valorized by late eighteenth-century moralists as 'sympathy,' then, is physiologically based. Galenic medicine had discussed sympathy, but only as the product of moving humours throughout the body. (12)[1]

The Scottish physician Robert Whytt wrote in his *Essay on the Vital and Other Voluntary Motions of Animals* (1751) that nerves "are endued with feeling, and ... there is a general *sympathy* which prevails through

[1] Also see John Mullan, *Sentiment and Sociability: The Language of Feeling in the Eighteenth Century*.

the whole system; so there is a particular and very remarkable *consent* between various parts of the body" (italicized sic). For him, "there is a still more wonderful sympathy between the nervous systems of different persons, when various motions and morbid symptoms are often transferred from one to another, without any corporeal contact" (qtd. in Bruhm 11, 14). This is in accordance with what Terry Eagleton declares the birth of modern aesthetic "as a discourse of the body" (13) during the eighteenth century. The early formulation of the concept in the work of the German philosopher Alexander Baumgarten (in his *Aesthetica* [1750]) referred primarily not to art, but "to the whole region of human perception and sensation, in contrast to the more rarefied domain of conceptual thought" (Eagleton 1990: 13). In other words, what aesthetics initially enforces is not between art and life, but "the material and the immaterial," "things and thoughts, sensations and ideas" (Burke 1958: 13). The phrasing Burke uses to address this "remarkable *consent* between various parts of the body" is a "general agreement" or "clear concurrence of all" (123) of all the senses. In a section on the beautiful in feeling, Burke writes: "There is a chain in all our sensations; they are all but different sorts of feeling, calculated to be affected by various sorts of objections, but all to be affected after the same manner" (120). In the same section, this sympathy between different bodily organs and senses is called "a similitude in the pleasures of these senses," which exists "if it were possible that one might discern colour by feeling, (as it is said some blind men have done) that the same colours, and the same disposition of colouring, which are found beautiful to the sight, would be found likewise most grateful to the touch" (121).

Burke's formula of the unity of perception could not be further different from that sense of "tactile, synaesthetic quality" (Mitchell 1978: 59) that the quaint romantic William Blake restores to pictorial form, nevertheless. W. J. T. Mitchell argues that in a history between oral, illustration and writing, Blake's significance is upon an emphasis of "the nonvisual sensations of heat, cold, wetness, dryness, hardness, and softness rather than the sensory alienation of visual distance" (Mitchell

1978: 60)[1]. This remains almost completely contrary to the classical definition of senses, which remains closer to an Aristotelian view of perception. For such a view, each of the five senses—sight, sound, hearing, taste, and touch—has a distinct and proper sphere of activity[2]. It is anything but the production of an associated mental image of a sense impression of one kind from a sense impression of another. Burke follows a separation of senses so as to make sympathy in between them work:

> The touch takes in the pleasure of softness, which is not primarily an object of sight; the sight on the other hand comprehends colour, which can hardly be made perceptible to the touch; the touch again has the advantage in a new idea of pleasure resulting from a moderate degree of warmth; but the eye triumphs in the infinite extent and multiplicity of its objects. (Burke 1958: 121)

This separated economy of senses is one means by which Burke makes a hierarchical ordering of perceptions and feelings, including the inter-subjective fellow feeling of sympathy. No wonder, William Blake, who consistently associates his art of writing with a synesthetic spectacle that "the eye of man hath not heard, the ear of man hath not seen, man's hand is not able to taste, his tongue to conceive, nor his heart to report" (qtd. in Mitchell 1978: 149) in the "age of paper[3]," was to feel "Contempt and Abhorrence" (qtd. in Monk 96) for Burke's philosophical enquiry. What is at stake for Burke seems to be the production of "experience, custom, tradition, and habit" (Mitchell 1986: 136) through a physiological ecology of sound:

> When the ear receives any simple sound, it is struck by a single pulse of the air, which makes the ear-drum and the other membranous parts vibrate according to the nature and species of

[1] Also see Marshall McLuhan in his *The Gutenberg Galaxy*, pp. 265-266.
[2] See John Gage, "Synaesthesia."
[3] See W. J. T. Mitchell, "Visible Language: Blake's Art of Writing," in his *Picture Theory*, pp. 111-150.

> the stroke. If the stroke be strong, the organ of hearing suffers a considerable degree of tension .... The tension of the part thus increases at every blow, by the united forces of the stroke itself, the expectation, and the surprise; it is worked up to such a pitch as to be capable of the sublime; it is brought just to the verge of pain. (Burke 1958: 140)

This economy of sound regarding aesthetics of the body runs against that of the proliferation of words in the "age of paper," which, with its graphic form of mechanic print, enhances the rupture between different sensory structures.

> Regarding our contemporary media paradigm shift, Jacque Derrida writes: What is happening to paper at present, namely what we perceive at least as a sort of ongoing decline or withdrawal, an ebb or rhythm as yet unforeseeable ... remind[s] us that paper has a history that is brief but complex, a technological or material history, a symbol history of projections and interpretations, a history tangled up with the invention of the human body and of hominization. (Derrida 2005: 43)

This chapter focuses on the origin of modern aesthetic and its sentimental economy upon the body. It is an attempt to outline a genealogy of the historical tangle by working with what G. S. Rousseau calls "physiological texts" and with some texts "*physiologically*". Regarding the poetic economy or the mentality of the West, Water J. Ong observes acutely:

> By removing words from the world of sound where they had first had their origin in active human interchange and relegating them definitively to visual surface, and by otherwise exploiting visual space for the management of knowledge, print encouraged human beings to think of their own interior conscious and unconscious resources as more and more think-like, impersonal and religiously neutral. Print encouraged the mind to sense that its possessions were held in

some sort of inert mental space. (Ong 1982: 129)

Burke devises an acoustic affective dimension of communication to run against this *visualizing* property of words that appears as an emergent form of mediation relevant to an increasing consumption of textuality[1]. This is especially the case when words are deployed to verbalize images, to create exact descriptions and imitations, and thus to increase means of communicating human sensorium. Description may be thought of as the moment in narration when the technology of memory—and what to be memorized: "experience, custom, tradition, and habit"—threatens to collapse into the materiality of its means. Description typically "stops" or arrests the temporal movement through narrative. It "spreads out the narrative in space," according to narratologist Gerard Genette[2]. W. J. T. Mitchell observes that in Burke's "antipictorial account of language," Burke embraces its effects as that being the product of "custom, habit, and acculturation" (Mitchell 1986: 138). Language, for Burke, is "primarily an oral, not a written, medium" (140). Verbal description with its unbounded cornucopia of rich details, often figured as the textual site of greatest wealth, has not come to what Foucault would call a "threshold of epistemologization[3]" yet in the writings of Burke. Instead, in his scenario, language still "operates ... by means of sounds which by custom have the effect of realities" (Burke 1958: 173). The ear wins over the eye in the transmission between a speaker and an audience. French narrative theorist Gerald Genette admits that the narration and description "frontier" may be nothing but a late development in the history of narrative structure. Indeed, it is a modern formation connected with *techne* of narrative in which

---

[1] See Walter J. Ong, *Orality and Literacy*, p. 120. This is something impossible to realize for Henry Home as suggested in the epigraph of this chapter.

[2] Gerard Genette, "The Frontiers of Narrative."

[3] See Michel Foucault, *The Archaeology of Knowledge and the Discourse on Language*, in particular Part IV, section 6, "Science and Knowledge," with its elucidation of several thresholds of emergence of a "discursive formation": the thresholds of positivity, epistemologization, scientificity, and formalization (186-187). For Foucault, these are events whose dispersion is anything but evolutive, which is where his archaeological spirit lies.

subjectivity and privacy "establish their 'classic' relation to the public sphere" (Mitchell 1994: 204) as W. J. T. Mitchell follows this argument in another context. For Burke, narration predominates over description. The "classic" extension of the private and subjective to the public and social, as suggested in histories of the rise of bourgeois social structure in the eighteenth century, has not reached its threshold of visibility yet. An amplifycation of the structural difference between narration and description by Genette would bring to light the political significance of Burke's aesthetics:

> Narration is concerned with actions or events considered as pure processes, and by that very fact it stresses the temporal, dramatic aspect of the narrative; description, on the other hand, because it lingers on objects and beings considered in their simultaneity, and because it considers the processes themselves as spectacles, seems to suspend the course of time and to contribute to spreading the narrative in space ... narration restores, in the temporal succession of its discourse, the equally temporal succession of events, whereas description must modulate, in discursive succession, the representation of objects that are simultaneous and juxtaposed in space. (Genette 136)

Thus, the Burkean temporal continuity is over spatial simultaneity, and the narrative restoration remains above discursive modulation. Against all historical accounting, Thomas Paine is no doubt right in suggesting that:

> Hard as Mr. Burke laboured the Regency Bill and hereditary succession two years ago, and much as he dived for precedents, he still had not boldness enough to bring up William Normandy, and say, *There is the head of the list, there is the fountain of honour*; the son of a prostitute and the plunderer

of the English nation. (Paine 103-104)[1]

It is primarily the aural aspect of language that operates at both the individual and collective levels of realities in Burke's epistemic schema. The English "experience, custom, tradition, and habit" that Burke advocates through his politics of aesthetic is regulated by the means of narration as a speaking inscriptive mechanism. This is an aesthetics of physiological embodiment to be replaced by that of abstraction regarding the way selfhood is *staged*. The theatricalized abstraction of selfhood is comparable to a reduction of human sensorium and perception to commodity and object of symbolic exchange in Adam Smith's political economy. It is analogous to what Hegel, a philosopher notorious for his system of abstractions, attributes to "morning prayer" in a comparison with reading:

> Reading the newspaper in early morning is a kind of realistic morning prayer. One orients one's attitude against the world and toward God [in one case], or toward that which the world is [in the other]. The former gives the same security as the latter, in that one knows where one stands. (qtd. in Buck-Morss 844)

If one takes what Marshall McLuhan defines communication by whatever media as "participation in common situations," [2] the predominant means of participation for Burke probably still remains more that of "morning prayer" than of modern newspaper. The latter of

[1] Different from Burke, Paine, in a very straightforward way, transforms America into an observable beginning for all governments: "The case and circumstances of America present themselves as in the beginning of a world; and our enquiry into the origin of government is shortened, by referring to the facts that have arisen in our own day. We have no occasion to roam for information into the obscure field of antiquity, nor hazard ourselves unto conjecture. We are brought at once to the point of seeing government begin, as if we had lived in the beginning of time. The real volume, not of history, but of facts, is directly before us, unmutilated by contrivance, or the errors of tradition" (*Rights of Man*, p. 185).

[2] McLuhan, "Notes on the Media as Art Forms" (1954), quoted in Paul Barker, "Medium Rare: With Big Brother Bestriding the Global Village, a Chance to Read What McLuhan Really Wrote," *Times Literary Supplement*, March 17, 2006, p. 3.

which, with its fictive and arbitrary nature, especially its "calendrical coincidence," [1] imposes the rituals of anonymous simultaneity on individuals, and thus creates collective, homogeneous identity among the larger group of numerous and scattered citizens of modern states. This is part of the theoretical arguments well developed by Benedict Anderson and Jürgen Habermas.

II.vii. Emotional Immediacy: Its Fate

There is no significant critical attention from Burke on the necessity for a well-informed active citizen to retreat to internalized and solitary reading of the newspaper in order to participate in the larger, public group political process of modern society, nevertheless. It is not that modern newspaper did not appear during Burke's time. As a matter of fact, two decades before Edmund Burke went to London, *The Daily Advertiser*, as the "first modern newspaper,"[2] already began publication. It included the following notice about its contents:

> This paper will consist wholly of Advertisements, together with the Prices of Stocks, Course of Exchange, and Names and Descriptions of Persons becoming Bankrupts; as also in Alphabetical Manner a Daily Account of the Several Species and Quantities of Goods Imported into the Port of London .... (qtd. in Stephens 160)[3]

Its success inspired all of London's growing number of morning dailies in the 1740s to feature such "commercial intelligence." [4] Newspapers are believed to have encouraged the rise of public opinion and spheres of publicity in the modern sense. The public sphere this modern media helps form channeling of sympathy more conveniently transferred. An extreme case exists in an investigation upon reports of

---

1 Anderson, *Imagined Communities*, pp. 25, 34, 36, 39.

2 See Stanley Morison, *The English Newspaper, 1622—1932*, pp. 123-151.

3 *Daily Advertiser*, Feb. 26, 1730.

4 Again see Stanley Morison, *The English Newspaper, 1622—1932*, pp. 123-151.

suicide in *Sleepless Souls* (1990), in which Michael MacDonald and Terence Murphy argue that "the style and tone of newspaper stories about suicides promoted an increasingly secular and sympathetic attitude towards self-killing" (qtd. in Briggs and Burke 72) in eighteenth-century England. The impression was created through the frequency of the reports that suicide was a commonplace event. On the other hand, coffee houses and clubs offer an immediate space of local conversations[1]. Conversation is a crucial term in the eighteenth century for illustrating "the flow *across* those newly reconstituted fields" of the private individual exchanges and the public ones, as Graham Burchell points out in the case of David Hume. It is "to describe the form ideally taken by the 'commerce' of ... [the political culture] of opinion, the appropriate cultural form of exchanges between individuals of the 'middling rank' immersed in 'common life'" (Burchell 1991: 129), and "'opinion' became emancipated from the bonds of economic dependence" (Habermas 33-34). Thus, there exists a heterogeneous system of media, which fosters different perceptual proclivities and spatialities. For instance, the dialogue form of the moral weeklies and essays published in such periodicals as *Tatler* and *Spectator*, "attested to their proximity to the spoken word" (34). Burke, with his emphasis on the oral aspect and affective message of the language, belongs to that category of the local, immediate, coffee house and personal.

What Burke's invocation of orality and affection through his local empiricism achieves is what Niklas Luhmann describes as "the impression of ... immediacy" (Luhmann 2000: 8), which runs throughout Romantic poetry[2]. The human sensorium of sound is taken as means to maintain presence and immanence. During the process, for Burke, sympathy registers and communicates "realities." It is also used to

[1] The coffee houses were in their golden age between 1680 and 1730. Not only coffee, but also tea and chocolate became the common beverages of at least the well-to-do strata of the population around the middle of the seventeenth century. Specifically, by the first decade of the eighteenth century London had already 3,000 coffee houses, each with a core group of regulars. See Jürgen Habermas, *The Structural Transformation of the Public Sphere*, p. 32.

[2] See Celeste Langan and Maureen N. McLane, "The Medium of Romantic Poetry," pp. 244-245.

identify with a sense of nationhood. At the end of his philosophical enquiry, Burke writes: "It may be observed that very polished languages, and such as are praised for their superior clearness and perspicuity, are generally deficient in strength. The French language has that perfection, and that defect" (Burke 1958: 176). Transparent mediation is taken as a polluting other, who, by executing the queen, just caused the collapse of "the unbought grace of life ... the nurse of manly sentiment and heroic enterprise ... that sensibility of principle, that charity of honor" (86). The era of sympathy, honor and chivalry is being succeeded by "that of sophisters, economists, and calculators," and "the glory of Europe is extinguished forever" (86). It is no more that of an age when "ten thousand swords must have leaped from their scabbards to avenge even a look that threatened her with insult" (86). "A look" at "her" would incorporate "ten thousand swords," establishing a "close-knit group" of sentiment, similar to that of the spoken word, as Walter J. Ong writes: "in its physical constitution as sound, the spoken word proceeds from the human interior and manifests human beings to one another as conscious interiors, as persons" (Ong 1982: 73). Burke's aesthetic theory is an elegy of the oral rhetoric at the emergent stage of textuality. Sympathy from English thereby "good" Europeans produces immediate personal tactility, the possibility of which is canceled by abstractions from "sophisters, economists, and calculators[1]"—that kind of proliferation of signs included in what Coleridge denounces as merely the "verbal truth[2]." More significantly, abstraction as mediated through words and numbers is

---

[1] Interestingly, Thomas Paine seizes upon a metaphor of Burke's—the nation as organic body—and superimposes upon it a characteristic geometric figure: "A nation is not a body, the figure of which is to be represented by the human body, but is like a body contained within a circle, having a common center in which every radius meets; and that center is formed by representation. To connect representation with what is called Monarchy is eccentric Government." (*Rights of Man*, p. 178)

[2] Coleridge makes a distinction between "verbal truth" and "moral truth": "By *verbal* truth we mean no more than the correspondence of a given fact to given words. In *moral* truth, we moreover involve the intention of the speaker, that his words should correspond to this thought in the sense in which he expects them to be understood by others. " Coleridge, *The Friend*, 2: 42. On the relations between Burke's historicism and Coleridge's, see James K. Chandler, *Wordsworth's Second Nature*, pp. 237-238.

aligned with a venomous sight of a revolution spectacle. A relation, in which face-to-face contact and immediate somatic feedback are the conditions of knightly performance, is taken away through artifactualization of words and numbers. The previous (and bygone) helps stage his feelings as immediate, natural, human and of course English[1]. "Oh! What a revolution! And what a heart must I have to contemplate without emotion that elevation and that fall!" (Burke 1958: 85-86), as Burke imitates an oral act of shouting with onomatopoeic exclamations, not to mention the processing consciousness of "I thought." In this act of creating an "illusion of oral mimesis,"[2] immediation is already embedded in mediation. No wonder Mary Wollstonecraft, in her *A Vindication of the Rights of Men*, finds Burke's own feelings false when referring ironically to the "compassionate tears" he "elaborately laboured to excite." She denounces his "sentimental exclamations," his "pampered sensibility," and the sentimental nostalgia of his political vision. His feelings are not only false and regressive. They also fail where real feeling is due: "Your tears," Wollstonecraft admonishes, "are reserved ... for the declamation of the theatre, or for the downfall of queens ... whilst the distress of many ... were vulgar sorrows that could not move your commiseration" (Wollstonecraft 2, 5, 6, 10, 27).

The myth of vocal and auditory immediacy conceals materiality of communication, such as the drop of ink, the line, the page, the brush of painting, the book, the print shop or the cognitive activities of the brain. Voice, as the vehicle of communication and expression, is

> a medium which both preserves the *presence of the object* before intuition and *self-presence*, the absolute proximity of the [subjective]

1 It is also worthy of noting that Thomas Paine appeals to the same economy of sympathy in his political language, as Jon P. Klancher points out: "Absorbing Burke's language of 'veils,' 'mystery,' or 'pantomimical contrivance' into the symbolic surplus of monarchy, the radical writer [Thomas Paine, that is] claims for his own language a firm representative order that 'exists not by fraud and mystery; it deals not in cant and sophistry; but in spires a language that, passing from heart to heart, is felt and understood" (Klancher 110).

2 A phrase used by Maureen N. McLane in her discussion on how James Beattie's *The Minstrel* published in 1771 offers a case of "print culture's solicitation and transmediation of oral materials" (McLane 2008: 32).

> acts to themselves... The subject can hear or speak to himself and be affected by the signifier he produces, without passing through an external detour. (Derrida 1973: 76)

Thus Derrida argues in his *Speech and Phenomena.* It belongs to what he names as a "white mythology[1]." It is a fiction of transparency and presence, and covers up an ideology of auto-affection that "has had a long, strange career in [Western] philosophy" (Terada 25). Its appearance of immediacy promises self-sufficiency and self-immediacy instead of self-difference and mediation. When "consciousness processes perception under the impression of their immediacy," Niklas Luhmann writes, "... the brain is actually executing operations that are highly selective, quantitatively calculating, recursively operative" (Luhmann 2000: 8). In Burke's scenario of mediated sentiment of "immediacy," sympathy functions with technologies of orality and aurality in communication, which itself is "nothing primordial, but an impression resulting from the differentiation of autopoietic systems of the brain and consciousness" (8). Burke's aesthetics thus covers up the processing of materiality and labor by achieving the effects of tactile presence and somatic immanence in realities. It is part and parcel of Burke's suspicion upon "the whole pictorial model of mind that dominated the empirical tradition" (Mitchell 1986: 166), which comes to occupy a significant place in the political economy of sympathy in the philosophy of moral sentiments developed by Adam Smith, who differs from many British Romanticists[2]. It seems that from Burke's disavowal and vituperation of mediation to Smith's welcoming embrace of it into one visual and theatrical mode there exists a transitional history of mediation.

---

[1] See Jacques Derrida, "White Mythology: Metaphor in the Text of Philosophy."

[2] For the antipictorial and antivisual attitudes as characteristic of Romantic criticism, see a brilliant study by Roy Park. Also see W. J. T. Mitchell, *Blake's Composite Art*, pp. 14-39. For a critique of the phonocentric tendency from a deconstructionist stance, see Jacques *Derrida's Of Grammatology* (1976) and *Writing and Difference* (1978). For the function of the pictorial mode of mind and how the British Romanticists treat it as a national difference between the English and the French, see W. J. T. Mitchell, *Iconography: Image, Text, Ideology*, pp. 131-149, and 164-167. We will return to this topic.

What a secret history of sentiment would this transition unfold? How does the moral sentiments taking on a putative life of its own help approach the so-called "Adam Smith problem," an alleged biographical rupture from a moral philosopher to a political economist? How is it metonymical of emergent distinctions of class, culture, social status, and divisions of labor, which cohabit with the collapse of classical mode of vision and the occurrence of a specific mode of theatricality? What does it mean to our everyday mode of beings? These are the questions I try to address throughout this current writing, with detours and mediations.

Chapter III

Practicing Passions: David Hume and His Philosophy in Writing

III.i. Sympathy, History and Writing

Adela Pinch argues that for most middle and late eighteenth-century aesthetic theorists, sympathy "described not only interpersonal relationships but also relations between persons and representations" (Pinch 29). Sympathetic sentiments are aroused through realistic objects or interpersonal relations, which can always move into aesthetic representations. One passage in David Hume's *Treatise*'s discussion of compassion clearly suggests this:

> A spectator of a tragedy passes thro' a long train of grief, terror, indignation, and other affections, which the poet represents in the persons he introduces. As many tragedies end happily, and no excellent one can be compos'd without some reverses of fortune, the spectator must sympathize with all these changes, and receive the fictitious joy as well as every other passion. (Hume 1978: 369)

This relation between sympathy and aesthetic representations begins to be common in the eighteenth century. Highly influenced by Hume, Adam Smith makes sympathy a more universal experience through the imagination of the spectators upon the agents in his *The Theory of Moral Sentiments* (abbr. as *TMS*). For him, we "form some idea of his sensations" and even feel something "which, though weaker in degree, is not altogether unlike them," and we do this by means of the imaginative experiment of placing ourselves in the agent's circumstance: "[W]e enter as it were into his body, and become in some measure the same person with him" (Smith 1984: 9). It is noteworthy that Smith emphasizes the aspect of the adverbial quality of sympathy—to feel *sympathetically*[1], that is, while Hume's stress is on the process that sentiment is fictitious and manufactured, which is the well-maneuvered process of "a long train of grief, terror, indignation, and other affections" resulting most likely in a "joy." In another passage on how sympathy is the "propensity" that we have "to receive by communication [others'] inclinations and sentiments, however different from, or even contrary to our own" (Hume 1978: 316), Hume writes on importance of processing representation in the economy of passions:

> 'Tis indeed evident, that when we sympathize with the passions and sentiments of others, these movements appear at first in *our* mind as mere ideas, and are conceiv'd to belong to another person, as we conceive any other matter of fact. 'Tis also evident, that the ideas of the affections of others are converted into the very impressions they represent, and that the passions arise in conformity to the images we form of them. (Hume 1978: 319)[2]

In this economy of sympathy, it is of significance to grasp the procedure between ideas, identifying, impressing and conforming, through which a strong sense of temporality is suggested. Sentiment is treated as "any other matter of fact." It is not subjective, and requires intellectual effort rather than affective labor to realize. This might be identified as a part of the eighteenth-century civic humanism that is suggested through Joseph Addison and Richard Steele in the first decade of the century, if not earlier.

In their writings, sympathy, and sociality are designated as the basis

---

1 See Alexander Broadie, "Sympathy and the Impartial Spectator," p. 163.

2 Also see Jerome Christensen, *Practicing Enlightenment*, p. 71.

for "a new kind of virtue, which served national interests by promoting civility and, not incidentally, by strengthening Britain's commerce with the rest of the trading world" (Poovey 152)[1]. The subscribers to their journal *The Spectator* "were directors of the Bank of England ... goldsmiths, private bankers or moneylenders," the largest group of which "included the 'great body of secretaries, commissioners, clerks, and agents in the various branches of government, civil and military, required to carry on the war abroad and manage affairs at home'"(Nicholson 55). Thus it becomes their natural concern

> to promote a polite and civilizing sense of participation in the new society being developed, acclimatizing its readers to market priorities and procedures and familiarizing them with codes and conventions of recognition and self-recognition appropriate to their place in a burgeoning world. (55)

What is of interest here, however, is to situate Hume in a history of emotions and history of the writing media. Hume's writing on passion and his act of writing itself mean more than establishing a "polite culture" that mediates "as a validating and confidence-building network of relationships" (55). They require a social constituency of a readership as imagined through the act of reading and writing. They self-consciously involve the changing essence of representation with regard to emotional realities and selfhood. For Hume, writing is an experience of the newly popular print medium, which affects a historical understanding of empirical philosophy and identitarian mediation.

Indeed, Hume carefully distinguishes the way passions derived from literature feel from those derived from real life. For him, the "*feelings* of the passions" caused by poetical fictions are fainter than "what they are when they arise from belief and reality": the passion "feels less firm and solid," and it is but a "mere phantom" of the passion caused by reality (Hume 1978: 631). The point is that absence of objects and circumstantial realities enhanced by increasing

---

[1] Also see Jerome Christensen, *Practicing Enlightenment*, p. 151, note 44.

communication and information flow [1] becomes an issue of late eighteenth-century aesthetic theory, which "frequently pondered how an emotional response to an image of a thing should be like and unlike a response to the thing itself" (Pinch 114)[2]. The issue becomes complicated in the Humean transposition of a representational work of self into the new forum of print medium through the work of writing. It is part of what Christensen detects "the significance of the printing press to Hume's philosophical project" (136)—the relation of causation in both his epistemology of sense data and history:

> When we infer effects from causes, we must establish the existence of these causes; which we have only two ways of doing, either by an immediate perception of our memory or senses, or by an inference from other causes; which causes again we must ascertain in the same manner, either by a present impression, or by an inference from *their* causes, and so on, till we arrive at some object, which we see or remember. It is impossible for us to carry on our inferences *in infinitum;* and the only thing, that can stop them, is an impression of the memory or senses, beyond which there is no room for doubt or enquiry.

For Hume, this "impression of the memory or the senses" exists merely in a procedural process. It is a means of mediation to something that, in another passage, is attributed to a remotely ancient historical past. Hume's historical knowledge, unlike that of Burke, has a visual beginning:

> Thus we believe that Caesar was kill'd in the senate-house on the ides of March; and that because this fact is establish'd on the unanimous testimony of historians, who agree to assign this precise time and place to that event. Here are certain characters and letters

---

[1] See Katherine E. Ellison, *The Fatal News* and Daniel R. Headrick, *When Information Came of Age*.

[2] For an elaboration on this observation in David Hume, William Wordsworth and Henry Kames, see Adela Pinch, *Strange Fits of Passion*, pp. 114-116.

> present either to our memory or senses; which characters we likewise remember to have been us'd as the signs of certain ideas; and these ideas were either in the minds of such as were immediately present at that action, and receiv'd the ideas directly from its existence; or they were deriv'd from the testimony of others, and that again from another testimony, by a visible gradation, 'till we arrive at those who were eye-witnesses and spectators of the event. (Hume 1978: 82-83)

The certainty of a historical knowledge is caused by a chain of narration, that is, a "visible gradation" to the original "eye-witnesses and spectators of the event." Hume seems to suggest that there is no room for doubt or enquiry beyond that. The historical causation is manufactured into an establishment of a relational connection and continuity between units previously atomic and disparate.

This sympathetic epistemological and historical relation with "the original, indubitable testimony of an eyewitness to the historical event" (Christensen 1987: 138) would gradate as the intermediary connections increase. It can be assured, nonetheless, through "the republic of letters" and "the art of printing": "One edition passes into another, and that into a third, and so on, till we come to that volume we peruse at present. There is no variation in the steps. After we know one, we know all of them" (Hume 1978: 146). Thus, "Europe is at present a copy, at large, of what Greece was formerly a pattern in miniature" (qtd. in Christensen 1987: 140). Representations make not merely historical knowledge possible. History becomes loyally printed copies of what were before. The process of mediation takes predominance over what is mediated. The intermediary, as a consequence of the saturation of the print medium in the eighteenth century, occupies such a significant role of representation that what is supposed to be represented turns into it. The means overwhelms and thus becomes the end. The proliferation of the medium *remediates* what goes before and what comes after. It becomes more than a mere technical instrument through which the historical and sympathetic—or, sympathetically historical—causation is communicated. This strong sense of reliance upon the printing press for communicating an authentic historical knowledge exists in Hume's epistemological, philosophical and affective project. For him, experience as reflected in empirical epistemology and philosophy is interwoven with an obsession with emotion and passion. Communicating an "authentic self" to "the republic of letters" through the print medium creates a specific sociality that could be identified as a "literary career" of the mid-century for him. The work of writing puts him "in a position where he can repeat himself over and over again" (Christensen 1987: 142). A career, a historical knowledge and a proprietary selfhood converge through the possibility made by the print medium. Indeed, as the historian of print culture Elizabeth Eisenstein suggests, the life-long literary career as a modern writer is made possible through the saturating printing technology. It is the work of writing in a

> duplicating process that made possible not only a sequence of improved editions but also a continuous accumulation of fixed records. For it seems to have been permanence that introduced progressive change. The preservation of the old, in brief, launched a tradition of the new. (Eisenstein 1979: 124)

This sense of accumulation and progress is built into a social history of modern subjectivity in its proprietary as well as existential aspects.

This is specifically about the role of social sympathy—or sympathetic sociality—in Hume's work of writing. An evil fanatic and the lord of a gloomy, gothic castle as regarded by more or less his contemporary James Beattie [1], Hume establishes an economy of sympathy, which is different from that of Wordsworth writing in the late eighteenth century. As "*a communication of sentiments*" (Hume 1978: 324), sympathy is a necessary part of the property transference in sentimental sociality:

> We can form no wish, which has not a reference to society. A perfect solitude is, perhaps, the greatest punishment we can suffer.

[1] See Adela Pinch, *Strange Fits of Passion*, p. 40, note 25.

> Every pleasure languishes when enjoyed apart from company, and every pain becomes more cruel and intolerable. Whatever other passions we may be actuated by; pride, ambition, avarice, curiosity, revenge or lust; the soul or animating principle of them all is sympathy; nor would they have any force, were we to abstract entirely from the thoughts and sentiments of others. Let all the powers and elements of nature conspire to serve and obey one man; Let the sun rise and set at his command; The sea and rivers roll as he pleases, and the earth furnish spontaneously whatever may be useful or agreeable to him; He will still be miserable, till you give him some one person at least, with whom he may share his happiness, and whose esteem and friendship he may enjoy. (Hume 1978: 363)

Here communicated and shared emotions are that of property, the importance of which to a Humean selfhood is even more than a transcendental possession of the universe. Solitude means scarcity and poverty. Sympathetic companionship implements a pleasurable and animating social selfhood. It is a sentimental sociality through a process of abstraction, during which Hume initiates *a necessity of writing* to make a self possible by not being a self, and to make a *medial* empiricism through the print media as a literary property in Western Enlightenment.

A recent discussion suggests that the "event" of Enlightenment, one that conventionally occupies roughly a half-century between the 1730s—1740s and the 1780s, emerged "as an effect of" "*proliferating mediations*[1]." Hume's writing and philosophy can be situated in this theoretical and historical light. It is similar to his accounts of taste, through which, as Hume puts it, "considering myself as a man in general, [I] forget, if possible, my individual being and my peculiar circumstances[2]." It is a creation of a public life, *bios politikos*, in the market place of a literary career, through deploying the pen, one of what

[1] See Clifford Siskin and William Warner, *This Is Enlightenment*, pp. 1-36, especially p. 11.
[2] David Hume, "Of the Standard of Taste," in *Essays, Moral, Political, and Literary*, p. 239.

Jürgen Habermas calls "public organs[1]", a specific political economy of social and literary labor as an apparatus. In "the context of incipient consumerism in the eighteenth century[2]," labor in representing is not as production but as performance, a performance in the literary marketplace that "is nothing other than a theater" (Christensen 1987: 118). Hume is aware of the danger of retreating (or advancing) "into a solitude (or a solidarity) that is either a solipsistic darkness or a violent method" (119), which would mean an absence of access to the public, and a loss of the ability of performing as a literary producer. With a fanatic, gloomy and gothic phobia upon such an obsession, he invests theatricality and performance as forms of literary and emotional labor through work of writing into the marketplace and theater of the printing press. Stephen Greenblatt observes that the new textual medium, indeed, presents a theater of performance through iterated function:

> At the deepest level of the [theatrical] medium itself the motivation is the ... renewal of existence through repetition of the self-constituting act. The character repeats himself in order to continue to be the same character on the stage. Identity is a theatrical invention that must be reiterated if it is to endure. (Greenblatt 201)

In other words, the theatrical space of the textual medium provides the spatial and material base for the invention of an iterable identity that can be produced and reproduced through revising. Thus the Humean theatricality becomes therapeutic of the disease of solitude, and the social sentiment of sympathy provides the cure, which is materialized through act of writing. Historically, the concept of sympathy, as in the phrase "sympathetic nervous system," belongs in Graeco-Roman physiology and medicine and in particular figured significantly in Stoic

---

[1] See Jürgen Habermas, *The Structural Transformation of the Public Sphere*, pp. 2-3.
[2] Jerome Christensen, *Practicing Enlightenment*, p. 118, note 24.

thought[1]. Hume may well have been familiar with the medical concept of sympathy. It is illustrated in a tripartite classification of causes of disease in parts of the body by James Crawford (d. 1732), a member of the Physiology Library to which Hume also belonged. Crawford was also a teacher of medicine at Edinburgh University where Hume was a student. He writes:

> That a Part is affected by *Protopathia*, when it is essentially in itself lesed [=diseased], and owes not its Origin to any Communication from another Part. Or by *Idiopathia*, when tho' it be essentially lesed, yet the hurt was at first propagated to it from some other Part. Or lastly, by *Sympathy* or Consent, when the Part in itself is yet whole and sound, and is only affected by the fault of some other Part ... Diseases by Consent are propagated from a Distance, (in which case only I shall consider them) either by long Muscles or Nerves[2].

This medical discourse of sympathy is frequently taken through the Scottish Enlightenment, and used "by physicians both in respect of physiology and physical sickness and also in respect of the psychology of physician/patient relations" (Broadie 161). Hume's anxiety of solitary sympathetic nerves motivates an *ad infinitum* theatricality in print medium through the iterable act of writing to foster a fragmentary identitarian existence, which obtains a sense of causation and continuity. Writing, while creating and curing more sympathy, is both poison and medicine[3].

---

[1] See Alexander Broadie, "Sympathy and the Impartial Spectator," p. 161.
[2] James Crawford, "Practical Remarks on the Sympathy of the Parts of the Body by the Late Dr. James Crawford Professor of Medicine in the Universe of Edinburgh," article XV, in *Medical Essays and Observations, Revised and Published by a Society in Edinburgh*, 1744, vol. 5, part 2; quoted in Alexander Broadie, "Sympathy and the Impartial Spectator," p. 161.
[3] As Jacques Derrida traces the Greek word "pharmakon." See his "Plato's Pharmacy" in *Dissemination*, pp. 61-171.

III.ii. Theatrical Presence in Print Medium and Masculinity in Media Modernity

In this sense, "sympathy," for Hume, refers to a feeling as well as a principle of communication of opinions. It correlates to issues of the emergence of modern subjectivity, individualism, and literary character through a history of mediation upon the body. In a phenomenological perspective upon the coming of modernity from the medieval to early modern theater, William Egginton argues that examining relations of space is more significant for investigating a historical origin of modern "subjectivity." He details the notion of "presence."—For Egginton, the medieval spatial conception that was "full":

> Rather than taking place in an empty, geometrically determined space in which stories can be played out in relative independence of the reality of the audience's world, the hyperbolic solidity of the space of medieval drama reflected the instability of the distinction between the reality being represented and the reality of the representation. (Egginton 55)

The Spanish sixteenth century, as Egginton suggests, begins to witness a flattened space designating "the border between the real and the imaginary." Thus it becomes a "screen" (108), along which exists the "empty space" of modern theater. This "theatrical space" "is constituted by the presence of bodies in it, as opposed to the place where bodies may be shown" (56). In regard to the relation between subjectivity and theatricality, Egginton writes:

> This telescoping of separable spaces requires audiences to negotiate different levels of reality, which they do by means of characters or avatars, virtual selves that become conditioned to this new, fundamentally scopic organization of space, in which they watch and are watched watching; they become bodies saturated by the gaze. (121)

Egginton's suggestion of theatricality as a term of media analysis[1] is helpful for our historical investigation of the print medium in the eighteenth century. This new form of theatricality is manifested through an obsession of spatial presence, and also exists in the print medium, which offers a culture of abstraction in the "empty space" to be filled by iterable performative identities through the work of writing. Identity becomes a spatial presence, the absence of which is darkness and means non-identity. Modern subjectivity comes through this act of *filling*, which is realized in Hume as *writing* and *communicating* through sympathy. It is analogous to the *ad infinitum* shifting visual perspectives of watching and being watched through the audience. Charles Taylor suggests that modernity can be read as that experience whose leitmotif is of inwardness and detachment from self, which allows the emergence of both the themes of self-control and of self-exploration. For him, this self is put into a visually "separate, autonomous sphere of inwardness, capable of being separated from itself—as agent and object—and acting upon, manipulating, or exploring itself in a state of disengagement":

> What one finds running through all the aspects of this constellation—the new philosophy, the methods of administration and military organization, the new spirit of government, and methods of discipline—is a growing ideal of a human agent who is able to remake himself by methodological and disciplined action. What this calls for is the ability to take an instrumental stance to one's given properties, desires, inclinations, tendencies, habits of thought, and feelings so that they can be worked on, doing away with some and strengthening others, until one meets the desired specifications[2].

---

[1] See especially William Egginton, *How the World Became a Stage*, chapter 5.

[2] Charles Taylor, "Inwardness and the Culture of Modernity," in *Philosophical Interventions in the Unfinished Project of Enlightenment*, p. 99. Quoted in William Egginton, *How the World Became a Stage*, pp. 128-129.

While the concept of "agency" may be alien to the eighteenth century, this observation and discipline of a modern "self" through engaging and disengaging is reflected in Hume's writing as periodic melancholy—a phobia of solitary being, away from the communicating space of writing, a lack of media sociality where the productivity of self is, that is. This phobia itself, in a way, is productive of a subjective self. It is a moment of producing an inward self that was not normal, but still gothic in the middle of the eighteenth century, several decades before the coming of modern mass media.

Contemporary moral philosopher Charles Taylor puts this into a philosophical language of reflexivity: "What we turn to in radical reflexivity seems to demand description as something 'inner.' This spatial metaphor is irresistible to describe the 'space' opened by self-scrutiny[1]." The moment of producing an inward interiority, a spatial self-scrutiny that takes enormous labor and sentimentality, produces gothic melancholy. This reflexivity—the "Inner Eye," according to Richard Rorty, is not new but an invention of the seventeenth century[2]. Prior to Descartes and Locke, Rorty explains, there was no

> conception of the human mind as an inner space in which both pains and clear and distinct ideas passed in review before a single Inner Eye ... The novelty was the notion of a single inner space in which bodily and perceptual sensations ('confused ideas of sense and imagination' in Descartes's phrase), mathematical truths, moral rules, the idea of God, moods of depression, and all the rest of what we now call 'mental' were objects of quasi-observation. (Rorty 50)

Egginton takes a less intellectual, more materialistic approach to this serious problematic of the seventeenth century. He suggests that this was "a theatrical experience of spatiality, one in which viewers had

---

[1] Charles Taylor, "Inwardness and the Culture of Modernity," in *Philosophical Interventions in the Unfinished Project of Enlightenment*, p. 103. Quoted in William Egginton, *How the World Became a Stage*, p. 196, note 48.

[2] See William Egginton, *How the World Became a Stage*, p. 138.

learned to become disembodied spectators of an action that only involved them as characters, as virtual rather than actual participants" (Egginton 138). It is a historical case that this "inner eye" is emblematic of a modern reflexive subjectivity, which originates from the seventeenth century. Along with it comes a shifting concept and practice of theatrical spatiality of presence. In the eighteenth century this presence proliferated, and this theatrical space expands with the coming of the modern print medium. Philosophically, this needs an association with the notion of disengagement, as Taylor puts it:

> Reason and human excellence requires a stance of disengagement. 'Disengagement' here is a term of art, meaning a stance toward something which might otherwise serve to define our identity or purposes, whereby we separate ourselves from it by defining it as at best of instrumental significance[1].

On a societal scale, Habermas calls this the public sphere. This subjectivity, "as the innermost core of the private, was always already oriented to an audience" (Habermas 49). The eighteenth-century Britain debated about taste and began to take disinterestedness as among its tradition of aesthetics. David Hume takes this as a device for disengaging, philosophically and experientially[2]. This very sense of disinterestedness is specifically suggested by David Home's change of his own family name. Considering Hume was the youngest son of a distinguished Scottish family in the system of primogeniture, he would

---

[1] Charles Taylor, "Inwardness and the Culture of Modernity," in *Philosophical Interventions in the Unfinished Project of Enlightenment*, p. 103. Quoted in William Egginton, *How the World Became a Stage*, p. 137.

[2] Though in Britain the word "aesthetics" did not achieve a triumph comparable to the Wolffian tradition in Germany until the end of the nineteenth century. See Marc Redfield *Phantom Formations*, pp. 6-7 and Jerome Stolnitz "On the Origins of 'Aesthetic disinterestedness'" in *Journal of Aesthetics and Art Criticism*, 1961, 20 (2), pp. 131-143. In a sense, it is that out of moral philosophy were developed aesthetics and economics, with economics probably originating from aesthetics. See Howard Caygill, *Art of Judgment* and John Guillory *Cultural Capital,* pp. 269-340. We will come back to this point while addressing Adam Smith.

not inherit his father's estate and must leave Home behind[1]. This change of family name is not merely about a new identity obtained, but also, more significantly, about a voluntary creation of identitarian spatial crevices between "home" and "not-home," the filling of which requires a mediation of sympathetic sociality as presence and thus literary property. This is fulfilled through a theatrical performance of the pen apparatus in the modern print medium, which establishes an exchangeable space for the eighteenth-century men of letters. Hume deviates or departs from a monolithic and normalized "I" so as to be productive of himself as a literary character and a literary career—"a versatile middleman" (Christensen 1987: 151).

In "Of Essay-Writing," Hume defines his identity as an "ambassador" between "the learned and conversable": "I shall give Intelligence to the Learned of whatever passes in Company, and shall endeavor to import into Company whatever Commodities I find in my native Country proper for their Use and Entertainment" (Hume 1985: 535). A role of the middle print medium is structurally possible out of its relation with the other two media: the scribal and learned usually taken as masculine, the oral and conversable as feminine[2]. It is suggested by his turn from a not successful moral philosopher—"the least entertaining and least political of all eighteenth-century genres" of knowledge producers (Poovey 146)—to an essay writer[3]. Essay writing is a new form of relationship and affiliation deploying the publicity of reason and emotion. In *An Enquiry Concerning the Principles of Morals*,

---

[1] See Jerome Christensen, *Practicing Enlightenment*, p. 57, note 14, and Adela Pinch, *Strange Fits of Passion*, pp. 27-28.

[2] It is noteworthy that this is defined in a commercial terminology, which was anticipated by Joseph Addison in *Spectator* no. 69, indicating that "factors in the trading world are what ambassadors are in the polite world" (qtd. in Christensen 151).

[3] In the eighteenth century, "because it both sought to generate knowledge—in the form of a conversation—and elicited identification with a more or less particularized speaker, the essay constituted the generic bridge between experimental moral philosophy and the novel, where yet another mode of knowledge production was being codified" (Poovey 198). For this turn and its relation to an epistemological shift regarding an emergent problem of liberal governmentality, see Mary Poovey, *A History of the Modern Fact*, chapter 4, pp. 144-213.

Hume makes this point:

> A gloomy, hair-brained enthusiast, after his death, may have a place in the calendar; but will scarcely ever be admitted, when alive, into intimacy and society, except by those who are as delirious and dismal as himself[1].

This suggests a strong sense of dependence regarding exertions and relations of co-workers in the social labor of writing. The dependence expresses an anxiety over the rising public: "The Public is the most capricious Mistress we can court[2]." In a strong repentant passage upon authorship, Hume writes:

> But I am so sick of all those Disputes and so full of Contempt towards all factious Judgments and indeed towards the Prejudices of what is call'd the Public, that I repent heartily my ever having committed any thing to Print. Had I a Son I shou'd warn him as carefully against the dangerous Allurements of Literature as James did his Son against those of Women; tho if his Inclination was as strong as mine in my Youth, it is likely, that the warning would be to as little Purpose in the one Case as it usually is in the other[3].

Interestingly, the public medium is portrayed as feminine, that is, "the most capricious Mistress," "dangerous Allurements of Literature" as analogous to "those of Women." The dangerous and consumptive public is represented as a feminine sphere, which creates a career for him and makes work of writing a property for him, and it replaces the son that he never had. Thus Hume expresses a strong sense of castration in his work. The development of a literary career is an articulated anxiety over the absence of an authentic masculinity that demands a constant work of writing to meet its requirements. As Jerome Christensen writes: "Hume not only did not father a son, but the enabling condition of his

---

[1] Quoted in Adela Pinch, *Strange Fits of Passion*, p. 17.

[2] David Hume, *The Letters of David Hume*, vol. 1, p. 222.

[3] David Hume, *The Letters of David Hume*, vol. 1, p. 461

career is to respond to the allure of the feminine public by a castration that makes authorship a necessarily barren romance" (1987: 96). As a matter of fact, Hume establishes "the imagery of mutilation and references to various texts as children" or as a corpulent body[1]. In a letter to David Mallet, he writes:

> The Truth is, I am entirely idle at present so far as regards writing; and I am very happy in that indolent State. My Friends tell me, that I will not continue long so, and that I will tire of having nothing to do but read and converse; but I am resolved to resist, as a Temptation of the Devil, any Impulse towards writing, and I am really so much ashamed of myself when I see my Bulk on a Shelf, as well as when I see it in a Glass, that I would fain revent my growing more corpulent either way[2].

The accumulative quantity of work of writing is made analogous to the economy of the writer's body. It communicates a sense of boredom and tedium upon literary labor, as well as a desire to be abstinent from an addiction to performative theatricality in the print medium. Hume seems to suggest that writing too much—production and reproduction in work, that is—would cause corpulence upon the body, and thus emaciate the body into that lacking sympathetic sentiments and virility. Mary Poovey argues that *A Treatise of Human Nature*, as Hume's first publication, was already intended

> to the marketplace of ideas, where writers competed for readers and respect. Without a university position and acutely aware of the rewards and punishments meted out to writers in the burgeoning age of print, Hume increasingly sought to turn what might have seemed like an unfortunate necessity—the imperative to please his audience—into a stylistic practice infused with philosophical and moral import. (Poovey 204)

---

[1] Jerome Christensen, *Practicing Enlightenment*, p. 197, note 12.
[2] David Hume, *The Letters of David Hume*, vol. 1, p. 369.

This audience imagined as feminine might reflect "a pervasive cultural ambivalence repeatedly expressed toward women by would-be arbiters of culture and morality in this period." It "expressed a mixture of loathing and admiration for the women whose consumption and production so indelibly marked the emergent consumer society" (Poovey 212). This is also suggested by recent feminist criticism of the work of Swift, Pope, and Richardson[1]. In the way that "money functions as the standard of value," "she functions strictly as the standard of taste" (Christensen 1987: 99). Before this standard, Hume is obsessed with his fertility, health, and offspring. In this sense, he provides a case, in which masculinity is a defense strategy adopted in the coming of the print and literary modernity.

III.iii. Personal History of Writing in a Grammatical Issue of Identity of the Enlightenment

This strategy is also manifested in the autobiographic piece "My Own Life," the last essay that Hume wrote in his life. At the beginning of its last paragraph[2], we read: "To conclude historically with my own character. I am, or rather was (for that is the style I must now use in speaking of myself, which emboldens me the more to speak my sentiments); I was, I say ....[3]" The literary death of an "I" or "Home" makes a transactional scarcity in the commerce of writing. It actualizes Hume's scribbling on "many a Quire of Paper, in which there is nothing contained but my own Inventions," which is put at the beginning of his *Treatise*. Writing, thereby, becomes an aesthetic tool for self-fashioning in an economy of capitalism. In his final composition Hume writes

---

[1] See Mary Poovey, *A History of the Modern Fact*, p. 212, note 78.

[2] Here is an opening paragraph of Hume's "My Own Life": "I was born on the 26th of April 1711, old style, at Edinburgh. I was of a good family, both by father and mother: my father's family is a branch of the Earl of Home's, or Hume's; and my ancestors had been proprietors of the estate, which my brother possesses, for several generations. My mother was daughter of Sir David Falconer, President of the College of Justice: the title of Lord Halkerton came by succession to her brother."

[3] David Hume, *The Letters of David Hume*, 1: 7.

retrospectively:

> It is difficult for a man to speak long of himself without vanity; therefore, I shall be short. It may be thought an instance of vanity that I pretend at all to write my life; but this Narrative shall contain little more than the History of my Writings; as indeed, almost all my life has been spent in literary pursuits and occupations[1].

Roy Pascal is not accurate when he comments that

> Hume's *Life*, important historically as one of the first extended accounts by a writer of his literary progress, fails to reach greatness because of Hume's unwillingness to tell us of anything but the facts directly relevant to his publications; from it one could scarcely guess at the content of his Essays[2].

It is exactly in this "little more than the History of my Writings," this writing argues, that we have a theatrical imposition in print medium to satisfy the created discrepancy. This is a social consequence of moving away from a society that was dominated by "strategy rather than economy[3]" into a literary culture of modern market economy. It reflects a shift from the primogeniture system into the literary career marketplace. Ronald Paulson argues that Joseph Addison

> modulates the austere virtue of civic humanism into politeness, and extends the amenities across a broader spectrum of society, noting that the 'man of a Polite Imagination' feels 'greater Satisfaction' in the Prospect of Fields and Meadows, than another does in the Possession. (Paulson 1996: 50)

For Paulson, this aesthetic pleasure is "precisely because it is *not* his

---

[1] David Hume, *The Letters of David Hume*, vol. 1, p. 1.
[2] Roy Pascal. *Design and Truth in Autobiography*. Quoted in Jerome Christensen, *Practicing Enlightenment*, pp. 45-46, note 2.
[3] R. H. Campbell, *Scotland since 1707: The Rise of an Industrial Society*, p. 7. Quoted in Jerome Christensen, *Practicing Enlightenment*, p. 40.

own property and he sees in it the perspective of commerce and paper money, rather than inheritance, upkeep, and tenantry" (50-51). In Hume, this sense of property in representation through work of writing is satisfied not merely in "the perspective of commerce and paper money," but more in inscribing emotions through working as part of an interiorized and thus propertied selfhood.

This mapping of interior emotions is a means to socialize the relation between the writer and its public readers. It is made very clear in one of the passages taken from the *Treatise*:

> We may infer from them [the fleeing men], that the uneasiness of being contemn'd depends on sympathy, and that sympathy depends on the relation of objects to ourselves; since we are most uneasy under the contempt of persons, who are both related to us by blood, and contiguous in place. Hence we seek to diminish this sympathy and uneasiness by separating these relations, and placing ourselves in a contiguity to strangers, and at a distance from relations. (Hume 1978: 322)

The local sympathy from blood relations or geographic closeness is rather detrimental, and thus makes a salubrious sympathy at distances more necessary. This role of benevolence of sympathy upon the body, whether of oneself or others, is among the moral philosophical agenda in the Scottish Enlightenment. For instance, Francis Hutcheson (1694—1746) takes sympathy as a fact that is included in his anti-Hobbesian doctrine. Unlike a warring-state between individuals, benevolence is natural to humans for Hutcheson. By sympathy or compassion, as Hutcheson writes:

> We are dispos'd to study the Interest of others, without any Views of private Advantage .... Every Mortal is made uneasy by any grievous Misery he sees another involv'd in, unless the Person be imagin'd evil, in a moral Sense: Nay, it is almost impossible for us to be unmov'd, even in that Case. (qtd. in Broadie 160)

In Hume, the provincial "strategy" gives way to economically relational "contiguity to strangers." Or, "ourself ... is in reality nothing" (Hume 1978: 340). What wants in geographic and physical "reality" needs fueling in global and representational "fiction" through writing, by which a "freely" self-actualizing personality is achieved. This economy of scarcity or a fictionalized self of sentimental deprivation is captured by Gilles Deleuze and Felix Guattari in their analysis of the capitalist deformation of desire: the "deliberate creation of lack as a function of the market economy is the art of a dominant class[1]." Thus the Humean self becomes a necessity of production in a literary career in the early commerce of capitalism, not *that* much away from his original occupation in a merchant's office. With those "as delirious and dismal as himself" and "in a contiguity to strangers, and at a distance from relations," the Humean self is always in the practice of a "process," to put it in the term that Northrop Frye used to characterize the artistic formations of the "age of sensibility[2]." It is a career of the men of letters, whose practice, like the society whose economy his career reflects, is "maintained at a continuous present by various devices of repetition[3]." A repetition of the imposition of a fictional self into a system of rational abstraction is a move "from observed particulars to general claims about universals like 'man' by claiming that their universals were somehow derived from an additive process that identified the 'greatest good of the greatest number' by looking at the philosopher's (representative) self" (Poovey 149). For the British and more frequently Scottish moral philosophers of the eighteenth century, "the problem epitomized by identity becomes the problem of philosophy" (201). "Considering myself as a man in general, [I must] forget, if possible, my individual being and my peculiar circumstances" (239), as Hume writes in "Of the Standard of Taste[4]."

Jerome Christensen argues that, for Hume and his fellow men of

---

[1] Gilles Deleuze and Felix Guattari, *Anti-Oedipus: Capitalism and Schizophrenia*, p. 28.
[2] Quoted in Jerome Christensen, *Practicing Enlightenment*, p. 12.
[3] Jerome Christensen, *Practicing Enlightenment*, p. 12.
[4] David Hume, *Essays: Moral, Political and Literary*.

letters, "the general term that subsumed 'discourse' and 'conversation' was 'correspondence'" and it is that "in the empiricist epistemology knowledge depends on the correspondence or analogy between sense impressions and mental ideas"(Christensen 1987: 10). Mary Poovey examines Hume's repudiation of experimental moral philosophy and his turn to the genre of the essay writing, and writes that

> eighteenth century attempts to produce knowledge about a universal subject through experiment coexisted with another kind of knowledge project, which sought not so much to generate facts about a universal subjectivity as to engage readers' subjective response in the service of producing something else, which eighteenth-century writers variously called conversation, moral emulation, and self-improvement. (Poovey 150)

The concluding part of Book I of Hume's *Treatise* (1739) suggests a case of this experiment with conversation, the epistemological correlation it promotes, and the sympathetic sociality such experiment and knowledge production build. Hume writes:

> But setting aside some metaphysicians of this kind, I may venture to affirm of the rest of mankind, that they are nothing but a bundle or collection of different perceptions, which succeed each other with an inconceivable rapidity, and are in a perpetual flux and movement. Our eyes cannot turn in their sockets without varying our perceptions. Our thought is still more variable than our sight; and our other senses and faculties contribute to this change; nor is there any single power of the soul, which remains unalterably the same, perhaps for one moment. The mind is a kind of theatre, where several perceptions successively make their appearance; pass, re-pass, glide away, and mingle in an infinite variety of postures and situations. (Hume 1978: 252-253)

Self is put into a flux of theatrical performance. The physical phenomena accessible to sight and perceptions succeeding each other "with an inconceivable rapidity" contribute to a constantly altering soul at any moment. To put it in another way, the identitarian existence becomes an experiment through its relation with various "others" to encounter "in a contiguity to strangers." Rather than realized in (moral) philosophical self-reflection, this self is more like a procession illustrated in a natural philosophy laboratory experiment that is indispensable with representations[1]:

> We must therefore glean up our experiments in this science from a cautious observation of human life, and take them as they appear in the common course of the world, by men's behavior in company, in affairs, and in their pleasures. Where experiments of this kind are judiciously collected and compared, we may hope to establish on them a science, which will not be inferior in certainty, and will be much superior in utility to any other of human comprehension. (Hume 1978: xviii-xix)

Self-reflection and premeditation yield to observation of "others," which is made possible by a burgeoning quantity of anthropological materials supplied through traders, travelers, missionaries, and colonial administrators in the century[2]. The treatise illustrates a sympathetic "science" to experiment with general human understanding "in company, in affairs, and in their pleasures." This ethnographical approach to experiential data as a necessary extension of self is expressed more explicitly in Hume's *An Enquiry Concerning Human Understanding*:

> Records of wars, intrigues, factions, and revolutions are so many *collections of experiments*, by which the politician or moral philosopher fixes the principles of his science, in the same manner as the physician or natural philosopher becomes acquainted with the

[1] Regarding the relation between the emergence of modern laboratory science and representation, see Steven Shapin and Simon Schaffer's *Leviathan and the Air-Pump*, and John B. Bender, "Novel Knowledge: Judgment, Experience, Experiment."

[2] Alan Bewell, *Wordsworth and the Enlightenment*, p. 19.

> nature of plants, minerals, and other external objects, by the experiments which he forms concerning them[1].

Selfhood is put under the gaze of a medical physician and a natural philosopher. It is, in a sense, objectified. Thus, subjectivity is achieved as a visual sympathy or understanding. It is theatrically established, and always remains in fluidity of conversable exchanges.

In a contemporary sense, this theatrical metaphor reminds of the theatrical spatiality of John Malkovich's body in Spike Jonze's film *Being John Malkovich* (1999). In the film, theatricality is also used to indicate the constant flux of the mind in the sense of visuality and ethnography of selfhood. The dispossessed human body of Malkovich's is similarly "no longer a self-contained vessel." It is "the vehicle of a no less self-contained soul" and does not demarcate "the internal self-containment of a subject" either. Thus it becomes "a kind of apartment house or, better, a dwelling for transients," "as a temporary container and as an observation post, something like a loge in a theater" (Weber 2004: 317). In the cases of Hume and this film, a strong sense of theatricality is displayed through the body and mind site. This reminds of Walter Benjamin's writing about Brecht's Epic Theater, in which he describes the actor's ability to "fall out of one's role artistically" and by implication to "fall" into another one (qtd. in Weber 2004: 317). The site of Malkovich's body is "thus the site of a struggle for 'possession' in which expropriation and reappropriation alternate" (Weber 2004: 318), as Samuel Weber puts it. The theatrical mind stage of Hume's is not a *tabula rasa* either. It is a social stage representing a causal continuity as a performative and articulating an identity. Hume famously writes:

> ... all the nice and subtile questions concerning personal identity can never possibly be decided, and are to be regarded rather as

---

[1] *The Philosophical Works of David Hume*, 4: 64, my emphasis. The practice of experimental moral philosophy in the eighteenth century is devised in the image of natural philosophy, as suggested in this passage. In Scottish universities, natural and moral philosophies not only coexisted but overlapped. See Mary Poovey, *A History of the Modern Fact*, pp. 175-176.

> grammatical than as philosophical difficulties. Identity depends on the relations of ideas; and these relations produce identity, by means of that easy transition they occasion. But as the relations, and the easiness of the transition may diminish by insensible degrees, we have no just standard, by which we can decide any dispute concerning the time, when they acquire or lose a title to the name of identity. All the disputes concerning the identity of connected objects are merely verbal, except so far as the relation of parts gives rise to some fiction or imaginary principle of union .... (Hume 1978: 262)

Out of the grammatical as well as the verbal, Hume composes a literary career. The sense of temporality in the transfer of different perceptions and relations of ideas regarding the organization of an identity leads to "the *History* of my Writings" (emphasis mine.): "Thus we feign the continu'd existence of the perceptions of our senses, to remove the interruption; and run into the notion of a *soul*, and *self*, and *substance*, to disguise the variation." Hume admits in the very grammar of his sentence:

> I cannot compare the soul more properly to any thing than to a republic or commonwealth in which the several members are united by the reciprocal ties of government and subordination, and give rise to other persons, who propagate the same republic in the incessant changes of its parts. And as the same individual republic may not only change its members, but also its laws and constitutions; in like manner the same person may vary his character and disposition, as well as his impressions and ideas, without losing his identity. Whatever changes he endures, his several parts are still connected by the relation of causation. And in this view our identity with regard to the passions serves to corroborate that with regard to the imagination, by the making our distant perceptions influence each other, and by giving us a present concern for our past or future pains or pleasures. (Hume 1978: 261)

The self is more like a segregation of different parts, which may change with relations and transitions of ideas. As a "fiction or imaginary principle of union," the identity issue is dependent upon "the relation of causation" to construct a future history. This sense of a multiplying self into segments takes an introspective interior dialogue as a means of self-government. It might not have stricken Hume's contemporaries as strange. Through a corroboration of "the passions" and "the imagination," it is part of new science of aesthetics of the century. Shaftesbury and his *Characteristics of Men, Manners, Opinions, Times* (1711) is one of its beginnings. For Shaftesbury, an introspective self resembles the "art or science" of surgery. Similar to Hume's, it suggests a social process of interaction:

> Accordingly, if it be objected against the above-mention'd Practice, and Art of Surgery, "That we can no-where find such a meek Patient, with whom we can in reality make bold, and for whom nevertheless we are sure to preserve the greatest Tenderness and Regard": I assert the contrary; and say, for instance, That we have each of us Our Selves to practise on. "Mere Quibble! (you'll say:) For who can thus multiply himself into two Persons, and be his own Subject? Who can properly laugh at himself, or find in his heart to be either merry or severe on such an occasion?" Go to the Poets, and they will present you with many Instances. Nothing is more common with them, than this sort of Soliloquy. A Person of profound Parts, or perhaps of ordinary Capacity, happens, on some occasion, to commit a Fault. He is concern'd for it. He comes alone upon the Stage; looks about him, to see if any body be near; then takes himself to task, without sparing himself in the least. You wou'd wonder to hear how close he pushes matters, and how thorowly (sic) he carrys (sic) on the business of Self-dissection. By virtue of this Soliloquy he becomes two distinct Persons. He is Pupil and Preceptor. He teaches, and he learns[1].

---

[1] Shaftesbury, *Characteristics of Men, Manners, Opinions, Times*, vol. 1, part 1, section 1.

The poetic soliloquy is a theatrical skill for self-examination, which creates a self-dissecting interiority. For Anthony Ashley Cooper, Earl of Shaftesbury—"devoted disciple of Renaissance neo-Platonism" (Eagleton 1990: 3), it is a punitive as well as pedagogical necessity. This surgical discourse is part of the emergent aesthetics of the eighteenth century, "a creative turn to the sensuous body, as well as an inscribing of that body with a subtly oppressive law" (Eagleton 1990: 9). The split and fragmentation leads to what Georg Wilhelm Friedrich Hegel (1770—1831) proposes as the modern "Spirit in Self-Estrangement" in his *Phenomenology of Mind*[1]. Different social and political positions are "united by the reciprocal ties of government and subordination," and would enhance a different somatic body of the republican self.

III.iv. Causation in Print Medium as Empirical Philosophy

What remains of significance for Hume is that of "relation of causation." It is not explicitly stated in Shaftesbury's aesthetics. As a key issue in Hume's philosophy, it is contoured by a principle of property in Hume's construction of aesthetics. This is correlated as an epistemological question. Hume writes in the "Appendix" to the *Treatise*:

> Philosophers begin to be reconcil'd to the principle, that we have no idea of external substance, distinct from the ideas of particular qualities. This must pave the way for a like principle with regard to the mind, that we have no notion of it, distinct from the particular perceptions. If perceptions are distinct existences, they form a whole only by being connected together. But connexions among distinct existences are ever discoverable by human understanding. We only feel a connexion or determination of the thought, to pass from one object to another. It follows, therefore, that the thought alone

[1] See Lionel Trilling, *Sincerity and Authenticity*, pp. 33-39.

> finds personal identity, when reflecting on the train of past perceptions, that compose a mind, the ideas of them are felt to be connected together, and naturally introduce each other. (Hume 1978: 635)

Introspective identity becomes that of an iterable process of being connected. An intellectual labor of "thought" is needed to make a "train," thus a history of perceptions and ideas so as to maintain a continuity of the "distinct existences." It creates crevices between fragments and parts, and anticipates what Ira Livingston detects as "disciplinarity" in the "portable panopticon" of the Romantic poetry: "a *plaid*, a pattern of patterns that works not by being radiated from a center but by generating correspondences among nodes in multiple networks" (Livingston 21). This poetics of processive parts is manifested in a materialist and property-like form through the publication history of the *Treatise*. Jerome Christensen examines this in details:

> Although the first edition was published in 1739 and 1740 (and remained unsold in 1756), sections of the *Treatise* appeared in *An Enquiry Concerning Human Understanding* (1748), *An Enquiry Concerning the Principles of Morals* (1751), and the essay 'Of Passions' (1752); another portion was intended for the 'Fourth Dissertation,' which was never set up in print. The *Treatise* appeared under the imprint of three publishers: books 1 and 2 were printed by John Noon; book 3 was originally published by Thomas Longmans; and Andrew Millar published all the later reworkings of the *Treatise* during Hume's lifetime. (Christensen 1987: 122)

In a metaphoric sense, human nature and understanding of an identity is never an organic unity. Rather, it consists of various parts materialized and realized through different compositions. The body of work finds it analogous in the forms of a book and aesthetics of selfhood. It demands intellectual labor and work of writing through a corresponding public organ of the pen. Christensen argues:

> It is not the immediate possession of the whole that defines the value of the *Treatise* for Hume or its interest for anyone else; rather, it is the relation in which those parts stand to one another and to the individual. The scattering of parts, as long as they are held together as property by copyright, is a means of turning scarcity into plenty. (124)

In other words, to establish a relation of this kind is Hume's strategy to accumulate his capital achieved on a limited labor and life time. The aesthetics upon a fragmentary self—what Shaftesbury calls the "Art of Surgery" of self-dissecting—has obtained a material history in the print medium of the eighteenth century. This poetics about parts constitutes the creation of an emotional selfhood through work of writing. The organization involved in working through constant revisions and publications in the men of letters since the emergence of a print culture reminds of what Antonio Gramsci holds as the difference between the orator and the new intellectual:

> The mode of existence of the new intellectual can no longer consist of eloquence, the external and momentary arousing of sentiments and passions, but must consist of being actively involved in practical life, as a builder, an organizer, 'permanently persuasive' because he is not purely an orator—and nevertheless superior to the abstract mathematical spirit[1].

As a process, the dispersion of the work of writing and the knowledge it produces is analogous to the constancy of revision, and partition. This uniformed replication allowed by the printing press makes the birth of the modern author. The copyrighted relation to the mechanically reproduced knowledge with the author is what "connects," which is a relation impossible previous to the print culture. According to Elizabeth Eisenstein,

---

[1] Quoted in Jerome Christensen, *Practicing Enlightenment*, p. 126.

> Scribal culture could not sustain the patenting of inventions or the copyrighting of literary compositions. It worked against the concept of intellectual property rights. It did not lend itself to preserving traces of personal idiosyncrasies, to the public airing of private thoughts, or to any of the forms of silent publicity that have shaped consciousness of self during the past five centuries. (Eisenstein 1979: 229-230)

It is part of the historical proposition made through modernity like the financial revolution of the 1690s, during which, as J. G. A. Pocock argues, a crisis in the traditional association of landed property with propriety was precipitated:

> Property moved from being the object of ownership and right to being the subject of production and exchange, and ... effect of this on the proposition that property was the basis of social personality [which] was to make personality itself explicable in terms of a material and historical process of diversification, refinement and perhaps ultimate decay and renewal. (Pocock 1985: 119)

The print medium creates a publicity of "personal idiosyncrasies," "private thoughts," and "consciousness of self" that maintain the continuity of identity through production (writing), exchange (publication), and reproduction (revision or refinement, or re-edition).

For Hume, the capital realized through the publicity of print medium is that of scarcity, which is unequally distributed through an economy of emotions: "There is no such passion in human minds, as the love of mankind, merely as such, independent of personal qualities" (Hume 1978: 309). Emotion exists merely as a reflection of a diversity of personalities. This, however, does not mean that there does not exist universality of human love or understanding:

> The skin, pores, muscles, and nerves of a day-labourer are different from those of a man of quality: So are his sentiments, actions and manners. The different stations of life influence the whole fabric,

external and internal; and different stations arise necessarily, because uniformly, from the necessary and uniform principles of human nature. Men cannot live without society, and cannot be associated without government. Government makes a distinction of property, and establishes the different ranks of men. This produces industry, traffic, manufactures, law-suits, wars, leagues, alliances, voyages, travels, cities, fleets, ports, and all those other actions and objects, which cause such a diversity, and at the same time maintain such an uniformity in human life. (Hume 1978: 402)

Analogous to the train of perceptions, feelings and opinions are made into a bundle of the grammatical issue of identity. The republic is composed of a diversity of careers, between which "a uniformity in human life" is somehow established through association and exchanges in the public. The "distinction of property" and "different ranks of men" work into a sentimental economy of accordance, similar to a processive construction of a personal identity. The necessary mediation from the government takes the "relation of causation" further into a distinction between nature and culture, self and society, external and internal, sensibility and commerce. It forms diversifications and fragments. This point anticipates William James in a moment of scientific psychology of *The Principles of Psychology* (1890):

In its widest possible sense ... a man's Self is the sum total of all that he CAN call his, not only his body and his psychic powers, but his clothes and his house, his wife and children, his ancestors and friends, his reputation and works, his lands and horses, and yacht and bank-account[1]. (italicized sic)

A self is a composition of *ad infinitum* partitions. It can claim itself as a property in its structural relation with others, physical and affective, exterior and interior. This probably explains, for Hume, that "History"

---

[1] William James, *The Principles of Psychology*, p. 291. Quoted in Daniel M. Gross, *The Secret History of Emotion*, p. 120.

of his self "shall be short." It is not merely because of what Hume claims as "difficult for a man to speak long of himself without vanity" (Hume 1985: xxxi), but more significantly, of just a practical impossibility to reiterate all the processes and qualities. Literally, it is beyond human to re-live the life as it has gone through different impressions, perceptions, and ideas in the Humean process of "identity." Nevertheless, it is beyond "little more than the History of my Writings" (xxxi).

Samuel Weber outlines a critical history upon theatricality as medium in Western tradition. In his short chapter on two contemporary films *Being John Malkovich* and David Cronenberg's *eXistenZ* (1999), he defines "theater" as what "signifies the *imposition of borders* rather than a *representational-aesthetic genre*." "Theatricality," for him, is a "*problematic process of placing, framing, situating* rather than as a process of representation" (Weber 2004: 315). It is exactly this "little more than the History of my Writings" in Hume that initiates and actualizes a grammatical and fictionalized Humean self-identity, which is a concrete example of objectifying the personal in an exchange economy of the print. After all, it is in between "Home" and "Hume"—"home" and "not being home"—that the name change was made at the first place. This initiation makes possible a realization of theatrical medium in a writing career through its "imposition of borders" and "placing, framing, situating" in a sentimental sociality of sympathy. Theatricality is realized in the presence in print and literary medium, which becomes iterable and iterated in Hume's empiricism and discourse of experience. This reminds of what Horkheimer and Adorno call the "totalitarianism" of the Enlightenment:

> For enlightenment is as totalitarian as any system. Its untruth does not consist in what its romantic enemies have always reproached it for: analytic method, return to elements, dissolution through reflective thought, but instead in the fact that for enlightenment the process is always decided from the start. When in mathematical procedure the unknown becomes the unknown quantity of the

> equation, this marks it as well-known even before any value is inserted .... Thinking objectifies itself to become an automatic, self-activating process; an impersonation of the machine that it produces itself so that ultimately the machine can replace it. (Horkheimer and Adorno: 24-25)

Writing, like the republic government, becomes a machine to produce and reproduce itself, a thing not being able to be captured through another writing about it. This is why "the history of my Writings" is almost impossible. Knowledge production, through initiating and maintaining a selfhood, is an enlightenment system made possible through a uniform process of *pressing* and *impressing* with presence through the print medium.

The "totalitarian" empiricist knowledge production, on the one hand, depends on the correspondence or analogy between sense impressions and mental ideas. On the other hand, it depends on continual and natural exchanges of ideas between one person and another. At the end of the discussion of how sympathy explains our esteem for the rich and powerful, Hume remarks: "The minds of men are mirrors to one another, not only because they reflect each other's emotions, but also because those rays of passions, sentiments and opinions may be often reverberated, and may decay away by insensible degrees" (Hume 1978: 365). Emotions, indeed, play a very significant role in the Humean empiricist epistemology upon selfhood. The affective correspondence with others—sympathy, that is—"appears to be a phenomenon that complicates the 'mechanistic' or Newtonian aspects of Hume's understanding of force, impression, and idea and reverses the unidirectional fading of force" (Pinch 37). The correspondence could be unidirectional, however, once it involves the relation between our own minds and the world of matter. The move is more from exteriority to interiority, from high social power to less so: "No internal impression has an apparent energy, more than external objects have. Since, therefore, matter is confess'd by philosophers to operate by an unknown force, we shou'd in vain hope to attain an idea of force by consulting our own minds" (Hume 1978: 633). This particular correspondence is situated in a particular relation of power, as Hume puts it in one of his ethical thought experiments:

> 'Tis evident, that tho' all passions pass easily from one object to another related to it, yet this transition is made with greater facility, where the more considerable object is first presented, and the lesser follows it, than when this order is revers'd, and the lesser takes precedence. Thus 'tis more natural for us to love the son upon account of the father, than the father upon account of the son; the servant for the master, than the master for the servant; the subject for the prince, than the prince for the subject. (341-342)

Or, as he explains in such terms: "… our passions, like other objects, descend with greater facility than they ascend" (221-222). Passions, like other materials, are more of communicative attitudes than of subjective feelings. They are maintained through a system of hierarchy and order, not without the trace of the eighteenth-century "great chain of being[1]". It is an issue of impression and force upon the mind, which are property-like regarding their significances to form a Humean identity. At another level, for Hume, passion is invested in labor in a democratic sense, which, in turn, produces property[2]. There is a form of literary labor "that annexes it to commodity production under the rubric of passion" (Christensen 1987: 100), as suggested in Hume's essay "Of Commerce": "Everything in the world is purchased by labour; and our passions are the only causes of labour" (Hume 1985: 261). Passion, as causes of literary labor, is put into the circulation of literary commodities, and the neutralizing literary market serves as the only standard to judge. It makes historical sense to situate Hume's ambivalence and his grammatical issue of personal identity in a society that begins to be

---

[1] See Arthur Lovejoy's classic study *The Great Chain of Being: A Study of the History of an Idea*.

[2] See Jerome Christensen, *Practicing Enlightenment*, p. 148.

dominated by a modern market economy.

III.v. Affective Property and Literary Copyright in Print Virtualization

A "physicist of emotions[1]," Hume puts his economy of identities in the light of the correspondence of feelings. Passions "are so contagious, that they pass with the greatest facility from one person to another, and produce correspondent movements in all human breasts," (Hume 1978: 605) Hume writes. Affective interiority is rather in a very flat situation, and exists in an epidemic syndrome. Passions come from without and subordinate individuals: "Hatred, resentment, esteem, love, courage, mirth and melancholy; all these passions I feel more from communication than from my own natural temper and disposition" (317). Exchangeable communication through sympathy, rather than solipsist solitude, is the means, form and content of affective labor. Transfer of feelings is similar to the very act of writing that composes "little less[2]" than a life for Hume. It is very constitutive of a personhood susceptible of darkness and skepticism, which could be the form of literary laziness and lack of sympathetic communication:

> Where am I, or what? From what causes do I derive my existence, and to what condition shall I return? Whose favour shall I court, and whose anger must I dread? What beings surround me? And on whom have I any influence, or who have any influence on me? I am confounded with all these questions, and begin to fancy myself in the most deplorable condition imaginable, inviron'd with the deepest darkness, and utterly depriv'd of the use of every member and faculty. (269)

---

[1] Jerome Neu, *Emotion, Thought, Therapy: A Study of Hume and Spinoza and the Relationship of Philosophical Theories of the Emotions to Psychological Theories of Therapy*, p.1. Quoted in Jerome Christensen, *Practicing Enlightenment*, p. 80.

[2] See an analysis of that "little more" above.

Hume also writes this in a less autobiographic way:

> Man is altogether insufficient to support himself; ... when you loosen all the holds, which he has of external objects, he immediately drops down into the deepest melancholy and despair .... Hence company is naturally so rejoicing, as presenting the liveliest of all objects, *viz.* a rational and thinking Being like ourselves, who communicates to us all the actions of his mind; makes us privy to his inmost sentiments and affections; and lets us see, in the very instant of their production, all the emotions, which are caus'd by any object. Every lively idea is agreeable, but especially that of a passion, because such an idea becomes a kind of passion, and gives a more sensible agitation to the mind, than any other image or conception. (352-353)

Passion communicates a sense of agreement between man and "all the holds" external to him. "Sentiments," "affections," "actions" and "emotions" become communicable in the sense of production, which keeps one away from "the deepest melancholy and despair." The point is not whether these passages of this kind are Hume "not on his best behavior," in "youthful indiscretion," in "a philosophical and emotional extravaganza," "melodrama," and "a kind of schizophrenia," as many times identified by modern critics[1]. Nor is it about whether Hume presents himself as a true skeptic or not. Rather, it is about the emotionality involved in the production of ideas and the communication of literary labor. Emotion has to be extravagant and excessive so as to appear authentically Humean, and to be of a productive literary identity and career. Literary labor is "nothing other than the technique for matching indirect passions with satisfaction indirectly acquired," and "the career of the man of letters is the most abstract labor of all" (Christensen 1987: 155). The trope of sympathy, more than images or conceptions and "nothing but the conversion of an idea into an impression by the force of imagination" (Hume 1978: 427), turns

---

[1] See Adela Pinch, *Strange Fits of Passion*, p. 40.

individuals into communicating bodies. In the public sphere of the coffee houses, "their public was recruited from private people engaged in productive work" (Habermas 34). The publicness of a writing career entails a necessity of self-fashioning for the sake of public secrecy. Emotionality has to be sincere in this production process. Similar to the independence of the male property owner in the market as complemented by the dependence of the wife and children[1], the personal and emotional makes possible a public and philosophical Hume. It produces the "firmness, or solidity, or force, or vivacity" of an impression, which "did once exist" "from the present idea" (Hume 1978: 106):

> For as this idea is not here consider'd, as the representation of any absent object, but as a real perception in the mind, of which we are intimately conscious, it must be able to bestow on whatever is related to it the same quality ... with which the mind reflects upon it, and is assur'd of its present existence. The idea here supplies the place of an impression, and is entirely the same, so far as regards our present purpose. (106)

"The present idea," "especially that of a passion," operates like a physical property, and to be measurable as such, as Adela Pinch points out[2]. It is that "little more than" in between "Hume and "Home," which is a theatrical space of the mind. "[The theater,] like sympathy at large, works as an implicit guarantor of property rights because appropriation conventionalized is not the theft of property but its transfer" (Christensen 1987: 72). Jerome Christensen argues that "Post-Cartesian representation of the passions contributed both to the stability of their possession and to the facility of their transfer in an exchange with another passion owner" (72). This, nevertheless, is not merely about ideas or Enlightenment thinking as Christensen proposes. It has a material base. The sense of "totalitarianism" in the empiricist epistemology presents the writing of a

---

[1] Jürgen Habermas, *The Structural Transformation of the Public Sphere*, p. 47.
[2] Adela Pinch, *Strange Fits of Passion*, p. 33.

Humean self as a medium, a process of abstraction and generality, and a seemingly transparent sociality of sympathy that produces by leaving the "firmness, or solidity, or force, or vivacity" of an impression or transferring it to another mind. It is a new form of materiality, virtual and immaterial, which presents a human being-figure in a bourgeois public sphere of the literary. It embodies an act of composition that

> unlike oratory, is a *labor* of conversion—the writer copying down his ideas (themselves copies of his impressions) and thus, whether we have reference to letter, fair copy, or published text, converting ideas into graphic, communicating impressions so that the reader can repeat the process in reverse, performing the same sort of labor. (106)

As communication, sympathy is established between the spectator and reader, who observe, and the agent and writer, who produce. The reader-like psychological interiority and subjectivity in modern literature and Romantic poetry as communication and imitation originates in Hume's moral philosophy of experience:

> When any affection is infused by sympathy, it is at first known only by its effects, and by those external signs in the countenance and conversation, which convey an idea of it. This idea is presently converted into an impression, and acquires such a degree of force and vivacity, as to become the very passion itself, and produce an equal emotion, as any original affection. However instantaneous this change of the idea into an impression may be, it proceeds from certain views and reflections, which will not escape the strict scrutiny of a philosopher, though they may the person himself, who makes them. (Hume 1978: 317)

It is a process of observing, being impressed, internalizing, and expressing. The philosopher—a position close to Smith's impartial spectator[1]—holds a position of a strict observer. This reminds of the role of natural philosopher upon objects and things as well as suggestive of the role of a supposedly transparent communicant medium of the print. The visual scrutiny could penetrate into the most obscure and private part of a self. Textuality becomes a process of emotional impression and evocation, which is materialized through a transmission relay in the exchange of ideas. It is

> stimulated by the luxury status of the impressions that an author makes (refining them from the truth that one already has) and that a reader receives (the new impressions are fundamentally a surplus version of that idea of herself that she already has. (Christensen 1987: 106)[2]

It necessarily involves production and reproduction of class, as Jürgen Habermas writes:

> The fully developed bourgeois public sphere was based on the fictitious identity of the two roles assumed by the privatized individuals who came together to form a public: the role of property owners and the role of human beings pure and simple. (Habermas 56)

The places where we see a gothic and gloomy Hume are exactly the self-reflexive places of the writing medium, through which Hume confirms his job of writing as literary market labor, rather than any noble activity that Hannah Arendt calls "work[3]." Work of writing unfolds itself in the literary laborer's subjectivity, which presents a case of virtualization through the writing medium used Hume and about Humean identities. No wonder we have a scene of this kind in Richard Ellman's biographic James Joyce: "Joyce suddenly asked some such

---

1 For the difference regarding economies of sympathy between Hume and Smith, see Alexander Broadie, "Sympathy and the Impartial Spectator."

2 Also see Jerome Christensen, *Practicing Enlightenment*, p. 112.

3 Hannah Arendt, *The Human Condition*, chapter 3 "Labor," pp. 79-135.

question as, 'How could the idealist Hume write a history?' Beckett replied, 'A history of representations'" (qtd. in Christensen 1987: 3).

In 1695, the Licensing Act[1], which had legalized censorship, was allowed to lapse. So did the monopoly rights it conferred on certain powerful printers and booksellers. In 1710, the English Copyright Act[2], though "in effect a qualified response to the Stationers' pleas for the protection hitherto provided under the licensing regime" (Johns 234), was passed to provide statutory protection for what was increasingly called "the property in the copy[3]." It was the first legal endorsement of what was to become copyright, whose intent is made clear through the statute's full title: "An Act for the Encouragement of Learning by Vesting the Copies of Printed Books in the Authors or Purchasers of Such Copies[4]." This legalized system of patenting of inventions or the copyrighting of literary compositions was impossible in a scribal culture, which worked against the concept of intellectual property rights[5]. Only the proliferation of a print culture would encourage publishers to advertise authors to advertise themselves. For Samuel Johnson, who lived through such an age and made a career similar to that of Hume, "Written work might be quite different from the products of a laborer worthy of his hire, or even, perhaps, the lands that a gentleman purchased or inherited" (Kernan 101), as Alvin Kernan points out in his thoroughly investigated history of Johnson's literary life in the age of print. The writer "created," not just made, bought, or received his property. Thus, "authors," as Johnson writes, had "a stronger right of property than that by occupancy; a metaphysical right, a right, as it were, of creation, which should from its nature be perpetual[6]." This birth of

---

[1] See Elizabeth Eisenstein, *The Printing Press as an Agent of Change*, p. 120. Also see Adrian Johns, *The Nature of the Book*, p. 130.

[2] See Adrian Johns, *The Nature of the Book*, pp. 215, 233-234, 353, 454-455, 620. Also see Elizabeth Eisenstein, *The Printing Press as an Agent of Change*, pp. 556-567.

[3] John Feather, "Book Trade in Politics," in his *Publishing, Piracy and Politics*, pp. 51-63.

[4] Also see Alvin Kernan, *Samuel Johnson and the Impact of Print*, pp. 91-117.

[5] See Elizabeth Eisenstein, *The Printing Press as an Agent of Change*, p. 229.

[6] Quoted in Alvin Kernan, *Samuel Johnson and the Impact of Print*, p. 101.

modern author[1] and intellectual copyright are described by Lionel Gossman as

> the identification of works with individual graphically recorded utterances [that] led to a conception of literary creation as absolutely original production, arising out of and in some way embodying a unique, substantial and autonomous self[2].

This "unique, substantial and autonomous self" was legalized and therefore objectified by the 1710 English copyright Act as "an invention distinctive enough to be patented[3]," to use a phrase from Northrop Frye. Mark Rose shows in his important book *Authors and Owners: The Invention of Copyright* that legal theorists such as Blackstone defined a literary work as consisting solely of its "style and sentiment." "These alone constitute its identity," Blackstone wrote, "The paper and print are merely accidents, which serve as vehicles to convey that style and sentiment to a distance." It was on the material "accidents" of "the paper and print" that the concept of literary property was formulated on the model of the landed estate by the eighteenth-century jurists of Blackstone's kind[4]. "Copyright as an absolute right of property, a freehold 'grounded on labour and invention'" (Rose 8) that is. Thus in this blending of literary and legal discourses in the context of the contest over perpetual copyright, "the literary-property struggle generated a body of texts—parliamentary records, pamphlets, and legal reports—in which aesthetic and legal questions are often indistinguishable" (Rose 6). The legal history of copyright, indeed,

---

[1] Also see, of course, the classic essays by Michel Foucault and Roland Barthes: "What Is an Author?" and "Death of the Author."

[2] Lionel Gossman, "Literary Education and Democracy," in *Modern Language Notes*, 1971, 86, pp. 761-789. Quoted in Alvin Kernan, *Samuel Johnson and the Impact of Print*, p. 102.

[3] Northrop Frye, *Anatomy of Criticism: Four Essays*, p. 90. "Poetry can only be made out of other poems; novels out of other novels. All this was much clearer before the assimilation of literature to private enterprise concealed so many of the facts of criticism" (pp. 96-97), as Frye writes pages later.

[4] See Mark Rose, *Authors and Owners*, p. 7.

> had important consequences for literature that went beyond purely legal considerations, for it helped to solidify the literary author as a man of original genius (the author's assumed gender in these discourses was invariably male) who created literary property by mixing his intellectual labor with the materials afforded him by nature—much as Locke had argued men created private property by mixing their labor with the land. (Hayles 31)[1]

Thus, the modern sense of literary labor and property comes from an older sense of legal and theological definition of physical property. For Locke, it is through labor that an individual might convert the raw materials of nature into private property, whose familiar passage from the *Two Treatises of Government* (1690) is worth quoting:

> Though the Earth, and all inferior Creatures be common to all Men, yet every Man has a *Property* in his own *Person*. This no Body has any Right to but himself. The *Labour* of his Body, and the *Work* of his Hands, we may say, are properly his. Whatsoever then he removes out of the State that Nature hath provided, and left it in, he hath mixed his *Labour* with, and joined to it something that is his own, and thereby makes it his *Property*. (305-306)

If the private property in the physical sense derives from a literal labor with physical hands, the literary and intellectual property is from an affective communication of a spatial theatricality of presence through the print medium as in the case of Hume. The physical body through the aesthetic labor becomes virtualized, expanded, theatricalized, and emotionalized. Jerome Christensen writes:

> If ... there are three discrete features of text production that the invention of the printing press highlighted—uniform replication, infinite reproduction, and indefinite dispersion—the last

[1] As N. Katherine Hayles argues in her *Writing Machines*.

> remained *in potentia* until the eighteenth century, when, in England at least, a distribution that could rapidly saturate a market came for the first time a real possibility. (Christensen 1987: 184)

Textualized presence thus becomes a communicable transparency of modernity. Circulation enhances the neutrality and objectivity of the print medium, which is analogous to qualities of commodities that began to pervade in the eighteenth century[1]. At the same time it creates a possible being of gloomy and gothic consciousness that remains absent from the theatrical space of the print medium. Thus we could locate the Humean self and its theatrically staged sympathetic sentimentality into the problematic of personal and literary identity that was being legalized and virtualized through the rise of a print media[2]. If, as Pierre Levy puts it, "virtualization" distinguishes itself above all through its tendency towards "deterritorialization" and through "a movement of becoming-other or heterogenesis[3]," Hume's self presents an early case of "virtualization" in print culture through deterritorializing identities from moment to moment in the form of his work of writing. Out of that he obviously made a good fortune, as stated in "My Own Life":

> But, notwithstanding this variety of winds and seasons, to which my writings had been exposed, they had still been making such advances, that the copy-money given me by the booksellers, much exceeded any thing formerly known in England; I has become not only independent, but opulent. I retired to my native country of Scotland, determined never more to set my foot out of it; and

[1] See the collection of essays in *The Consumption of Culture 1600—1800: Image, Object, Text.*

[2] For an intellectual history of this problematic as it had distressed British thinkers ever since John Locke in his *An Essay Concerning Human Understanding* (1690) challenged tradition and located personal identity in consciousness, see Christopher Fox, *Locke and the Scriblerians: Identity and Consciousness in Early Eighteenth-Century Britain.*

[3] Quoted in Samuel Weber, "The Virtuality of the Media," p. 297.

> retaining the satisfaction of never having preferred a request to one great man, or even making advances of friendship to any of them. (Hume 1985: xxxviii)

This "nothing but a bundle or collection of different perceptions, which succeed each other with an inconceivable rapidity, and are in a perpetual flux and movement" (Hume 1978: 252), as Hume puts it, is performed in his work of writing and is a theatricality realized in the print media. Sympathetic sentiment materialized through the pen offers him a financial opulence instead of a corpulence of the body, and thus secures a cozy solitude from any friendship. It is only in this sense we can see the significance of Hume's declaration that "the passions are so contagious, that they pass with greatest facility from one person to another, and produce correspondent movements in all human breasts." In this light, a media history of emergent interiority in the inter-subjective correspondence of sentiments is realized in transferring between "Home" and "Hume." Jerome Christensen writes:

> Although inexperienced in the trade, Hume pursued his interests with considerable acumen. And from the very first those interests were understood in terms of future, successive, and altered editions of the *Treatise* ... Hume managed the *Treatise* not as a child, attached to him by bonds of nature, but as his property, which, as we have seen, subsists not in simple possession but in a *mode* of possession. (Christensen 1987: 123)

This "*mode* of possession," nevertheless, not merely consists of specific work, not even specific modes of work[1]. More significantly, it is a *mode* of experience taken as part of the empiricist philosophy upon identities as an issue of representation. Work of writing shapes a literary career not only in the materialistic sense, but also in the

[1] Like that of correction, as illustrated by Christensen's argument. See Jerome Christensen, *Practicing Enlightenment*, chapter 5 "The Commerce of Letters," pp. 120-200.

ontological sense. A deterritorialized crevice between "Home" and "Hume" makes possible a mode of emotional identity as mediated in this emergent textual media culture.

Chapter IV

Poetic Mediality and Feminine Sentiments in William Wordsworth's Early Poems: Gender, Modern Literature, and Textual Mediation

IV.i. Man of Feeling and Romanticism in a History of Mediation

The expressive mode of emotion in Western modernity gives rise to anxieties about affective authenticity and sincerity. It suggests a new kind of personality, which we call an "individual." Literary critic Lionel Trilling puts it in this way: "At a certain point in history men became individuals" (Trilling 24). For Trilling, this is reflected in the impulse to write autobiography, establishing "one's only authority" over "the truth of one's experience and the intensity of one's conviction of enlightenment" (23). Thus, the expressive mode is also about the increasing importance of representation in the making of modern self in the eighteenth century[1]. The proliferation of feelings in the century and our accessibility to them itself argue for the point that the existence of emotion reflects not just the content of mental representations but the fact that they are representations[2]. The realm of language is constructed

---

[1] Also see David E. Wellbery, *Lessing's "Laocoon,"* pp. 9-42.

[2] See my discussion on the making of a literary representation of an identity in the previous chapter on David Hume. Also see Rei Terada, *Feeling in Theory*, p. 18. Words like "emotion," "passion," "feeling," "affect," "sensibility," "sympathy," and "sentiment" are used in an impressionistic fashion unless noted otherwise. This is done intentionally.

as an autonomous epistemological field in the seventeenth century, through which modern knowledge becomes possible[1]. This new mode of representation could be discussed with the concept of "theatricality," concerning a selfhood individuated and privatized against an increasingly hypostatized "society." For Trilling, this could have been included into a group of vocabulary now of capital importance that comes into use in their present meanings in the last decades of the eighteenth century and in the first half of the next: "industry," "democracy," "class," "art" and "culture[2]." "Society," as an aggregate of individual human beings, becomes "something other than human, and its being conceived in this way, as having indeed a life of its own but not a human life" (19). It is what Bruno Latour asserts about modernity, which is constituted by language as the domain of stories, texts, and discourses[3]. In the case examined in this chapter, this period of history sees a vernacularization process. Sheldon Pollock identifies it as "literization," which is the commitment of oral and vernacular poetic forms to writing, as forms of modern literature in the production of modern text-artifact[4]. By 1800, James Raven points out, "print issued from hundreds of presses operating in London and almost every small town in the country[5]." Against this background, representations of sentiment and emotion are examined as politics of authenticity and

---

Historically speaking, as Adela Pinch remarks, "the many names for emotion travel as freely as the emotions themselves" (16) and these terms are almost interchangeable in the eighteenth- and nineteenth-century writing. What these terms have in common is much more significant than what differentiates them from each other in this current writing. Theoretically, I follow Rei Terada's methodology: "I try to steer a middle course between imposing a single vocabulary on all discussions of texts and giving up on terminological discussions altogether" (4). For a brief discussion on the shades between "emotion," "feeling," "passion," and "pathos," see Rei Terada, *Feeling in Theory*, pp. 4-5.

[1] See Michel Foucault, *The Order of Things*, pp. 41, 86.

[2] As they are also examined by Raymond Williams in his *Culture and Society*, especially pp. xiii-xx.

[3] Bruno Latour, *We Have Never Been Modern*, p. 88.

[4] Sheldon Pollock, "Indian in the Vernacular Millennium: Literary Culture and Polity, 1000—1500," p. 41; "The Cosmopolitan Vernacular," p. 9. Also see Michael Silverstein, "Metapragmatic Discourse and Metapragmatic Function," especially p. 38.

[5] See James Raven, "The Book Trades," p. 1.

sincerity, both of which occur in the space of hybridity between the source text—conceived as the oral—and a modern textual medium of the book in the eighteenth century[1]. A new literary culture encapsulates a work of writing that generates forms of subjectivity. And it invents a nature through representations that are both historical and historicizing. Indeed, as Walter J. Ong argues, "writing restructures consciousness[2]." This new textual culture positions the oral as the dangerous other, from which literacy as the province of rational morality is promoted. This probably starts with what Frances Yates names "the inner deep-seated changes in the psyche during the early seventeenth century"—"the vital period for the emergence of modern European and American man[3]."

By the end of the eighteenth century, William Wordsworth attributes this formation of a "society" to "a multitude of causes unknown to former times" that "are now acting with a combined force" (Wordsworth 1974: 232). This includes both "the great national events which are daily taking place" and the more gradual processes of modernization, such as "the increasing accumulation of men in cities, where the uniformity of their occupations produces a craving for extraordinary incident which the rapid communication of intelligence hourly gratifies" (232). For him, "the change has been silently going on ever since we were born; the disease has been growing, and now breaks out in all its danger and deformity," as he writes in an 1812 letter to Catherine Carkson[4]. The mission of Romantic poetry is to counteract "the gross and violent stimulants," to which the human mind is vulnerable when exposed to "frantic novels, sickly and stupid German Tragedies, and deluges of idle and extravagant stories in verse"

---

[1] See Richard Bauman and Charles L. Briggs, *Voices of Modernity: Language Ideologies and the Politics of Inequality*, p. 16. Also see Maureen N. McLane, *Balladeering, Minstrelsy, and the Making of British Romantic Poetry*, p. 251 and Susan Stewart, "Notes on Distressed Genres," p. 7.

[2] Walter J. Ong, *Orality and Literacy*, chapter heading for pp. 78-116.

[3] F. Yates, "Bacon and the Menace of English Lit.," p. 37.

[4] The letter was written from London: "The lower orders [who] have been for upwards of 30 years accumulating in pestilential masses of ignorant population." Wordsworth to Catherine Clarkson, 4 June 1812, *The Letters of William and Dorothy Wordsworth*, 3: 21. Also see his *The Prelude*, Book VII.

(232). In other words, Wordsworth proposes an economy of selfhood different from that stimulated from emotional extravagance. He sees a mature British literary technology and system being contaminated by "the rapid communication of intelligence" from the media of foreign Gothic novels. His project is against the conformity with "this tendency of life and manners" that "the literature and theatrical exhibitions of the country" commit. For him, this major feature of his contemporary popular literature distances a large population of displaced laborers, peddlers, and beggars away from being susceptible to the socializing influences of nature: "A primrose by a river's brim / A yellow primrose was to him / And it was nothing more" (218-220). Instead, they are all too susceptible to "whatever vice / The cruel city breeds" (274-275). Wordsworth addresses this "disease," "danger and deformity," and "vice" through handling, hierarchizing, and authorizing medially disparate sources. He develops a complex system of anthropological *poiesis* with lyrical ballads, which is a genre of writing different from novels in its oral features[1]. Through distinguishing his poetry from "the popular Poetry of the day" not by rejecting but by using its figures[2], Wordsworth explores that edge,

---

[1] For the genre of British "novel" as institutionalized as a modern work of writing in the eighteenth century, see Clifford Siskin, *The Work of Writing,* especially chapter 7 "The Novel, the Nation, and the Naturalization of Writing." For how collection of ballads, "full of the majiestick Simplicity which we admire in the greatest of the ancient Poets" (as Joseph Addison ratifies its cultural value in *The Spectator* 74 [25 May 1711]), is both of an articulation of tradition-based cultural difference (thereby antiquarian) and a new construction of Britishness in the eighteenth-century Britain, see Susan Manning, "Antiquarianism, Balladry and the Rehabilitation of Romance."

[2] "The Popular poetry of the day" includes portrays of the "species of unfortunates" in the 1780s and 1790s, among whom were also prostitutes. See Robert Mayo, "The Contemporaneity of the Lyrical Ballads." The Susan figure from his "Poor Susan," along with many others, may be one of the characters taken from there, as judged from the original poem's last stanza, which was excised by Wordsworth. This leads to controversial debates about the ambiguous moral character of Susan's, which Charles Lamb bothers to close by clearly assuming Susan as a prostitute. For interpretations of this poem against the developments of early industrial England—the capitalization of agriculture in the country and the growth of an urban underclass in London, and how a gendered discourse—whether late eighteenth-century poem or contemporary historicist criticism—maps the ideologies of country versus city onto the figure of a woman, see Adela Pinch, *Strange Fits of Passion*, pp. 98-106.

geographically and medially, and renders his lyrical ballads as a quasi-anthropological trope[1]. His critique of the contemporary reading public amounts to an attempt to replace debased readers with readers who have been "purified and exalted." Jon P. Klancher writes:

> Out of his [Wordsworth's] prefaces, supplements, and letters emerged a whole vocabulary with which literary history and the sociology of culture came to distinguish the transmission of cultural works: their 'reception' by some readers, their 'consumption' by many others, and the abyss between serious and mass culture that has only recently begun to be critically explored. (Klancher 135)

The form of ballads, in which appear "the figure of the primitive, the popular, and the authentically emotive, whether encountered at home or abroad" (McLane 2008: 223), and the deluge of feelings are domesticated into the emergence of a modern literary medium in Wordsworth's poetry writing. It manufactures a vehicle of self-representation: "I breathed (for this I better recollect) / Among wild appetites and blind desires, / Motions of savage instinct, my delight / And exaltation" (*Home at Grasmere*, MS. B, lines 912-915)[2]. It is a poetic project of trans-mediation that encompasses various media activities, including reading, singing, watching, collecting, and transcribing.

It has been admitted as a critical fact that Wordsworth—at least for many of his early readers—was notorious for "the disproportionate nature of his emotions" (Pinch 72). Lucy Aikin remarks in her review of Wordsworth's *Poems in Two Volumes* (1807) upon the poet's "unfortunate habit ... of attaching exquisite emotions to objects which excite none in any other human breast[3]." Another reviewer puts Wordsworth's emotional extravagances in gendered terms: "Mr.

---

[1] An anthropological vision is at the core of Wordsworth's poetry writing. See Alan Bewell, *Wordsworth and the Enlightenment: Nature, Man, and Society in the Experimental Poetry*.

[2] Which is the prospectus to *The Reclus* (a "philosophical poem, containing views of Man, Nature, and Society").

[3] Lucy Aikin in *Annual Review*, quoted in Marlon Ross, *The Contours of Masculine Desire: Romanticism and the Rise of Women's Poetry*, p. 50.

Wordsworth ... gave considerable testimony of strong feeling and poetic powers, although like a hysterical schoolgirl he had a knack of feeling about subjects with which feeling had no proper concern[1]." Samuel T. Coleridge, the collaborator of the lyrical ballad project, agrees that Wordsworth demonstrated

> an intensity of feeling disproportionate to *such* knowledge and value of the objects described, as can be fairly anticipated of men in general, even of the most cultivated classes; and with which therefore few only, and those few particularly circumstanced, can be supposed to sympathize[2].

Wordsworth refers himself as the "sentimental traveller" in a note to *Descriptive Sketches* (1793)[3]. In his anthologized poetry album as a gift for Lady Mary Lowther, more than half of poems consist of the poetry of women[4]. He expropriates the conventionalized images of women's suffering as the medium, through which a transmission of feeling and of a romantic *poiesis* is (re)produced[5]. Wordsworth's editorial practice, Adela Pinch argues,

> suggests that for the poet and his contemporaries, what motivated the anthologizing of women's poetry was a desire to represent women's voice as the production of a certain kind of lyric feeling predicated on women's suffering. (Pinch 75)

Seeking for "appropriate human centers" is a very significant means for the central figure of Wordsworth's poetry to locate himself in a

---

[1] Quoted in Marlon Ross, *The Contours of Masculine Desire: Romanticism and the Rise of Women's Poetry*, pp. 51-52.

[2] Samuel T. Coleridge, *Biographia Literaria*, 2:136.

[3] Quoted in James H. Averill, *Wordsworth and the Poetry of Human Suffering*, p. 10.

[4] It includes the poems of Anne Finch, countess of Winchelsea, texts by Ann Killigrew and Laetitia Pilkington, clearly drawn from *Poems by Eminent Ladies* (1755), a popular anthology of women's poetry. See Adela Pinch, *Strange Fits of Passions*, chapter 3 "Female Chatter: Gender and Feeling in Wordsworth's Early Poetry," pp. 72-110, especially p. 72.

[5] See Adela Pinch, *Strange Fits of Passion*, pp. 74-75.

"hurrying world" (Wordsworth 1979b: 143). It differs from Henry MacKenzie's lachrymose man of feeling Harley, whose response to an insane girl cry—similar to Wordsworth's Mad Mother—is to "burst into tears[1]," an explicit instance of emotional extravagance. Wordsworth's contemporaries did not miss this point. His "reworking and intensification of what sentimentalism conventionally labeled 'the pathetic'" (Averill 1980: 11) is well recognized. For instance, William Hazlitt writes in "My First Acquaintance with Poets":

> [I]n *The Thorn, The Mad Mother,* and *The Complaint of a Poor Indian Woman,* I felt that deeper power and pathos which have been since acknowledged, 'In spite of pride, in erring reason's spite,' as the characteristics of this author; and the sense of a new style and a new spirit in poetry came over me[2].

Coleridge, who initiates the project of "interiority" into Romanticism[3], defines Wordsworthian economy of poetic sentiment more regarding its narrative structure:

> a meditative pathos, a union of deep and subtle thought with sensibility; a sympathy with man as man; the sympathy indeed of a contemplator; rather than a fellow-sufferer or co-mate, (spectator, *haud particeps*) but of a contemplator, from whose view no difference of rank conceals the sameness of the nature; no injuries of wind or weather, or toil, or even of ignorance, wholly disguise the human face divine. (Coleridge 1983: 150)

---

[1] Harley's encounters include a tableau of suffering, such as the mad girl, the beggar and his dog, the discharged soldier Edwards. See James Averill, *Wordsworth and the Poetry of Human Suffering*, pp. 10-11.

[2] *The Collected Works of William Hazlitt*, XII, p. 270; review of *Poems in Two Volumes* in *Edinburgh Review* 11 (1807), rpt. in Elsie Smith, *An Estimate of William Wordsworth by His Contemporaries 1793—1822*, p. 76.

[3] See Robert Miles, "Romanticism, Enlightenment, and Mediation: The Case of the Inner Stranger," in *This Is Enlightenment*. Especially Miles's analysis of Coleridge's "Frost at Midnight."

For him, Wordsworth, with Goethe, "both have this peculiarity of utter non-sympathy with the subjects of their poetry. They are always, both of them, spectators *ab extra*,—feeling *for*, but never *with*, their characters[1]." Charles Altieri argues that Wordsworth's 1802 "Preface" attempts "to provide a passionate rendering about the effects of passion, which then makes sense only if one provisionally adopts the projected state of mind[2]." Wordsworth admits his economy of emotions, especially in his discussion of "the pathetic" in the 1815 "Essay, Supplementary to the Preface." There are two "emotions of the pathetic": one as "simple and direct" that "participates of an *animal* sensation," another as "complex and revolutionary." More significantly, "there is also meditative, as well as a human, pathos; an enthusiastic, as well as an ordinary, sorrow; a sadness that has its seat in the depths of reason, to which the mind cannot sink gently of itself—but to which it must descend by treading the steps of thought." "The depths of reason" and "treading the steps of thought" create a space of reflection and a medial distance towards immediacy. Thus, Wordsworth lists "Sensibility" second among "the powers requisite for the production of poetry," commenting that "the more exquisite it is, the wider will be the range of a poet's perceptions; and the more will he be incited to observe objects, both as they exist in themselves and as re-acted upon by his own mind[3]." A poet's perceptions and ability to observe is of primary significance for the production of poetry for Wordsworth, that is. In the note to "The Thorn," Wordsworth stresses the intrinsic connection between a poetic language and passion: "Words, a Poet's words more particularly, ought to be weighed in the balance of feeling, and not measured by the space they occupy upon paper. For the Reader cannot be too often reminded that Poetry is passion." Thus, the history of poetry is also a "history or

---

[1] Samuel T. Coleridge, *Specimens of the Table Talk of the Late Samuel Taylor Coleridge*. Quoted in *Biographia Literaria*, p. 150, note 1.
[2] Charles Altieri, "Wordsworth's Poetics of Eloquence: A Challenge to Contemporary Theory," p. 372.
[3] William Wordsworth, *The Prose Works of William Wordsworth*, vol. 3, p. 26.

science of feelings[1].” The dual focus of the emotional object and subject makes Wordsworth’s poetry writing possible. And his sense of observational neutrality or impartiality in the management of sentiments from the “objects of distress” is discernible in his marginal figures like women, beggars, old men, and maniacs among others. In the American context, it is not until the late nineteenth century when “the discourse of virility so central to the rhetoric of literary realism” becomes “part an attempt to keep distinct ‘quality’ writing from the creeping sensuality of romance[2].” In the British context, as this writing argues through this chapter, Wordsworth’s political economy of feelings is gendered as female in the making of British Romantic poetry, which is gendered as male. This *poiesis* seems like what Henry Mackenzie explains as the genesis of *The Man of Feeling*: “I was somehow led to think of introducing a Man of Sensibility into different Scenes where his Feelings might be seen in their Effects[3].” However, for Wordsworth, a relation between the oral (either singing, or reading) and the print (or the “textual”) is transposed, presenting the poet as a mediator. It thus positions a poetic “author” in the British Romantic poetry as a *bona fide* transmitter, which is a performative medial role absent in the fragmentary episodes of the life of Harley in Henry Mackenzie. In this sense, literary form, and its proprieties of authorship and consumption absorb the nature of gender, which runs through a history of modern media[4]. In this cultural history of modes of containment and management, a textual culture presents itself as *neutral* and *objective* in a historical period that Jeremy Bentham categorizes as “the regime of

---

[1] William Wordsworth, *The Poetical Works of William Wordsworth*, vol. 1 , p. 240.

[2] Lauren Berlant makes this historical argument, as she writes: “Realist novels that included sentimental-romance elements tended either to denigrate actively those modes of ‘feminine’ excess or to embrace those plots, motivated by a desire to speak female discourse better (technically and perceptually) than the woman herself.” See Berlant, “The Female Complaint,” p. 244.

[3] Henry MacKenzie, *Letter to Elizabeth Rose of Kilravock on Literature, Events, and People, 1768—1815*, p. 16.

[4] For an American example, see Lauren Berlant, “The Female Complaint,” p. 244.

publicity[1]," whereas the oral, female, sentiment always as that of the other. The other of writing (reading, singing, speech), of culture (the voice of nature), of the modern (a pre-modern, pre-linguist past), that is. Stylistic strategies and modes of narration required of modern publics absorb viewers into textually constructed positions of general subjectivity, which also serves the historical convergence of social and economic objectives[2]. It is from here, I argue, a poetics of interiority is deployed and well developed in the growth of a poet's mind, which maintains an economy of exclusion that otherwise marks the domestic sphere.

Contemporary media theorists Jay David Bolter and Richard Grusin, following Marshall McLuhan, call the constant remix of older media forms by newer ones and vice versa as "remediation," the goal of which, as reform, is "to refashion or rehabilitate other media" (Bolter and Grusin 55-56). Their influential formulation is invoked by N. Katherine Hayles in *Writing Machine* into a simpler formula: "*Remediation*, the cycling of different media through one another" (5). In the light of this theoretical framework, Wordsworth *remediates* what he calls "the gross and violent stimulants" and "frantic novels, sickly and stupid German Tragedies, and deluges of idle and extravagant stories in verse." Out of this process the oral is transposed into the textual. This conjuring of "orality" in textual culture invites us to reckon with what another media theorist Friedrich A. Kittler calls "a transposition of media[3]." It is an attempt to recoup the voice of orality in all its presumed authenticity of context. What matters here is to see what theatrical presence Wordsworth performs in transposing feminine sentimentality into poetic work in "the history or science of feelings." This would be

---

[1] It is a phrase drawn from Bentham's *An Essay on Political Tactics*, which was printed in 1791 but not published until 1816. According to Andrew Franta, it was Bentham who introduced "publicity" into the English language. See Andrew Franta, *Romanticism and the Rise of the Mass Public*, pp. 1-2.

[2] Another illustrating example would be from American early cinema. See Miriam Hansen, *Babel in Babylon*.

[3] Friedrich A. Kittler, *Discourse Networks, 1800/1900,* in particular the section "Untranslatability and the Transposition of Media," in "Rebus," pp. 265-273.

of significance to throw light upon an investigation of the making of sentiments and feelings in moral philosophy, literature, political economy and science from the middle of the eighteenth to the late nineteenth centuries, which is a history of media as "historical subjects" in their full historical and historicizable complexity[1]. Raymond Williams takes "mediation" as "an active relationship, or, more interestingly, a specific transformation of material" (Williams 1977: 158), as "a way of emphasizing the material production" (163)[2]. The print medium of communication is, for Williams, also a "means of production[3]." The current writing follows this Marxist vein of realism, and locates how the man of feeling appropriates what Maureen McLane calls "the glamor of the oral" (214) in the Romantic period to configure the real in the emergence of a textual media culture. Robert Miles argues:

> Romanticism is distinguished by a self-consciousness that simultaneously looks backward toward a state of naivety from which history has permanently deviated, and forward toward new forms of expression .... Thus one of the fundamental ironies of Romanticism: it is often most modern when most 'nostalgic,' or backward-looking. (Miles 185)[4]

In a history of media, it could be addressed as less a transition stage and more a "cusp" that partakes both the oral and the print, the reader and the writer, interiority and media[5].

---

[1] See Lisa Gitelman, *Always Already New: Media, History, and the Data of Culture*, especially "Introduction: Media as Historical Subjects," pp. 1-24.

[2] See Raymond Williams, *Marxism and Literature*, pp. 158-164.

[3] Raymond Williams, "Means of Communication as Means of Production."

[4] He follows Charles Taylor's argument on secularization in *A Secular Age*.

[5] As Robert Miles, following Taylor's argument, situates Romanticism between Providential Deism and modernity.

IV.ii. Sensibility as Gendered, Authenticity, and the Scriptural System

In the eighteenth century, as Michel Foucault suggests:

> The entire female body is riddled by obscure but strangely direct paths of sympathy; it is always in an immediate complicity with itself, to the point of forming a kind of absolutely privileged site for the sympathies; from one extremity of its organic space to the other, it encloses a perpetual possibility of hysteria. The sympathetic sensibility of her organism, radiating through her entire body, condemns woman to those diseases of the nerves that are called vapors[1].

This problematic relation between control and anxiety upon the female body is a reflection upon the long-time existent discourse upon women's susceptibility to "passions," which leads to hysteria, the depictions of feminine sensibility and disorder. Robert Whytt, for example, writes in his *Observations* of 1765:

> It is true that in women, hysteric symptoms occur more frequently, and are often much more sudden and violent, than the hypochondriac in men; but this circumstance, which is only a consequence of the more delicate frame, sedentary life, and particular condition of the womb in women, by no means shows the two diseases to be, strictly speaking, different[2].

Woman's liability to disorder is particularly associated with her reproductive capacities, which is the womb. Several pages latter, Whytt defines the problem through the nervous system. "WOMEN, in whom the nervous system is generally more moveable than in men, are more

---

[1] Michel Foucault, *Madness and Civilization*, pp. 153-154.

[2] Robert Whytt, *Observations on the Nature, Causes, and Cure of those Disorders which have been commonly call'd Nervous, Hypochondriac, or Hysteric*, p. 105.

subject to nervous complaints, and have them in a higher degree[1]." Certainly this discursive attribution of sensibility to women does not merely exist in medical treatises. John Mullan writes:

> In many of the novels of the eighteenth century which elevate sentiment, and most notably in *Clarissa* and *Sir Charles Grandison*, the investment in sensibility is an investment in a particular version of the feminine—tearful, palpitating, embodying virtue whilst susceptible to all the vicissitudes of 'feeling.' (Mullan 218)

Terry Eagleton calls this into a broad "feminization of discourse" (Eagleton 1982: 14) that is represented in Richardson. E. J. Clery argues that this constitutes a "feminization debate," in which the growing status and influence of women was "variously condemned as cause and symptom of national decline, or celebrated as an index of increasing refinement or civility" (Clery 1). Thus, through the century, different discourses, medical or literary, attribute to women "an elevated sensibility, an especially vivid imagination, a highly tuned sympathy, and a susceptibility to narratives of misfortune and suffering" (Brown 113)[2]. Feminine sensibility and disorder "is, and continues into the nineteenth century to be, the object of a male scrutiny which is by turns suspicious, enraptured, and dismissive" (216-217). This is partially true of Wordsworth's first published composition, "Sonnet on Seeing Miss Helen Maria Williams Weep at a Tale of Distress," the title of which already suggests a tinge of scrutinizing voyeurism into a sentimental

---

[1] Robert Whytt, *Observations*, p. 118

[2] For how feminine sensibility or sentimentality is promoted largely because of the influence of civic humanism in the first half of the eighteenth century (like in Addison and Steele), and how it begins to be a factor in a commercial society in the second half of the century (in Richardson, for instance), see E. J. Clery, *The Feminization Debate in Eighteenth-Century England*, pp. 1-12, and chapter 5-6, pp. 95-170. For a brief analysis on the apprehension of "effeminacy" in the eighteenth-century England that covers the traditional ideology of civic humanism to the innovative ideology of sensibility, see Michael McKeon, "Historicizing Patriarchy: the Emergence of Gender Difference in England, 1660—1760."

reading scene, sedentary, domestic and private[1]. The poem, as one of the many youthful poems of Wordsworth's, was published pseudonymously in the *European Magazine* of March 1787 under the Latin name of "Axiologus," which means "words' worth." Miss Helen Maria Williams's *Poems, in Two Volumes* was published in 1786, and short poems of recognition to a fellow poet were a minor genre popular in the late eighteenth century[2]. In many ways, however, this first composition is not simply an exercise for Wordsworth[3]. Neither there lies any significance to see that James Averill argues the development of "a connection between sympathetic emotion and moral improvement" started from *The Ruined Cottage* and *Peter Bell*[4]. Instead, it reveals much about Wordsworth's self-consciously established relationship to contemporary popular culture and to a history of sentiment as materialized in textual media, with its extraordinary dramatic complexity and tensions within Wordsworth's early experimental poems. As a matter of fact, the theatrical strategy of posing himself not only as a writer but as a viewer and a cultural transmitter, with a sophisticated manufactured perception of and proximity to feminine sentimentality, is throughout Wordsworth's rhetoric of sentiment. It is also among the century-long "attempts to raise the dead, to hear what has vanished, to re-animate the scene" that "become coupled with the authors' desire to fix their own history in perpetuity—that is, to control the future of language as well" (Stewart 8). It is one of the primary means that British Romantics deploy for the production of their literary work and project themselves as productive and valuable through

---

[1] The voyeuristic pleasure for an absorbed reader, long before Wordsworth, is well constructed in the amorous fictions by Behn, Manley, and Haywood, such as *Love Letters*, *The New Atlantis*, and *Love in Excess*. See William Warner, *Licensing Entertainment: The Elevation of Novel Reading in Britain, 1684—1750*, pp. 216-217.

[2] See James H. Averill, *Wordsworth and the Poetry of Human Suffering*, p. 33.

[3] Esher Schor claims it is. See Esther Schor, *Bearing the Dead: The British Culture of Mourning from the Enlightenment to Victoria*, p. 69.

[4] See James Averill, *Wordsworth and the Poetry of Human Suffering*, p. 38.

their work of writing[1].

In this first published poem of Wordsworth's, he moves swiftly across gender lines in expressing a response to another person's emotion as a beholder in an elaborate and fictitious situation devised through the work of writing:

SHE wept.—Life's purple tide began to flow
In languid streams through every thrilling vein;
Dim were my swimming eyes—my pulse beat slow,
And my full heart was swell'd to dear delicious pain.
Life left my loaded heart, and closing eye;
A sigh recall'd the wanderer to my breast;
Dear was the pause of life, and dear the sigh
That call'd the wanderer home, and home to rest.

The sonnet's language is conventional and derivative, with a strong overdependence on adjectives, and much of the vocabulary echoing that of Helen Maria Williams[2]. In the late eighteenth century, there exists a type of sentimental figure responding to sentimental objects, who mediate between human suffering and its ultimate audience—figures such as Yorick, Tristram, Belford, Harley, and even Rasselas[3]. Probably this is why this poem has not been given that much critical attention and significance, and was often brushed aside mainly as a "marginal poem" or "an exercise in a certain style of late eighteenth-century poetic diction" (Pinch 76). The original pathos, however, is placed further from the reader than it had ever been in other similar literary texts—such as Henry Mackenzie's *The Man of Feeling*. In this poem, the real or present objects of distress is not accessible to the reader, to whom is

---

[1] Perhaps this could explain why the British Romantic poets are the six males. This is especially obvious in the work of Thomas De Quincey—as the author of both *Confessions of an English Opium-Eater* (1822) and *The Logic of the Political Economy* (1844), who is a Romantic aspiring to be something of a political economist. See Catherine Gallagher, *The Body Economic*, pp. 29-31.

[2] See James H. Averill, *Wordsworth and the Poetry of Human Suffering*, p. 34.

[3] See James H. Averill, *Wordsworth and the Poetry of Human Suffering*, pp. 28-29.

presented a mediated occasion to view Miss Williams's reading or hearing a tale of distress—both as oral activities. Her book or tale is enclosed to the reader, and in this textualized situation merely a sentimental woman figure is manufactured[1]. In place of a presentation of the moving incidents from the tale Williams was reading (qtd. in Averill 1980: 208)[2], there is the drama of consciousness, sentimentality, and somatically involved trepidation. Wordsworth authors a context as well as an artifact. Right at the beginning, we have the poetic incident presented through a short but significant predication—"SHE wept," which, different from "a void of physical sensation" (Averill 1980: 200) in Wordsworth's later poems such as "The Pedlar[3]," initiates a "descent" into the meticulous somatic details of the poet's body in the octet: the purple tide, the thrilling vein, the slow pulse, the swollen, "loaded" heart, the closing eye[4]. It suggests what Paula McDowell discerns "a renewed fascination with the human body as a powerful (and potentially universal) communications medium" (McDowell 2010: 241) in the eighteenth century. The quickening impulse comes from the contemplation of the sentimental. It reminds of Coleridge's description of *The Recluse* as a poem that would involve a history of the progress of sensation in its relation to conjectural history popular around that historical period: it treats "man as man, a subject of eye, ear, touch, and taste, in contact with external nature, and informing the senses from the mind, and not compounding a mind out of the senses[5]." Peter Murphy argues that

> in the modern world the written self may appear to be more capricious and free, but that self is sutured ever closer to the bodily

---

[1] As a matter of fact, Wordsworth did not have chances to meet Williams until 1820. See James Averill, *Wordsworth and the Poetry of Human Suffering*, p. 40.

[2] "... incidents are among the lowest allurements of poetry," as Wordsworth writes to Coleridge, in *The Letters of William and Dorothy Wordsworth: The Early Years, 1787—1805*, p. 234. Also see Geoffrey Hartman, *Wordsworth's Poetry*, pp. 157-162.

[3] On which James Averill comments: "Its suffering is silent, and its narrative without 'bodily form,' 'scarcely palpable,' ill adapted 'to the grosser sense'" (Averill 1980: 200).

[4] See Adela Pinch, *Strange Fits of Passion*, p. 77.

[5] Samuel T. Coleridge, *Specimens of the Table Talk of the Late Samuel Taylor Coleridge*, p. 38. Also see Esther Schor, *Bearing the Dead*, p. 70.

> self, since its career generates profits that the bodily self wants, and which culture becomes ever more capable of overseeing and collecting. (Murphy 134)

Vision, as a metaphor of encounter and interaction between subject and suffering object, becomes contagious and tactile, through which what Earl Wasserman has called the "doctrine of sympathy[1]" is achieved. It already initiates Wordsworth as a Romantic poet, who stands for "a particularly powerful form of sympathetic relationship between author and reader" (Franta 55)—what Coleridge writes in the following way:

> And therefore it is the prime merit of genius and its most unequivocal mode of manifestation, so to represent familiar objects as to awaken in the minds of others a kindred feeling concerning them and that freshness of sensation which is the constant accompaniment of mental, no less than of bodily, convalescence[2].

This self-sentimentalizing move collapses the distance between the sympathizing observer and the weeping subject he contemplates upon. It is among the tendency of Wordsworth's contemporary sentimental literature, which is "to bring the reader self-consciously into literary structure" (Averill 1980: 37), and to remind of "a literary situation in which the reader had been aware of himself as reader and of the work as literary artifact" (45)[3]. It subordinates the concreteness of lived relations to an imaginary, which thereby substitutes and cancels the unruly detail and flux of the real through gestures of suppression and absorption. This is a gesture of confining it in the feminine sentimental scene so that it is possible to reassert orality as a nurturing mode rather than the corrupting influence of popular literature. Maureen McLane categorizes this as

---

1 See Earl R. Wasserman, "The Pleasures of Tragedy," passim.

2 Samuel T. Coleridge, *Biographia Literaria*, 1: 81.

3 For an illustration of a dynamic relation between reader-like expectations and the structure of the poetic experience, and how a psychology of writing, reading and response is established, specifically in "Simon Lee, the Old Huntsman," see James Averill, *Wordsworth and the Poetry of Human Suffering*, pp. 162-166. Also see Andrew L. Griffin, "Wordsworth and the Problem of Imaginative Story: The Case of 'Simon Lee.'"

"the romance of orality" in the transformation of a Romantic *poiesis*, an "emergence of a new literary orality" in eighteenth-century Britain[1].

The central role of language is placed a significant position by Wordsworth in the formation of moral sentiments and beliefs. In a criticism of the contemporary moral philosophy, he suggests that moral philosophers set an "undue value ... upon that faculty which we call reason" and, therefore, appeal to us in "lifeless words, & abstract propositions." They are "impotent over our habits," as he writes. For him, only if a language is directed toward the body can our passion and habit be reshaped:

> Can it be imaged by any man who has deeply examined his own heart that an old habit will be foregone, or a new one formed, by a series of propositions, which, presenting no image to the [? mind] (sic) can convey no feeling which has any connection with the supposed archetype or fountain of the proposition existing in human life? (Wordsworth 1974, 1: 103)

And a text—like what Miss Williams is reading as well as the artifactualized text through Wordsworth's work of writing—should "melt into our affection[s]" and "incorporate itself with the blood & vital juices of our minds" in the act of reading, so as to inform "us how men placed in such or such situations will necessarily act ... thence enabling us to apply ourselves to the means of turning them into a more beneficial course" (qtd. in Bewell 11)[2]. Thus the ethos of a reading audience is interpellated through the regulation of an expanding cultural economy of intimacy, and a rhetorical relationship between readers and the writer is established. It is through presenting the illusion that he and the actual readers share the activity of constructing a literary reality. Reader and writer are conflated in the act of watching through a sense of complicity,

---

[1] See Maureen N. McLane, *Balladeering, Minstrelsy, and the Making of British Romantic Poetry*, chapter 7, "British Romantic mediality and beyond: reflections on the fate of 'orality," pp. 212-251. Also see her "Ballads and Bards: British Romantic Orality."

[2] William Wordsworth, *The Prose Works of William Wordsworth*, vol. 1: 139.

which merges reader and writer in the "action" of the poetic text. This is different from moral philosophy[1]. A sense of contextual realism is negotiated through a developed sense of closeness between narrator and audience. It follows the empirical mode of sentimentalism prevalent in the eighteenth century[2]. The dramatic monologue form of the poem initiates what Robert Langbaum recognizes as the impulse toward the "poetry of experience" stemming from the late eighteenth century[3].

There is not merely a transition of poetic objects, presumably from the feminine sentimental scene "SHE wept" to descriptions of its "physiological effects" (Pinch 77) upon the poet's body, however. More than that, this description of the internal response to the tale of feminine sentimentality is a transposition of media, from the visual and aural (and even tactile) to the literary and in the extension from the mimetic into the realm of pure language. It anticipates—if not already an instance of—what Celeste Langan identifies print as quite "recognizable as a medium" by 1800: "[T]he medium of print becomes recognizable as a medium ... by its attempt to 'deliver' audiovisual information[4]." Literature as part of the emergent modern print medium invents and legitimates the personal and familial in the oral forms as "a nostalgia for the presence of the body and the face-to-face, a dream of unmediated communication that, of course, could never be approximated even in the

[1] The "science of MAN" as David Hume termed it. David Hume, *A Treatise of Human Nature*, p. xv. Wordsworth was writing at exactly the moment when the field of moral philosophy was about to "break up into the modern disciplines of anthropology, sociology, psychology, philosophical ethics, economics, history, and political science" (Bewell 13).

[2] As is suggested by Walter Scott's comment upon Henry Mackenzie, whose work is to represent "the effect of incidents, whether important or trifling, upon the human mind" and "to follow the fluxes and refluxes of the mind when agitated by the great and simple affections of our nature," see Walter Scott, *Lives of the Novelists*, p. 298. For a detailed analysis on the relation between empiricism and Romanticism, see Cathy Caruth, *Empirical Truths and Critical Fictions*, pp. 2-4.

[3] Robert Langbaum, *The Poetry of Experience*.

[4] Celeste Langan, "Understanding Media in 1805: Audiovisual Hallucination in the Lay of the Last Minstrel."

oral—a dream of an eternal present, a future-past" (Stewart 23)[1]. If, starting from the early eighteenth century, "in works such as *The Dunciad* and *A Tale of a Tub*, Pope and Swift reflect on and register threatening oral practices as part of their extended meditation upon the problems and possibilities of print[2]", orality including the readerly activity of reading, in a later period of the century, is sanctioned and revivified by its acquisition of an imaginary feminine scene. Penny Fielding, in her *Writing and Orality*, notes that when the "romance of orality" is "constructed by a dominant ideology it begins to look suspiciously like writing" (10). It would be fixed, authoritative, monologic, and culturally hegemonic. Some forms of orality are better than others. In a "graphocentric society" (10), it is the elite literati who sift and determine the values and meanings of the oral. Or what Friedrich A. Kittler claims that "all the passion of reading consisted of hallucinating a meaning between letters and lines: the visible or audible world of romantic poetry" (40).

The poetic subjectivity perceives, hears of, and even (possibly) physically approximates the weeping female poet, and presents all through the actual work of his writing on the somatic details. This agrees with the picture of the Enlightenment anthropology, which, though guided by an ethnocentric belief that all cultures are on the way to becoming European, nevertheless assumes a greater degree of reciprocity in this relationship[3]. Wordsworth, strongly influenced by moral philosophical texts[4], follows the moral philosopher constructing his "science of man." He remains far removed from the societies that provided the raw materials of his theories, and presents philosophical speculations in the form of textual activities[5]. In this poem, it is partially

---

[1] This is also why in the works of Maupassant, Peter Brooks identifies "an urban literature, self-consciously a commodity in a marketplace, which nonetheless returns again and again to fictive situations of oral communication." See Brooks, "The Tale vs. the Novel."

[2] Paula McDowell, "Mediating Media Past and Present: Toward A Genealogy of 'Print Culture' and 'Oral Tradition," in *This Is Enlightenment*, p. 238.

[3] See Alan Bewell, *Wordsworth and the Enlightenment*, p. 22.

[4] See Alan Bewell, *Wordsworth and the Enlightenment*, pp. 13-17.

[5] See Alan Bewell, *Wordsworth and the Enlightenment*, p. 22.

true that "it is not clear how many characters people the sonnet" (Averill 35). It is also partially true that

> the speaker's detachment from his object, his leaving her spontaneously and immediately to retreat into his own response, is balanced by a blurring of the boundaries between his body and hers, as if his feelings were physically propped upon hers, rather than reflecting or imitating them. (Pinch 77)

That is, a possibility (or ambiguity) of ventriloquism exists in the poem. All of this, however, may be read more broadly as an index of "mediality," a term proposed by Friedrich A. Kittler, of which David Wellbery amplifies as "the general condition within which, under certain circumstances, something like 'poetry' or 'literature' can take shape[1]." Wordsworth takes this occasion of "SHE wept" to stage himself as that person of feeling, and doing the work of writing. The female vocal activity is used to conjure a sense of "orality" in modern literature, which is made possible by a "general" medium of print. Regarding the historical relation between literacy and orality, Celeste Langan argues, in the case of Walter Scott:

> Once print has achieved its would-be transparency—once literacy has become *general* (I use "general" rather than "universal" here to signify that literacy had become both an acknowledged goal and a norm though not an actuality), the storage system of 'oral literature' would seem to be obsolete. But precisely for that reason, it becomes available as the ostensible content of the broadcast medium of print. (Langan 70)

This is also true of this first poem of Wordsworth's, in which the oral is configured in an artifactualized Miss Williams weeping. Sentimentalism's orientation toward response, which fastens attention exclusively upon a sympathetic economy of the emotions of the

---

[1] See David E. Wellbery's "Foreword" to Friedrich A. Kittler, *Discourse Networks, 1800/1900*, p. xiii.

perceiver[1], is made into a dialectics between orality (weeping), literacy (reading), and viewing ("I" and the implicated reader) in this "transparency" economy of the print medium. This process of transmission is exactly what Friedrich A. Kittler calls "the transposition of media," through which the male writer—as words' worth—of the poem becomes what might be aptly captured as the "participant observer" in the parlance of cultural anthropology [2] in the discourse of sentimentality. The weeping female (poet or not) is positioned as that of an anthropological object[3]. If, indeed, it is that "an imperative issues from the realization that the transposition of media is always a

[1] As Northrop Frye suggests, "Where there is a sense of literature as process, pity and fear become states of mind without objects, moods which are common to the work of art and the reader, and which bind them together psychologically instead of separating them aesthetically" ("Toward Defining an Age of Sensibility," p. 316).

[2] Johannes Fabian suggests that the "denial of coevalness" of actually coexisting peoples is a "constitutive phenomenon" of the modern discipline of anthropology, a discipline whose origins he traces to this period. See Matti Bunzl, "Foreword" to Fabian's *Time and the Other: How Anthropology Makes Its Object*, pp. x-xi. Indeed, as Maureen N. McLane observes, "the late eighteenth-century problem of representing ballad informants—indeed, whether to represent them at all—forecasts the kinds of debates scholars like Johannes Fabian, Edward Said, James Clifford, and others have animated regarding twentieth-century ethnography and more broadly the representation of 'others.'" See Maureen N. McLane, "Mediating Antiquarians in Britain, 1760—1830: The Invention of Oral Tradition; Or, Close Reading before Coleridge" in *This Is Enlightenment*, p. 251.

[3] This anthropologist attitude is also expressed in Wordsworth's acknowledgement of the existence of a peasant's written culture, for instance, in a letter to Francis Wrangham, 5 June 1808: "I find, among the people I am speak of, half-penny Ballads, and penny and two-penny histories, in great abundance; these are often bought as charitable tributes to the poor Persons who hawk them about (and it is the best way of procuring them); they are frequently stitched together in tolerably thick volumes, and such I have read; some of the contents, though not often religious, very good; others objectionable, either for the superstition in them (such as prophecies, fortune-telling, etc.) or more frequently for indelicacy. I have so much felt the influence of these straggling papers, that I have many a time wished I had talents to produce songs, poems, and little histories, that might circulate among other good things in this way, supplanting partly the bad; flowers and useful herbs to take place of weeds. Indeed, some of the Poems which I have published were composed not without a hope that at some time or other they might answer this purpose." And yet rustics themselves do little reading, and there does not exist a public sphere of letters in the bourgeoisie sense: "The labouring man in agriculture generally carries on his work either in solitude, or with his own Family, persons whose minds he is thoroughly acquainted with, and with whom he is under no temptation to enter into discussions, or to compare opinions." *The Letters of William and Dorothy Wordsworth*, 2: 247-248.

manipulation and must leave gaps between one embodiment and another[1]," here we have the gaps between the male observer and the female sentiment, reading, watching and writing. Alan Bewell argues that

> Wordsworth's anthropology is distinct from most of the work done prior to the twentieth century in that it is grounded on direct observation and participation in fieldwork, not on the distanced synthesis of ethnographic documents ... denies any neutral form of observation or description ... continually draws our attention to the place, function, and intellectual limits of the observer in anthropological narratives. (Bewell 91)

Indeed, this more complex and self-conscious manner of anthropological discourse in the poem establishes a staging situation, where the poetic narrator's body must be of meticulous somatic details so as to be authentic and sincere: not merely the authenticity and sincerity of the authorial "I," but also that of the female weeping reader. This accords well with the century's attempt to represent honest feeling honestly, as suggested through the critical work of Michael Fried on French eighteenth-century painting and David Marshall on Shaftesbury, Defoe, and Rousseau[2]. It suggests a mode of excess in sensibility, when the "society" is saturated of mass media. What the conservative poet Robert Southey names "the sentimental classes, persons of ardent or morbid sensibility" in 1823 (qtd. in Williams 282) already has its historical precursors in the eighteenth century. It exists as an undefined antagonist, for which Fried designates "theatrical"—what Jon Klancher defines as "the stances of both radical rhetoric and mass-cultural display," and "it is worth pointing out that theorists of this *kind* of reader/spectator nearly always fabricate a hybrid antagonist, composedly equally of

---

[1] As proposed by Friedrich A. Kittler, *Discourse Networks, 1800/1900*, p. 267.

[2] While Fried and Marshall's arguments are more textually based, the current analysis tries to situate this proliferation of sentiments into a saturated history of media and mediation. See Michael Fried, *Absorption and Theatricality*; David Marshall, *The Surprising Effects of Sympathy*.

radical discourse and mass culture" (Williams 191)[1]. What draws Wordsworth's reforming impulse in his preface to the second edition of the *Lyrical Ballads* is prominently the prevailing taste of the gothic novels—what Wordsworth calls "frantic novels[2]." The exemplar of this taste is "an implicit endorsement of a mindless but entertaining practice of absorptive reading that requires a willing suspension of disbelief" (Warner 291) in Horace Walpole's novel *The Castle of Otranto* (1764). For Wordsworth and Coleridge his collaborator, an authentic-deep-self has to be established for accessing the substance of interiority[3]. This might be also the primary reason why the first generation of English Romantic poets finds "simulation"—the creation of virtual realities, through panoramas, billboards, or phantasmagorias—especially noxious[4]. The strategy of blurring the boundaries between his body (and consciousness) and hers is a shrewd camouflage of projecting the textual media of poetry-writing as male and the oral form of weeping as female[5]. In other words, Wordsworth seems very aware of what de Certeau summarizes as the pedagogical function of the book at the heart of the Enlightenment: a certain concept of education as mimicry, with a "scriptural system" that assumes: "[that] although the public is more or less resistant, it is molded by (verbal or iconic) writing, that it becomes similar to what it receives, and that it is imprinted by and like the text which is imposed on it" (167)[6]. In this way, Wordsworth accomplishes

---

[1] For Klancher, this "kind" of theorists includes Samuel T. Coleridge, see chapter 5 in *The Making of English Reading Audiences, 1790—1832* for his discussion. This tactic is indeed—as Jon P. Klancher points out—throughout media culture, whether literature or otherwise, see Jon P. Klancher, p. 191, note 46. For a Chinese case regarding the historical development of a musical medium *Qin*, see Ronald Egan, "The Controversy over Music and 'Sadness' and Changing Conceptions of the Qin in Middle Period China." I thank Professor Ling Hon Lam for this reading.

[2] Also see Martha Woodmansee, *Author, Art and the Market*, p. 114.

[3] Also see Clifford Siskin, *The Historicity of Romantic Discourse*, pp. 11-13.

[4] See Gillen D'Arcy Wood, *The Shock of the Real*, passim.

[5] See Adela Pinch, *Strange Fits of Passion*, p. 78.

[6] John Locke's theory of the mind as a *tabula rasa* presents the mind of the marginal people in the British Enlightenment—idiots, children, savages and illiterates, who are also recurrent figures that Wordsworth observes and writes about—as in its natural state, where innate ideas could possibly be written. See de Certeau, Michel, *Practice of Everyday Life*.

the emotional authenticity claim as realized in the somatic details of the writing poet through mimicry, while distancing the oral reader of Miss Williams into an anthropological object.

IV.iii. Political Economy of Romantic Literary Labor in Media History

Here it claims the author and the first person "I" as the authentic producer of literary value—words' worth. It does not address Miss Helen Maria Williams as a writer at all but as a sentimental reader distanced from a reading audience. Interestingly, in the eighteenth century, the novel-addicted reader in Britain is usually gendered female[1], and "this figure of the woman reader can function as an admonitory figure for men as well as for women: because novels render readers sensitive and erotic, they menace men with feminization" (Warner 141). Miss Helen Maria Williams, the actual woman writer, is poeticized into a prevalent figure of a popular female reader but admonitory for men who perform as the producer of literary work. The actual pedagogical process—Wordsworth the young learner, Miss Williams the established poet to be learned from—is reversed: the women reader as the pedagogical subject[2]. And a first-person narrative, unlike the third-person narratives in early fictions by Behn, Manley, and Haywod[3],

---

Also see James Ross Holstun, *A Rational Millennium: Puritan Utopias of Seventeenth-Century England and America*, pp. 34-39 and 110-115, for an insightful discussion of the political uses of the *tabula rasa* metaphor in seventeenth-century utopian texts.

[1] See William Warner, *Licensing Entertainment: The Elevation of Novel Reading in Britain, 1684—1750*, p. 140.

[2] This corresponds to Wordsworth's politics of a poetic language in general, about which Jon P. Klancher argues that the poems of 1800 "compose the textual countermove against that vast social transformation that since Wordsworth's birth has been turning one (full) culture into another (empty) culture, as the peasants who speak 'the very language of men' become historically the future urban readers who, at further and further textual removes, can at best read only *about* such a language in the poems the poet offers them. Thus the increasingly bleak strategy of a writer who casts the act of *reading* against ineluctable historical development itself" (Klancher 144).

[3] See William Warner, *Licensing Entertainment: The Elevation of Novel Reading in Britain, 1684—1750*, p.151.

would not take the reader into an affect-laden, supercharged sympathy with the thoughts and sensibilities of the characters, but with that of the author *à la* the observer. It is a fully self-conscious authorial response to that media culture eroticized and feminized by womanizing consumption and women production: the body of the author is instrumentalized along with his pleasure and experience through an act of voyeurism. His power comes from standing apart but nevertheless watching, the classic gesture of the anthropological participant observer, through which we can see an embryonic structure of narrator, audience, and victim complicated in later poems of Wordsworth's. This exteriority to the scene he contrives offers an evidential "I," with which the reader is persuaded to identify. It lies outside any overwhelming and sentimental consumption of reading, and is thus able to produce work for readings. This "I"—a figure of what Geoffrey Hartman has called "the ocular man in Wordsworth[1]"—develops an ethos that facilitates the serialization of the life of a reader into a sequence of absorbing adventures: it could be about Miss Helen Maria Williams or anyone else that takes the role of textualized characters weeping and reading. From this a sense of steady, cost-free accumulation of experience becomes possible, and a print media becomes addictive.

This sentimental sympathy in Miss Helen Maria Williams's reading scene—NOT in her writing scene—as watched with an erotic tinge by a Wordsworthian "I" becomes a necessary condition for the visibility of her virtue in print[2]. It helps situate the literary value of a Wordsworth, whose work keeps readers free from the contagious feminizing reading-tale activity. Womanizing reading and writing women are resolved with this strategy of the "containment of the contagion," to use a phrase by Paula McDowell used in a different context[3]. Writing here indeed

[1] Geoffrey Hartman, *Wordsworth's Poetry, 1787—1814*, p. 148.

[2] This reminds of the way Samuel Johnson introduces Samuel Richardson to the readers of the *Rambler* as the writer who "has taught the passions to move at the command of virtue." See Johnson, *Rambler*, head note to Richardson's guest appearance in no. 97, Feb. 19, 1751.

[3] See Paula McDowell, "Defoe and the Contagion of the Oral: Modeling Media Shift in *A Journal of the Plague Year*."

structures simultaneously poison and cure[1]. The rift is at once temporal, epistemological, and ethical. An implicit as well as complicit contract is formed between "I" in the poem and its reader. Thus a hierarchy of writing and reading, literary producer and consumer is established along the gender axis to reassure the distancing authority of the author in the reader that enters the sentimental scene and goes away unscathed. There lies the whole possibility of a carefree absorption of the reader in transition between reading, weeping and listening. It is reminiscent of a similar gesture that we see in Francis Bacon's experimental philosophy of the British Enlightenment:

> For as yet we are but lingering in the outer courts of nature, nor are we preparing ourselves a way into her inner chambers. Yet no one can endow a given body with a new nature, or successfully and aptly transmute into a new body, unless he has attained a competent knowledge of the body so to be altered or transformed. (Bacon 7)

In Bacon's method, nature is subjected to our will to transform it, under a penetrating gaze of a knowledge gendered male. The feminine nature enables a possibility of knowledge in a sexualized cartography, which, in turn, grants an aggressive masculinity and male dominion over nature many times identified as modernity[2].

In the same way, Wordsworth takes the imitation-inducing powers ascribed to an absorptive reading with an emergent feminine sentimentality,

---

[1] See Jacques Derrida, "Plato's Pharmacy," in *Dissemination*, pp. 61-172.

[2] This is also manifested in what Wordsworth identifies as a universal "music of humanity"—or "we have *all* one human heart"—in his language politics, as Jon P. Klancher's analysis suggests: "To 'select' from, 'adopt,' or 'adapt,' above all to 'imitate' a 'real language' of the peasant poor, is to assert that such a language exists ontologically apart from the language of the urban middle class, that the very framework of representation—where one language 'imitates' another—will at last reveal yet a third language. Neither peasant nor middle-class, this language is the very 'music of humanity.' Here the ambitious, profoundly moral act of writing produces an audience that may escape its unacknowledged prison house of language, its own class-limited cultural position, and gaze into the far freer realm of a humanity that 'suffers' rather than 'craves'" (Klancher 140). For Bacon's sexualized epistemological cartography, also see Carolyn Merchant, *The Death of Nature*; Evelyn Fox Keller, *Reflections on Gender and Science*.

and then harnesses them to the cause of virtue through the authorial mediation of print in the sestet of the poem:

That tear proclaims—in thee each virtue dwells,
And bright will shine in misery's midnight hour;
As the soft star of dewy evening tells
What radiant fires were drown'd by day's malignant pow'r
That only wait the darkness of the night
To cheer the wand'ring wretch with hospitable light.

The relation of the oral to the literate within literature is projected as a theatrical performance and medium in print, a type of theatricality exploitative to female sentimentality and female writers, which at the first place, provides a means of entering the poetic arena. The transmission relays established through Wordsworth makes the poem an open social channel for readers to internalize. It serves an intermediary linguistic bridge between Williams, "I," Wordsworth and the reader that link between "soul" and "self" in the unusual figure of the "stranger within" of the eighteenth century[1]. Anna Letitia Barbauld's "A Summer Evening's Meditation" (1773) presents a case of an inner self, or "soul" of providential deism projected across the heavens in an act of imaginary interstellar level[2]. The sublime

[1] For a more detailed analysis of this "stranger within" in Edward Young and Samuel T. Coleridge, see Robert Miles, "Romanticism, Enlightenment, and Mediation: The Case of the Inner Stranger," in *This Is Enlightenment*, pp. 173-188.

[2] … is there not
A tongue in every star that talks with man,
And wooes him to be wise; nor wooes in vain:
This dead of midnight is the noon of thought,
And wisdom mounts her zenith with the stars.
At this still hour the self-collected soul
Turns inward, and beholds a stranger there
Of high descent, and more than mortal rank;
An embryo GOD; a spark of fire divine,
Which must burn on for ages, when the sun,
(Fair transitory creature of a day!)
Has clos'd his golden eye, and wrapt in shades
Forgets his wonted journey thro' the east.

See Robert Miles, "Romanticism, Enlightenment, and Mediation: The Case of the Inner Stranger," p. 177, p. 186.

"God" from within in "this dead of midnight" as "a spark of fire divine"—to which the transported "self-collected soul" turns inward—is replaced by the inter-subjective and inter-medial sentimental and virtuous (and vivifying) tear of either Williams, "I," Wordsworth and the reader, with its cathartic affect achieved upon each. It is this mediating practice in between subjects and media that performs cultural work for words' worth. The earlier inward turn to Providence in the "self-collected soul" converts to a more buffered zone of medial space for representation, reflection and response. The vertiginous effects, which the eighteenth century typically gained by contemplative projection into outer space[1], is achieved by Wordsworth as about interiority and consumptive reading. By absorbing the older (female) forms of sentimental scenes (weeping, as well as writing for Williams) into the new (male) buffered zone as its content, the print media both contain the older forms and draw strength from it as it develops into new practices[2]. In this characteristically Wordsworthian transparency[3], he lays it bare his own history of received transmissions—the voyeuristic gesture—and his profound, painful internalization, the agonized power he himself invests in his work. The poet's body is made internalized textual—weeping as a consequence to reading activity—possibly a silent solitary reading[4], with Williams's as the oral. The narration itself works the change. The transmission relays work to invite a re-oralization from the actual readers of that historical

---

[1] See James Averill, *Wordsworth and the Poetry of Human Suffering*, p. 92, and especially note 8 on that page.

[2] This performative and anthropologist gesture also exists in Wordsworth's politics of language, what Jon P. Klancher calls his "metalanguage,"—"a framework of highly qualified 'poetic' language that carefully 'selects,' 'adapts,' 'adopts,' or 'imitates' a 'real language of men' as its object": "Deprived of the real by the corruption of his own language, the self-conscious poet must now hypothesize another language—the language of the peasant poor—that preserves all the crucial referentials the poet can no longer summon himself" (Klancher 139).

[3] Also see Maureen N. McLane, *Balladeering, Minstrelsy, and the Making of British Romantic Poetry*, p. 231.

[4] Chartier warns that the distinctly modern shift toward silent solitary reading was far from complete or unidirectional, see Chartier, *Order of Books*, p. 20.

period[1]—what Coleridge realizes as "the devotees of the circulating libraries[2]" and "the luxuriant misgrowth of our activity: a Reading Public![3]" Don H. Bialostosky even argues that Wordsworth does not view the poet as "a maker in the medium of language but a maker of poems representing speaking persons[4]." If the eighteenth century had access to interpretation of catharsis likening the effect of tragedy to physical purgation, the expulsion of what Samuel Johnson calls "impurities of tragedy from the human body[5]," the "darkness of the night" is enlightened or refined into "hospitable light" in the practice of writing and reading. It is another place where Wordsworth situates his poetics in eighteenth-century philosophy and "conjectural history[6]," which "takes up a specific stance toward marginal individuals, viewing them as keys for

---

[1] Also see Maureen N. McLane, *Balladeering, Minstrelsy, and the Making of British Romantic Poetry*, p. 230.

[2] In his *Biographia Literaria.* Quoted in Andrew Franta, *Romanticism and the Rise of the Mass Public*, pp. 4-5.

[3] In his "The Statesman's Manual: A Lay Sermon." Quoted in Paul Keen, *Revolutions in Romantic Literature*, p. 19. Of course, Coleridge's history of the book as part of the emergent nineteenth mass media is rather dreary, which retrogrades from "religious oracles" to "venerable preceptors," "instructive friends," "entertaining companions," and finally "culprits to hold up their hands at the bar of every self-elected, yet not the less peremptory, judge" (57). He claims in *Biographia Literaria* that "[t]he same gradual retrograde movement may be traced, in the relation which authors themselves have assumed toward their readers" (58): "Poets and philosophers, rendered diffident by their very number, addressed themselves to '*learned* readers;' then, aimed to conciliate the graces of 'the *candid* reader;' till, the critic still rising as the author sunk, the amateurs of literature collectively were erected into a municipality of judges, and addressed as THE TOWN! And now finally, all men being supposed able to read, and all readers able to judge, the multitudinous PUBLIC, shaped into personal unity by the magic abstraction, sits nominal despot on the throne of criticism" (59). For a convincing historical argument on Coleridge's attitudes towards a reading public, see Jon P. Klancher, *The Making of English Reading Audiences, 1790—1832*, pp. 150-170.

[4] Bialostosky, *Making Tales*, p. 19.

[5] James Boswell, *Life of Johnson*, III, 39. Quoted in James H. Averill, *Wordsworth and the Poetry of Human Suffering*, p. 131, note 24.

[6] "Conjectural history" is also called "stadial theory" of history, elaborated through Scottish Enlightenment historiography—a model summarized by Adam Smith thus: "The four stages of society are hunting, pasturage, farming, and commerce" (Smith, *Lecture on Jurisprudence* 1). Other exponents of this theory include Adam Ferguson in his *Essay on the History of Civil Society*, William Robertson in *A View of the Progress of Society* and *History of the Discovery and Settlement of America*, and Henry Home, Lord Kames in his *Sketches of the History of Man.*

unlocking otherwise insoluble problems about human origins" (Bewell 25). Sentimentality gendered as feminine is used to lend support for textual speculation and production. The meticulous somatic details of the poet's body in the octet are not for nothing but the sake of individual—as well as textual—sincerity and authenticity, pure and hygienic. This is what Wordsworth suggests as the labor of a poetic genius in his 1815 "Essay":

> Of genius, in the fine arts, the only infallible sign is the widening the sphere of human sensibility, for the delight, honor, and benefit of human nature. Genius is the introduction of a new element into the intellectual universe: or, if that be not allowed, it is the application of powers to objects on which they had not before been exercised, or the employment of them in such a manner as to produce effects hitherto unknown. What is all this but an advance, or a conquest, made by the soul of the poet? Is it to be supposed that the reader can make progress of this kind, like an Indian prince or general—stretched on his palanquin, and borne by his slaves? No; he is invigorated and inspirited by his leader, in order that he may exert himself; for he cannot proceed in quiescence, he cannot be carried like a dead weight. Therefore to create taste is to call forth and bestow power, of which knowledge is the effect; and *there* lies the true difficulty. (Wordsworth 1974, 3: 82)

This male literary laboring scene from the Romantic genius is a trope prevalent in Romantic anxiety upon literary value. Jerome J. McGann observes it as "A Romantic Agony": "Imagination and poetry do not offer a relief and escape but a permanent and self-realized condition of suffering" (McGann 131)—efforts of Romantics to identify their work as labor in the coming of political economy[1]. This political economy is conditioned upon feminine and female sentimentality, through which the musing male's settling into the vivifying virtue and hospitable

[1] A typical case of in between Romanticism and political economy would be Thomas De Quincey, whose *The Logic of Political Economy* (1844)—whose significance lay "in its impulse to draw out and examine the issue of subjective desire in political economy. In doing so, he [De Quincey] anticipated the political economy of the end of the century..." (30), as Catherine Gallagher points out. See Catherine Gallagher, *The Body Economic*, p. 30.

light is primarily a response to mediation and the process of writing. Wordsworth poeticizes this sentimental scene in the tradition of eighteenth-century empirical philosophy, through the writing of which "a specific group of marginal and otherwise anonymous people entered into writing and history ... structured to meet the demands of these texts and to function as an idiom or working grammar within the language of empiricism" (Bewell 28). Elsewhere Wordsworth writes: "Poetic excitement, when accompanied by protracted labour in composition, has throughout my life brought on more or less bodily derangement[1]." This "bodily derangement"—as a form of what Robert Whytt identifies as "the hypochondriac"—needs the feminine sentimental virtue to vivify, as the baby is wanting the motherly eyesight. It provides a virtue of pleasure and productivity[2]. Different from Richardson, who engages what Madeleine Kahn calls "narrative transvestism"—hiding himself behind an alluring story of a sexually embattled fifteen-year-old girl[3], Wordsworth presents a relational mediality between the sentimental feminine reading, the authorial "I" seeing, and the readerly experience, drawing a space represented as individualistic and private into the public sphere of print. This poetic strategy throughout his career locates the poetic subjectivity in the isolated as well as sharing position, in similar cases of which Walter Benjamin sees in the novelist in his "The Storyteller: Reflections on the Work of Nicolai Leskov":

> The storyteller takes what he tells from experience—his own or that reported by others. And he in turn makes it the experience of those who are listening to his tale. The novelist has isolated himself. The birthplace of the novel is the solitary individual .... (Benjamin 87)

[1] William Wordsworth, *The Poetical Works of William Wordsworth*, vol. 3, p. 542.

[2] A pleasure and productivity perhaps not unrelated to the brief surge of sales in poetry during the first decades of the nineteenth century, which was an anomaly attributable to the inflated price of paper during the Napoleonic wars. As Lee Erickson argues in *The Economy of Literary Form*, the consequently inflated cost of books increased the value of condensed language, and temporarily encouraged the rereading that Wordsworth and Coleridge had both proposed as the particular pleasure of poetry and as the demand it places on consumers. See Erickson, *The Economy of Literary Form*.

[3] See Madeleine Kahn, *Narrative Transvestism*.

For instance, *The Prelude*, the great unread poem—unread because published posthumously—of the Romantic period, emphasizes the necessity of literacy needed, the ability to read, to be able to discover human emotional subjectivity, which is the object of a poetic epistemology. In a sense, this suggests the emergence of a lonely male writer and reader in the bourgeoning textual culture:

> When I began to enquire,
> To watch and question those I met and speak
> Without reserve to them, the lonely roads
> Were open schools in which I daily read
> With most delight the passions of mankind,
> Whether by words, looks, sighs, or tears, revealed;
> There saw into the depth of human souls,
> Souls that appear to have no depth at all
> To careless eyes. [Wordsworth 1979b: 160-168]

The need to "inquire / To watch and question" these individuals—as an act of silent reading, the means by which the "passions of mankind" and the "depth of human souls" can be "daily read"—is a process of education and socialization for the poetic subjectivity. The observer, rather than the observed, is educated with a literacy of reading deep into souls. And this is conducted in a domestic context, restricting a knowledge formed from observations to and conversations with people, with whom he held "familiar talk [1]." The solitary poetic voice (as suggested by travelling on "the lonely roads") technologizes an oral tradition—part of "low and rustic life"—into that of literacy: a specifically oral medium to be eventually supplanted by the more efficient technology of reading. Through the oral, an interior subjectivity—"the depth of human souls"—is produced as a consequence of literate reading. It is

[1] For how Wordsworth's employment of the language of moral speculation as a domestic anthropology is different from the prevalent discourse of an eighteenth-century anthropology—where ethnographic descriptions of other peoples are provided by travel narratives (which were Wordsworth's favorite reading), see Alan Bewell, *Wordsworth and the Enlightenment*, p. 30.

what a process of "glamor"—the way Walter Scott defines it in *The Lay of the Last Minstrel* (1835): "Glamour, in the legends of superstition, means the magic power of imposing on the eyesight of the spectators, so that the appearance of the object shall be totally different from the reality" (Scott 1835: 41). Penny Fielding points out that, in Scottish culture, "the association of writing with magic is preserved, as 'grammar', or book-learning, became 'glamour', or magical power" (Fielding 66) [1]. It is as if the Scottish does work upon Wordsworth in a figural sense. In the case analyzed here, this poetic strategy is realized in the beginning of his literary career in a virtualized familiarity with Miss Williams through Wordsworth's reading of and learning from women sentimental poems in the 1780s. The magic of literacy makes possible the somatic reactions of the poetic subjectivity from "She weeps." It could be identified as what Kittler calls "alphabetism" in a larger context of historical media: "Around 1800, the book became both film and record simultaneously—not, however, as a technological reality, but only in the imaginary of readers' souls. General compulsory school attendance and new technologies of alphabetization helped to bring about this new reality" (Kittler 1997: 39).

IV.iv. Sympathetic Life in Things, Silence and the Sublime

This erasure of female literary labor in "poetic mediality[2]" is not specifically that of Wordsworth, nor merely of this poem. Adela Pinch points out that "Sonnet on Seeing Miss Helen Maria Williams Weep at a Tale of Distress" is similar to other contemporary poems addressed to women poetesses—Anna Seward, Charlotte Smith, Hannah More, Ann

---

[1] Walter Scott, as the editor of the *Minstrelsy of the Scottish Border*, "in seeming to mediate between oral texts and a literate readership ... maneuvered himself into a position which kept orality and literacy firmly apart". See Penny Fielding, *Writing and Orality*, p. 66. For how the necromantic or etymological relation between "glamour" and "grammar" is situated in a historical transition from orality to literacy by Walter J. Ong in the case of Walter Scott, see Celeste Langan, "Understanding Media in 1805: Audiovisual Hallucination in the Lay of the Last Minstrel," p. 59.

[2] Also see Maureen N. McLane, *Balladeering, Minstrelsy, and the Making of British Romantic Poetry*, p. 231.

Yearsley and Williams—that populated the poetry sections of the magazines in the 1780s[1]. This general textual media strategy is deployed for control and anxiety upon the possibly hysterical woman body at a time decades after "the female body came to be understood no longer as a lesser version of the male's (a one-sex model) but as its incommensurable opposite (a two-sex model)" (Laqueur viii)[2]. The female body and passion are so potentially contaminating that in another poem of Wordsworth's—written in 1799 or 1800—there has to be a literary death:

A Slumber Did My Spirit Seal
A slumber did my spirit seal;
I had no human fears.
She seemed a thing that could not feel
The touch of earthly years.

No motion has she now, no force;
She neither hears nor sees;
Rolled round in earth's diurnal course,
With rocks, and stones, and trees.

The poem's sources in the ballad tradition have long been

---

[1] See Adela Pinch, *Strange Fits of Passion*, p. 79. James Averill writes: "Certainly the genre flourished in the poetry section of the *European Magazine*. In 1786, six such poems appeared, five of them addressed to poetesses. There are 'Stanzas to Mrs. Barbauld,' a 'Sonnet, Addressed to Miss Seward,' three sonnets to Mrs. Smith, and an 'Ode to the Author of the Triumph of Benevolence'" (Averill 33). In the American context, it was not until the 1830s, an intimate public sphere of femininity "constituted the first subcultural, mass-mediated, market population of relatively politically disenfranchised people" (Berlant 2008: xii). Berlant's pessimistic optimism, as "located in the centrality of aesthetics and pedagogy to shaping fantasies, identifications, and attachments to particular identities and life narratives" (xii), is shared in this current writing. See Lauren Berlant, *The Female Complaint*.

[2] "Orgasms that had been common property were now divided. Organs that had been seen as interior versions of what the male had outside—the vagina as penis, the uterus as scrotum—were by the eighteenth century construed as of an entirely different nature. Similarly, physiological processes—menstruation or lactation—that had been seen as part of a common economy of fluids came to be understood as specific to women along" (Lacqueur viii). See Thomas Lacqueur, *Making Sex: Body and Gender from the Greeks to Freud*.

recognized[1]. The literary death of the female figure reminds of a similar female informant mentioned in Thomas Percy's headnote to his "Edom O'Gordon, a Scottish ballad" (1765): "We are indebted for its publication (with many other valuable things in these volumes) to Sir David Dalrymple, Bart., who gave it as it was preserved in the memory of a lady that is now dead[2]." The figure of a dead lady informant becomes part of what Edinburgh moral philosopher Dugald Stewart calls "the culture of memory" and "the principles on which the culture of memory depends[3]"—a mnemonics constituted by the coming of the modern print[4].

In an important essay, Geoffrey Hartman argues that many of the spectral qualities that we associate with marginal figures in Wordsworth's poetry derive from their genealogical link to the world of ballads and romance. "The archaic or literary forms subsumed by Wordsworth," he writes, "are the literal spooks of Gothic ballad or tale, and the etiolated personifications endemic to poetic diction[5]." This Gothic tincture of female figures in Wordsworth's poetry is more explicitly stated in a primal scene of terror that happens in "The Thorn"—"one of the strangest poems in *Lyrical Ballads*" (Hartman 146), according to Geoffrey Hartman[6]—before the narrator has a language to poeticize it. While climbing among the hills, when the old sailor first

---

[1] Especially in Robert Anderson's "Lucy Gray of Allendale" (1798) and Percy's *Reliques*, specifically "The Children in the Wood," see Alan Bewell, *Wordsworth and the Enlightenment*, p. 204.

[2] Thomas Percy, *Reliques*, p. 140.

[3] Dugald Stewart, *Elements of the Philosophy of the Human Mind*, Part I (1792), reprinted in William Hamilton, *The Collected Works of Dugald Stewart*, 2: 391.

[4] Dugald Stewart situates this in a progressive conjectural history of communications development: "[T]the means of communication afforded by the press, have, in the course of two centuries, accelerated the progress of the human mind, far beyond what the most sanguine hopes of our predecessors could have imagined" (10: 54).

[5] "The Use and Abuse of Structural Analysis: Riffaterre's Interpretation of Wordsworth's 'Yew-Trees,'" p. 169. For Wordsworth's simultaneous critique and appreciation of the conventions of the gothic, also see, for example, Karen Swann, "Public Transport: Adventuring on Wordsworth's Salisbury Plain," *ELH*, 1988, 55 (4): 533-553, and Michael Gamer, *Romanticism and the Gothic: Genre, Reception, and Canon Formation*.

[6] Geoffrey H. Hartman, *Wordsworth's Poetry 1787—1814*.

comes to this seaside village and has not yet "heard of Martha's name" (173), he is caught in a terrible storm:

> 'Twas mist and rain, and storm and rain:
> No screen, no fence could I discover;
> And then the wind! in sooth, it was
> A wind full ten times over.
> I looked around, I thought I saw
> A jutting crag, —and off I ran,
> Head-foremost, through the driving rain,
> The shelter of the crag to gain;
> And, as I am a man,
> Instead of jutting crag, I found
> A woman seated on the ground.
> I did not speak—I saw her face;
> Her face!—It was enough for me;
> I turned about and heard her cry,
> "Oh misery! oh misery!" [177-191]

Seeking a rock, the poetic voice comes upon what seems an isolated woman, her body figuring so close to the earth that she becomes part of it, suffering, like mad Lear, the brunt of the storm[1]. S. M. Parrish contends that the narrator does not actually see Martha Ray, only "a gnarled old tree hung with moss" (Parrish 101). The encounter establishes itself as a literary artifact, reminiscent of Wordsworth's writing of "Sonnet on Seeing Miss Helen Maria Williams Weep at a Tale of Distress" before he actually met Miss Williams[2]. In this Lucy poem of Wordsworth's, the object-like spectral "she" "neither hears nor sees." "She" becomes part of the inanimate "earthly years," "rolled," "earth's diurnal course" with rocks, and stones, and trees, which, in turn, strikes of interest because of being provided by consciousness of the human

---

[1] Also see Alan Bewell, *Wordsworth and the Enlightenment*, p. 167.

[2] Wordsworth did not have chances to meet Williams until 1820. See James Averill, *Wordsworth and the Poetry of Human Suffering*, p. 40.

presence—the eyesight of the narrator, the sympathetic erotic "touch," and their implied visual and aural sensorial abilities. Literature is presented as work and nature as that work. The entire absence of the readerly experience of the "audiovisual hallucinations" presents another experience of the "blanking" from the auditory screen of the blank verse (Langan 53). Readers are thus presented at a crucial moment in an almost primitive encounter when standing before the other, as a figure of inarticulate feeling, seeking sympathetic understanding that underlies and makes possible the mediation from writing. Only after an evocation from the sensuality of the touch could the narrator claim knowledge and the right to speak the truth and reconstruct the primeval world, which is pre-human and pre-linguistic: she dies, as Geoffrey Hartman has observed, "at the threshold of humanization" (Hartman 1964: 60).

Condillac, in his *Essay on the Origin of Human Knowledge* (1746), situates his account of the origin of language in a postdiluvian period, when "that some time after the deluge two children, one male, and the other female, wandered about in the deserts, before they understood any sign." "Who knows?" he asks, "but some nation or other owes its original to an event of this kind?[1]" Wordsworth, as almost certain to have been familiar with this *Essay*[2], seems to invest an origin of a poetic language through the erotic "touch of earthly years" communicated to the female figure. It accomplishes a transition from natural to instituted signs in a gesture of what Charles Taylor calls "the affirmation of ordinary life[3]"—"earth's diurnal course," that is[4]. It agrees with the way in which "Enlightenment theories of the origin of languages regarded poetry as the most archaic form of discourse, and meter and rhyme chiefly as mnemonic devices for the preservation of cultural history in

---

[1] Quoted in Alan Bewell, *Wordsworth and the Enlightenment*, p. 74.

[2] See Alan Bewell, p. 74; also see Hans Aarsleff, "Wordsworth, Language, and Romanticism," in his *From Locke to Saussure*, pp. 372-381; and James Chandler, *Wordsworth's Second Nature*, pp. 216-234.

[3] Charles Taylor, "Conditions of an Unforced Consensus on Human Rights.

[4] Of course, Wordsworth "found in stones the sermons he had already hidden there" (Wilde 173), as Oscar Wilde remarks.

the *absence* of writing" (Langan 50)[1]. Celeste Langan argues that

> the problematic archaism of a written poetry culminates with the development in the eighteenth century of print capitalism as a truly massive medium .... The most widespread solution to this evident dilemma is to identify poetry as the language of the passions; poetry represents that excited utterance which, according to grammarians of the eighteenth and early nineteenth centuries, is registered in prose only by the unmeaning interjection (oh! ah! alas!). (Langan 50)

"A Slumber Did My Spirit Seal" presents an exemplary illustration of this solution through an entire absence of the oral communication of passions, since the touch is tactile.

This insinuated fertility of the feminine suggested in the poem is not strange in Wordsworth's poetics: "For the Vale profound / Is overflowing with the sound" suggesting a voice and womb from the Solitary Reaper, who, "o'er the sickle bending," sings "a melancholy strain" of "natural sorrow, loss, or pain," or of "old, unhappy, far-off things," a primordial song whose power over the listener / narrative voice is pre-linguistic, connecting the ancient past with the present[2]. The south-to-north "progress of poetry"—as well as its east-to-west / downward-to-upward movement, is an ascent contrary to the descent in "Sonnet on Seeing Miss Helen Maria Williams Weep at a Tale of Distress." This movement accords well with a progress from exteriority to interiority—"The music in my heart I bore, / Long after it was heard no more[3]," visuality to

---

[1] See, for instance, Hugh Blair's "Critical Dissertation on the Poems of Ossian" (1763), where he explicitly links the characteristics of Ossian's oral poetry to his "very remote area": "there are four great stages through which men successively pass in the progress of society. The first and earliest is the life of hunters; pasturage succeeds to this, as the ideas of property begin to take root; next agriculture; and lastly, commerce. Throughout Ossian's poems, we plainly find ourselves in the first of these periods of society" (qtd. in McDowell, 2010, p. 245, note 23).

[2] Like language, which is believed to have been born "among Arabian sands," her song moves northward, breaking "the silence of the seas / Among the farthest Hebrides." See Alan Bewell, *Wordsworth and the Enlightenment*, 177.

[3] This is suggestively discussed by Geoffrey Hartman, "Blake and the Progress of Poesy," in *Beyond Formalism*.

aurality, and more significantly, the female poetic object to the male poetic subject that realizes the ethnographic poetic project, with a strong sense of landscaping ownership obtained[1]. This characterizes the transformation of the temporality of speech into the spatiality of writing. Susan Stewart argues that: "The movement of time into space is often a device for the legitimation of territory and property, both private and national, by means of narrative or textual evidence" (23). The acoustically conscious singing culminates in a silencing move of the ascending male poetic consciousness: "I listen'd till I had my fill. / And, as I mounted up the hill, / The music in my heart I bore, / Long after it was heard no more." Work of writing aspires to achieve an Enlightenment ideal of transparent communication of a silent medium, where "print is the medium of a *virtual* community of speakers" (Langan 50)[2]. The silent reader of the blank verse, "no longer subjected to the *immediate* sensory input of verbal melody," "gain access to the *mediated* (i. e., narratively evoked) musical sense of the poem" (Langan 53). The construction of the poetic is rather interiorized sound and vision in the poem.

Between the medium itself and this "community" always already exists a process of mediation—a constant inter-textual activity. Wordsworth remarks of "The Solitary Reaper": "This Poem was suggested by a beautiful sentence in a MS. Tour in Scotland written by a

---

[1] From here, we can see that Walter J. Ong is not right when he comments that "Popular ballads, as the Border ballads in English and Scots, develop on the edge of orality," whereas "the novel is clearly a print genre, deeply interior, de-heroicized, and tending strongly to irony" (Ong 1982: 156). For how landscape is relevant to a rise of individualistic possession-ship, see John Berger, *Ways of Seeing*.

[2] The fact that Wordsworth worked up this poem not from an actual encounter recalled from his and Dorothy's 1803 tour of Scotland but more directly from "a beautiful sentence" in his friend Thomas Wilkinson's manuscript—*Tours to the British Mountains*—offers another case of poetry-writing as an inter-textual production, always already mediated and in the process of mediation, which dismantles the Enlightenment and Romantic myth of origins. See Peter Manning, "Will No One Tell Me What She Sings?: *The Solitary Reaper* and the Contexts of Criticism," chapter 11 of his *Reading Romantics: Texts and Contexts*, pp. 241-272.

Friend, the last line being taken from it *verbatim*[1]." In an entirely inverse gesture, the death of sentimentality and dearth of the magical repository of "audiovisual hallucinations" in "A Slumber Did My Spirit Seal" gives the birth of the writer, assuming a common cause with the ethnologist and the archaeologist, who, as Michel de Certeau puts it, "arrive at the moment a culture has lost its means of self-defense" (de Certeau 1986: 123). By the 1780s, indeed, as Paula McDowell points out, "one detects the crystallization of a new confrontational model of balladry, whereby an earlier, more 'authentic' tradition of 'minstrel song' is seen as having been displaced by commercial print" (McDowell 2010: 242). It is a confrontation stated very explicitly in John Pinkerton's preface "Dissertation on the Oral Tradition of Poetry" to his Scottish Tragic Ballads: "In proportion as Literature advanced in the world Oral Tradition disappeared" (qtd. in McDowell 2010: 243). The erotic and tactile touch is revealed as time, a gesture of classifying and ordering of objects. It produces a structure of rationalization, a legitimation of an end that only the present can bring to consciousness. The acoustic and visual faculties of the poetic figure are surrogated by a silent reader. It is the historical emergence of mass literacy identified by Friedrich A. Kittler as "around 1800," which teaches "a silent and private way of reading." "[A]s a 'sad surrogate of speech' could easily consume letters bypassing the vocal organs" (Kittler 1997: 38), so that "one believes one hears what one merely reads" (39)[2]. It reminds of Wordsworth's attempts to sink "deep into the mind of Man," into "the darkest Pit / Of the profoundest Hell, chaos, night" (*Home at Grasmere*, MS. B, lines

---

[1] See his note to the poem in *Poems, in Two Volumes, and Other Poems*, p. 415. Jared Curtis, the editor of *Poems, in Two Volumes*, identifies the friend as Thomas Wilkinson, and adds that his "*Tours to the British Mountains* (London, 1824) circulated among friends in MS. for years before it was published; the passage reads: 'Passed a female who was reaping alone: she sung in Erse as she bended over her sickle; the sweetest human voice I ever heard: her strains were tenderly melancholy, and felt delicious, long after they were heard no more' (12)" (415). See Maureen N. McLane, *Balladeering, Minstrelsy, and the Making of British Romantic Poetry*, p. 231, note 25.

[2] Friedrich A. Kittler, "Gramophone, Film, Typewriter," in *Literature*, *Media*, *Information Systems*. This argument is elaborated in *Discourse Networks, 1800/1900*.

984-989) bred by superstition and fear, to reconstruct imaginatively the "vulgar metaphysics" of the world's first humans through a poetic media[1]. Lucy here is so objectified that she shares in the "rolling," after being rolled by "obscurely animate, motion and force of that earth[2]" into periods of darkness, measure of early days and years that occupies the threshold between nature and man linking the two states. A spiritualizing progress is very rudimentary: "[W]hat has been immortalized is not a spirit, but the body, which rolls interminably, as a 'thing' hardly different from 'rocks, and stones, and trees,' in an elemental material nature" (Bewell 203). It is "transformed into a genius loci, an expression of the 'law and impulse' of nature[3]"—"Rolled round in earth's diurnal course," that is. What Herbert Lindenberger observes as the "rhetoric of interaction" throughout *The Prelude* and elsewhere in Wordsworth's poetry[4], charges the poetic incident through mirroring "my spirit," "she," and "early" rocks, stones, and trees. Before this, she is claimed as a "thing," a literary as well as sentimental dearth. The human figure is fused into her sympathetic relationship with natural objects[5]: "in all shapes ... a secret & mysterious soul, / A fragrance & a spirit of strange meaning." "[M]oral life" is given to "every natural form, rock, fruit, & flower / Even the losse stones that cover the highway[6]." This remains similar to what Geoffrey Hartman has perceptively noted in the old man of the leech gatherer: "a relict of the spiritual flood ... a 'sea-beast' stranded by the ebbed side" (Hartman 1966: 33). The feminine body,

---

1 Also see Alan Bewell, *Wordsworth and the Enlightenment*, p. 94.

2 For a narratological interpretation of this poem, see J. H. Miller, "Narrative."

3 See Alan Bewell, *Wordsworth and the Enlightenment*, p. 204. This comment addresses another "Lucy Poems"—"Three Years She Grew in Sun and Shower," but well to our discussion here.

4 Lindenberger uses this phrase to describe the recurrent imagery of transference and mirroring. See *On Wordsworth's "Prelude,"* pp. 41-98.

5 This pantheistic tendency has long been noticed, for instance by H. W. Piper, *The Active Universe*; E. D. Hirsch, *Wordsworth and Schelling: A Typological Study of Romanticism*; and Jonathan Wordsworth, *The Music of Humanity*, pp. 184-232. See James Averill, *Wordsworth and the Poetry of Human Suffering*, p. 135, note 31.

6 *"The Ruined Cottage" and "The Pedlar,"* p. 181. Quoted in James H. Averill, *Wordsworth and the Poetry of Human Suffering*, p. 135.

through affective dearth, is reduced to a state of nature and can now epitomize, having regained the spirit through the erotic touch of writing, the transition from nature to culture. It is here one sees the poet that Hazlitt describes as scanning

> the human race as the naturalist measures with earth's zone, without attending to the picturesque points of view, the inequalities of surface. He contemplates the passions and the habits of men, not in their extremes, but in their first elements. (Hazlitt 11)

As the poet of the Lake District, Wordsworth wanders through a primeval landscape, engaged in the hazardous task of gathering a poetic language capable of withstanding the historical flow of time—a leech-gatherer of words, that is. He writes that he feels a "wide ... vacancy" separating himself from his past, yet nevertheless he feels that "those days" have

> such self-presence in my mind
> That sometimes when I think of them I seem
> Two consciousnesses—conscious of myself,
> And of some other being. [Wordsworth, 1979b: 28-33]

This double self, an identity split into two parts—"the means by which he recovered that 'other being' within himself" (Bewell 35)—constitutes a condition as well as a product of his "poetic mediality." Poetry-writing works to create means of mediation between them to interiorize the outward glance—the objects of which are either nature, "uncouth vagrants," female sentiments, or females reading and creeping—into a way of looking inward. Jean-Luc Nancy and Philippe Lacoue-Labarthe argue that "since [Walter Scott], since a certain break or rupture that took place with [Scott], [poetry] is no longer what was understood by this word, but rather the agency (or insistence) of the letter in the unconscious. [Poetry] is the letter and hence what passes in and through the unconscious[1]." In Wordsworth we have one of the

[1] Jean-Luc Nancy and Philippe Lacoue-Labarthe, *The Title of the Letter: A Reading of Lacan*, pp. 22-23.

beginnings regarding this technology of writing in relation to an emergent form of the unconscious through media and mediation[1].

Wordsworth, loving a nature felt "all in all" and setting a larger interactive history embodied in the site of Tintern Abbey, learns

> To look on nature, not as in the hour
> Of thoughtless youth; but hearing oftentimes
> The still, sad music of humanity. (Wordsworth 1952—1959, 2: 260)

The shift from "looking on" nature as a "thoughtless youth" to "hearing ... music" is mediated by the coming of a poetic consciousness, which is realized in the work of writing. A landscape made significant to a savage eye is poeticized into an acoustic *literacy* of the social ear to domesticate the sublime topographical landscape into an individualized listening experience[2]. This is probably why Wordsworth places the site of the poem "a few miles above Tintern Abbey" to manufacture "the landscape of the opening passage" to be "prehistoric rather than unhistorical, prefiguring the abbey that is not so much absent entirely as not yet there, but waiting downriver in the flow of time[3]." The facility for objectification and for distancing compels a poetic mediation from the work of writing to *mean* historically. The failure of the landscape is

---

[1] Penny Fielding historicizes this in the last quarter of the nineteenth century, which "saw the emergence of the sign as an object of scientific scrutiny first in the anthropological obsession with the totem as a sign of social groupings, and then with the beginnings of psychoanalysis," and "if the speech / writing opposition is recast in the terms of psychoanalysis, the visual sign (writing or the phallus) becomes associated with the creation of the conscious while the oral is repressed into the unconscious and is unable to bear the same symbolic function as writing" (17). It could have started from *The Dunciad* in the early eighteenth century: "It is to The Dunciad," McLuhan pronounces, "that we must turn for the epic of the printed word .... For here is the explicit study of plunging of the human mind into the sludge of an unconscious engendered by the book. See Marshall McLuhan, *The Gutenberg Galaxy*, pp. 147, 255.

[2] The poem's relation to the picturesque tradition has often been noted, especially on how Wordsworth has learned from William Gilpin's *Observations on the River Wye*. See Meyer Howard Abrams, "Structure and Style in the Greater Romantic Lyric;" and Marjorie Levinson, *Wordsworth's Great Period Poems: Four Essays*, pp. 16-18.

[3] James A. W. Heffernan, *The Re-Creation of Landscape: A Study of Wordsworth, Coleridge, Constable, and Turner*, pp. 16-18.

to meet the actual motivation for the composition of the poem, which is suggestive of what Andrew Franta identifies of "Romantic poetry's aspiration to achieve the kind of durability that will allow it to reach its readers" (Franta 15). It is an illustration of "the self-regarding quality of Romantic poetry—and of the poet 'who sits in darkness, and sings to cheer its own solitude with sweet sounds,'" which is "a formal acknowledgement of the necessity of transmission" (15). This media transmission is interwoven with a new and distinctly modern historical consciousness, which print culture historian Elizabeth Eisenstein attributes to "the printing press as an agent of change[1]." With the introduction of printing, Eisenstein suggests,

> less effort was required to preserve and pass on what was known .... Successive generations began to pride themselves on knowing more than had their forebears ... Human history itself acquired the character of an indefinitely extended unfolding sequence. (Eisenstein 1986: 6)

In this sense, the rise of a poetic consciousness in Wordsworth, as materialized through a saturating print technology, creates a historical sense. And this involves an engagement with his contemporary situation, as Coleridge comments upon *The Recluse*: after surveying "the pastoral and other states of society," it was to have presented "a melancholy picture of the present state of degeneracy and vice," which would serve as proof of the "necessity for, the whole state of man and society being subject to, and illustrative of, a redemptive process[2]."

This redemptive historical sense cannot dispense with the sublime nature, the anthropological figures of which Wordsworth resituates into a domestic circumstance: idiots, children, villagers, and women, the blind, the deaf, and the mute. What we call their sublimity is actually our "dim and undetermined sense" that they represent "unknown modes of being"

---

[1] Elizabeth L. Eisenstein 1979, *The Printing Press as an Agent of Change*, p. 184.
[2] Samuel T. Coleridge, *Specimens of the Table Talk of the Late Samuel Taylor Coleridge*, 37-38.

(Wordsworth 1979b: 51), like the leech-gatherer, who seems a figure "met with in a dream" (110). No wonder John Keats writes to Richard Woodhouse of "the Wordsworthian or egotistical sublime[1]." In the fragmentary essay "The Sublime and the Beautiful," Wordsworth claims that

> as we advance in life, we can escape upon the invitation of our more placid & gentle nature from those obtrusive qualities in an object sublime in its general character; which qualities, at an earlier age, precluded imperiously the perception of beauty which that object if contemplated under another relation would have been capable of imparting. (Wordsworth 1974, 2: 349)

The sublime and the beautiful, simultaneously existing in nature, works differently to a maturing poetic mind, which is affected first by the "obtrusive qualities in an object sublime" and later by a more "placid and gentle nature[2]." James Averill argues that Wordsworth "finds such power in the traditional sources of literary energy inherited from previous generations of poets, the complex of images and responses collectively known as the 'sublime'." The four such sources of "sublimity" include "the cosmic space vision, the 'mountain glory,' the 'graveyard' and the 'psychological sublime'" (Averill 1980: 91). A sense of tranquility and catharsis achieved in "A Slumber Did My Spirit Seal" is through a convergence of these four sources: earth, rocks, death and slumber[3]—nature as the "agent *invisible*" (Hobbes' phrase[4]) materialized through the touch. The performative function of narrative is well maintained through these two stanzas: "she" literarily has to become a "thing," to which the narrator can claim an epistemological

---

[1] John Keats, *The Letters of John Keats, 1814—1821*, 1, p. 387.

[2] Also see Alan Bewell, *Wordsworth and the Enlightenment*, p. 140.

[3] Another place of this realization of the sublime in nature would be in *Peter Bell*:

> The moon uneasy look'd and dimmer,
> The broad blue heavens appear'd to glimmer,
> And the rocks stagger'd all around. [518-520]

[4] *The English Works of Thomas Hobbes*, 3, p. 95.

truth, and she does. The exploitative theatricality becomes even ghoulish. If "words" are "not only as symbols of the passion, but as things, active and efficient, which are of themselves part of the passion," as Wordsworth conceives in his Note to "The Thorn," in making "words" into a poem "she" has to become a "thing" and thereby part of the "words." The silence—"slumber"—of the poetic voice represents not tragic catharsis but a form of sublimity, and comes through with vacuity, darkness, solitude and a general privation of humanity rendered into earthly things and a printed image[1]. The doctrine of Love of Nature and Love of Mankind are merged by an economy of sympathy not in scarcity, but almost in excess. Wordsworth, not proposing a Burkean emotionalism, has a more self-conscious "moral discipline" towards feelings, some of which he considers to be "coarse sympathies[2]". Too much excitement from poetry should be tranquilized rather than celebrated, and excessive emotionalism could only be attributed to the marginal characters of his poems. The textual media, indeed, serves as the Freudian "superego" in the work process of writing and transmission. For instance, Wordsworth writes:

> The end of Poetry is to produce excitement in coexistence with an overbalance of pleasure. Now, by the supposition, excitement is an unusual and irregular state of the mind; ideas and feelings do not in that state succeed each other in accustomed order. But if the words by which this excitement is produced are in themselves powerful, or the images and feelings have an undue

---

[1] Herbert Lindenberger, in *On Wordsworth's "Prelude,"* sees the dichotomy between "violent emotions" and the "calm and gentle" as a betrayal of Wordworth's learning in the ancient Quintillian's rhetorical distinction of *pathos* and *ethos*: "... when Wordsworth speaks of 'a natural delineation of human passions, human characters, and human incidents,' he refers to *pathos* and its various attributes under the term 'passions,' to *ethos* under 'characters' and 'incidents'" (25). "Sonnet on Seeing Miss Helen Maria Williams Weep at a Tale of Distress," and "A Slumber Did My Spirit Seal" might be seen respectively as cases of *pathos* and *ethos* in this way. However, as throughout this analysis, the distinctions of these two rhetorical practices might not hold rigidly in Wordsworth's poems, the cross-fertilization between which makes possible a work through writing.

[2] William Wordsworth, *The Poetical Works of William Wordsworth*, vol. 1, p. 334.

> proportion of pain connected with them, there is some danger that the excitement may be carried beyond its proper bounds. (Wordsworth 1974, 1: 146)

He finds "the great social principle of life, / Coercing all things into sympathy" (Wordsworth 1979b: 87). It reminds of some abiding sense of calm that Coleridge finds in sympathy with the real or imagined life of objects: "The rocks and Stones put on a vital semblance; and Life itself thereby seemed to forego its restlessness, to anticipate in its own nature an infinite repose, and to become, as it were, compatible with Immovability[1]." Albert O. Wlecke argues that for Wordsworth, as for Coleridge, "the true source of the sublimity of anything, physical object or idea, is always the subject," and "sublime consciousness" becomes "a structure of awareness in which all conceptions tend to recede from shapeliness, and the mind is left groping in the darkness of its own subjectivity[2]." A sublimating self-consciousness incarnates the poetic subjectivity in the object-like things like "she," trees and stones, and words, or a companionship of Dorothy Wordsworth, who "enters the poem [*The Prelude*] not in her own right but in answer to the poet's and the poem's needs[3]." The sublimity of subjectivity is made possible through a necessary aesthetic distance between the observer and the object associated with sentimentality. If in the previous poem, the readers could still afford to have an access to Miss Helen Maria Williams's poems published in the magazines of the 1780s, along with those by Anna Seward and Charlotte Smith, Wordsworth bases his poetic vision and possibility in the literary death of the female body when more

---

[1] *The Notebooks of Samuel Taylor Coleridge*, I, 1616. Though in general this Wordsworthian tendency to sympathize with things and objects was denounced by Coleridge, as pointed out by Averill. See James Averill, *Wordsworth and the Poetry of Human Suffering*, p. 135.

[2] Albert O. Wlecke, *Wordsworth and the Sublime*, p. 79, p. 81. Quoted in James H. Averill, *Wordsworth and the Poetry of Human Suffering*, p. 107, note 24.

[3] See Margaret Homans, "Eliot, Wordsworth, and the Scenes of the Sister's Instruction," in *Writing and Sexual Difference*, p. 53.

into his career of being a poet[1]. Thus, the movement of Wordsworth from sentimental to topographical verse could be observed: the poetic energies that originally focus on sentimental human objects shift to "the infinite variety of natural appearances[2]," in both of which sources of "sublimity" are located and achieved in mediation, whether what Meyer Howard Abrams terms as "visual peripety[3]" is devised. It is in this way that female figures and sentiments are forged, collected, annotated, surveyed, transcribed, and edited into the conditions of existence in an emergent textual media culture.

IV.v. Nurturing Economy of Feelings, and Phobia of Feelings in Work of Writing

Indeed, William Wordsworth draws an eighteenth-century myth of origins in which feelings are learned from women[4]. An example of this myth would be Richard Steele describing how he learns to feel by seeing his mother weeping in a 1710 entry of *The Tatler*:

> There was a Dignity in her Grief amidst all the Wildness of her Tranport, which, methought, struck me with an Instinct of Sorrow, which, before I was sensible of what it was to grieve, seized my very Soul, and has made Pity the Weakness of my heart ever since .... Having been so frequently Overwhelmed by her Tears before I knew the Cause of any Affliction, or could draw Defences from my own Judgement, I imbibed Commiseration, Remorse and an unmanly Gentleness of mind. (qtd. in Pinch 81)

---

[1] "A Slumber Did My Spirit Seal" was published in 1799 or 1800—one or two years after the publication of *Lyrical Ballads* as a collaborate enterprise between Wordsworth and Coleridge, as identified by Harold Bloom. See *The Best Poems of the English Language: From Chaucer through Robert Frost*, p. 332.

[2] William Wordsworth, *The Poetical Works of William Wordsworth*, vol. 1, p. 319. For an analysis of the same movement from sentimental to topographical verse in "A Ballad" and "Sonnet on Seeing Miss Williams Weep" to *An Evening Walk*, see James Averill, *Wordsworth and the Poetry of Human Suffering*, pp. 47-51.

[3] Meyer Howard Abrams, *Natural Supernaturalism*, pp. 376-377.

[4] Also see Adela Pinch, *Strange Fits of Passion*, p. 81.

The transmission of emotion is taken "as a spontaneous, pre-cognitive process that seems to preclude the possibility both of ever deriving a feeling directly from a real 'cause,' and of ever making feeling itself an object of reason" (Pinch 81). This is very reminiscent of what Wordsworth defines as "good poetry" in his "Preface" to *Lyrical Ballads*: "for all good poetry is the spontaneous overflow of powerful feelings" (230)[1]. It helps create an image of Romanticism in general: im-mediated, natural, sincere, and authentic. This kind of transmission of affect taken as "having the continuity of bodily substances" (Pinch 81) also happens to Wordsworth's famous account of origins of feelings in *The Prelude*, the Blessed Babe passage of book II:

> ... the Babe,
> Nurs'd in his Mother's arms, the Babe who sleeps
> Upon his Mother's breast; who, when his soul
> Claims manifest kindred with an earthly soul,
> Doth gather passion from his Mother's eye! (Wordsworth 1979b: 79)

James Averill points out that scenes of this kind might come out as consequences of Wordsworth's reading of Erasmus Darwin's *Zoonomia*[2], its chapter on "Diseases of Increased Volition." For Darwin, in cases of acute puerperal depression, for instance, the doctor suggests that "the child should be brought frequently to the mother, and applied to her breast, if she will suffer it, and whether she at first attends to it or not; as by a few trials it frequently excites the storgè, or maternal affection, and removes the insanity[3]." And in Wordsworth's "The Mad Mother," previous to *The Prelude*, the woman is given a relieved poetic voice:

> Suck, little babe, oh such again!

---

[1] Wordsworth and Coleridge, *Lyrical Ballads*, p. 230.

[2] In a historical time "when a knowledge of medicine was understood as a prerequisite for empirical speculation," it probably would not have been unusual for a poet, seeking material for *The Recluse*, to have turned to Erasmus Darwin's *Zoönomia*, as pointed out by Alan Bewell. See Alan Bewell, *Wordsworth and the Enlightenment*, p. 145.

[3] Erasmus Darwin, *Zoonomia, or the Laws of Organic Life*, II, p. 360. Quoted in James H. Averill, *Wordsworth and the Poetry of Human Suffering*, p. 156.

> It cools my blood; it cools my brain;
> Thy lips I feel them, baby! they
> Draw from my heart the pain away. (Wordsworth 2006: 82)

This could almost be read as a paraphrase of Steele's periodical essay. Here Paul de Man's seminal analysis in his *The Rhetoric of Romanticism* may be helpful to dismantle the Romantic myth of immediacy. Considered "Wordsworth's essay on the origins of language as poetic language" (de Man 90), this is indeed a place expressive of "an active verbal deed, a *claim* of 'manifest kindred' which is not given in the nature of things" (91). Contrary to the myth of immediacy in Romanticism, however, here lies a case of "the enigmatic phrase: to 'gather passion,'" which refers to "a process of exchange" that goes much beyond "continuity of bodily substances." It is

> the possibility of inscribing the eye, which is nothing by itself, into a larger, total entity, the 'same object' which, in the internal logic of the text, can only be the face, the face as the combination of parts which the mind, working like a synecdoche trope, can lay claim to—thus opening the way to a process of totalization which, in the span of a few lines, can grow to encompass everything, '*All* objects through *all* intercourse of sense.' (91)

Wordsworth's epistemology of passions, as also observed by Cathy Caruth, is "governed by the figure of passage, present here in the word *passion* as a sort of original movement" (Caruth 50). Passion is like milk and the eye like the breast in this nursing scene, in which the word "'eye'… displace[s] 'breast' where one would most naturally expect it" (de Man 90). It is merely one of Wordsworth's references to "maternal passion" (either "connubial or parental[1]," as he later notes) and its "subtle windings." This is against a historical media shift from the patronage system into a commercial market—alienating to Romantic poets, as Jonathan Arac suggests:

[1] William Wordsworth and Dorothy Wordsworth. *The Letters of William and Dorothy Wordsworth: The Middle Years*, vol. 1, p. 336.

> Once poetic authority was lost, once the previously existing social demand for poetry had been transformed, once the writer was no longer producing on direct demand by patrons, or even subscribers, but was isolated in the marketplace producing for unknown readers whose taste could not be predicted but might with luck be formed, once, in other words, a certain condition of alienation prevailed, then the possibility of literary autonomy also came into existence. The process of internalization by which Wordsworth not only defended but also formed a new literary human nature—the human nature that makes psychoanalysis possible—cannot be understood apart from such externalities. (Arac 49)

This "process of totalization" "underlies all perception, beginning the assembly of a world," and "the infant metaphor grows up to be a [Romantic] myth" (Terada 54), which enriches an individual into a mature moral and affective being so that an otherwise barren sublimity could be made fertile and beautified:

> But joy to him,
>
> Oh, joy to him who here hath sown, hath laid
> Here, the foundation of his future years!
> For all that friendship, all that love can do,
> All that a darling countenance can look
> Or dear voice utter, to complete the man,
> Perfect him, made imperfect in himself,
> All shall be his: and he whose soul hath risen
> Up to the height of feeling intellect
> Shall want no humbler tenderness; his heart
> Be tender as a nursing mother's heart;
> Of female softness shall his life be full,
> Of humble cares and delicate desires,
> Mild interests and gentlest sympathies. (Wordsworth 1979b: 471)

However, as de Man writes, "this same face-making, totalizing power is shown at work in a process of endless differentiation," a "sea of infinite distinctions in which we rush to drown" (de Man 92). In other words, it is here we have the work "by a man who being possessed of more than usual organic sensibility had also thought long and deeply" (230), to use Wordsworth's own words in his "Preface." Several pages later in his "Preface," Wordsworth returns to this subject in a more elaborate way:

> It [poetry] takes its origin from emotion recollected in tranquility: the emotion is contemplated till by a species of reaction the tranquility gradually disappears, and an emotion, similar to that which was before the subject of contemplation, is gradually produced, and does itself actually exist in the mind. (Wordsworth 239)

Thereby, it is less of "emotion recollected in tranquility" than of the development and evocation of sentimentality during the act of writing and producing. The Romantic myth of immediacy could be dismantled through finding passages of what de Man terms as "endless differentiation" and "infinite distinctions," passages in between mediated moments of the infant gathering passions and his mother's eye. In other words, it is in the passages of what Rei Terada captures as "the transmission of substance" where errors and mistakes could happen: "The child could mistake what he believes he sees: if the mother's eye is reflective, the face he lends his mother may be his own" (Terada 54), for instance. Exactly in order to avoid this kind of failures in the transmissions of substance poetic or emotional, Wordsworth writes poems as he does in "Sonnet on Seeing Miss Helen Maria Williams Weep at a Tale of Distress" and "A Slumber Did My Spirit Seal." It is a work of writing, separating and manipulating feminine sentimentality by the means of language and representation in which "a fictive transfer of properties occurs" but more than in the metaphorical sense[1]. It could be read partially as a concern with a "figural survival of the traditional medical discourse on hysteria" (Bewell 143).

> For centuries, as Alan Bewell suggests through a reading of William Harvey—a seventeenth-century English physician: [I]n highly metaphoric descriptions of female physiology, medicine had explained the disease in terms of 'unnatural states' of the womb—the hungry up-and-down wanderings and complicated windings of the uterus, or the poisonous and corrupt 'vapors' rising from a diseased womb. Hysteria (or the Mother, the Incubus, spleen, vapors) was usually accompanied by a sensation of 'suffocation,' pressure felt on the chest or a choking feeling in the throat. (143)

Hysteria becomes an exemplary disease of the imagination. The powers of the imagination and bodily imitation are made visible to the eye, not as abstract principles, but as forces "monstrous and terrible to behold," which are palpably operating on women's bodies, behavior, and speech[2]. The possibility of "suffocation," "poisonous and corrupt 'vapors'" and the forces "monstrous and terrible to behold" are contained, domesticated, mediated into a Romantic myth in a safe-distancing work of writing. It permeates in the production of literature to such a degree that decades later in a Brontë novel *Wuthering Heights*, Lockwood has to defend himself from Cathy's terrifying oral ghost by piling up books against the broken window, which is a gesture of "enacting an episode of special importance to the construction of social morality in the nineteenth century" (Fielding 19). The eye-contact of the Romantic child with maternal feeling, like the "erotic touch of earthly years," finds in women figures a medium of speculative argument. It is

---

[1] Rei Terada, *Feeling in Theory*, p. 54. And this leaves a history hidden from a progressive history of modern literature, a history that covers hysterical women sentiments (or represents "hysteria" as feminine and thereby abnormal), similar to Mrs Hogg's rebuke of Scott for having "spoilt" her ballads by printing them: "[T]hey were made for singin' and no' for readin'" (qtd. in McLane 2010: 254).

[2] Edward Jorden, *A Disease Called the Suffocation of the Mother*, p. 26.

a means for observing and forcefully delineating, like Wordsworth writing at a historical time "when a knowledge of medicine was understood as a prerequisite for empirical speculation[1]" (Bewell 145). Aware of the possibility of pollution from the physiological hysteria and its imagination, Wordsworth writes, while commenting on George Crabbe's poetry in 1808, that "the Muses have just about as much to do [with 'mere matters of fact'] as they have with a Collection of medical reports, or of Law cases[2]." Noting in connection with *Lyrical Ballads*, the manner in which "language and the human mind act and react on each other[3]"—a key to understanding the mysteries of "a mind beset / With images, and haunted by itself" (Wordsworth 1979b: 195)[4], Wordsworth deploys a differentiating poetic strategy[5] to present a mode of writing designated for a poetic argument, which is well suited to the observation, dramatic display, and interpretation of the workings of the imagination.

In another classic statement of the anthropological into the autobiographical[6], Wordsworth has his sister Dorothy performing the motherly figure in "Lines Written a Few Miles above Tintern Abbey," whose "wild eyes" (119, 148) link her directly to the "wild secluded scene" that Wordsworth can no longer adequately experience.

---

[1] "Locke's *Essay*," as Alan Bewell points out, "by combining ethics and physiology, had placed medical theory at the center of philosophical debate so that, by the end of the eighteenth century, as Han-Jürgen Schings has shown, the 'philosophical doctor' had become a popular literary type" (Bewell 145). Also see G. S. Rousseau, "Nerve, Spirits, and Fibres," p. 151.

[2] *The Letters of William and Dorothy Wordsworth: The Middle Years*, 1, p. 268.

[3] William Wordsworth, *The Prose Works of William Wordsworth*, vol. 1, p. 120.

[4] In a genealogical sense of the future of the unconscious in the technology of writing—the proliferation of the sign, this is linked to Freud's turning to "hysterical women" as a scientific point of departure for psychoanalysis a century later—another close reading upon the body, that is, especially on his "A Child Is Being Beaten," "The Uncanny," "A Case of Paranoia" along with Jacques Lacan's "The Agency of the Letter in the Unconscious *or* Reason since Freud." The next chapter will elaborate upon this point.

[5] Or "anxiety of influence," to use a catchy phrase from Harold Bloom.

[6] Indeed, Wordsworth's anthropological concerns lay behind his turn to autobiography, as Alan Bewell argues throughout his book *Wordsworth and the Enlightenment*, especially p. 45, p. 86.

Wordsworth claims that there are "conformities" between her present "wild ecstasies" (138) and what he once felt, when "like a roe / I bounded o'er the mountains" (67-68). He has a way out of the impasse he had earlier reached, by reading *her* present experience as a "survival" of *his* past feeling:

> For thou art with me here upon the banks
> Of this fair river; thou my dearest Friend,
> My dear, dear Friend; and in thy voice I catch
> The language of my former heart, and read
> My former pleasures in the shooting lights
> Of thy wild eyes. Oh! yet a little while
> May I behold in thee what I was once,
> My dear, dear Sister! (Wordsworth 1952—1959, 2: 262)

The poem offers a mediation of two worlds—his and her—in "the meeting or 'self-presence'" celebrated and documented in the poem. It is a "historical and educational framework linking them" (Bewell 38) through a reciprocal semiotic exchange:

> If Dorothy has allowed her brother to recover an experience that he has passed beyond, Wordsworth offers his sister the possibility, when her ecstasy has 'matured / Into a sober experience', of recovering in his absence her own history, now in a textual form, in the poem. (Bewell 39)

The documentation makes possible a textual media of poetry. Instead of seeing this as a criticism of the exoticism of eighteenth-century anthropology, more of interest to this writing is to examine the sense of familiarity and historical continuity—between the two worlds—domesticated into work of writing, which is consumed as a household activity.

Indeed, when Wordsworth urges Dorothy, in "solitude, or fear, or pain, or grief," to "remember me, / And these my exhortations!" (144, 146-147), he imagines that his poems not only record his own 'healing thoughts' but will bring solace to its readers (145)[1]. It is performed in a mediated anthropological way. A marginal comment on a passage in Richard Payne Knight's *Analytical Inquiry into the Principles of Taste* dealing with the syntax of primitive speech makes Wordsworth's "poetic mediality" quite clear:

> What means all this parade about the Savage when the deduction as far as just may be made at our own firesides, from the sounds words gesticulations looks &c (sic) which a child makes use of when learning to talk. But a Scotch Professor cannot write three minutes together upon the Nature of Man, but he must be dabbling with his savage state, with his agricultural state, his Hunter state &c &c (sic)[2].

The anthropological methods of the Scottish Enlightenment, which often suggests a full-scale "history of the species, in its progress from the savage state to its highest civilization and improvement[3]", is rather ridiculed. In its place, we have a primitive speech made available at home: "at our own firesides," by observing "the sounds, words gesticulations, looks" that a child makes in learning to speak. A necessary mediation between the primitive (Dorothy's "wild eyes") and the domestic pedagogy (child learning) is established through poetry writing and reading, not grounded in the anthropological field but in the "lines" offered to Dorothy and, by extension, to his readers as a structured and shareable experience—a mode of engagement[4]. That is placed into what Homi Bhabha calls "the location of culture" rather than the psychology or mentality of the author, through which sentiments, subjects and a seemingly transparent print as a "general medium" (to use

---

[1] See Andrew Franta, *Romanticism and the Rise of the Mass Public*, p. 6.

[2] Cited in Edna Aston Shearer, "Wordsworth and Coleridge Marginalia in a Copy of Richard Payne Knight's *Analytical Inquiry into the Principles of Taste*."

[3] Henry Home, Lord Kames, *Sketches of the History of Man: considerably enlarged by the last additions and corrections of the author*, 1:1.

[4] In the nineteenth century, J. S. Mill's dictum "that eloquence is *heard*; poetry is *over*heard" explicitly epitomizes the Victorian identification of poetry with the privacy of lyric expression. J. S. Mill, "What Is Poetry?," p. 109. Also see Andrew Franta, *Romanticism and the Rise of the Mass Public*, p. 12.

Celeste Langan's phrase) come into being in a structural way. In a famous passage in the revised *Preface* to the *Lyrical Ballads* of 1802, Wordsworth distinguishes between "the knowledge of the Poet and the Man of Science" in this way:

> The knowledge both of the Poet and the Man of Science is pleasure; but the knowledge of the one cleaves to us as a necessary part of our existence, our natural and inalienable inheritance; the other is a personal and individual acquisition, slow to come to us, and by no habitual and direct sympathy connecting us with our fellow-beings. The Man of Science seeks truth as a remote and unknown benefactor; he cherishes and loves it in his solitude: the Poet, singing a song in which all human beings join with him, rejoices in the present of truth as our visible friend and hourly companion. Poetry is the breath and finer spirit of all knowledge: it is the impassioned expression which is in the countenance of all Science ... In spite of soil and climate, in spite of things silently gone out of mind and things violently destroyed, the Poet binds together by passion and knowledge the vast empire of human society, as it is spread over the whole earth, and over all time[1].

IV.vi. Conclusion

If we agree that it is by the 1730s the new discipline of aesthetics begins to displace the traditional rhetoric[2], it is at the end of that century, as in the case of William Wordsworth, that a saturated print media culture brings a new degree of mediation between subjects and their representations. The subjects of female sentimentality in the oral

---

[1] William Wordsworth, *Preface to the Lyrical Ballads*, Additions of 1802, in Wordsworth and Coleridge, *Lyrical Ballads*, p. 259.

[2] As David Wellbery argues: "In one and the same movement, art becomes the subject matter of theory and aesthetic experience is transformed into something that takes place between subjects and their representations, without the mediation of inherited bodies of erudition and independently of a locally defined cultural site" (Wellbery 232).

become mediated through a male sympathizer in the seemingly transparent work of writing. John B. Bender argues that the British realistic novel between 1719 and 1779 has developed a technical convention of transparency whereby "character and reflective conscience are isolated" (Bender 3). For Bender, that realistic pretension of being "a transparent, unmediated form of knowledge" (8) about the process of daily life is epitomized in the social system by the penitentiary of the novel[1]. In Wordsworth, as this writing argues, we have a representation of female sentiments processed as form of knowledge mediated through print and writing. This Wordsworthian *poiesis* of the modern print culture contains, confines, and encloses female sentiment, from which it is nurtured at the first place. Thus, it produces the print media through sympathizing in a scopic regime, or the experience of quasi-seeing, which is called aesthetic illusion in the eighteenth century[2]. Indeed, the poetic texts of Wordsworth's induce that subjective absorption in the represented world by inviting modern readers to re-oralize female sentimentality through reading (like Miss Helen Maria Williams or the Blessed Babe), which is true of the representational aesthetic theory of the eighteenth century[3]. Rei Terada points out that "the existence of emotion reflects not just the content of mental representations but the fact that they are representations" (Terada 18). In Wordsworthian *poiesis*, female emotions and sentiments are theatrically represented through the words of worth in the emergence of a historical print media culture. If theatricality is medium[4], we have a medium of manufactured interiority in the print media of Romantic poetry through the male words of worth. Sympathy with feminine sentimentality is produced into theatrical situations through representing print media culture with its *oral* and *oralizing* properties as realized in the British Romantic poetic medium. In other words, Wordsworth's economy of feminine

[1] John B. Bender, *Imagining the Penitentiary*.

[2] David E. Wellbery, *Lessing's "Laocoon,"* p. 72.

[3] For this aspect of the representational aesthetic theory of the eighteenth century, see David Wellbery, *Lessing's "Laocoon,"* p. 72.

[4] See Samuel Weber, *Theatricality as Medium*.

sentimentality is a variety of what Bourdieu calls "*officializing strategies,* the object of which is to transmute 'egoistic,' private, particular interests ... into disinterested, collective, publicly avowable legitimate interests." And it enables him to augment the "capital of authority necessary to impose a definition of the situation, especially in the moments of crisis when the collective judgment falters [and] to be able to mobilize the group by solemnizing, officializing, and thus universalizing private incident[1]." Paula McDowell points out that in the eighteenth century, "the dramatic proliferation of print and the specter of future mass literacy generated widespread consideration of the nature and implications of media shift" (McDowell 246). Wordsworth manufactures his poetic medium in making over feminine sentiments into the emergent literary medium of print, which anticipates a political economy of consciousness / unconsciousness and emotions in the nineteenth century. It is through this that an officialized medium of literature, and print mediation becomes possible in the British Romantic period[2], and the middle-class audience—who, in Coleridge's terms, "dieted" at the "two public *ordinaries* of Literature, the circulating libraries and the periodical press[3]"—come into historical being in the early nineteenth century of Western modernity, when a "society" begins to be "something other than human."

---

[1] See Pierre Bourdieu, *Outline of a Theory of Practice*, p. 9. Also see Jerome Christensen, *Practicing Enlightenment*, p. 87.

[2] In a way, as Andrew Franta points out: "It is not too much to say that 'Wordsworth' and 'Romanticism' are interchangeable" (Franta 55). Jerome McGann, for instance, also makes a version of this claim in *The Romantic Ideology*: "The patterns I shall be marking out are widespread in the works of the period. I shall concentrate on Wordsworth, however, because his works—like his position in the Romantic Movement—are normative and, in every sense, exemplary" (82). For a powerful argument about the critical tendency to "[subsume] Romanticism under Wordsworth," see Robert J. Griffin, *Wordsworth's Pope: A Study in Literary Historiography*, p. 1.

[3] Samuel T. Coleridge, *Lay Sermons*, p. 38.

Chapter V

Theatricality of Moral Sentiments, Institutions of Sympathy, and Adam Smith: Empire and the Coming of the Unconscious

In 1936 Walter Benjamin published his "Work of Art in the Age of its Technical Reproducibility," and in 1938 Martin Heidegger gave a lecture that turned into a published essay bearing the title, "The Age of the World-Picture." In 1992 post-structuralist theorist Samuel Weber read these two essays together in his Mari Kuttna Lecture on Film, entitled "Mass Mediauras, or: Art, Aura and Media in the Work of Walter Benjamin." For Weber, the Heideggerian world-as-picture—the pictorialization of the world, that is—"consists in a highly ambivalent oscillation of bringing-forth (*her-stellen*) and setting-before (*vor-stellen*), with the aim of securing the foundations of the subject *at* and *as* the center of things" (Weber 1996: 80). Aura, also designated by Benjamin as the "unique appearance of a distance, however close it may be" (qtd. in Weber 1996: 87), is

> never uniquely itself but always constituted in a process of *self-detachment*: detachment *from* the self as demarcation *of* a self. The aura would then be something like an enabling limit, the *emanation* of an object from which it removes itself, a *frame* falling away from a picture and in its fall. (Weber 1996: 87-88)

The theoretic as well as historical frameworks raised by these three theorists are useful for our discussion on the moral philosophy of sympathetic sentiment proposed by Adam Smith. In a similar sense, Smith's theory of moral sentiments is approached through a methodology that could be named as "historical analogy." This chapter sees Smith's economy of moral sentiments as analogous to the proliferation of print medium and mediation in the second half of the eighteenth century. This is historically as well as theoretically feasible in that both share some specific epistemological modes of uniformity and reproducibility. Sympathy is formed and communicated as if through a reading activity. In this way, reading and its cognate activities affect the emergence of a modern interiority: "bring-forth" and "setting-before" feelings, as well as the "detachment *from* the self as demarcation *of* a self." Reproducibility, in this sense, is more than what Weber defines as "the *mediauric*": "auratic flashes and shadows that are not just produced and reproduced by the media but which *are* themselves the media" (Weber 1996: 106). It also helps to reproduce the part of irreproducibility—that part detached and demarcated, which is identified as the "unconscious" in its mature form in another wave of the technology of writing—that of psychoanalysis—after moral philosophy and political economy.

V.i. Adam Smith Problem, His System-Building and the Impossible of the Chinese

As could be imagined, Smith's substantial theory of sympathy did not escape Burke's notice[1]. In a private letter to Smith[2], Burke ("an Irish

---

[1] As Dixon Wecter pointed out, from biographies of Edmund Burke by Robert Bisset and James Prior, we hear that Burke had made his careful study of George Berkeley in hope of being appointed *circa* 1752 to the chair of logic at Glasgow, a position eventually vacated by Adam Smith. This could be another reason for Burke's attention upon Smith's work. See Dixon Wecter, "Burke's Theory concerning Words, Images, and Emotion," p. 176, note 30. Also see Dixon Wecter's essay "The Missing Years in Burke's Biography," p. 1109.

[2] Dated 10th September, 1759. See D. D. Raphael and A. L. Macfie, "Introduction," pp. 27-28.

Gentleman, who wrote lately a very pretty Treatise on the Sublime," as David Hume informed Smith[1]) comments acutely:

> I own I am particularly pleased with those easy and happy illustrations from common Life and manners in which your work abounds more than any other that I know by far ... there is so much elegant Painting of the manners and passions, that it is highly valuable even on that account. (qtd. in Raphael 28)

It seems that Burke is very sensitive on the means of mediation reflected in Smith's work, which, for him, are illustrations and paintings of "common Life and manners," or "manners and passions." In the review he wrote for his periodical the *Annual Register*[2], Burke repeats some of the comments made in the letter: "The illustrations are numerous and happy, and shew the author to be a man of uncommon observation. His language is easy and spirited, and puts things before you in the fullest light; it is rather painting than writing" (qtd. in Raphael 28). Again, Smith's emphasis on the visual dimension of the sympathetic sentiment is captured by Burke, who is said to be "a man of uncommon observation." The theory of moral sentiments approaches the effects of the visual medium of painting through a presentation of "manners and passions" in the verbal medium of language. These should not be read as passages of self-denial of what is outlined above in his aesthetics of the sublime and the beautiful. Rather, here the stress is more upon "manners and passions," "common life and manners," with which Burke is more than concerned with, and they are more likely to be *narrated* than *described* in Burke's ideological packaging. It is possible that Burke sees in Smith's book a new stage of visuality in language and representation, regarding its communication of English "manners and passions," which explains his sense of resignation—"I own ..." All of

---

[1] Dated 12 April, 1759, a letter from London by Hume, who sent copies of Smith's *The Theory of Moral Sentiments* to the Duke of Argyll, Lord Lyttelton, Horace Walpole, Soame Jenyns, and Edmund Burke. See D. D. Raphael and A. L. Macfie, "Introduction," pp. 25-26.

[2] Year 1759. See D. D. Raphael and A. L. Macfie, "Introduction," p. 28.

this may as well go with a sense of identity politics for Burke as well. Difference can be tolerated within the imperial boundaries of the British, whether Irish or Scottish. Thus it does not matter very much if these "illustrations" and paintings suggest Smith's aspiration to pictorial realism, which Burke's aesthetics holds as French.

Probably much less provincial than Burke, Adam Smith makes a grand claim of universality in the formation of an ethic and epistemological subject visually, which is realized in his *The Theory of Moral Sentiments*. It was published in 1759 and since then put under constant revisions until its sixth edition coming out in 1790, a few weeks before the death of its author. The very first sentence of this book addresses the question of sympathy as a universal principle of human beings:

> How selfish soever man may be supposed, there are evidently some principles in his nature, which interest him in the fortune of others, and render their happiness necessary to him, though he derives nothing from it except the pleasure of seeing it. Of this kind is pity or compassion, the emotion which we feel for the misery of others, when we either see it, or are made to conceive it in a very lively manner. (Smith 1984: 9)

Sympathy here is theorized as a moral issue upon luck: upon either happiness or miseries of others. Even the "greatest ruffian, the most hardened violator of the laws of society" (9) Smith argues, is not altogether without this pity or compassion. As a moral philosophical argument, this suggests a strong influence upon him from the moral philosophical agenda in the Scottish Enlightenment, chiefly because of the role of accorded sympathy by Hutcheson and Hume[1]. It is also very obvious that the words such as "soever," "evidently," "nature" are among the universalism vocabulary of the British Enlightenment. Perhaps this can be made in defense of Smith against criticism of Thomas Reid's kind, which is that Smith establishes an essentially

---

[1] See Alexander Broadie, "Sympathy and the Impartial Spectator," p. 160.

"selfish" system of sympathetic sentiment since it forms a moral judgment about a person's attitude or behavior based on how *I* would feel if *I* were in that person's situation[1]. This leads to an interesting observation upon a *naturalizing* and *universalizing* gesture reflected in another place, interest in the economic welfare of humanity this time in the opening pages of *The Wealth of Nations*:

> It is not from the benevolence of the butcher, the brewer, or the baker, that we expect our dinner, but from their regard to their own interest, we address ourselves, not to their humanity but to their self-love, and never talk to them of our own necessities but of their advantages. (Smith 2000: 16)

In 1762, a year after the second edition of *The Theory of Moral Sentiments* and five years before the third, Smith was lecturing on the material that grew into *The Wealth of Nations*[2]. The latter was published in 1776, two years after the fourth edition of *TMS*. So different and opposed do *The Theory of Moral Sentiments* and *The Wealth of Nations* appear at the first glance that for some years scholars refer to the task of their reconciliation as the "Adam Smith problem". For these scholars, the moral philosopher who makes sympathy the basis of social behavior in *The Theory of Moral Sentiments* does an about-turn from altruistic to egoistic theory in *The Wealth of Nations* owing to the influence of the French Physiocratic thinkers whom Smith met in his French trip. The argument goes that his economic theory and moral philosophy conflict with each other, with sympathy as a contrast to self-interest. Smith could have forgotten his economic ideas, while revising his moral philosophy till the last phase of his life, or vice versa. H. T. Buckle suggests a duality-hypothesis upon human nature from Smith's theories:

---

[1] See J. C. Stewart-Robertson and David F. Norton, "Thomas Reid on Adam Smith's Theory of Morals." Also see Alexander Broadie, "Sympathy and the Impartial Spectator," p. 163.

[2] Alexander Broadie, "Sympathy and the Impartial Spectator," p. 165.

one sympathetic and the other selfish[1]. How shall we deal with these two universal but seemingly different economies of humanity, one based on sympathetic emotions, another on economic if not materialistic interest? I will try to address this question from a preliminary reading of his *The Theory of Moral Sentiments*. This would be an interpretation of the emergent forms of abstraction and exchangeability in the history of capitalism. My argument sees this Janus-faced Adam Smith in his moral philosophy and political economy as a figure strategically corresponding to a social transition from the local to the global in the formation of the British Empire. This chapter takes "empire" not as an empirical process that takes place "out there" in the world, as many historians and social scientists have presumed it to have been. Rather, I show "the empire" as an instituted affective economy that involves the entire economy of the subject's perceptual and cognitive, various framing devices of a mental theater, and figured conditions of communication like market and the print medium. Following Sanjay Krishnan's "reading the global," I advance an approach to the comparative study of cultures that is attentive to epistemic and affective apparatuses[2]. What it involves is an attention to the texture in which perceptual and cognitive framing of self is produced of contextual unevenness and heterogeneity, so as to learn "how to displace or unsettle its lines and rules of perception" (Krishnan 5) in order to activate other/less conformist ways of feeling and knowing about transactions between self, mediation and institutions of subjectivities. Through Adam Smith's political economy of sentiments, a theatrical selfhood, language and rhetoric, we see an apparatus of empire upon the borders between home and world, the private and the public, the foreign and the intimate.

Adam Smith's theories, either on moral sentiment, rhetoric and belles letters, or political economy help to posit a specific category of subjects as the abstract and the universal, "the idea of a system" as set

---

[1] See *TMS*, editors' Introduction, pp. 20-24; Laurence Dickey, "Historicizing the 'Adam Smith Problem': Conceptual, Historiographical, and Textual Issues;" Alexander Broadie, "Sympathy and the Impartial Spectator," pp. 164-165.

[2] In the sense Agamben uses this word, see Agamben, "What Is Apparatus?"

out by Smith himself in his "History of Astronomy[1]". Edward Gibbon admired *The Wealth of Nations* as a "science" and a "system": "the most profound and systematic treatise" and "an extensive science in a single book[2]." This very strongly conscious gesture of system-building and theory-developing in the British Enlightenment can be unpacked with help from postcolonial and feminist theories of difference. What is of interest is that Smith, right in the first sentence, draws an ethics of the Enlightenment category "Man" as spontaneous reaction—"interest," that is—to actual or imagined visual pleasure into his picture of a sympathetic moral sentiment. Sight and its pleasure principle offer (sometimes processed as "live" by the brain[3]) a buffer zone between a gravitating[4] ego center and its periphery, which makes this "man" extensively universal. It reminds of James Woodrow, who compares Smith's accounting for the principal phenomena in the moral world from the one general principle of sympathy, with "that of gravity in the natural world[5]." This nature of Smith's system-building guarantees the existence of "some principles," which, in turn, produces an economy of extension through emotional reflux. It accords well with the rising significance of visuality in print medium in the eighteenth century, through which the imperial subjects can anticipate the nature of tactile contact with distant objects. Sight becomes foresight and pre-mediates knowledge of other places[6].

For Adam Smith, fellow-feeling can contract distances: "As we

---

[1] See J. C. Bryce, "Introduction," pp. 34-37. For how "the system" not only works as an idea, but as a genre in the British Enlightenment, and how it originates through Newton's *Opticks* and *Principia*, see Clifford Siskin, "Mediated Enlightenment: The System of the World," in *This Is Enlightenment*, pp. 164-172.

[2] Edward Gibbon, *The Letters of Edward Gibbon*, vol. 2, pp. 166, 335.

[3] The mind works after the eye, that is. A process inverse to what is defined as impossible by Lord Kames in his *Elements of Criticism*.

[4] In early natural philosophy, bodies classed as heavy were said to gravitate, and bodies classed as light to levitate, in consequence of their tendency to 'seek their own place'. See *OED* online, under the entry of "gravitate."

[5] In his letter to the Earl of Buchan. Quoted in J. C. Bryce, "Introduction," pp. 34-35.

[6] As illustrated by George Berkeley several decades before Smith. See David E. Wellbery, *Lessing's "Laocoon,"* p. 27.

have no immediate experience of what other men feel, we can form no idea of the manner in which they are affected, but by conceiving what we ourselves should feel in the like situation" (Smith 1984: 9). It substitutes situations through the mediated experience of imagination. Thus, sympathy acts as an imaginative act, as an agreement between sentiments, one possible way out of man's affective solipsism through a geographical extension of oneself. At the same time, paradoxically, this is out of the realization of mutual inaccessibility between autonomous individual minds. For instance, in a remarkable thought experiment added to his discussion on "the Influence and Authority of Conscience" in 1790[1], Smith suggests the impossibility of practicing the sympathetic impartial spectator from an average European, who, "from the place and with the eyes of a third person," makes moral adjudication between two parties in a physically distant place of the "great empire of China" in the consequence of an earthquake[2]. As part of the inward shift of a split self caused by distant and non-communicating human beings, this mention of China in the framework of a fictitious moral case dates back to *Rameau's Nephew* and *The Paradox of Acting* by Denis Diderot (1713—1784), who, as Carlo Ginzburg writes, "took his example from a Jesuit treatise on casuistry" (Ginzburg 1994: 50). It goes through François-René de Chateaubriand (1768—1848) and Honoré de Balzac (1799—1850)[3]. Though he might, in the initial shock, writes Smith, "make many melancholy reflections upon the precariousness of human life," or in a soberer moment consider "the effects which this disaster might produce upon the commerce of Europe," he would eventually return to his normal life "with the same ease and tranquility, as if no such accident

[1] The entire section "Of the Influence and Authority of Conscience" appeared only for the first time in the second edition of 1760, which substantially revised the text of the first 1759 edition. Smith's book remained more or less unchanged until its sixth edition, printed in 1790. See Eric Hayot, *The Hypothetical Mandarin*, p. 3. Also see D. D. Raphael and A. L. Macfie, "Introduction."

[2] This was discussed by Carlo Ginzburg in his "To Kill a Chinese Mandarin: The Moral Implications of Distance," in *Wooden Eyes, Nine Reflections on Distance*. This essay was also published in *Critical Inquiry*, 1994, 21 (1), pp. 46-60.

[3] See Ginzburg's essay "Killing a Chinese Mandarin: The Moral Implications of Distance."

had happened" (136). The distant millions would not be registered in the European sympathy economy. But consider, Smith writes, that

> the most frivolous disaster which could befall himself would occasion a more real disturbance. If he was to lose his little finger to-morrow, he would not sleep to-night; but, provided he never saw them, he will snore with the most profound security over the ruin of a hundred millions of his brethren, and the destruction of that immense multitude seems plainly an object less interesting to him, than this paltry misfortune of his own. To prevent, therefore, this paltry misfortune to himself, would a man of humanity be willing to sacrifice the lives of a hundred millions of his brethren, provided he had never seen them? (136-137)

Seeing is believing and feeling. The distant geographical location (as well as cultural alienation) of China and its not being accessible by a discourse of free circulation and commerce of the Western capital[1] make it an emotional other that could not be accommodated into this sympathy economy. This historical period that saw dramatic expansion of the human and geopolitical space toward which the average members of society are supposed to be emotionally and morally responsible[2]. Nevertheless, moral sympathetic strangeness seems more difficult to overcome than simply geographical distance. Though, almost two decades before the publication of Smith's treatise, David Hume already

---

[1] See David Porter, "A Peculiar but Uninteresting Nation: China and the Discourse of Commerce in Eighteenth-Century England."

[2] Regarding the Anglo-American sympathetic economy to Chinese, Gertrude Stein was asked a similar question by the philosopher Hutchins Hapgood. As Stein writes in her *Everybody's Autobiography*, Hapgood "liked to think of the number of angels on the point of a needle ... and ... always complained of me that I had too good a time for anybody who was so virtuous." One day, frustrated by Stein's "virtue," Hapgood asked her a "test question. Would I if I could by pushing a button would I kill five thousand Chinamen if I could save my brother from anything. Well I was very fond of my brother and I could completely imagine his suffering and I replied that five thousand Chinamen were something I could not imagine and so it was not interesting" (qtd. in Hayot 205). In a sense, this impossibility of sympathizing with Chinese is an integrated part of Western modernity and modernism, as Eric Hayot argues throughout *The Hypothetical Mandarin*.

remarked in a section of his *A Treatise of Human Nature* entitled "Of Contiguity and Distance in Space and Time": "A *West-Indian* merchant will tell you, that he is not without concern about what passes in Jamaica; tho' few extend their views so far into futurity, as to dread very remote accidents" (Hume 1978: 429), he probably would also "ignored the moral and juridical implications of it" (Ginzburg 1994: 56)[1], like the average European person in Smith's moral philosophy of sentiments.

Indeed, one can take the popular trope of sympathy of the eighteenth century as what builds affective affinities between the circulating commercial markets, credit, and public opinion acting at great distances. It was a century with increasing social mobility as the British empire was being formed. To this observation, we can adduce David Marshall's comment that sympathy is "structured by theatrical dynamics that ... depend on people to represent themselves as tableaux, spectacles, and texts before others" in order to suggest how closely the identifications, on which sympathy depends, rely both in practice and in theory, on a notion of "exchange" that includes representational and economic dimensions[2]. Exchanges between persons, places, and commodities became more necessary than they had once been. In chapter 7 of the first volume of his sentimental novel *The Life and Opinions of Tristram Shandy (1759—1767)*, Laurence Sterne describes a village midwife, who, as

> she had all along trusted little to her own efforts, and a great deal to those of dame nature,—had acquired, in her way, no small degree of

---

[1] For an analysis about this specific passage of Hume's, see Carlo Ginzburg, "To Kill a Chinese Mandarin: The Moral Implications of Distance," pp. 56-59. In a relevant passage that might be an influence upon Adam Smith, Hume writes: "Accordingly we find in common life, that men are principally concern'd about those objects, which are not much remov'd either in space or time, enjoying the present, and leaving what is afar off to the care of chance and fortune. Talk to a man of his condition thirty years hence, and he will not regard you. Speak of what is to happen tomorrow, and he will lend you attention. The breaking of a mirror gives us more concern when at home, than the burning of a house, when abroad, and some hundred leagues distant." (Hume 1978: 428-429).

[2] David Marshall, *The Surprising Effects of Sympathy*, p. 5. Also see Eric Hayot, *The Hypothetical Mandarin*, p. 263.

> reputation in the world;—by which word world, need I in this place inform your worship, that I would be understood to mean no more of it, than a small circle described upon the circle of the great world, of four English miles diameter, or thereabouts, of which the cottage where the good old woman lived, is supposed to be the center. (Sterne 1: 10)

The additional proclamation of a provincial English parameter of four miles indicates a world much beyond the local midwife's reputation, whose existence Sterne's readership is obliged to imagine and anticipate. The world is so obviously global that Sterne's message of irony could be easily missed. This is the world in which Adam Smith was writing. His *Theory of Moral Sentiments* is what Janet Todd calls "the end of a line of British moral philosophy" that admits "the sentimental aim of trying systematically to link morality and emotion[1]." Sympathy thus offers us a window into the trans-subjective condition of affective 'mediality' at the moment of modern mobility[2].

V.ii. Visuality in a Distended Selfhood

Marshall McLuhan argues that the seventeenth and eighteenth centuries were crucial periods of adaptation to the "new model[s] of perception," when "the initial shock gradually dissipates as the entire community absorbs the new habit of perception into all of its areas of work and association." And this, for McLuhan, comes "[w]ith the advent of the printed word," by which "the visual modalities of Western life increased beyond anything experienced in any previous society" (McLuhan 23). The printed word produces more information and disseminates to the far-away places. Indeed, it is clear that the

---

[1] Janet Todd, *Sensibility: An Introduction*, p. 27. Todd identifies sentimental literature's heyday as the period from 1740 to 1770, tracing its decline through adjectives applied to the term "sensibility" (pp. 7-8).

[2] For the concept of "mediality," see David E. Wellbery, 'Foreword' to Fredrich A. Kittler, *Discourse Networks, 1800/1900.*

eighteenth century was what Susan Crawford aptly calls an "information-conscious society" (qtd. in Ellison 17) with its changes of reading habits, the construction of new systems and offices of information management. Popular consciousness was adapting, to use Pocock's phrase, "to a world of moving objects" (221) and to an increasingly detached and mobile population. It is in a congenial relation to this expansive British Empire building that Adam Smith advocates a theory of emotional impartiality, which is realized through sympathy. As that "amiable virtue of humanity," it is the principle by which sentiments are communicated. The unfortunate, by

> relating their misfortunes in some measure renew their relief. Their tears accordingly flow faster than before, and they are apt to abandon themselves to all the weakness of sorrow. They take pleasure, however, in all this, and, it is evident, are sensibly relieved by it; because the sweetness of his sympathy more than compensates the bitterness of their sorrow, which, in order to excite this sympathy, they had thus enlivened and renewed. (Smith 1984: 15)

There forms a mutual relation between the spectator and the agents of feelings. Sense of the bitterness from misfortune has to be "enlivened and renewed" to achieve its communicating effect upon the spectator, and it produces a therapeutic side-effect to the tellers-agents. Sympathy thus achieved is highly mediated through representations: telling as well as tearing. It is not a simple process, and involves oral, aural as well as visual skills from the plural form of tellers-agents to the singular form of the spectator. More than this therapeutic function of healing consolation that the very articulation of misfortune brings forth by offering a sympathetic interlocutor, sympathy also creates the highest pleasure in observing "in other men of fellow-feeling with all the emotions of our own breast" (13). Interiority in this affective transmission communicates through observation and creates a sense of benevolence to either the agent or the spectator. It is not achieved through immediate experience of what others feel, but "by the imagination only that we can form any conception of what are his sensations" and

> by the imagination we place ourselves in his situation, we conceive ourselves enduring all the same torments, we enter as it were into his body, and become in some measure the same person with him, and thence from some idea of his sensations, and even feel something which, though weaker in degree, is not altogether unlike him. (9)

Several decades before Smith's treatise, Joseph Addison writes that the function of "imagination" "fills the Mind with the largest Variety of Ideas [, and] converses with its Objects at the greatest Distance, and continues the longest in Action without being tired or satiated with its proper Enjoyments[1]." It is interesting to see that imagination, as a principle of pleasure, is a function of writing on the *tabula rasa* of mind through an engagement with objects in a geographic sense. It establishes sympathetic affinities between things and the subjective agent through overcoming an objective distance by conversing, which is an impossible verbal activity with things, but may be carried out in the visual sense. Smith's sympathetic figure, that of an observer, follows this vein "in producing and reproducing the feelings of others" (Festa 27) through a strategy of situational substitution. More in between subjective agents and a spectator, sympathy is "an intense labor" upon oneself, a construct of "a replica of another's feeling from within the citadel of the self." For Smith, "empathy is anything but spontaneous and natural" (27-28). It is specifically significant to see this point against a backdrop of the rise of individualism and the construction of the subject, both as central issues in eighteenth- and nineteenth-century studies[2]. The practice and idea of modern personhood and personification is developed further than that by moral philosophers like David Hume, who writes in his *A Treatise of Human Nature*:

---

[1] See *The Specator*, Saturday, June 21, 1712, "Addison on the Pleasures of the Imagination." Quoted in Erin Mackie, *The Commerce of Everyday Life*, p. 387.

[2] See Adela Pinch, *Strange Fits of Passion*, p. 13. Also see Niklas Luhmann, "The Individuality of the Individual: Historical Meanings and Contemporary Problems;" C. B. Macpherson, *The Political Theory of Possessive Individualism*.

> But setting aside some metaphysicians of this kind, I may venture to affirm of the rest of mankind, that they are nothing but a bundle or collection of different perceptions, which succeed each other with an inconceivable rapidity, and are in a perpetual flux and movement. Our eyes cannot turn in their sockets without varying our perceptions. Our thought is still more variable than our sight; and all our other senses and faculties contribute to this change; nor is there any single power of the soul, which remains unalterably the same, perhaps for one moment. (252-253)

In another place, Hume writes: "Nice and subtile questions concerning personal identity can never possibly be decided, and are to be regarded rather as grammatical than as philosophical difficulties" (Hume 1978: 262). For Hume, identity consists of "a succession of related objects" through an act of association because of their "resemblance, contiguity, or causation" "from daily experience and observation" (255). A subjective interiority is more contagious and of temporal continuity. Highly influenced by Hume, Smith also takes sympathy as a feeling "to which the mechanism of sympathetic communication has made an essential contribution" (Broadie 165). Nevertheless, in his moral philosophy of sympathy, there are two significant differences from that of Hume's or Addison's "imagination." For Smith, sympathy seems more of a visual as well as situational sentimental substitution and exchange, which involves more an aesthetic sense of labor upon a sympathetic spectatorial self. Less philosophical and contemplating, a Smithian spectator makes efforts to modify his sentiments so they agree with the agent's. He must "endeavor, as much as he can, to put himself in the situation of the other;" he must "strive to render as perfect as possible, that imaginary change of situation upon which his sympathy is founded" (Smith 1984: 21). A person's "natural feeling of his own distress, his own natural view of his own situation, presses hard upon him, and he cannot, without a great effort, fix his attention upon that of the impartial spectator" (148). Also, "[t]he compassion of the spectator must arise altogether from the consideration of what he himself would feel if he was reduced to the same unhappy situation, and, what perhaps is impossible, was at the same time able to regard it with his present reason and judgment" (12)[1]. The sentimental efforts are more of a visual mode of observation and identification of the situations of the agents, who are more of common life, as Burke already comments. It probably suggests that Smith situates himself more in a political economy of print, when the saturation of the technology of writing reaches a representational economy dovetailing with a mature commercial society. Sense of theatricality as spatial presence as we see in Hume is soon materialized in the form of monetary capital that can be achieved only from hard labour. At the same time, a rising transparent exchangeability brings with it an inscrutable deepness in a sentimental mode, which cannot be resolved through the visual form of money, but creates another form of writing technology about the psyche—psychoanalysis, that is—which is different from that of moral sentiment of sympathy. Interiority and exteriority co-exist and co-evolve in a splitting and complementary way to each other.

Representational theatricality is built into a modern selfhood. In a sympathetic economy, sentimental subjectivity relates to the physical circumstances of the impartial spectator. John B. Bender identifies this blurring line between "fiction and reality" as a problematic in "the predicament of a culture" (35), which exists through the English philosophical tradition from Locke, through Hume, to Bentham[2]. This fictionalizing and theatrical labor upon self-making is more of a visual process. It involves an apparatus towards others, and takes interiority as a work towards a split self through that of visuality. Smith writes in this way:

> We must look at ourselves with the same eyes with which we look at

---

[1] Also see Alexander Broadie, "Sympathy and the Impartial Spectator," pp. 170-171.

[2] The blurring of boundaries between fact and fiction is also one of the commonplace strategies of the early realist novel. For an application of Foucault's work to the novel and to take the genre as a discursive practice in this regard, see Lennard J. Davis, *Factual Fictions: The Origins of the English Novel*.

others: we must imagine ourselves not the actors, but the spectators of our own character and conduct, and consider how these would affect us when viewed from this new station, in which their excellencies and imperfections can alone be discovered. (Smith 1984: 111)

David Marshall argues that, for Smith, one "becomes a spectator to oneself in order to determine if one can enter into one's own feelings ... Smith seems to separate the self from the one self it could reasonably claim to know: itself" (Marshall 175-176). Smith's theory of sympathy thus relies "upon an eclipsing of identity, a transfer of persons in which one leaves oneself behind and tries to take someone else's part[1]." In this process, "this relation to emotion as one's own becomes more and more distended" (Festa 28). A self is increasingly further away from itself, which is realized through visual mediation. This gesture of distension runs analogous to but seems more psychoanalytical than what "the Sense of Feeling" evoked by "Sight" produces as reflected in Joseph Addison essay-writing—"a Notion of Extension, Shape, and all other Ideas that enter at the Eye." It is further away from what Shaftesbury defines as the aesthetic type of "divine example"—"a Platonic abstraction, defined in mathematical terms of balance and harmony" (Paulson 1996: 3)[2]. Shaftesbury writes in his *Inquiry concerning Virtue and Merit* (1699, 1711): "This ... is certain that the admiration and love of order, harmony, and proportion, in whatever kind, is naturally improving to the temper, advantageous to social affection, and highly assistant to virtue, which is itself no other than the love of order and beauty in society" (qtd. in Paulson 1996: 3). This Shaftesburian divine creation is "figured as order (beauty is to deformity as regularity is to irregularity) of both the world and of man's individual mind, which as an example can improve the already benevolent man" (Paulson 1996: 3). Instead, for Smith, a selfhood of fragmentation

---

[1] See David Marshall, "Adam Smith and the Theatricality of Moral Sentiments," p. 599. Also see Lynn Festa, *Sentimental Figures of Empire in Eighteenth-Century Britain and France*, p. 28.

[2] Ronald Paulson, *The Beautiful Novel, and Strange: Aesthetics and Heterodoxy*.

comes into its place. It displays as uniform exchange means of the capital, on the one hand. On the other hand, it is realized as deeply subjective psyches, to which the clues are hard to recognize and analyze[1].

> Addison's series of essays came out around four decades previous to Smith's treatise[2]. His visual act of "Sight"seems designed to supply all these Defects, and may be considered as a more delicate and diffusive kind of Touch, that spreads it self over an infinite Multitude of Bodies, comprehends the largest Figures, and brings into our reach some of the most remote Parts of the Universe[3].

With conceptualization of the cultural location "that would be occupied by print-media culture and the elevated novels of Richardson and Fielding" (Warner 233), Addison takes that the cultivation of a disinterested spectator is through the abstracting power of sight's operation at a distance so as to "[consider] the world as a theater, and [desire] to form a right judgment of those who are the actors on it[4]". David Wellbery argues that in the eighteenth century, representation, as "the essential activity of the soul," is "a fundamental category of thought …, a governing notion, or rather a matrix of notions, that pre-structures the fields in which thought and inquiry move[5]." For Addison as well as Adam Smith, sight serves as a significant means of collecting data and representing the objective world objects all over[6]. It offers an

---

[1] For a similar historical argument, see Lionel Trilling, *Sincerity and Authenticity*. Trilling's approach is more of close reading of literary texts and intellectual thoughts. He never, as could be imagined from such a conservative literary critic, takes a point out of historical materialism.
[2] See Erin Mackie, *The Commerce of Everyday Life*, pp. 387-396.
[3] See Note 130.
[4] *The Spectator*, Monday, March 12, 1711. In Erin Mackie, *The Commerce of Everyday Life*, p. 90.
[5] See David E. Wellbery, *Lessing's "Laocoon,"* p. 9.
[6] Of course, one can relate this to the popular argument of the rise of the visual in the modern Western society. See Martin Jay, *Downcast Eyes: The Denigration of Vision in Twentieth-Century French Thought*; Hal Foster, *Vision and Visuality*. For a useful historical analysis about the literature of this argument and how it can be used in the Chinese situation, see Shu-mei Shih, *Visuality and Identity: Sinophone Articulations across the Pacific*, especially "Introduction," pp. 1-39.

extended selfhood, and reflects its relation with the subject, and realizes the soul and its mediate or immediate objects. In Addison's world at the beginning of the eighteenth century, this visuality is very tactile, embedded within the skin and the flesh, and assimilated to the body—"as a more delicate and diffusive kind of Touch," that is. Thus, the sense of corporeal "touch" as such—as the longest entry in the *OED* dictionary[1]— involutes with "Sight." Imagination in Addisonian sense remains as what Aristotle proclaims in *De Anima* as the "medium of the tangible[2]," maintaining a classic unity of the entire psychological sphere. If we understand the historical process of modernity and modern media—following arguments from Karl Marx, Max Weber, Georg Simmel, Georg Lukács, Guy Debord and Jean Baudrillard—as one of abstraction, Adam Smith's theory of moral sentiments remains very significant in this genealogy. It imbricates with his theories on rhetoric and language, and on political economy as well, all three of which add up to his sense of the Enlightenment system[3]. Reading it with a postcolonial historical hindsight would enhance our understanding of globality as an affective issue of sensorial organization of a selfhood.

V.iii. Sentimental Labor and Sympathetic Communication

For Smith, this distension of selfhood consists in a very visually presented tripartite division of the spectator, the actor and the third person, the mechanism of which works through sympathy as a matter of duplicating another's feelings. All sympathy is constitutively agreeable. As a matter of fact, "we" take delight in perceiving imitation. The spectator, Smith argues, derives pleasures from

> the emotion which arises from his observing the perfect coincidence between his sympathetic passion in himself, and the original passion

---

[1] See Didier Anzieu, *The Skin Ego*, p. 13.

[2] Aristotle, *De Anima* (*On the Soul*), p. 423.

[3] See J. C. Bryce's "Introduction" to Adam Smith's *Lectures on Rhetoric and Belles Lettres*, specifically part 5, "System and Aesthetics," pp. 34-37.

> in the person principally concerned. This last emotion, in which the sentiment of approbation properly consists, is always agreeable and delightful. The other may either be agreeable or disagreeable, according to the nature of the original passion, whose features it must always, in some measure, retain .... Two Sounds, I suppose, may, each of them taken singly, be austere, and yet, if they be perfect concords, the perception of this harmony and coincidence may be agreeable[1].

The sound analogy reminds of the flute that functions as a Romantic literary trope[2], and it appears to an atomistic and seemingly solipsist world resolved in harmony and coincidence. Emotions, like the two sounds for Smith, are essentially communicative, as observed by Daniel M. Gross[3]. Nevertheless, rather than another rehearsal of the romantic trope of the musical transference of the Spirit, sentiment—specifically sympathy—is from being natural and spontaneous. It offers the bodily sensations or sensorial organization as sites of cultivation and labor through a *theatrical* tripartite of the spectator, the actor and the third person. Adam Smith was writing at the time when the body was turned into the market of laboring and consuming through a development of an inner life of its own, visible and audible. Self, with its business of meaning and feeling, and market (with its capacity to capitalize) are two of the same machine or mechanism, equivalent to what Smith calls "the Idea of a System" that runs rampant through the Enlightenment. Hannah Arendt once argues:

> Nothing, in fact, is less common and less communicable, and therefore more securely shielded against the visibility and audibility of the public realm, than what goes on within the confines of the

---

[1] This, as a footnote, was added to the second edition of *TMS*. An earlier draft of it was enclosed by Smith with letter 40 addressed to Sir Gilbert Elliot, dated 10 October 1759. See the editorial note by D. D. Raphael and A. L. Macfie on p. 46 of *TMS*.

[2] See Abrams' discussion of the Aeolian lyre and the imagery of inspiration in "The Correspondent Breeze: A Romantic Metaphor."

[3] See Daniel M. Gross, *The Secret History of Emotion*, p. 173.

> body, its pleasures and its pains, its laboring and consuming. (Arendt 112)

Rather than "the confines of the body" as natural, nevertheless, this privacy of the body is invented by the public realm of production and reproduction so as to be explored in its laboring and consuming, including its affective pleasures and pains. This system moves what Foucault calls "the concepts of money, price, value, circulation, and market" from their seventeenth- and eighteenth-centuries' "rigorous and general epistemological arrangement" to a more visible "system of identities and differences." After this paradigm shift,

> all wealth is *coinable*; and it is by this means that it enters into *circulation*—in the same way that any natural being was *characterizable*, and could thereby find its place in a *taxonomy*; that any individual was *nameable* and could find its place in an *articulated language*; that any representation was *signifiable* and could find its place, in order to be *known*. (Foucault 1970: 175)

A profound space common to body and money, to both wealth and representation, was opening up. Circulation became one of the fundamental categories of analysis, socially as well as physiologically. It is in this historical background we take Smith's moral philosophy of sympathetic sentiment and his political economy of society resonates rather than conflicts with each other.

For Smith, sympathy is not a "selfish" system for which Thomas Reid criticized him[1]. The sympathetic spectator imagines not being himself in the agent's situation but being the agent in that situation:

> But though sympathy is very properly said to arise from an imaginary change of situations with the person principally concerned, yet this imaginary change is not supposed to happen to

---

[1] See J. C. Stewart-Robertson and David F. Norton, "Thomas Reid on Adam Smith's Theory of Morals." Also see Alexander Broadie, "Sympathy and the Impartial Spectator," p. 163.

> me in my own person and character, but in that of the person with whom I sympathize. (Smith 1984: 317)

It is an economy of substitution and situation, close to identification but never the same, especially in two extreme situations, bereavement and death. If I sympathetically grieve with you in your bereavement, my "grief ... is entirely upon your account, and not in the least upon my own. It is not, therefore, in the least selfish" (317). Thus, there exists difference between sentiments of the spectator and the agents. The "as it were" in "we enter as it were into his body" and "in some measure" in "we become in some measure the same person" suggest significant difference between the agent's feeling and the spectator's, the latter of which is brought into existence and sustained through the imaginative act of sentimental labor[1]. His being sympathetic "excites some degree of the same emotion, in proportion to the vivacity or dullness of the conception" (9):

> What they [the spectators] feel, will, indeed, always be, in some respects, different from what he [the agent] feels, and compassion can never be exactly the same with original sorrow; because the secret consciousness that the change of situations, from which the sympathetic sentiment arises, is but imaginary, not only lowers it in degree, but, in some measure, varies it in kind, and gives it a quite different modification. (22)

The correspondence, although imperfect, is, however, "sufficient for the harmony of society" and "this is all that is wanted or required[2]." Alexander Broadie argues that Smithian sympathy is not about the singularity of each feeling or perception, but of a kind of universality through which "the spectator has the feeling—he has it *sympathetically*" (Broadie 164). In other words, it is a voluntary attitude and sentiment to involve and engage the other as part of self:

---

[1] See Alexander Broadie, "Sympathy and the Impartial Spectator," p. 169.

[2] See Alexander Broadie, "Sympathy and the Impartial Spectator," pp. 169-170.

> His agonies, when they are thus brought home to ourselves, when we have thus adopted and made them our own, begin at last to affect us, and we then tremble and shudder at the thought of what he feels. (Smith 1984: 9)

This mode of universality is very significant for Smith. It is more about a mode of understanding and perceiving, as suggested in his *Lectures on Rhetoric and Belles Lettres*. In which a historian has to produce a wide range of sympathetic responses in the reader:

> The accidents that befall irrationall (sic) objects affect us merely by their externall (sic) appearance, their Novelty, Grandeur, etc., but those which affect the human Species interest us greatly by the Sympatheticall (sic) affections they raise in us. We enter into their [*sc.*human beings'] misfortunes, grieve when they grieve, rejoice when they rejoice, and in a word feel for them in some respect as if we ourselves were in the same condition. The design of historicall (sic) writing is not merely to entertain: (this perhaps is the intention of an epic poem); besides that it has in view the instruction of the reader. It sets before us the more interesting and important events of human life, points out the cause by which these events were brought about and by this means points out to us by what manner and method we may produce similar good effects or avoid similar bad ones. (Smith 1983: 90)[1]

Smith's moral philosophy depends a great deal on the "illusion of the imagination" involved in this act of sympathy. The spectator takes the situation of the agents, as a text analogous to "the design of historical writing," through a willing observation upon which he does a contextual (or situational) reading. The physiological effects—"tremble," "shudder," or otherwise—upon the spectator are a consequence upon identifying and accommodating what is read as part of an affective self. This adverbial sense of sympathy realizes the theatrical presentation and

---

[1] Also see Alexander Broadie, "Sympathy and the Impartial Spectator," p. 164.

representation of division of labor among the spectator, actor and third person regarding their perception, epistemology and communication. Smith's writing defines this as

> arranged and digested, both in their coincidence and in their succession, into so complete and regular a system ... not unlike that which it derives from the contemplation of a great system in any other science[1].

This moral philosophy of sentiment presents itself as a strong system-building symptomatic of Western Enlightenment.

V.iv. Property and Propriety in Making Inferiority

This Smithian sympathetic sentiment is critical in the evolution of eighteenth-century management of "information overload" in the rise of a saturating textual media and acts of reading[2]. For Smith, it is not merely sentimental, subjective or perceptive. It is also corporeal and physiological: "Persons of delicate fibres and a weak constitution of body complain, that in looking on the sores and ulcers which are exposed by beggars in the streets, they are apt to feel an itching or uneasy sensation in the correspondent part of their own bodies" (Smith 1984: 10). The exterior appearance here is easily projected into the interior of another and thereby puts in danger the latter's physical health, owing to their weaker constitution that causes strong sensibility. Sympathy seems almost a telepathic correspondence. The pleasures of seeing and feeling become in effect a physiognomic metaphor for the mobile and polymorphous features of the society that depends on universally managed correspondence. "Persons of delicate fibres and a weak constitution of body" thus have chances of being exposed to

---

[1] Quoted in J. C. Bryce, "Introduction," p. 35.

[2] See Katherine Ellison's recent study on reading and information overload in early eighteenth-century literature, *The Fatal News: Reading and Information Overload in Early Eighteenth-Century Literature*.

specters of destitution and dearth, socially and economically. On the other hand, Smith's sympathetic figure is detached and casual, unbound by ritual, communal, or tribal loyalties. It is free from social constraints and conventions. It is, indeed, a syndrome of Western modernity not irrelevant to the increasing flow of information, commerce and people of the eighteenth century, which requires a writing of a political economy of commodities as well as a moral philosophy of sympathy to regulate. Smith is quite certain, in fact, that sympathy withers in primitive and "barbarous" communities and thrives in "civilized" society, because it is only with man's release from the immediate exigencies of survival that he becomes free to extend and expect sympathy:

> Before we can feel much for others, we must in some measure be at ease ourselves. If our own misery pinches us very severely, we have no leisure to attend to that of our neighbour: and all savages are too much occupied with their own wants and necessities, to give much attention to those of another person. (Smith 1984: 205)

In another place, he continues: "Our imagination which in pain and sorrow seems to be confined and cooped up within our own persons, in times of ease and prosperity expands itself to every thing around us" (183). By virtue of its opulence and its division of labor, a commodity economy would boost the supply of sympathy, that is. On the other hand, the sympathetic sentimental process, "a parallel with the sequence of surprise, wonder, and admiration that Smith discusses at length in his 'History of Astronomy'" (Broadie 176), is mutual between the spectator and the agent. For Smith the spectator is able to affect a change upon the agent from whose situation he sympathizes, for the agent desires to be approved of and seeks "to see his own situation through the eyes of the spectator" (177-178). Then, he might for the first time "grasp the real significance of previously noted features of his situation":

> In light of these new perceptions, gained by an exercise of his creative imagination, his feelings will naturally change, probably toward conformity with the feelings of the spectator. Disagreement

> in feeling will be transformed into agreement, and in effect each will come to sympathize with the other. (Broadie 178)

The sentimental consensus thus achieved is analogous to Smith's famous sequence of "truck, barter and exchange" as well as to the tripartite structure of reader-text-writer. A pleasurable agreeing relation is made through exchanging sentiments between the spectator and the agent, similar to the bartering business around the commodity that finalizes the deal[1]. The text becomes pleasurable, and textuality permeates into everyday practice of representation and reading.

It takes something to build "a thoughtful, critical observer" that matters to Smith. The spectator-observer is "directed by virtuous considerations, whether of the intellectual sort or some other, and seeking to understand" (177). Indeed, for the eighteenth-century reader, propriety and property often resonate with each other. The long-standing association of honor and decorum with ancient and prescriptive rights in the land is being replaced by its much less aristocratic but more bourgeoisie-like capitalistic counterpart. As historian Jean-Christophe Agnew points out: "In drama as in life, honor was increasingly understood to be a particularly stable and solid form of credit, whereas land was coming to be seen as an especially illiquid form of capital" (175). Sympathy, in some sense, joins in the first of this pair, "a particularly stable and solid form of credit," that is. Access to this agreement of sentiments is *economic*, through bodily management as well as social capital. Let's take a look at another passage from *The Theory of Moral Sentiments*:

> ... it is chiefly from [the] regard to the sentiments of mankind that we pursue riches and avoid poverty. For to what purpose is all the toil and bustle of this world? What is the end of avarice and ambition, of the pursuit of wealth, of power and preeminence? ... From whence ... arises the emulation which runs through all the different ranks of men and what are the advantages which we propose by that great purpose of human life which we call better our

[1] See Alexander Broadie, "Sympathy and the Impartial Spectator," pp. 177-178.

> condition? To be observed, to be attended to, to be taken notice of with sympathy, complacency, and appreciation, are all the advantages which we can propose to derive from it. It is the vanity, not the ease or the pleasure, which interests us. But vanity is always founded upon the belief of our being the object of attention and approbation. (Smith 1984: 50)

To be seen, to be sympathized with become a kind of competitive economy. Attention and sympathy turn into "a limited commodity for which isolated individuals competed" (Agnew 181). Individuals are portrayed as driven by the fear of possible indifference and mortification. Theatrical sentiment more notoriously turns into capitalization. "Nothing is so mortifying as to be obliged to expose our distress to the view of the public, and to feel, that though our situation is open to the eyes of all mankind, no mortal conceives for us the half of what we suffer" (Smith 1984: 60) as Smith writes pages later. Sympathy here joins honor, virtue, and decorum to be part of a bottomless line of credit. It functions in an economy of scarcity rather than a natural or equal distribution. Those blessed with "ease and prosperity" are more sympathetically regarded by others, or more easily moved into the adverbial sympathetic positions. Their words, gestures, and actions are "observed by all the world," in stark contrast to the poor, who come and go unnoticed, without visibility and deprived of theatrical presence[1].

In a passage on the influence of fortune upon merit and demerit, Smith writes:

> If, between the friend who fails and the friend who succeeds, all other circumstances are equal, there will, even in the noblest mind, be some little difference of affection in favour of him who succeeds. (Smith 1984: 183)

Which is also why Adam Smith argues that a "wild child"—one recurrent figure of the marginal people in the anthropological discourse

---

[1] To use a concept that we discussed in the chapter on David Hume.

of the British Enlightenment[1]—also lacks an idea of self. It is because he lacks the "mirror" provided by others that he could ever afford to entertain:

> Were it possible that a human creature could group up to manhood in some solitary place, without any communication with his own species, he could no more think of his own character, of the propriety or demerit of his own sentiments and conduct, of the beauty or deformity of his own mind, than of the beauty or deformity of his own face. All these objects which he cannot easily see, which naturally he does not look at, and with regard to which he is provided with no mirror which can present them to his view. Bring him into society, and he is immediately provided with the mirror which he wanted before. (Smith 1984: 110)

"Who we are," as well as "who we think we are," depends on our ability to see ourselves reflected in the actions and eyes of others. The "solitary place" represents a strong sense of death drive, sentimental dearth, social impropriety and propertied poverty. Others provide us with the means of seeing ourselves, which we "cannot easily see" or which we "naturally" do "not look at." Conscience is also a product of our identification with what we imagine to be the sentiments of the spectators of our actions[2]. Smith observes:

> We suppose ourselves the spectators of our own behaviour and endeavour to imagine what effect it would, in this light, produce upon us. This is the only looking-glass by which we can, in some measure, with the eyes of other people, scrutinize the propriety of our own conduct. (112)

This property of interiority is necessary to maintain a bourgeoisie autonomous individual selfhood, and manifested in the figure of the impartial spectator. Smith calls this "the man within the breast" in his

---

[1] See Alan Bewell, *Wordsworth and the Enlightenment*, pp. 50-71.
[2] Also see Alan Bewell, *Wordsworth and the Enlightenment*, p. 77.

account of the faculty of conscience:

> The all-wise Author of Nature has, in this manner, taught man to respect the sentiments and judgments of his brethren .... But though man has, in this manner, been rendered the immediate judge of mankind, he has been rendered so only in the first instance; and an appeal lies from his sentence to a much higher tribunal, to the tribunal of their own consciences, to that of the supposed impartial and well-informed spectator, to that of the man within the breast, the great judge and arbiter of their conduct. The jurisdictions of those two tribunals are founded upon principles which, though in some respects resembling and akin, are, however, in reality different and distinct. The jurisdiction of the man without, is founded altogether in the desire of actual praise, and in the aversion to actual blame. The jurisdiction of the man within, is founded altogether in the desire of praise-worthiness, and in the aversion to blame-worthiness; in the desire of possessing those qualities, and performing those actions, which we love and admire in other people; and in the dread of possessing those qualities, and performing those actions, which we hate and despise in other people. (Smith 1984: 128-131)

Thus, the formation of a subjective interiority is a social act of communication and reflection. Interiority and exteriority correspond to each other in a sympathetic way of correspondence. The "supposed impartial and well-informed spectator," not the ideal observer, cannot dispense with "the man without," whose "desire of actual praise" and "aversion to actual blame" result from a socializing process. It relates to an approximation to propriety that could be attained:

> There exists in the mind of every man, an idea of this kind, gradually formed from his observations upon the character and conduct both of himself and of other people. It is the slow, gradual, and progressive work of the great demigod within the breast, the great judge and arbiter of conduct. This idea is in every man more

> or less accurately drawn, its colouring is more or less just, its outlines are more or less exactly designed, according to the delicacy and acuteness of that sensibility, with which those observations were made, and according to the care and attention employed in making them .... Every day some feature is improved; every day some blemish is corrected. (247)

It is noteworthy that the impartial spectator, "the judgment of the ideal man within the breast" (147), is not a version of the "ideal observer theory" that has been on the agenda of moral philosophers at least since the work of Roderick Firth[1]. It is simply a demigod—as Smith repeatedly uses this term—not God at all. Sympathy, as a "primal human form of imitation" (Bewell 77), becomes possible with a strong dependence upon a socialized domestic imagination, which produce resemblance under certain social conditions. Otherwise, it becomes not possible for sympathy to register encounters with difference, and thereby a self would be stranded in a situation of affective poverty.

For instance, in the midst of a crowd, the pauper finds himself "in the same obscurity as if shut up in his own hovel":

> The poor man ... is ashamed of his poverty. He feels that it either places him out of the sight of mankind, or, that if they take notice of him, they have, however, scarce any fellow-feeling with the misery and distress which he suffers. He is mortified upon both accounts. (Smith 1984: 51)

This shame economy of affective dearth (no attention, no fellow-feeling), this overriding compulsion to become or to remain "the object of attention and approbation," serves as a goad to industry, like the same "propensity to truck, barter, and exchange one thing for another" (Smith 2000: 14), the latter of which is the same abstract entity driving the competing individuals "the butcher, the brewer, or the baker" in *The*

---

[1] See Roderick Firth, "Ethical Absolutism and the Ideal Observer." Also see Alexander Broadie, "Sympathy and the Impartial Spectator," p. 184.

Wealth of Nations. In Smith's description, this affective economy is so imperative that the isolated murderer, like Peter's education in Wordsworth's poem *Peter Bell*[1], is compelled to return to society to face the judgment of others. It is because his "exposure," as David Marshall has noted, "before the imagined spectators the man must personate in his solitude," is more frightening than a real court of justice[2]. It is similar to what William Warner sees in William Hazlitt's *Lectures on the Comic Writers* regarding a classic history of the rise of the novel in figures like Richardson, Fielding, Smollett, and Sterne of the period of George II (1727—1760). Hazlitt correlates this with the rise of the middle class, whose political demands for representation are manifested through self-expressing "in books as well as Parliament." It is a turn-away from the "vices, miseries, and frivolities of the great" as expressed in the continental romance and novella, toward "an account of themselves" as winning for themselves "a security of person and property, and freedom of opinion." This, according to Warner's analysis, makes a more popular and "domestic" culture in that the English reader of the novel thereby wins a certain "life" and "liberty," and becomes propertied—"each individual had a certain ground-plot of his own to cultivate his particular humours in." Thereby, according to Warner's analysis on Hazlitt, the English novel "allows every English citizen to realize a claim to the Lockean trinity of life, liberty, and property (Locke, *Second Treatise of Government*, VII: 87)" (Warner 25)[3].

For Smith, sympathetic sentiment's correlation with an attentional and visual economy is set to exclude some individuals from the "moralizing gaze of others" (Poovey 33), who "sunk in obscurity and darkness": "His conduct is observed and attended to by nobody, and he is therefore very likely to neglect it himself, and to abandon himself to

---

[1] See Alan Bewell, *Wordsworth and the Enlightenment*, p. 103.

[2] David Marshall, "Adam Smith and the Theatricality of Moral Sentiments," p. 603.

[3] William Warner, *Licensing Entertainment: The Elevation of Novel Reading in Britain, 1684—1750*. This, of course, as Warner makes it clear, is a very "Whiggish interpretation of the free golden age of the Whig mid-eighteenth century, written from the vantage point of Hazlitt's conception of English democratic identity" (Warner 25).

every sort of low prodigality and vice" (Smith 1984: 134). The *natural* impulse to keep oneself from moral and visual oblivion, and mankind's "dull insensibility to the afflictions of others," compel the sufferer to take the part of his spectators toward himself, since it is only by such measures that the sufferer could discover at what level he needs to cast the expression of his own feelings to win their sympathy. Though such sympathy offers him "his sole consolation," the sufferer could "only hope to obtain this by lowering his passion to that pitch" which his spectator finds tolerable. He has to "flatten," in Smith's words, "the sharpness of its natural tone, in order to reduce it to harmony and concord with the emotions of those who are about him" (22). Only certain kinds and degrees of emotions can be counted as evidence, as testimony. The person in question is addressed with these enunciative and signifying rules in mind. In order to reach that momentary imaginary change of situations, upon which sympathy is founded, the sufferer turns instead to a more deeply theatrical and collusive set of relations with his audience:

> As they [the audience / spectators] are continually placing themselves in his situation, thence conceiving emotions similar to what he feels; so he is as constantly placing himself in theirs, and thence conceiving some degree of that coolness about his own fortune, with which he is sensible that they will view it. (19)

In this mutual process between the spectators and the agent of feelings, "strange fits of passion"—to use half a line from William Wordsworth's "Lucy Pomes"—need be reducible to be observable so as to be sympathized with. It takes efforts from both sides to establish a communicative process of analysis and imitation. Emotions should be tailored so as to enter into equilibrium and to be exchangeable. In this realm of emotional production and communication, what remains of interest is not what is "in the true" or "in the private," but what is "in the evidentiary" or what could be made "in the circulatory"—the aspect of "exchange value" if we use Karl Marx's formula of "commodity." It reminds of what Samuel T. Coleridge takes as "man of letters": "He imagines a man of type capable of being indefinitely reset[1]." Jerome Christensen argues that as consequence of commercialization of the print, the Romantic authorship becomes "no longer figured as an instrument for spreading light," but along with the print machine, "churned out ephemeral commodities, exacted soul-destroying labor, and chained genius to the caprices of a debased reading public" (Christensen 1987: 9). For Coleridge, whose two therapeutic substitutes for the man of letters are the individual poet and the corporate clerisy[2],

> with the greatest possible solicitude avoid authorship. Too early or immoderately employed, it makes the head *waste* and the heart empty; even were there not other worse consequences. A person, who reads only to print in all probability reads amiss; and he, who sends away through the pen and the press every thought, the moment it occurs to him, will in a short time have sent all away, and will become a mere journeyman of the printing-office, a *compositor*. (qtd. in Christensen 1987: 8)

Adam Smith's "flattening" strategy in representing emotions reads akin to the necessity of production and reproduction of the authorship: merely becoming "a journeyman of the printing-office, a *compositor*," that is. Both are manufactured into anonymous commodities in a logic analogous to the permeation of print and reading.

V.v. Sentimental Humanity and a Stadial European History

Writing on structural transformation of the public sphere as a category of bourgeois society, Jürgen Habermas explains rather cryptically that [i]ncluded in the private realm was the authentic "public

---

[1] Jerome Christensen, *Praising Enlightenment*, p. 8. Also see Jerome Christensen, *Coleridge's Blessed Machine of Language*, pp. 163-167, and "The Impropriety of Coleridge's Literary Life," pp. 156-167.

[2] Jerome Christensen, *Coleridge's Blessed Machine of Language*, p. 9, note 12.

sphere," for it was a public sphere constituted by private people (Habermas 30). This quite dialectical dynamics between the public and the private is further elucidated by Clifford Siskin in his analysis of the social role of writing in that differentiation. Siskin quotes Anne Dutton's defense of "PRINTING any Thing written by a Woman" (1743), more than a decade before the first publication of Smith's work:

> Communicating one Mind in *Print,* is as *private,* with respect to particular *Persons,* as if one did it particularly unto every one by *himself* in one's *own House.* There is only this *Difference.* The one is communicating one's Mind by *Speech,* in one's *own* private House: The other is doing it by *Writing,* in the private house of *another* Person. Both are still *private.* (qtd. in Siskin 164)

For Siskin, in Dutton's reading, it is print that "overwrites the category of public-as-state, by instituting, within the private realm of society, a new kind of publicness—one that is accessed and thus produced in private terms" (Siskin 164). In other words, print, as a technology and an art of transmission, enhances a world of moving objects, images and other means of representations. It would be technologically determinist to claim print as the incubator of social mobility. What interests this current writing more is the social increase of this "new kind of publicness" that "is accessed and thus produced in private terms" around the middle of the eighteenth century. Dutton's quite functionalist acknowledgement of the difference between the oral (*speech*) and the tactile (*writing*), without substantiating the effects of this difference, exactly suggests her ignorance of the modality of impersonality, transparency, and mediated exchangeability created by the *social* and *public* properties of writing. Spontaneous, communal speech and its audile mechanism begin to co-exist with an emergent mode of communication and its visual mechanism. One even can detect a transition from orality to literacy, to use a simplified model of communication theory by Walter J. Ong. The sense of immediacy—"as if one did it particularly unto every one by *himself* in one's *own*

House"—from which Dutton tries to salvage a sense of security—"in one's *own* House," thereby safe—turns out exactly to be what writers must find ways to achieve as a memorable quality of writing owing to words' separation from their "living present" (Ong 82). The world is becoming larger than that of the village midwife of Laurence Sterne's. Habermas, in his influential study with this point, describes the late seventeenth- and early eighteenth-centuries of commerce of communication and the way in which the press was a major factor in the emergence of the public sphere:

> The great trade cities became at the same time centers for the traffic in news; the organization of this traffic on a *continuous* basis became imperative to the degree to which the exchange of commodities and of securities became continuous. (Habermas 16)

This sense of imperative traffic and commerce displays itself also *immaterially*, which is the way a neutralizing strategy of *excessive* emotions works. It throws a significant historical light upon the theatrical and collusive set of relations between the sufferer and his audience in the sentimental economy. The way Adam Smith, as a would-be political economist then, designates emotions to be regulated, disciplined and transferred as evidences and testimonies for communicative sympathy correlates with these crucial periods of adaptation to an increasing commerce and mobility. This also explains that David Hume fixes on conversation as an antipode to "that forelorn (sic) solitude" mentioned above. Conversation is a crucial term in the eighteenth century for illustrating "the flow *across* those newly reconstituted fields" of the private individual exchanges and the public ones generated out of their multiplicity (Siskin 164). Graham Burchell points out that Hume "describe[s] the form ideally taken by the 'commerce' of … [the political culture] of opinion, the appropriate cultural form of exchanges between individuals of the 'middling rank' immersed in 'common life'" (Burchell 129). This necessity of interchangeability between things, perceptions and feelings require all of them to develop neutralized and well-disciplined platforms for the other, whether in the forms of commodities (and its exchange value), the visually demanding literacy, or sympathy.

Of course, labors are involved in translating different visual positionalities and making them "in the evidentiary" to the collective editorial "we" that Smith uses through his system. This ability to liquidate suffering and pain to make emotions *transparent* and *translatable* enough to be exchangeable, analogous to money as embodiment of exchange values of different commodities from different worlds, is rather theatrical and self-reflexive in Smith's theatre of sympathy. It seems unevenly distributed and much less accessible, in Smith's system, to the poor in the midst of the crowd, the street beggar with sores and ulcers, and the fair sex:

> The reserve which the laws of society impose upon the fair sex, with regard to this weakness [i.e., passionate love], renders it more particularly distressful in them, and, upon that very account, more deeply interesting. We are charmed with the love of Phaedra, as it is expressed in the French tragedy of that name, notwithstanding all the extravagance and guilt which attend it. That very extravagance and guilt may be said, in some measure, to recommend it to us. Her fear, her shame, her remorse, her horror, her despair, become thereby more natural and interesting. (Smith 1984: 3)

"Natural and interesting" here applies not to a set of proper emotions already tailored to circumstances, but to extravagant emotions such as Phaedra's fear, shame, remorse, horror, and despair "rendered (and thereby appropriate) by the art of the dramatist" (Gross 174). Here exists a touch of what Michel de Certeau calls "the ethnographic operation" (78). It is the epistemological-technical process, through which the emotions of "primitive" others become visually archivable, are brought into representations and translations, and are transcribed by social researchers or political economist of emotions. It is a hermeneutics of the emotionally other inscribed by and through certain forms of intelligibility, visuality and civility, as we already see in the literary media strategy of William Wordsworth. It may not be a ethnographic writing *per se*, as it is in the original de Certeau scheme, but the strategy remains the same. The editorial "we" that Smith used throughout the work is to "invoke the presumptive authority of common experience, thereby denying or, again, dissembling the emotional isolation that lay at the heart of his system" (Agnew 185-186). The common experience offers as the site of exchange and the nodal point of transference and translation. It remains categorically analogous to some other peculiar forms of modern abstractions, which are variously designated as the *commodity*, *reification*, and the *fetish*. The increasing problems of the production and administration of this sort of abstract space closely dovetail with the history of Western modernity. Smith weaves all social relations into versions of measurable exchange, and individuals as instantiations of the same abstract entity, whether it is sympathy, the moralizing impartial spectator or the "propensity to truck, barter, and exchange one thing for another." He designates this as a way to deal with the informational mobility in an increasingly globalized and capitalized world—"a world of moving objects."

In an etymological study, Rafael Capurro suggests that information became an entity to be regarded objectively as "something to be stored and processed" (qtd. in Ellison 8) between the seventeenth and eighteenth centuries. Katherine Ellison contextualizes Capurro's definition of information as "a kind of abstract stuff present in the world, disconnected from the situations that it is *about*" (qtd. in Ellison 9), which is "physically and spatially associated with surface, depth, and meaninglessness" (Ellison 9). In Smith's *The Theory of Moral Sentiments*, the impartiality of the sympathetic remains historically coincident with and logically analogous to the overloading information age of the eighteenth century, with its establishment of public post office, the publication of books[1], the "moving objects" (Pocock again), and the

[1] The word "publish" appears in Samuel Johnson's famous dictionary of 1755: "To put forth a book into the world"—suggestive of the expansive nature of book publishing, which is at once an act of production and dissemination.

moving people. It even "began to flow out along the arteries of European commerce in search of its victims" (229) as Peter Hulme writes. Antonio Damasio, one of the contemporary brain scientists of emotion, muses that the history of civilization is, to some extent, "the history of a persuasive effort to extend the best of 'moral sentiments' to wider and wider circles of humanity" (qtd. in Gross 170). Talal Asad refers this kind of civilizing moral sentiment as "the desire to impose what they [the European rulers] considered civilized standards of justice and humanity on a subject population—that is, the desire to create new human subjects," which is "humanizing the world"(Asad 110). This imperialist humanitarian effort of sentiment and sympathy aims to create a new sense of humanity and imperial subject. It has its historical predecessors. For instance, Lord Milner, undersecretary for finance during the British occupation of Egypt that began in 1882, describes Britain's imperial task in that country as follows:

> This then, and no less than this, was meant by 'restoring order.' It meant reforming the Egyptian administration root and branch. Nay, it meant more. For what was the good of recasting the system, if it were left to be worked by officials of the old type, animated by the old spirit? 'Men, not measures,' is a good watchword anywhere, but to no country is it more profoundly applicable than to Egypt. Our task, therefore, included something more than new principles and new methods. It ultimately involved new men. It involved 'the education of the people to know,' and therefore to expect, orderly and honest government—the education of a body of rulers capable of supplying it. (qtd. in Asad 110)

The imperialist reformation involves not merely the bureaucratic administration, but more essentially, the essence of a new humanity. It necessarily takes coercion and violence to eradicate traditional practices, and more so to establish a new affective mode of humanity. In this pedagogical process of learning to be "fully human," as Asad points out, "only some kinds of suffering were seen as an affront to humanity, and their elimination sought" (Asad 111). It remains integrated to the imperialist reform project to retain "suffering that was necessary to the process of realizing one's humanity—that is, pain that was adequate to its end, not wasteful pain" (111). For Eric Hayot, it is an end of taking the body as an imperialist "epistemological heuristic, as, that is, a way of knowing the world and a way of grasping the body's relation to it," and

> an understanding of suffering, its recognition and its classification, as epistemological processes, as mechanisms for the production of social truth and for the location of self in relation to world, and thus an awareness of the body's paradoxical status as both 'mode and object of knowing.' (Hayot 18)

The necessity of the existence of some pain, some suffering is to establish an epistemology of affect, which manifests itself as a condescending sympathy towards "traditional practices" that brings forth pain, misery and suffering. It therefore justifies Western modernity to affirm the development of a Western sense of self as modern, to take the body as site of anthropological observation, and to eliminate those "now branded as 'repugnant to justice and morality' or as 'opposed to natural morality and humanity,' or even sometimes as 'backward and childish'" (Asad 110-111). This Western liberalistic discourse of emotions and sentiments accords very well with the orthodoxy story of capital in Karl Marx—how it travels from the west to the east, that is—along with its ideology of the "Asiatic mode of production" in various forms[1]. It is interesting to note that etymologically, the word "Mandarin" is defined through the *OED* as "any obscurantist, esoteric, or exclusive variety of a language[2]"that remains outside of circulation and exchangeability. Eric Hayot suggests that this probably "borrows from the mandarin's economic and governmental stereotype the sense of mobility without movement, or activity without change" (Hayot 33), to which Adam

---

[1] See Perry Anderson, *Lineages of the Absolutist State*, pp. 462-550.

[2] See *OED* online, under the entry of "mandarin," definition 2b.

Smith also makes a discursive contribution[1]. It is no surprise that Adam Smith could be cited as an intellectual antecedent of this imperialist project of global sentiment[2]. There is also a historical heritage from the "conjectural," "hypothetical," "natural" history constructed by the Scottish Enlightenment that was popular and characteristic of eighteenth-century empiricist discursive genres[3]. Dugald Stewart (1753—1828), in his discussion of Adam Smith's *Dissertation on the Origin of Languages,* summarizes in this way:

> When, in such a period of society as that in which we live, we compare our intellectual acquirements, our opinions, manners, and institutions, with those which prevail among rude tribes, it cannot fail to occur to us as an interesting question, by what gradual steps the transition has been made from the first simple efforts of uncultivated nature, to a state of things so wonderfully artificial and complicated[4].

Smith's contribution to the four-stage theory helps to give rise to "an account of the progress of civil society which reinterpreted European history at the expense of non-European cultures. It made the extension of the concept 'history' to these difficult and even deniable" (Pocock 280)[5]. For him, the man of middling rank can afford to cultivate those bourgeois sensibilities—compassion first among them—that constitutes a civilized nation. Living in such a flux of mobility, one has to "flatten" (to use Smith's word) a little bit, and has to manage to remain connected, to be wired into medial possibilities. Otherwise, one would be "sunk in obscurity and darkness." This *flattening* or *abstracting* theatrically alternates between embodiment and disembodiment. Thus,

---

[1] See David Porter, "A Peculiar but Uninteresting Nation: China and the Discourse of Commerce in Eighteenth-Century England."

[2] See Daniel M. Gross, *The Secret History of Emotion*, p. 170.

[3] See Alan Bewell, *Wordsworth and the Enlightenment*, p. 59.

[4] "Account of the Life and Writings of Adam Smith, LL.D.," in Adam Smith, *Essays on Philosophical Subjects*, p. 292-293.

[5] J. G. A. Pocock, "Adam Smith and History," p. 280.

Smith's sympathetic subject creates an example of what Robert Mitchell and Phillip Thurtle examine as a creative process of information, and an instance of the convergence of individualism with capitalism in an early part of Western modernity. Significantly, such a story of information flow and convergence concerning emotions is class, gender and region based, as analyzed above.

Coda

In a history of the body as it is realized through photography, detectives and early cinemas, Tom Gunning tells a case of female paranoia analyzed by Freud. A young woman was obsessed of being photographed, because she heard a knock or click that she believed came from the snapping of a camera shutter. Freud identifies the source of this "aural hallucination" (Gunning 37) as the woman's body, and the click being an aural displacement of the throb of her excited clitoris[1]. In the long history given by Gunning on the pre-history of cinema, this is one of the places he reads "the conflation of the body with the processes of the camera" (37). What remains of interest here is this turn of the mechanic machine as part of the female body. A somatic interiority becomes externalized as the apparatus, which functions as an observing and diagnosing machine or mechanism. The deep female psyche is presentable through the snapping of a camera shutter, which comes from the body itself. This turning the body inside out as observable, exchangeable, and alienable is throughout Western modernity. It starts from the period of history we investigated, if not earlier, in the rise of the print medium, and various social practices this technology has brought forth. An affective maintenance of a selfhood is a social practice of fellow-feeling, the realization of which is made possible through a print logic enhanced through the daily saturation of textually based cultural

---

[1] Sigmund Freud, "A Case of Paranoia Running Counter to the Psycho-Analytic Theory of the Disease." See Tom Gunning, "Tracing the Individual Body: Photography, Detectives, and Early Cinema," p. 37.

practice of representation. This leads to the economy of sympathy increasingly visual and abstract, as our history from Edmund Burke to Adam Smith suggests.

In the mid-nineteenth century, photography, as relevant to the Freudian story here, accompanied the "autonomization of sight," by which, Jonathan Crary argues, the sense of sight becomes dissociated from touch, and thereby detaches "the eye from the network of referentiality incarnated in tactility and its subjective relation to perceived space." As a result, according to Crary, "The new objects of vision ... assume a mystified and abstract identity." And it is because the imagery has been cut off from any relation to the observer's position in space. In the century, like "older types of images," photography unifies "all subjects within a single global network of valuation and desire," and could be located as "an element of a new and homogeneous terrain of consumption and circulation in which an observer becomes lodged[1]." The paranoia of being photographed from the young woman is suggestive of an obsession of the proliferation of the photography technology in everyday life. Probably it is also an anxiety of being watched and scrutinized by this "element of a new and homogeneous terrain of consumption and circulation," whether manifested through photography, cinema or print. It is a human sensitivity against a culture of abstraction promoted through the saturation of different mass media in modernity, which produces a communication and reproduction "from the network of referentiality incarnated in tactility and its subjective relation to perceived space." In a rough way, this is referred to as "alienation" in various Marxist traditions. More of significance to our history of emotion—specifically "sympathy"—is the fact that the "aural hallucination" of the young woman is identified by Sigmund Freud the psychoanalyst as a part of the activity of the female body itself. It is not about any general part, but the throb of her excited clitoris, which is a most private and inscrutable part of a female body. The Freudian penetrating power of the masculine visuality is parallel with the

[1] Jonathan Crary, *Techniques of the Observer*, pp. 13, 19.

panopticon mode of scrutiny, whether it is from the mass media of print, photography and cinema, medical treatises, or moral philosophy et cetera. All of them can be labeled as the apparatuses of modernity in a general way. They turn the female body as hypersexual or hypersentimental, just abnormal enough to be in the necessary need of being normalized. The female body becomes a harbinger to the "mass" as Benjamin sees in one of the notes published later as "Central Park": that "mass of organs" on which the surgeon—and the political economist, the psychoanalyst, and the cameraman—"operate." It is an allegory of "the transformation of the body from an organic form into an allegorical 'mass' that the apparition of the passerby both announces and conceals" (Weber 1996: 96) as Samuel Weber points out. In this process of the discipline or penetration of the female comes masculinity in various modern technologies. This is what is usually called the process of "modernity." It is at the expense of the aurality psychoanalyzed as female in the Freudian way. Of course, this is an allegory, and the sacrificed aurality of the young woman in the science of psychoanalysis is referred to as the "Unconscious," which occurs to places, classes and genders identified as the other in the story of Western modernity.

Chapter VI

Specters of Crowds in Late Qing Print Culture: Nationalism, Subjectivity and the Rise of Modern Chinese Textual Media

The previous section of this writing addresses the inward turn of emotion as it correlate with the "mechanical reproducibility" of modern writing in the eighteenth-century Britain. Sentiment and emotion become mediated through a saturating modern textual culture into forms of individual subjectivity. Our discussions on David Hume and William Wordsworth suggest that sentiments proliferate along with the rise of a textual media, and become a necessary component of the media. The moral philosophy of sentiments in Adam Smith regulates representations of modern subjectivity, and gives rise to a subject-less writing medium. At the turn of the nineteenth century, this medium becomes that of transparent exchangeability. At the same time, it leaves the un-representable interiorized emotions into the deep Unconscious, which pre-mediates the emergence of the psychoanalytic self. As an extended comparison and contrast to this genealogy of Western modern selfhood and writing, this chapter suggests a trace of an evanescent moment of collective being in late nineteenth-century Chinese pictorial culture. Rather than an interiorizing activity as reflected in writing, this historical moment presents itself through visual mediation in pictorial culture before the coming of the modern vernacular literature. It releases a collective subject-less subjectivity in urban crowds at the beginning of Chinese modernity, which provides a specter of comparison to the stories of Western individuality we outline in the previous sections. The comparison is spectral in that it is made between two different places, historical periods and media. If all the previous chapters in this dissertation try to theorize upon forms of individual subjectivity in textual media, this chapter traces an evanescent moment of inter-medial phenomenal collective existence in pictorial culture. All are examinations of the technology of self through media and mediation. In this sense, the spectrality of comparison may be justified by the spectral quality of this subject-less subjectivity before the coming of the modern Chinese literature as well, which is manifested through a hybridized visual culture. In this may lie a lost moment in media history, when we once had a hope of being different from the individualistic subjectivity often attributed to Western modernity. It is a hope with which this dissertation concludes as a critique of subjectivity of modernity developed through writing—a hope beyond critical discussions upon subjectivity.

This chapter uses *The Dianshizhai Pictorial* (see Figure 1 at the end of this chapter) as its specific archive, in which crowds are represented as audience as well as participants of image-making in late imperial Chinese pictorial culture located in the late nineteenth century. In the pictorial newspaper, there emerges an appearance of some amorphous state of modern and collective state of being in mediation, and it is to be replaced by a more intensive individual subjectivity. This historical shift reflects different attitudes towards visuality and textuality. The latter is reflected in the beginning of modern Chinese literature, which takes as its task to enlighten the crowds through literary education. This chapter argues that the pictorial culture in late nineteenth-century China embraces an accommodation of multi-media fertilization in the pictorial over a repressive regime of textuality. In between the pictorial culture and the modern Chinese literature to come there lies a specific sense of absorption and theatricality, and it produces a spectral existence of collective crowds at the emergence of a modern media culture, which intersects illustrated magazines, pictorial newspapers, modern popular theater, and early cinematic exhibition.

For about two decades now, the late Qing period has been labeled as that which was impregnated with signs of "incipient modernities"(Wang 1997: 1), with regard to its literary and cultural productions. This argument was most famously developed in Der-wei Wang's work on late Qing fiction writing, which he takes as "part of a Chinese contribution to global modernity predating the May Fourth period" (1). For Wang, this kind of "incipient modernities" were repressed and dismissed in the discourse of the Chinese modern to come in the New Culture Movement. A more recent work by Alexander Des Forges titled *Mediasphere Shanghai: The esthetics of Cultural Production* categorizes the aesthetic forms through which Shanghai cultural production (mainly fictions) and social practice are organized in the late nineteenth and early twentieth centuries into four tropes—simultaneity, interruption, mediation and excess, that is[1]. With an investigation of the literary and visual dimensions of what Des Forges calls "these four narrative tropes, as well as their social and material effects," Des Forges, through deploying Régis Debray's neologism *mediasphere*, argues that

> These forms give shape and meaning to the sensory and emotional overload ... that confronts individuals who come face-to-face with the city; they allow these individuals to impose a comprehensible and compelling order on that overload and convert a chaotic set of impressions into a coherent understanding of "what Shanghai is." In so doing, these forms constitute a conceptual foundation on which Shanghai's "social reality" is built, construct a frame through which the city can be perceived, and supply a template for the reader's own experiences there. (Des Forges 2)

[1] Des Forges, *Mediasphere Shanghai*, pp. 1-2. I acknowledge the recommendation of Des Forges' work from Professor Kirk Denton, which is very useful for rethinking the arguments made in this essay. I wish I had known Des Forges' work earlier. I agree with many arguments made in Des Forges' book, and it seems that one of the differences is that he focuses more on the installment fiction set in Shanghai from the 1890s to the 1930s (*haishang xiaoshuo*), whereas my work, owing to the limit of its length and scale, is only taking a look at one moment in media transition between pictorial and print cultures, with a focus on the lithographical reproduction of the *Dianshizhai*.

Working with, if not challenging, this thread of scholarship on late Qing and early twentieth-century China, this chapter draws the relational shift between pictorial newspaper and printed literary work into this historical picture of a formative Chinese modernity. It suggests a trace of an evanescent moment of inter-medial phenomenal collective being in late nineteenth-century Chinese pictorial culture presented through visual mediation in pictorial culture before the coming of Chinese modern vernacular literature, which is located in Liang Qichao's reform propositions of the Chinese fiction in 1898 if not earlier. In this may lie a lost moment in media history and a form of being different from the individualistic subjectivity often attributed to (the dissemination of) Western modernity.

The major object of study in this chapter is the staging of crowds in the *Dianshizhai Pictorial* (Touching stone studio, 1884—1898). It is examined in conjunction with the coming of the individual at the beginning of the twentieth century. In this pictorial newspaper, crowds appear as audience as well as participants of image-making. There emerges an amorphous state of modern and collective state of being in mediation, and that is to be replaced by a more intensively individuated subjectivity. This historical shift involves how different ways of identitarian sensing are phenomenalized in visual and textual media. In his very thorough examination of installment fiction set in Shanghai from the 1890s through 1930s, Des Forges takes *mediasphere*—a neologism from Régis Debray the French mediologist, and gives it a particular and "a more productive level of historical specificity" (16). For him, *mediasphere* as "a form of cultural production" consists of:

> (1) a visual and textual field characterized by the drive to expand without limit; (2) the simultaneous and regular appearance of the wide range of cultural products that make up this field—fiction and nonfiction books, newspapers, magazines, illustrated collections, and eventually, recorded performances, film, and radio; and (3) frequent connections and references between these cultural products across

> boundaries between different texts, genres, and media. (Des Forges 16)

It seems that Des Forges' concern is more of media convergence—the coming together of different media and mediation, which explains the way he organizes various forms of materials for critical inquiry, including "fiction and nonfiction books, newspapers, magazines, illustrated collections, and eventually, recorded performances, film, and radio," and "different texts, genres, and media." He takes "mediasphere" as

> a type of cultural production characterized by aspirations to comprehensiveness and omnipresence, an interest in defining the various genres of texts and images relationally rather than absolutely, and a commitment to complex interaction between cultural producers and consumers. (91)

What this chapter, through the case of the *Dianshizhai* pictorial print culture, focuses, is more of a kind of media divergence. It is to argue that different forms of media and mediation help to create different sensing and subjectivities. The textualization of media, categorized as the print modern in this essay, is reflected in the beginning of modern Chinese literature, which takes as its mission to enlighten the crowds through literary education in the written vernacular, for instance. Thus, the pictorial culture in late nineteenth-century China embraces an accommodation of multi-media fertilization in the pictorial over a more individuated regime of textuality to come. In between the pictorial culture and the modern Chinese literature there lies a specific sense of absorption and theatricality, with regard to audience making in a modern mass media environment. This produces spectral existence of collective crowds at the emergence of a modern media culture, which inter-textualizes illustrated magazines, pictorial newspapers, modern popular theaters, and early cinematic exhibitions.

The *Dianshizhai Pictorial* is one of the earliest modern pictorial newspapers in Qing China. It was issued first as a newspaper supplement to the Shanghai-based newspaper *Shenbao* every 10 days in a consecutive span of 15 years. Also one of the most popular pictorial newspapers of its time[1], it publishes on contemporary news, Shanghai urban life, local customs and folklore stories among many other things. It perhaps can be taken as a continuation of the Chinese tradition of encyclopedias for daily use (日用类书, *riyong lei shu*) that began to become increasingly popular in late Ming[2]. What was covered on the *Dianshizhai* may fall into the following categories: military battles, military transportation technologies, geography, medical technologies, strange or supernatural phenomena, governmental policies and administrative acts, social phenomena, news on family issues[3]. Its coverage suggests its distribution and marketing strategy. The *Shenbao* describes the pictorial's mission as the dissemination of new knowledge:

> ……外洋新出一器，乍创一物，凡有利于国计民生者，立即绘图译说，以备官商采用。既扩见闻，亦资利益，故自开印以至今日，销售日盛一日。
>
> ... Once those foreign countries invented a new technology or device, as far as we think it would be beneficial to the commonwealth of our nation, we would introduce it through pictorial representations, so that this can catch attention from the government and merchants

---

[1] As the *Shenbao* reported on June 19, the first three issues of the *Dianshizhai* were immediately out of supply once it went into market, and the press had to print several other thousands, which sold out right away: "后卷嗣出，前卷已空，由后补前，司石司墨者日辄数易手，犹不暇给" ["Once the reprinted came out, the first-time printed already sold out. Those which came later supplied the market needs created by the popularity of those printed earlier. There were several work shifts of personnel responsible for lithography and ink within 24 hours, and still the market was not satisfied"], Cf. Xiong Yuezhi and Zhang Min, 《上海通史・晚清文化》(*Shanghai tongshi Wanqing wenhua*) [*A Survey History of Shanghai: Late Qing Culture*], p. 483.

[2] See Shang Wei, "The Making of the Everyday World: *Jin Ping Mei Cihua* and Encyclopedias for Daily Use."

[3] Wu Meifeng, 《从〈点石斋画报〉看晚清时期的民间信仰意识》(*Cong Dianshizhai huabao kan wanqing de minjian xinyang yishi*) ["Folk Belief and Mentality in Late Qing through an Analysis of the *Dianshizhai*"]; Guo Enci and Su Jue, 《中国现代设计的诞生》(*Zhongguo xiandai sheji de dansheng*) [*The Birth of Modern Chinese Design*], p. 113. Also see Xiaoqing Ye, *The Dianshizhai Pictorial: Shanghai Urban Life, 1884—1898.*

for them to apply it. This broadens our view of the world, and brings actual interests. Thus, since its first print, the sale of the pictorial has been increasing.

Wang Ermin writes:

凡关外洋新知、西洋文化生活、中外时事要闻……大部分是由摄影照片以及西洋传来画片照选择，再交由画家画出……《点石斋画报》画家是由英人美查所主导和供给照片。

Of all new knowledge from foreign countries, cultural and living fashions in Western countries, news of China and other nations .... Most of them were selected from photographical copies or printed pictures from Western countries, and then given to the painters in charge .... The painters of the *Dianshizhai* were chosen mainly by the English merchant Ernest Major and they were offered photographical pictures by Major[1].

It is a dynamic integration of different popular traditions and information, and suggests a sense of realism different from the long history of literati painting dominating in the previous centuries[2]. The pictorial's reportage on new knowledge and contemporary news obviously attracts attention from Lu Xun (Lu Hsun), A Ying, Bao Tianxiao and Zheng Zhenduo. In his 《上海文艺之一瞥》(Shanghai wenyi zhi yipie) ["A Glimpse upon the World of Literature and Arts in Shanghai"] written in 1931, Lu Xun writes:

这画报的势力，当时是很大的，流行各省，算是要知道“时务”——这名称在那时就如现在之所谓的“新学”——的人们的耳目。

[1] Wang Ermin, 《近代文化生态及其变迁》(*Jindai wenhua shengtai ji qi bianqian*) [*Cultural Ecology of Modern Times and Its Changes*], pp. 428-429.

[2] For how the Yangzhou school of painting in the eighteenth century is different from the outlook of Shanghai culture in the nineteenth century, see Richard Vinograd, *Boundaries of the Self*.

> The influence of this pictorial was very wide then. Its popularity was spread among many provinces, and it was the ears and eyes of those who desired to be informed of the "current affairs"—the same thing begins to be called "new knowledge" nowadays[1].

A Ying writes in his 《中国画报发展之经过》(Zhongguo huabao fazhan zhi jingguo) ["An Experience of the Development of Chinese Pictorials"]:

> 因《点石斋画报》之起，上海画报日趋繁多，然清末数十年，绝无能与之抗衡的。

> From the rise of the *Dianshizhai,* there began to have increasing pictorials in Shanghai. However, none of them could rival the popularity of the *Dianshizhai* in the last decades of the Qing Dynasty.

For him, it was because other pictorial newspapers either "画笔实无可观" ["Their painting techniques are not decent"] or they disregarded pictorial newspapers' mission to "强调时事记载" ["focus on realistic records of current events of the world"][2].

Zheng Zhenduo goes further in complementing the combination of contemporary news and painting as "乃是中国近百年很好的'画史'" ["a very good 'painting epic of its historical time' in China within the last hundred of years"][3].

Existing scholarship on the pictorial either takes a socio-historical approach, reading it as an illustrated guide to late nineteenth-century Shanghai urban life (Ye Xiaoqing, Rudolf G. Wagner, Hsiao-t'i Li, Chen Pingyuan), or locates it in the changing landscape of perceptual

---

[1] Lu Xun 鲁迅,《鲁迅全集》(*Lu Xun quanji*) [*Complete Works of Lu Xun*], vol. 4, p. 293.

[2] A Ying 阿英,《晚清文艺报刊述略》(*Wanqing wenyi baokan shulue*) [*A Brief History of Newspapers and Periodicals in Late Qing*], pp. 90-100.

[3] Zheng Zhenduo,《郑振铎艺术考古文集》(*Zheng Zhenduo yishu kaogu wenji*) [*Collected Essays on Art and Archaeology by Zheng Zhenduo*], p.193. Regarding comments on the *Dianshizhai* from Lu Xun, A Ying and Zheng Zhenduo, also see Chen Pingyuan, 《导论：以"图像"解说"晚清"》("Daolun: yi 'tuxiang' jieshuo 'wanqing'") ["Introduction: an Interpretation of 'Late Qing' from the Perspective of 'Pictures and Images'], p.4.

paradigms in late nineteenth-century Shanghai (Bao Weihong, Laikwan Pang).[1] The argument in this chapter, following these two threads of scholarship on this pictorial newspaper, identifies an evanescent trace of collective state of being in the modes of theatricality and absorption in the visual activities in the pictorial, and takes these modes as they correlate with other urban visual activities in Shanghai, including a garden culture and early cinema watching. It outlines an inter-media spectral phenomenal being spectrally existent in between media, tradition and modernity, word and image.

Zheng Zhenduo's comment of "画史" ["painting epic of its historical time"] is not merely upon Wu Youru, the major artist for the pictorial[2]. It is a recognition of the technological innovation that the *Dianshizhai* made in what Catherine Yeh calls a "visual revolution" happening in the Chinese pictorial newspapers in late nineteenth-century

---

[1] Ye Xiaoqing, *The Dianshizhai Pictorial*; Rudolf G. Wagner, 《进入全球想象图景：上海的〈点石斋画报〉》("Jinru quanqiu xiangxiang tujing: Shanghai de *Dianshizhai huabao*) ["Joining the Global Imaginary: the *Dianshizhai Pictorial* in Shanghai"]; Hsiao-t'i Li, 《上海近代城市文化中的传统与现代——1880 年代至 1930 年代》("Shanghai jindai chengshi wenhua zhong de chuantong yu xiandai: 1880 niandai zhi 1930 niandai") ["Tradition and Modernity in Shanghai Urban Culture: 1880s through 1930s"], in 《恋恋红尘：中国的城市、欲望和生活》(*Lianlian hongchen: Zhongguo de chengshi, yuwang he shenghuo*) [*Ashes of Time: China's City, Desire and Life*]; Chen Pingyuan, 《导论：以"图像"解说"晚清"》("Daolun: yi 'tuxiang' jieshuo 'wanqing'") ["Introduction: an Interpretation of 'Late Qing' from the Perspective of 'Pictures and Images'], in《图像晚清》(*Tuxiang wanqing*) [*Pictures and Images in Late Qing*]; Bao Weihong, "A Panoramic Worldview"; Laikwan Pang, "The Pictorial Turn."

[2] Zheng Zhenduo, in his《〈中国古代绘画选集〉序言》("*Zhongguo gudai huihua xuanji* xuyan") ["Preface to *Selected Paintings from Ancient China*"], writes on technique innovations of paintings in late Qing: "更多地表现那个'时代'的社会生活，乃是一个新闻画家吴嘉猷，他的《吴友如画宝》(石印本) 保存了许多的中国半封建、半殖民地社会的现实主义的记录" ["More of representing the social life of 'that period' are works by Wu Jiayou, a painter, whose subjects are social news. His *Treasured Paintings by Wu Youru* (lithographical edition) keeps many realistic records of the Chinese society in its semi-feudal and semi-colonial stage"], in《郑振铎艺术考古文集》(*Zheng Zhenduo yishu kaogu wenji*) [*Collected Essays on Art and Archaeology by Zheng Zhenduo*] , p.185. Also see Chen Pingyuan, 《导论：以"图像"解说"晚清"》("Daolun: yi 'tuxiang' jieshuo 'wanqing') ["Introduction: an Interpretation of 'Late Qing' from the Perspective of 'Pictures and Images'"], p.4.

China[1]. The founder of the famous *Dianshizhai* Lithographic Press (点石斋石印局, *Dianshizhai Shiyinju*), Ernest Major, was among the first to use the newly introduced visual technology of lithography into mass reproduction of dictionaries, ancient and rare books, newspapers and pictorials[2]. Indeed, this adoption of lithographic printing "made cheap mass production of pages crammed with detailed images possible," and "the image of the urban crowd" "no longer the exclusive property of the sovereign (or the elite classes)", but "a commodity available to many members of that same crowd" (Des Forges 73). It is among the techniques fulfilling what Laikwan Pang identifies as the "realist desire" (Pang 2007: 16) produced through cross-cultural contacts between Shanghai and the Western world. This desire of realism for objective descriptions is most effectively achieved through visual media, which, as many theorists have pointed out, serves as the privileged site to gain symbolic access to the modern world order[3]. The introduction of lithography to China by the missionaries in the 1820s and its wild adoption in the 1870s was instrumental in constructing a sense of Western perspectivalism in portraying Chinese customs, events and objects, when Shanghai was witnessing the beginning stage of a mass media of modern newspapers.[4] Along with this new "arena of print and visual media" (Des Forges 75), a new readership and audience were emerging.

In late nineteenth-century China, Western visual techniques were often valued over traditional Chinese painting, the latter of which was often taken as one of the explanations for China lagging behind the

---

[1] Catherine Vance Yeh, "Creating the Urban Beauty: The Shanghai Courtesan in Late Qing Illustrations," p. 397; Catherine Vance Yeh, *Shanghai Love*, chapter 6.

[2] Lithography was introduced to China first by Western missionaries, and not widely used until 1876, when Shanghai's *Xujiahui Tujiawan Yinshuasuo* (徐家汇土家湾印刷所) started to use it to publish Christian hymns. See Laikwan Pang, "The Pictorial Turn," pp. 19-21.

[3] Also see Laikwan Pang, *The Distorting Mirror*, p. 17.

[4] For Xiong Yuezhi and Zhang Min, the historical development of Shanghai's newspapers in late Qing falls into three periods: the formative period, 1850—1872; the molding period, 1872—1895; the developed period, 1896—1911, pp. 39-40.

modernity project. In August 1898, just when the *Dianshizhai* came to its last issue,《论画报可以启蒙》("On How Pictorials Can Enlighten"), an essay published in the *Shenbao* probably as an elegy for the pictorial, critiques Chinese painting for its too much emphasis on the spirit of things and too little attendance upon verisimilitude of objects. It writes:

> 此种笔墨，非不夺天地造化之妙，然究为文士玩好之物，而非有裨于实用也。
>
> This sort of painting steals the essential beauty from the creation between the earth and the heaven. Nevertheless it descends to the dilettante connoisseurship for the literati, and turns out to be of no practical use.

On the other hand, it takes skills and institutions of visual media as the foundation of Western civilization:

> 泰西以图画为重，不特天文地舆之学，精益求精，不差累黍，即人物器具，无不巧绘成图，使物物皆存于图，俾人人皆知是物。世但知其格致之妙，制造之精，而不知其绘图之妙也。又设蜡人馆、博物院、电照法，以补画工所不及。所以欧西之人，见闻日广，才识日增，而华人莫与比也[1]。
>
> The West lays more significance on the visual effects of painting. In the sciences of astronomy and geography, more precision and accuracy are demanded. Even people and instruments are painted with high skills, so that every instrument can be precisely recorded in visual archives for them to be recognizable. Many know the wonders of the west in acquiring natural knowledge, and the precision of the

[1] 《论画报可以启蒙》("Lun huabao keyi qimeng") ["On How Pictorials Can Enlighten"], the *Shenbao* August 29, 1898. This essay might have been written to express dissatisfaction on the closure of the *Dianshizhai Pictorial*. For speculations of its intent, see Chen Pingyuan, 《导论：以"图像"解说"晚清"》("Daolun: yi 'tuxiang' jieshuo 'wanqing') ["Introduction: an Interpretation of 'Late Qing' from the Perspective of 'Pictures and Images'], p.13.

> west in manufacturing. But few understand the beauty of its paintings. In addition to painting, visual institutions such as waxworks, museums, and X-rays are established to complement the painters' works. Therefore, it came as no surprise that the Westerners obtains increasingly more information, and acquires increasingly more learning on a daily basis, while nothing comparable can be found in Chinese.

The intent of the *Dianshizhai*, as stated by Ernest Major in 《点石斋画报缘起》["The Initiation of the *Dianshizhai Pictorial*"], was to entertain its audience with actual events as well as urban amusements in the aftermath of the Sino-French war (August 1884—April 1885):

> 爰倩精于绘事者，择新奇可喜之事，摹而为图……俾乐观新闻者有以考证其事，而茗余酒后，展卷玩赏，亦足以增色舞眉飞之乐。

> Then those who excel in painting choose novel and entertaining incidents as their subjects, and put them into pictorial representations ... so that those interested in knowing social news could verify whether they are true while enjoying the pictures over cups of tea or wine. This is enough to bring forth pleasures and sensations.

In this "Initiation" essay, Ernest Major compares the difference between Chinese painting and Western visual techniques:

> 盖西法娴绘画者务使逼肖，且十九以药水照成，毫发之细，层叠之多，不少缺漏，以镜显微，能得远近深浅之致，其傅色之妙，虽云影水痕，烛光月魄，晴雨昼夜之殊，无不显豁呈露。故平视则模糊不可辨，窥以仪器，如身入其境中。而人物之生动，尤觉栩栩欲活。中国画家拘于成法，有一定之格局，先事布置，然后穿绰以取势，而结构之疏密，气韵之厚薄，则视其人学力之高下，与胸次之宽狭，以判等差。要之，西画以能肖为上，中画以能工为贵，肖者真，工者不

必真也。既不皆真，则记其事又胡取其有形乎哉。然而如《图书集成》《三才图会》与夫器用之制，名物之繁，诸书以图传者，证之古今，不胜枚举。顾其用意所在，容虑夫见闻混淆，名称参错，抑仅以文字传之，而不能曲达其委折纤悉之致，则有不得已于画者，而皆非可从例新闻也。虽然，世运所至，风会渐开，乃者泰西文字，中土人颇有识其体例者，习处既久，好尚亦移[1]。

The Western style of painting puts many efforts to establish the verisimilitude effect, nine out of ten through the help of medical potion. As tiny as the turn of a hair, as many details as there are, all of them would be reflected, as if put under a microscope. Its coloring is so wonderful, that every difference between cloud shadows and water trace, candle light and moon rays, clear day and rainy weather, broad day and nighttime, becomes manifest to observe, whether in the vicinity or from afar. A scene looks blurry and indistinguishable when it is looked at with the naked eye; but with the instrument [of a photographic camera], one will experience the scene as if he himself is placed within it. Particularly the characters within paintings, they are so vividly represented as to come into life. Chinese painters, restrained by conventions and customs, have sets of patterns in their mind, and would arrange a framing first before they configure the space for the power of painting. Whether the pictorial structure is loose or tight, the spirit intense or light, is dependent on the depth of the painter's learning and the extension of the painter's vision. The essential difference is that verisimilitude is the priority in Western paintings, and delicate spirit in Chinese paintings. For the painting to be verisimilar, it has to be realistic, while it does not necessarily take realistic efforts to achieve delicate spirit. Since not all of it is realistic, it becomes not necessary to represent the incident through its appearance and shape. True, the Chinese tradition has books such as *Complete Collection of*

[1] Zunwenge Zhuren, the *Dianshizhai Pictorial*, Issue I, May 8, 1884.

> *Illustrations and Writings from the Earliest to Current Times* and *Collected Illustrations of the Three Realms*, the systematization of materials and instruments, and the sophisticated naming and ways of describing things. But, books of this kind communicate knowledge on things, materials and systems with illustrations from the ancient times to the present. Examples are countless. Its primary purpose is to avoid confusions in naming. Its primary means is words, which cannot convey the precision and accuracy of matters concerned. Some matters have to appeal to the power of paintings, and even those paintings are not following conventionalized styles of social news pictures. Nevertheless, now we are at a historical time when the world is where it is, and increasing open space becomes possible for foreign things. It becomes the case that some Chinese begin to familiarize themselves with styles of Western culture, and as they learn things gradually, social customs begin to move to new directions.

Major affirms the stereotypical dichotomy between the mimetic tradition of Western painting and the expressive modes that characterize Chinese painting, and attributes the verisimilitude of Western painting largely to the effect of photography. We will return to this point in the space below.

Crowds occupy a significant presence of the spectacles in the *Dianshizhai*. They very often appear as collective spectators, which are portrayed as urban spectacles in turn. Historically speaking, there were crowds thronging into Shanghai in the late nineteenth century when the urban environment in Shanghai had undergone drastic transformations. That creates what Meng Yue calls the "chaotic cosmopolitan culture in Shanghai" (Meng 100). This is a reflection of the demographic dynamics of the city. Refuges from wars, droughts, crimes among other natural or social misfortunes in neighboring provinces flooded to Shanghai, which became a treaty port in 1843 owing to the Treaty of Nanking (Nanjing) of the Opium War signed by the British and Qing governments. As early as in 1861, the *Shanghai Xinbao*, the first modern newspaper in Shanghai, writes in its founding issue: "In a place like Shanghai people from all over are mixed together. This creates obstacles to doing business, such as the inability to manage one another's dialects and the failure to hear about news" (qtd. in Lee 362). The increasing growth and diversity of its populace has changed Shanghai's urban geographic landscape[1]. Along with its demographic changes came its social and cultural encounters with the modern. Since the middle of the nineteenth century, modern facilities were introduced into Shanghai very quickly: modern banks in 1848, Western-styled streets in 1856, gas lamps in 1865, telephone in 1881, electricity in 1882, tap water in 1884, automobiles in 1901 and trolley bus in 1908[2]. The city became a place of high cultural diversity and social dislocation. It was "the great newspaper-exporting city" (Lee and Nathan 368). Art historian Jonathan Hay identifies that a sense of "big-city edginess" (Hay 87) existed in late Qing Shanghai school of painting. The city was the harbinger of Chinese modernity. A liminal space is thus cultivated at the edge of the Qing Empire with a bourgeoning mass media of print.

In their still classical study on the emergent mass culture from late Qing through the republican period, Leo Ou-fan Lee and Andrew J. Nathan point out that, in treaty-port concessions like Shanghai, many political and commercial journals sought registration often in the name of foreign agents for the purpose of avoiding government repression[3], and "[m]odern printing machines, which are essential to rapid production of a large number of copies of a periodical, were available only in large treaty ports, as was the imported paper that these machines required" (Lee and Nathan 368). According to Christopher Reed's historical study, Shanghai publishing industry witnessed a rapid growth from the 1880s forward, and by 1937 "an overwhelming 86 percent of all books published in China appeared under a Shanghai imprint" (qtd. in Des Forges 17). Thanks to an efficient transmission network,

[1] For Shanghai's changing cartography in the late nineteenth century, see Ye Kaidi, "Nali shi Shanghai?" (Where was Shanghai?).

[2] See Leo Ou-fan Lee, *Shanghai Modern*, pp. 6-7.

[3] See Leo Ou-fan Lee and Andrew J. Nathan, "The Beginnings of Mass Culture," p. 368.

including new roads and railroads, Chinese Post Office, local post offices (书信馆, *Shuxin guan*) from various nations, bookstores, traditional letter-carrying hongs, riverine paddle-boats and the like, "the urban-centered press achieved wide distribution throughout the nation" (Lee and Nathan 370). Newspapers from Shanghai or Tokyo could easily reach such distant inter-land places as Gansu and Sichuan. This enhanced the accessibility of the visual media of print pictorials under discussion here.

Regarding the rise of a "scopic regime"[1] and its correlative relation with Western modernity, art historian Jonathan Crary argues that changes of vision and visuality since the seventeenth- till the nineteenth-centuries are part of the larger rationalizations for reshaping the human faculty of sight, and that they came along with inventions of certain optical devices like *camera obscura* and the stereoscope. For Crary, vision and visuality relate to changing perceptions of human subjectivity and identity, and the observer become "the site of certain practices, techniques, institutions, and procedures of subjectification" (Crary 1990: 5). The observer in the nineteenth-century West is that of abstraction through modernity experience, who "increasingly had to function within disjunctive and defamiliarized urban spaces, the perceptual and temporal dislocations of railroad travel, telegraphy, industrial production, and flows of typographic and visual information" (11). Different from this history of vision and visuality in Western modernity, the Chinese case of pictorial culture presented here promotes a liminal space of sensorial freedom, a way of being imposed by neither the Western possessive individualism nor Chinese feudalistic imperial subjectivity. In between the classical literacy institution and an emergent modern vernacular literature to come in late Qing China, the visual cultural practice does not fit into the configuration of Western modernity. Instead, it presents a liberating though evanescent moment of cross-fertilized subjectivity through modern media and mediation. This is what this chapter tries to salvage by examining representations of crowds in between the pictorial

[1] This terminology is taken from Martin Jay's "Scopic Regimes of Modernity."

and the literary.

The *Dianshizhai Pictorial* presents crowds in various public viewing events, and they are often public and "collective voyeurs" (Bao 2005: 445-446). In a piece from the *Shenbao* on September 20, 1896, a reporter was writing about his viewing experience in a Strange Garden (奇园, *Qiyuan*) of a huge painting from the United States depicting its Civil War. The reportage was written in classical language, which was accessible only to those with trained literacy. Historically, as early as in 1876, newspapers using vernacular Chinese appeared in Shanghai, the first of which was the *People Newspaper* (民报, *Minbao*). A broad vernacular movement occurred in between 1876 and the end of the Qing Dynasty [1]. It was not until 1905 that the institution of imperial examination was still practiced, and the classical language, which was its official language for longer than a thousand of years, still enjoyed its supremacy of official status. As a language of the elite and the gentry, it is distinctively different from spoken vernaculars and takes years of training for its literacy. This is to say that, writings in the middle- to high-brow *Shenbao*, unlike illustrations in the *Dianshizhai*, discriminate classes of readers according to their literacy ability. It came as no surprise that literacy in urban areas was much higher. According to a historical study from Evelyn Rawski, male adult literacy in Daoguang era (1821—1850) in Guangzhou could be at 80 to 90 percent.[2] It should also be mentioned that there exists a gendered literacy rate. In the Qing Dynasty, basic literacy in the nineteenth century was beteen 30 and 45 percent for adult males, and between 2 and 10 percent for adult females[3].

---

[1] There were more than 140 vernacular newspapers in China, with 27 based in Shanghai. Xiong Yuezhi and Zhang Min, 《上海通史·晚清文化》(*Shanghai tongshi Wanqing wenhua*) [*A Survey History of Shanghai: Late Qing Culture*], p. 496. For a list of select vernacular newspapers published in Shanghai, see pp. 501-502. Also see Ma Guangren, *Shanghai xinwen shi 1850—1949* (*History of Journalism in Shanghai, 1850—1949*), pp. 282-287; Zhang Zhen, *An Amorous History of the Silver Screen*, pp. 21-23.

[2] Rawski, *Education and Popular Literacy in Ch'ing China*, pp. 11-12, 17. Also see Des Forges, *Mediasphere Shanghai*, p. 10.

[3] Evelyn Rawski has suggested that literacy was quite widespread in late imperial China, especially among urban males. See Rawski, *Education and Popular Literacy in Ch'ing China*, pp. 10-13, 140-146. Also see Des Forges, *Mediasphere Shanghai*, p.10.

This "奇园观油画记" ("Qiyuan guan youhua ji") ["Viewing a Painting in the Strange Garden"] of the *Shenbao* reads:

> 画为南北美利坚交战之图，经泰西画史穷十余年之心力，始克渲染告成。巨笔淋漓，大可蔽数亩。岁丙申，日人之好事者度地本邑泥城桥畔，支板为屋，命曰'奇园'将书幅陈列其中，招人观览。中秋前二日，轻寒薄暖，细雨如丝。午后，园主折柬以招，乃偕友散步而往。门者速之入，初行小弄中，朦胧如黑夜。旋见一灯如豆，始知梯在是。蹑而登，不觉豁然开朗，别有一天……日色黯淡，阴云蔽空，李华《吊古战场文》恐亦无此惨状。考南北美利坚战务起于一千八百六十年，其始只缘黑奴故耳……迨至一千八百六十五年，新总统旋凯庆贺，而已。[1]

> The painting is a war scene in the American Civil War, and it took over a decade's hard work by Western master painters to get accomplished. Its painting brushes are incisive, and its size is as large as several *mu* of land. In 1896, some interested Japanese measured a piece of land by the side of a Muddy Town Bridge in this county, set up boards as an exhibition house titled as *Qiyuan* for the painting to be visited by people. Two days before the mid-Autumn festival, the weather was chilly, and only slightly warm. It was drizzling. In that afternoon, I, as invited by a letter from the host of *Qiyuan*, walked to there with a couple of friends. We entered the door, and strolled in a small lane under darkness like walking in nighttime, for a while. Then, we saw a light ahead small like one pea, from which we recognized the direction of a staircase. Light-stepped, we climbed onto and across it. All of a sudden, everything is enlightening and there came a whole new world .... The sunlight became grey and the sky was full of clouds. It looks even more miserable than in Tang Dynasty Li Hua's *Elegy to the Ancient Battlefield.* A brief research would tell that the American Civil War was ignited in 1860, merely because of the black slave issue. It went on until 1865 when a new

[1] Quoted in Laikwan Pang, *The Distorting Mirror*, p. 174.

president celebrated its victory over the South. That is all.

A glimpse of this reportage suggests that the author entertains a cosmopolitan kind of knowledge of the world: the US, the West, Japan, the American civil war, slavery of African-Americans, Tang China.

On the September 2, 1896 issue of the *Shenbao*, the exhibition of this American civil war painting has been advertised:

> 开设英大马路近跑马场高大圆房便是：奇园南北花旗大战图，内设炮台营垒兵马战将交锋炮火连天尸横遍野……
>
> This is in the high and large round house next to the race house on the main road in the British Concession: A painting of Americans fighting each other between the South and the North in *Qiyuan*: a picture of artillery fort, military barracks, soldiers and horses, shooting everywhere, corpses rampant.

However, what seems an exhibition of a museum kind open to the public in the *Shenbao* advertisement turns out to more of a private outing activity in the reportage. It was staged two days before the traditional Chinese mid-autumn festival, and many details were laid out previous to the activity. In the reportage we read how the *Qiyuan* was established by a Japanese resident, and how the painting took more than ten years to come to its completion, and what the weather was like. Historically speaking, it was in 1868 that Shanghai built its first museum, namely, the Museum of Natual History by the Jesuits[1]. The way of describing in the *Shenbao* reportage reminds of conventional Chinese literati travelogue. It presents a sense of sociality recognizable in conventional literati travel writings, which is manifested through the contrast between the indoor space of enlightenment ("豁然开朗") and the threshold of darkness ("朦胧如黑夜")[2], the mention of Tang

[1] 徐家汇博物馆 (Xujiahui bowuguan) [Xujiahui Museum], established by Pierre Heude, a French Jesuit. See Xiong Yuezhi and Zhang Min, 《上海通史・晚清文化》(*Shanghai tongshi Wanqing wenhua*) [*A Survey History of Shanghai: Late Qing Culture*], p. 203-204.

[2] See Laikwan Pang, *The Distorting Mirror*, pp. 174-175.

Dynasty Li Hua's *Elegy*, and the moralization made upon the American civil war. That disillusionment through the long channeling of darkness was probably expected to be morally elevating, and the enlightenment afterwards shows a moment of awakening from media immersion. The literati writer of this *Shenbao* reportage enjoys "the primacy of spiritual vision and anti-illusionism," "precisely the burden of the literati tradition that modern minded Chinese radicals were trying to unload" (Wang 2001: 101). He probably did not realize what was realism and how it was considered as progressive by late Qing and Republican intellectuals. Or, this might be one strategy taken to accommodate the sense of shock of modernity—which the newspaper advertisement and public museum-kind exhibition intend to arouse, and the new institution of public visuality is remediated into a tradition of literati gathering. This is a process of media shift. The old media of literary writing takes over the public space involved in museum visiting. Within this short reportage several kinds of media are hybridized together—painting (the American painting), gardening (*Qiyuan*), touring (the mid-autumn festival atmosphere and rainy day), historiography (Li Hua's *Elegy to the Ancient Battlefield*, written in the eighth century about wars in centuries B.C.), and history (the American civil war).

What remains of more significance is to see the similarities as well as differences between this literary description and its visual representation, since there exists one *Dianshizhai* lithographical representation of the American Civil War painting watching experience of the 1896 *Shenbao* reportage on the *Qiyuan* event. The textualized news information reported in the *Shenbao* piece was "transposed" into a pictorial representation—an example of what media theorist Friedrich A. Kittler would call "a transposition of media."[1] And according to Des Forges, this "transposition of a textual aesthetic into a new 'extratextual' dimension" was becoming a fashion when "'diversion' [消闲, *xiaoxian*] has taken on a new prominence in the theories of literature," and this

[1] Friedrich A. Kittler, *Discourse Networks, 1800/1900*, in particular the section "Untranslatability and the Transposition of Media," in "Rebus," pp. 265-273.

"brings the world and the text together in a dystaxic or intercutting relationship, putting narrative lines inside and outside the text to a certain extent on equal footing" (Des Forges 86). In the *Dianshizhai* lithographic representation (奇园读画, Reading the Pictorial in the Qi Garden, Figure 1), we see a painting engulfing the viewers, who stand inside the railing at the lower left-hand corner[1]. The railing serves as a blurred media framing between the painting and its audience. The overwhelming visual impression from the painting seems almost not to be contained within the sensorial control of the audience. There is a tension of visual confrontation between those in the painting and the crowds watching it, and the boundary, which the framing tries to maintain, at the first sight, is not easily recognized. It is noteworthy that the verbal descriptions of the painting in both the inscription within the lithographic representation and the *Shenbao* reportage work to create a realistic dimension: the painting is reported to have been accomplished by a Western painter spending more than 10 years on it, and it is as large as able to cover several *mu* (亩, about 0.0667 hectares) area of land, almost as large as the garden in which it was exhibited.

Most of the *Dianshizhai* pictorials consist of journalistic paintings, battle depictions or portraitures, and the realistic effect was always a major concern for the management of the journal. Ernest Major claimed that Western perspectivalism and photography are superior techniques and technologies comparing to Chinese painting[2]. The painting of the American Civil War reproduced in the *Dianshizhai* is drawn in the Chinese lithographic style of the time, and that is different from the realist art in Western tradition. Zheng Yimei (郑逸梅) thinks that the effect of observational realism in the *Dianshizhai* is even comparable to what was to be realized in those 1920s pictorials, which used direct copies from photography[3]. However, the Chinese painters associated

[1] The analysis of this lithographical representation in the *Dianshizhai* is greatly inspired by Laikwan Pang in her *The Distorting Mirror,* p. 175.

[2] See Zunwenge Zhuren, the *Dianshizhai Pictorial,* Issue I, May 8, 1884.

[3] See Zheng Yimei, 《上海的画报潮》("Shanghai de huabao chao") ["Waves of Pictorials in Shanghai"], p.244.

with Ernest Major and the Shenbao Press, the most famous of whom was Wu Youru (?—1893), distinguished their work from traditional literati painting. They were among the first group of modern Chinese professional painters, and their livelihood depended on mass market. The objects of their work were more likely to be realistic things and scenes[1]. These artists, employed by the *Dianshizhai* pictorial, were paid to paint what they had never seen before—Western geography, natural plants and animals, new technological innovations and machines, et cetera. The objects of the painting art were changed into the contemporary things and events that the world was experiencing, rather than the previous generic themes of traditional Chinese painting, such as flowers, birds, worms, fishes or characters, hills or waters. Nevertheless, their work, as demonstrated in the lithographic pictorials in the *Dianshizhai*, contained traces of features from traditional calligraphy and painting. The cross-fertilization of their forms of art, traditional and modern, realistic and spiritual, helped to achieve commercial success for the *Shenbao* press. A piece from 《北华捷报》(*Beihua jiebao*) [*North-China Herald*] on May 25, 1889, titled as《上海石印书业之发展》("Shanghai Shiyin shuye zhi fazhan") ["The Development in Lithography and History of the Book in Shanghai"], writes:

> 石印的另一优点是比木刻容易保存书法的优美，石印局都雇有若干书法好的人，报酬较高。
>
> Another strength in lithography is that it is easier to keep the beauty of calligraphy in it than in woodblock. The lithography office employed several hands great at calligraphic work and paid them with very decent salaries[2].

[1] See Rudolf G. Wagner,《进入全球想象图景：上海的〈点石斋画报〉》("Jinru quanqiu xiangxiang tujing: Shanghai de *Dianshizhai huabao*) ["Joining the Global Imaginary: the *Dianshizhai Pictorial* in Shanghai"], p. 84.

[2] Cited from Chen Pingyuan,《新闻与石印——〈点石斋画报〉之成立》("Xinwen yu shiyin—*Dianshizhai huabao* zhi chengli"), ["News and Lithography: the Establishment of the *Dianshizhai Pictorial*"], p. 64.

On July 24, 1897, the *Shenbao* published an advertisement for the *Dianshizhai* — 《照相石印各种名画发售》 ("Zhaoxiang shiyin gezhong minghua fashou") ["Marketing for Various Famous Paintings in Photographical Lithography"]:

> 本点石斋用照相石印之法，印成各种画幅，勾勒工细，神采如生，久蒙中外赏鉴家誉不绝口。兹又印成各种名画，与初写时不爽毫厘者若干种，特一一开列于下，诸君早日赐顾为盼。
>
> Our Touching Stone Studio adopted a device of photographical lithography, printed various kinds of pictures, which are vividly made with precision and accuracy. This became widely acclaimed by connoisseurs home and abroad. Now, our studio begins to replicate various kinds of famous paintings, and they are almost as they were originally painted. The catalogue is as follows and we expect to see you as soon as possible.

A new sense of visuality was emerging, in the process of which there existed many cases of experimentation, anxiety and crises[1]. In Chinese painting, the positions of its objects are always arranged through long traditions, the stability of which assures the sense of world order imposed upon the external world. The new objects brings a new way of knowing, which underlines objectivity, positivity and scientific methods. The combination of Chinese painting of this kind and the print technology of lithography produce a different sense of realism, and it brings forth a distinctive aesthetics of perceptual structures, subjectivity and sociality.

Laikwan Pang observes that "line is the main graphic element in Chinese lithographic art" and "natural elements like trees, mountains, and rivers are often depicted in the traditional Chinese style, whereas modern items like urban buildings and modern transportation devices are

[1] See Guo Enci and Su Jue, 《中国现代设计的诞生》 (*Zhongguo xiandai sheji de dansheng*) [*The Birth of Modern Chinese Design*], pp. 130-146.

drawn with rigid lines and solid surfaces" (Pang 2007: 44). Based on Pang's point, this chapter argues that their combination suggests an embryonic state in between tradition and modern, and it produces amorphous representations that could be identified as "spectral." It is a strange sense of hybridization of traditional Chinese painting and new things and social events, and it does not always come together. This is a manifestation of complicated modernity where a new mode of perceptual self comes into being through an imbrication of different media, Chinese or Western, old or new, verbal or visual. In the compositional structure of this lithography pictorial of the *Qiyuan* event, "the reception space and the pictorial space were rendered in the same style, further reinforcing the impression that the representation and its reception were within the same reality" (175). The crowd spectators are not discrete from their viewing objects, almost immersed into the war spectacle represented in the realistic American painting of civil war. A further look indicates that the inscription in the uppermost of the pictorial tells not merely the current location, its history of making, and its subject of the painting, but also "provides some hint of narrative" (175):

> 有中炮而血肉纷飞者，有受弹而僵踣于地者，有方为墙之进者，有因败衄而逃者。山麓之间，尸横枕藉……
>
> Some were shot by guns and cannons. Their limbs flew out of bodies. Some, hit by bullets, fell down. Some, seeing a wall, chose to hide themselves behind it. Some, seeing they were losing, chose to run away. Corpses were everywhere, between hills and rivers.

This description is very suggestive of the causal relation of the incidents portrayed, which is communicated through a "progression of time" (175). Some happen to see a wall and hide themselves behind it, and some run away because they feel that they are losing. Along with descriptions of the verbal descriptions of the progressive time, the affective and psychological states of mind of the soldiers portrayed become accessible to the audience. This explanation of the pictorial within the lithography is made by the writer of the inscription and largely taken from the *Shenbao* reportage, the latter of whose classical style precludes those not trained in classical literacy. In late nineteenth-century China, pictorial paintings, inscriptions within paintings' pictorial compositions, and newspaper articles on the pictorial are usually by different authors[1]. This means that the *Shenbao* reportage, the lithographic representation of the viewing experience, and the inscription within that representation could be from different hands. It suggests that the authorial subjectivity emerging through early modern in the West—as suggested through the death of author arguments by Roland Barthes and Michel Foucault[2]—is not applicable in our investigation upon the relation between the image, and the two verbal descriptions. Narration in classical language is processed through trained literacy, and it speaks only to those sophisticated readers.

On the other hand, visual representation has a broader audience, and comes as pleasurable cultural products for consumption[3]. Half a century after the last issue of the *Dianshizhai* in 1898, Bao Tianxiao, a novelist in the republican period, writes about his experience of the *Dianshizhai* in his *Memoirs of Kushiro Studio*:

> 我在十二三岁的时候，上海出有一种石印的《点石斋画报》，我最喜欢看了。本来儿童最喜欢看画，而这个画报，即使成人也喜欢看的。每逢出版，寄到苏州来时，我宁可省下了点心钱，必须去购买一册。这是每十天出一册，积十册便可以线装成一本。我当时就有装订成好几本。虽然那些画师也没有什么博识，可是在画上也可以得着一点常识。因为上海那个地方是开风气之先的，

---

[1] Xiaoqing Ye, *The Dianshizhai Pictorial*, p. 52.

[2] Michel Foucault, "What Is an Author"; Roland Barthes, "The Death of the Author."

[3] Here it involves the structural difference between narration and description. For the narratologist Gerard Genette, description may be thought of as the moment in narration when the technology of memory—and what is to be memorized: "experience, custom, tradition, and habit"—threatens to collapse into the materiality of its means. Description typically "stops" or arrests the temporal movement through narrative. It "spreads out the narrative in space" (Gerald Genette, "The Frontiers of Narrative," p.136).

外国的什么新发明、新事物，都是先传到上海。譬如像轮船、火车，内地人当时都没有见过的，有它一编在手，可以领略了。风土、习俗，各处有什么不同的，也有了一个印象。其时，外国已经有了气球了，画报上也画了出来[1]。

When I was 12 or 13, Shanghai published a lithographically-made *Dianshizhai huabao*, which became my favorite. Indeed, children like pictures very much, and this pictorial was enjoyed by adults as well. Whenever it was published and disseminated to Suzhou, I would sacrifice my pocket money for snacks to get a volume. It had one issue coming out every 10 days. One could bind ten issues together and make a book out of it. Back then, I made several books of them. Though those painters did not have broad knowledge, one could always learn something from the pictures. Because Shanghai was a place of fashion, many new inventions and fashionable things, like steamship and trains, first went to Shanghai before people in the inter-lands even had chances to hear of them. With the pictorial, one could see what they were actually like. At that time, foreign countries already invented flying balloons, which appeared in the pictorial right away.

Thus, the pictorial newspaper could be enjoyed by a child of limited literacy, whose viewing experience of modernity is absorptive and pleasurable like consumption of snacks. Visual representations of modernity are thus more easily accessible to those at the margin of the traditional literacy institution, and they brought in new experiences of Western perceptual modernity. As a matter of fact, the balloon images in the pictorial were prominent, and literary scholar Chen Pingyuan takes it as part of the novel flying vehicles that appeared in popular science journals of the 1870s, illustrated newspaper such as the *Dianshizhai,* and science fiction at the turn of the twentieth century. For Chen, this is

[1] Bao Tianxiao, *Memoirs of Kushiro Studio* (《钏影楼回忆录》, *Chuanyinglou huiyilu*), p.114.

suggestive of the public fascination with the novel flying vehicle as embodying a new world consciousness and scientific imagination[1]. Bao Weihong sees these balloon images "as a figure of a new mode of visuality which is both embodied in the image of the balloon and also realized in the image composition of the pictures where the balloon appears" (Bao 2005: 436).

Verbal description within lithographic pictorials of the *Dianshizhai* often comments through a worldview of ancient historiography or the ethics of heaven or conventional Chinese wisdom. It tends to be more traditional, as indicated through the mention of Tang Dynasty Li Hua's *Elegy to the Ancient Battlefield* in the case under discussion. What remains more significant to this lithography is the similar positioning of the inscription and the viewers in the reception space, who are rendered as if they are reacting to the sound, sight, and affective intensity of the Civil War painting. The sense of realism, as reflected in the large size civil war painting through its rigid lines and solid surfaces, is maintained within the Western-styled balustrade, while the balustrade tries to keep the viewing group of the *Qiyuan* distinct from their viewing object. The boundary between these two seems hard to maintain: the painting medium and its audience of media consumption in the *Qiyuan* almost come into each other, especially when some of the audience are stretching their necks to look beyond. One of the viewers dresses himself in Western clothing and mingles his appearance with the American soldiers in the painting[2]. This, like the buzzy zone structure between performance space and other kinds of space in the Peking Opera theater of the same historical period[3], might be taken as an "immaturity" of late Qing modern visual media. It might result from the technical difficulties that the *Dianshizhai* painters had to accommodate

---

[1] See Chen Pingyuan,《以图像为中心——关于点石斋画报》, (Yi tuxiang wei zhongxin—guanyu *Dianshizhai huabao*) [Centering Picture—on the *Dianshizhai Pictorial*], p.94.

[2] See Laikwan Pang, *The Distorting Mirror*, pp. 164-183.

[3] For a historical investigation of the development of Peking Opera, see Joshua Goldstein, *Drama Kings*.

an American realistic painting and a museum-like garden visual experience into one pictorial frame[1]. It is exactly this kind of "awkwardness" that creates a "spectral" possibility of representations in the beginning of modern Chinese mass media. This is emblematic of the cultural hybridity in late nineteenth-century Shanghai. The audiences are intensively absorbed in their relation with the American painting, and turn out to be staged for the audience of the overall lithographic pictorial. The experience of Western modernity in viewing a modern war is thus mediated through a theatrical buffer zone in between representation and reality. This blurred boundary between absorption and theatricality throws light upon new forms of subjectivity and consciousness in an amorphous, embryonic and mediated state of being. The sight, sound, psychology of the American Civil war is represented lithographically to a group of audience. They, in turn, become a spectacle to the targeted audience of the *Dianshizhai*, who, owing to their limited literacy, may not be able to approach the *Shenbao* verbal reportage of the same visual event. This is an incipient sign of the perceptual modern in its spectral mediation before the coming of the well-defined May Fourth literary print modern. Its existence is framed through various layers of mediation and sensorial activities.

The *Qiyuan duhua* pictorial of the *Dianshizhai* is presented either as an ongoing reality or a stage performance. It is not a still picture. All of the viewers, standing inside the railing at the lower left-hand corner, are also portrayed in a theatrical situation, watching as well as being watched. Their attention upon the spatial environment is directed to the American civil war painting within the pictorial as well as to something without, probably the viewers of the lithography. If soldiers in the war are situated in a realistic war scene and choose to ignore its audience, the viewers of the war painting within the balustrade show a sense of awareness of its being watched. They are theatrically-staged, that is to say. The American civil war is mediated to its late Qing Chinese

---

[1] Cf. Guo Enci and Su Jue,《中国现代设计的诞生》(*Zhongguo xiandai sheji de dansheng*) [*The Birth of Modern Chinese Design*], pp. 130-146.

audience through their watching in the *Qiyuan*, whose geographical location mediates the war event through its mass spectators to the audience of the pictorial. It is a cross-fertilized media event represented through the lithographical technology, and its composition presents us an almost multi-media environment of painting, museum, theater, print and garden. All media activities squeeze into this one pictorial frame with meticulous details. This lithographic pictorial representation far exceeds what photography claims as its distinction from lithography—realistic mimesis, that is.

In the "Preface" of the *Dianshizhai*, Major compares the differences between Chinese and Western paintings. He affirms the stereotyped dichotomy between mimetic tradition of Western painting and expressive modes that characterize Chinese painting. The verisimilitude effect of Western painting is largely attributed to the modern technology of photography[1]. The miraculous mimetic power of photography is manifest, as Major observes: "A scene looks blurry and indistinguishable when it is looked at with the naked eye; but with the instrument [of a photographic camera], one will experience the scene as if he himself is placed within it." The photographic apparatus is accorded a quality of objectivity that complements the subjective—"as if he himself is placed within it." The naked eye, instead, is a too subjective and embodied device to be able to make abstract objective lines and realities. The "blurry and indistinguishable" effect in the *Qiyuan* pictorial, however, complements a multi-media framing and provides an enriching mediated experience that "as if he himself is placed within it." Rather than a clearly demarcated single media representation, the *Dianshizhai* produces a form of media immersion made possible through the lithographic pictorial print culture in late nineteenth-century China. The viewers of the war painting within the pictorial are self-reflexively aware of their being staged for the audience of the pictorial, the latter of whom are mirrored by the viewers within. The urban crowds become modern through their mediated presence in a relation to the sense of

[1] See Bao Weihong, "A Panoramic Worldview," p. 443.

realism as displayed in an American civil war painting. The mediating stage within the lithographic pictorial may be read as a metaphor of Chinese means of accommodating the impact of modernity in late nineteenth century. The ambivalent status of being in between watching and being watched indicates an embryonic collective experience of theatrical modernity, differing from consciousness or subjectivity that is individuated, the latter of which was to be fabricated in the coming New Culture Movement 1919.

As a comparison, the emergence of Western modern art in eighteenth and nineteenth centuries experiences a strong sense of what W. J. T. Mitchell terms as "the purism of modernist abstraction," which is a strong sense of the "negation of the beholder's presence" (Mitchell 2006: 44). Rather than cleansing the presence of viewers and their beholding experience, the *Dianshizhai* embraces them, and thus presents layers of theatrically mediated crowds. Spectators and viewing of this kind appear in almost every picture of the *Dianshizhai*[1]. Bao Weihong argues that the collective viewing experience through a mediating device seems to "parallel the rather recent technological mediation of vision and experience that constitute public readership or spectatorship" (Bao 2005: 444) and she locates the exhibition of early Western cinema in China as thriving on a pictorial print culture[2]. Following this argument, this essay argues that the visual activities of urban culture reflect the existence of substantial urban crowds, and their spectral access to visual culture is self-reflexively represented in the theatrical experience located in between the visual and the print. The visual literacy of the crowds and their consumptive activities of staging and viewing are less than apparent to be traceable. Bao Tianxiao, who was to become a writer, offers a portal to examine this trace of visual consumption of modernity through literary writing. Our knowledge of his experience is made possible through his ability to write as a novelist. In other words, the access to a history of the cross-fertilized inter-media immersion is

---

[1] See Bao Weihong, "A Panoramic Worldview," p. 444
[2] See Bao Weihong, "A Panoramic Worldview," p. 448

mediated through a modern Chinese literary writing. Bao's autobiographical writing embraces individuated literary subjectivity, and this is suggested by its title—*Memoirs of Kushiro Studio*, which indicates a domesticated and interiorized memory. Many members of the chaotic crowds may not be able to perform what this literacy institution requires, and this makes it difficult to capture this spectral inter-media state of immersion. In this sense, the pictorial *Dianshizhai* is one of the sites where trace of spectral crowds of this kind becomes locatable.

Laikwan Pang reads the *Shenbao* piece on the *Qiyuan* event along with another report found in the *Youxibao* (*Newspaper of Leisures*) in 1897, in which a first-time moviegoer elaborately describes a film show that he saw in *Qiyuan*, and details his feelings of shock and amusement after watching the actuality films. Widely considered to be the first documentation of the earliest film viewing in China[1], the essay begins:

> 近有美国电光影戏，制同影灯而奇妙幻化皆出人意料之外者。昨夕雨后新凉，偕友人忘奇园观焉。座客既集，停灯开演，旋见现一影，两西女作跳舞状，黄发蓬蓬，憨态可掬。又一影，两西人作角抵戏……
>
> There was an electric light shadow-play from the United States, with magical effects beyond anyone's expectations. Yesterday evening was breezy. After the rain, some friends and I went to the *Qiyuan* to watch the show. When all the viewers had been seated, the lights were turned off. All of a sudden we saw an image of two Western women dancing. Their hairs were yellow, and their manners were cute and lovely. Then, it was followed by anther image, in which two Westerners seemed to be playing acrobatics .... [2]

Stylistically, it seems that both this writer and the reporter of the American civil war painting viewing event were prepared to confront the

[1] Anonymous,《观美国影戏集》"Guan meiguo yingxiji" [Watching American Shadow Plays], *Youxibao* [*Newspaper of Leisures*], September 5, 1897.
[2] Quoted in Laikwan Pang, *The Distorting Mirror*, p. 174.

fantastic images. Pang notices that "the ritual of traveling through a dark passage had the effect of separating cinematic or painting spectacles from everyday life," and "the passages helped them to rationalize the alternative reality presented in the theatrical space" (Pang 2007: 177). Through this ritual of travelling, the American new media of actuality film is accommodated to its Chinese audience, for whom the American acrobatics is comparable to Chinese *Jiaodixi*. Both this *Youxibao* writer and the *Shenbao* reporter went to the same *Qiyuan*, which, as "part of an elaborate culture of 'watching'" (179), housed motion pictures, the American Civil War painting, and probably many exciting horse races popular then in Shanghai. This highly kinetic viewing environment is "part of the new entertainment culture," and "their [visitors'] ability to move in and out of the spectacles should be understood as a manifestation of their pride in their newly acquired modern identity and as an upper-middle-class privilege" (181). The ability of literary writing and publishing in newspapers like *Youxibao* and *Shenbao* to disseminate this knowledge of their viewing experience is correlated with this burgeoning upper-middle-class modern urban culture. In other words, that they went through "ritual of traveling through a dark passage" into "the alternative reality presented in the theatrical space" is performed through their privilege of being able to enjoy the institution of literacy. It becomes possible by the means of the reflexive effect of acts of writing coming after the visual experience. In both the *Youxibao* writing and the *Shenbao* report, a passage of travelling is clearly drawn before the viewing, and this is the style of traditional literati travelogue, which shows how Western new media such as the actuality film is accommodated into the Chinese institution of literacy. Their social and class status is also suggested by the cultural capital of the *Qiyuan* that they visited. In contrast, the lithographic representation of the same *Qiyuan* experience in the *Dianshizhai* is without any foreplay of travelling or disillusionment. In the lithographical pictorial, crowds rather than literary individuals reflect themselves spectrally through an inter-media unconscious. They act and react spontaneously, naturally, but not without mediation. They have a spectral existence in and without media representations in late nineteenth-century Shanghai. It is an amorphous form of collective spectatorship as reflected inter-medially.

The regime of visuality in the *Dianshizhai* case is of inter-media immersive absorption and theatricality, and its difference from writing brings significant light upon the perceptual difference between word and image. Let's take another look at the 1896 *Shenbao* report. The *Qiyuan*, located west of the Muddy Town Bridge on Grand Avenue in the British Concession ("英大马路泥城桥西首有奇园焉"), was a temporary lodge built by Japanese ("日人之好事者") expressly to show this painting. In the second part of the *Shenbao* reportage one finds its author sentimentalizing upon his past experience of the civil war painting, which is not mentioned at all in the verbal inscription of the lithographic pictorial: Six years ago, when China and Japan were in peaceful relations with each other, he saw this Civil War painting in a Tokyo Bodhisattva temple ("东京浅草观音寺之畔"), with three of his Chinese friends—two as Qing Dynasty officials, one as scholar—and three of his Japanese friends. One of the Qing officials died in the war, one of the Japanese died of illness, and the rest of them either lost contact with each other, or could do nothing about the deteriorating political tension between the two nations. Thus,

> 偶观斯画，益不禁枨触于怀已。至于画之新奇，则海上人诚见所未见，风清日丽，盍往观乎？
>
> Accidentally seeing this painting again, I cannot help feeling sentimental. As to the novelty of the painting, it is surely something people in Shanghai had no chance to see yet. When weather is nice, why not go and see it?

A personal visual experience is connected with the geopolitical relations and the the War of Jiawu. This passage relating the personal with the political is reported only in the newspaper *Shenbao* in classical Chinese, and its accessibility requires considerable literary education. This is not presented in the *Dianshizhai* pictorial, the "reading" of which demands neither any substantial literary education nor any sense of enlightened subjectivity that goes with it. The sense of political education and enlightenment may be well beyond the understanding of Bao Tianxiao in his 12 or 13, who paid for the *Dianshizhai* his pocket money originally for snacks. The *Shenbao* was established in 1872, and here was its original ideal audience:

> 求其纪述当今时事，文则质而不俚，事则简而能详，上而学士大夫，下及农工商贾，皆能通晓者，则莫如新闻纸之善矣。
>
> Its purpose is to record contemporary events. Its language style should be plain but not colloquial, the events in it should be simple and with details. There is nothing better than newspapers, which is approachable not merely to literati and officials, but also to every walk of life[1].

Unfortunately, this was not fully realized and part of the actual audience of the newspaper was probably the sentimentalized gentry class[2]. The sentimentalized political knowledge that the *Shenbao* reportage contains may have been entirely incomprehensible to many members of the urban crowds audience of the pictorial, many of whom were refugees from inter-land wars and famines without any chances of

---

[1] Ernest Major, 《本报告白》 ("Benbao gaobai") ["A Statement from This Nespaper"], in the first issue of the *Shenbao*, April 30, 1872.

[2] See Rudolf G. Wagner, 《进入全球想象图景：上海的〈点石斋画报〉》 ("Jinru quanqiu xiangxiang tujing: Shanghai de *Dianshizhai huabao*) ["Joining the Global Imaginary: the *Dianshizhai Pictorial* in Shanghai"], pp. 161-162. The *Minbao* was established in March 26, 1876, and its editors-in-chief were Cai Erkang (蔡尔康) and Shen Yujia(沈毓佳). "此报专为民间所设，故字句俱如寻常说话。每句及人名地名尽行标明，庶几稍识字者便于解释。" ["This newspaper was established specifically for common people. Thus its vocabulary comes from everyday vernacular language. Every sentence, every name and address are all well marked, so that they are accessible to those with very basic literacy."] This was the earliest vernacular newspaper that was not established by the missionaries. It is a pity that it didn't survive long. Its targeted readership, those with very basic literacy, were struggling for survival in their everyday life and simply could not afford to enjoy reading newspapers. See Ma Guangren, 《上海新闻史：1850—1949》 (*Shanghai xinwen shi: 1850—1949*) [*A History of News in Shanghai: 1850—1949*], p.69.

trained literacy. These crowds of refugees probably would not have the privilege to initiate the Gongche Shangshu movement upon the signing of the Treaty of Shimonoseki in 1895—in the aftermath of the the War of Jiawu—as Kang Youwei and Liang Qichao did. In the late nineteenth century, classical Chinese writing reached its limit to make a populist enlightenment for the salvation of the nation and experience of modernity. Historian Zhang Pengyuan estimates the per-copy readership of some late Qing periodicals at ten to twenty persons.[1]

In the case of a pictorial like the *Dianshizhai*, the per-copy readership could be wider. An advertisement on July 1886, 《画报招登告白启》 ("Huabao zhaodeng gaobai qi") ["Public Notice of Inviting Publications for the Pictorial"], from the pictorial makes the point very clear:

> 今又承各巨商切属踵行，谓："天下容有不能读日报之人，天下无有不喜阅画报之人。近今告白借图以传，日报已有行之者，画报专精艺事，行之必有大效。"
>
> As told by all important merchants: 'There might be people who don't read newspapers, but people who dislike the pictorials don't exist. Recently public notice is disseminated through help from pictures. There are also daily newspapers with pictures. Thus it is predictable that pictorial newspapers, well versed in arts and literature, would be very efficient to that effect.'

The editorial "On How the Pictorial Can Enlighten," from the *Shenbao* August 29, 1895, three years previous to the last issue of its *Dianshizhai*, writes similarly:

> 上海自通商以后，取效西法，日刊日报出售，欲使天下之人咸知世务，法至善也。然中国识字者少，不识字者多，安能人人尽阅报章，亦何能人人尽知报中之事？于是创设画报，月出数册。
>
> Since its opening as a trading port, Shanghai learned from the

[1] Cf. Lee and Nathan, "The Beginning of Mass Culture," p. 372

West. The publishing of the newspaper is to enlighten people with the knowledge of the world. However, in China there are more illiterates than literates, and how can we let everyone read newspapers so as to know what is reported? For this purpose, we publish the pictorial at the base of several volumes monthly.

The rhetoric of enlightenment of modernity sounds not far from the correlation of the personal and the political in the *Shenbao* piece on the *Qiyuan* visual event. Both are communicated through the medium of writing. It comes very close to the pedagogy and enlightenment function attributed to the literary fiction by Liang Qichao in 1902 in his 《论小说与群治之关系》("Lun xiaoshuo yu qunzhi zhi guanxi") ["On the Relation between Fiction and the Government of the People"]:

欲新一国之民，不可不先新一国之小说。故欲新道德，必新小说；欲新宗教，必新小说；欲新政治，必新小说；欲新风俗，必新小说；欲新学艺，必新小说；乃至欲新人心，欲新人格，必新小说。何以故？小说有不可思议之力支配人道故。

In order for a nation of people to become modernized, that nation's fiction should be modernized first. Thus, to modernize morals, modernize fiction first; to modernize religion, modernize fiction first; to modernize politics, modernize fiction first; to modernize customs, modernize fiction first; to modernize learning and workmanship, modernize fiction first; to modernize people's heart, to modernize people's character, modernize fiction first. How so? Fictions can have amazing power over people.

Liang's essay was published on the first issue of 《新小说》(*Xin xiaoshuo*) [*New Fiction*] in November 1902. The difference lies in their respective technological approaches. One proposes to use the pictorial newspaper evoking visual literacy, and another the literary print fiction for political enlightenment. Liang pinpointed four basic "powers" of fiction: its power to "incense" (熏), to "immerse" (浸), to "goad" (刺), and to "uplift" (提) the reader. For Liang, the power of uplifting the reader to a higher plane of the hero and to persuade him to emulate the hero's exemplary behavior is of the greatest value of fiction writing to reform a whole nation's morality, religion, politics, customs, arts, and personhood[1]. As early as in his 1898《译印政治小说序》("Yiyin zhengzhi xiaoshuo xu") ["Preface to the Published Series of Translations of Political Fiction"], Liang attributes the political progress made in various modern nations to the dissemination of the political novel:

> 彼美、英、德、法、奥、意、日各国政界之日进，则政治小说为功最高焉。
>
> For the increasing social progress one observes in the political works of the USA, the UK, Germany, France, Austria, Italy and Japan, political fictions have been its primary driving force[2].

Liang managed to elevate fiction to "a position of unprecedented intellectual respectability in China" (Lee and Nathan 379-380) because of its identitarian function in the reformation of a dynasty into a modern nation-state. It is an individualistic as well as societal campaign through the means of the literary print. The spectrality of crowds as reflected inter-medially in the lithographic pictorial is lost ever since. Crowds become the object of political education and mobilization that are realized through the modern technology of writing and reading. They are targets of political enlightenment and are turned into potential citizens and members of a modern nation-state in the making. The kind of *qun* in Liang's scenario might be able to find its origin in Kang Youwei's political conviction of "以群为体，以变为用" ["Take *qun* as form, and change as essence"]. However, when Liang developed his theory of "新民" ["New People"] in 1902—the same year he wrote this

[1] "自化其身焉，入于书中，而为其书之主人公" ["One melts oneself into the book, and becomes its protagonist."]《论小说与群治之关系》("Lun xiaoshuo yu qunzhi zhi guanxi") ["On the Relation between the Novel and the Government of the People"].

[2] 《清议报》(*Qingyibao*) [*The China Discussions Newspaper*], Issue 1, December 1898.

"On the Relation between the Novel and the Government of the People," his concept of *qun* began to turn radically from Kang's harmonious picture of a dynastic *Tianxia* people into an idealized political order between individuals and communities under the category of a modern nation-state[1]. Indeed, critics argue that for Liang of this period, *qunzhi* [governance of crowds] and *xinminshuo* [theories on new people] are exchangeable terms[2]. The political significance of this *qun* lies in its connection with modern nation-state consciousness. As early as in his 1897《说群自序》("Shuo qun zixu") ["Preface to Discussions on *Qun* by Oneself"], Liang already attempted to make this point clear:

> 善治国者，知君之与民，同为一群之中之一人，因以知夫一群之中所以然之理。所常行之事，使其群和而不离，萃而不涣，夫是之谓群术。

> The best governing is to know both king and common person are equal members of a *qun*, and thus to know how a *qun* is what it is. What should be done is to harmonize rather than disintegrate a *qun*, to gather rather than disassemble a *qun*. This is called the art of governing *qun*[3].

This rhetoric of enlightenment seems necessarily to require a gendered—particularly male—stance of literacy, which entails a denigration of visuality. Liang's argument on the pedagogical function of fiction in the Enlightenment project can be seen as early as in Liang's《变法通义》("Bianfa tongyi") ["The General Meaning of Reform"] published before 1898 in《时务报》(*Shiwubao*) [*Newspapers of Current Affairs*], and might be attributed both to Kang Youwei's

[1] See Hao Chang, *Liang Ch'i-ch'ao and Intellectual Tradition in China*, pp. 150-155.

[2] Chen Jianhua,《从革命到共和：清末至民国时期文学、电影与文化的转型》(*Cong geming dao gonghe: qingmo zhi minguo shiqi wenxue dianying yu wenhua de zhuanxing*) [*From Revolution to Republicanism: Transformations in Literature, Cinema and Culture from Late Qing to Republican China*], p. 81.

[3]《时务报》(*Shiwubao*) [*Newspaper of Current Affairs*], Issue 26, May 1897, pp. 1729-1730. Cf. Chen Jianhua, p. 80.

influence in the latter's《日本书目志》(*Riben shumu zhi*) [*A Catalogue of Japanese Books*] and to Liang's exposure to Meiji Japanese literature and culture, especially the political novel of《佳人奇遇》(*Jiaren qiyu*) [*Strange Encounters with Beautiful Women*][1]. Liang's "On the Relation between Fiction and the Government of the People" was published in the initial issue of *The New Fiction* (*Xin xiaoshuo*), a periodical established by him in Yokohama, Japan. The title of the journal was taken from its namesake of two Japanese journals respectively founded in 1889 and 1896. There is an explicit Japanese influence[2]. *Xin Xiaoshuo* was one of the journals which published Liang's articles on national Enlightenment to propagate his thoughts to the whole nation:

> 自是启超复专以宣传为业，为《新民丛报》《新小说》等诸杂志，畅其旨义，国人竞喜读之；清廷虽严禁，不能遏；每一册出，内地翻刻本辄十数。二十年来学子之思想，颇蒙其影响。
>
> Since then [around 1900] Qichao takes political propaganda as his mission, has written for such periodicals as *Xinmin Series Newspaper* and *The New Fiction* to make fully clear of his political thoughts. Fellow countrymen loved reading them. Though the Qing court ordered to ban their dissemination, people still managed to obtain them. Once an issue was published, it would be reprinted a dozen times in the inter-land. For the last two decades, the thoughts of young people and students were

[1] Especially in 《时务报》(*Shiwubao*) [*Newspapers of Current Affairs*] , Issues 16-19, January-March, 1897. Cf. Xia Xiaohong, 《觉世与传世——梁启超的文学道路》(*Jueshi yu chuanshi: Liang Qichao's wenxue daolu*) [*To Enlighten the World and to Be Valuable for Posterity: Liang Qichao's Literary Career*], pp. 13-21, pp. 201-208.

[2] Xia Xiaohong,《觉世与传世——梁启超的文学道路》(*Jueshi yu chuanshi: Liang Qichao's wenxue daolu*) [*To Enlighten the World and to Be Valuable for Posterity: Liang Qichao's Literary Career*], p. 194.

strongly influenced by these essays[1].

Liang's move to elevate the position of fiction above other genres of literature, including traditional classics and poetry, came along with a political reality in which an emergent kind of crowds and individuals were moving to the center of history, particularly to "young people and students." They were to be staged at the center of the New Culture Movement in the 1910s[2]. For Liang, the function of literary fiction is political, national, and nothing but closely related to a sort of radical cultural picture of the Chinese nation-state imaginary[3].

Between 1903 and 1905, the *Xin xiaoshuo* journal published a serialized novel titled *The Strange State of the World Witnessed over Twenty Years* by Wu Yanren. In chapter twenty-two of the novel, the protagonist—the narrator "I"—comes back from outside:

> 只见我姊姊拿着一本书看，我走近看时，却画的是画，翻过书面一看，始知是《点石斋画报》。便问哪里来的。

---

[1] Liang Qichao,《清代学术概论》(*Qingdai xueshu gailun*) [*A General Survey of Qing Dynasty Scholarship*], p.85. Also see Cao Juren's memoir: "《新民丛报》虽是在日本东京刊行，而散播之广，乃及穷乡僻壤。清光绪年间，我们家乡去杭州四百里地，邮递经月才到，先父的思想文笔，也曾受梁氏的影响；远至重庆、成都，也让《新民丛报》飞跃三峡而入，改变了士大夫的视听。" ["Though *Xinmin congbao* was published in Tokyo Japan, it was widely disseminated even far to poor villages and remote land. Under the reign of Emperor Guangxu in the Qing Dynasty, our home was four hundred *li* away from Hangzhou, and it took around a month for a post to be delivered. The way my father thinks and writes was once under the influence of Liang Qichao. As far as to Chungking and Chengdu, the *Xinmin congbao* can be delivered through the Three Gorges, and it changed literati class's vision."] Cao Juren,《文坛五十年》(*Wentan wushinian*) [*Fifty Years of Literary Career*], p.31.

[2] For Liang's influence on Hu Shih in his stay in 1904—1910 Shanghai, see《我的信仰》in《胡适文集》vol. 1, p. 10. For a discussion on the generational divides of intellectual figures and their interrelations with each other in late Qing and the early twentieth century, see Jiang Tao,《公寓里的塔：1920年代的文学与青年》(*Gongyu li de ta: 1920 niandai de wenxue yu qingnian*) [*The Ivory Tower in Apartments: Literature and Youth in the 1920s*], pp. 1-23. Please also see Xu Jilin,《中国知识分子十论》(*Zhongguo zhishi fenzi shilun*) [*Ten Essays on Chinese Intellectuals*], p.82.

[3] See Chen Jianhua,《从革命到共和：清末至民国时期文学、电影与文化的转型》(*Cong geming dao gonghe: qingmo zhi minguo shiqi wenxue dianying yu wenhua de zhuanxing*) [*From Revolution to Republicanism: Transformations in Literature, Cinema and Culture from Late Qing to Republican China*], pp. 65-84.

姊姊道："刚才一个小孩拿来卖的，还有两张报纸呢。"说罢，递了报纸给我。我便拿了报纸，到我自己的卧房里去看。

Seeing my sister holding a book and reading, I walked to find what it was about. It turned out to be a pictorial. I turned it over, and came to know that it was *The Dianshizhai* pictorial. I asked how she obtained, and my sister answered: 'a moment ago a child came over to sell it, and there are two other newspapers there.' Right away she gave me the newspapers. I went away with them to my bedroom, reading. (Wu 216)

The novel does not bother to comment upon the pictorial, but leaving it to the sister, while the male protagonist takes with him the verbal newspapers. This seemingly insignificant detail makes a subtle but important distinction between pictorial newspaper and verbal newspaper, pictures and words, and their distinctively gendered consumptions. Visual literacy is attributed to be that of feminine consumption, whereas verbal literacy taken as masculine and enlightening. In the last decade of the nineteenth century, the literacy rate "was 1 percent—more or less—of China's population … the audience still consisted of the highly literate minority … the 'masses' were not being reached by modern media" (Lee and Nathan 373)[1]. Although at the turn of the twentieth century Shanghai, the modern reader figure is addressed in straightforward fashion in newspapers and guidebooks,[2] and it might be historically true that "by the 1890s women at a certain level of Shanghai society—and at least some men at every level—could and did read newspapers, *tanci* (narratives that consisted of both prose and verse portions), and novels" (Des Forges 10), it could be hypothetically true that a gender-based

[1] Nevertheless, the literacy rate in late nineteenth-century Shanghai was higher: about 60 percent of adult men and between 10 and 30 percent of adult women were able to read fairly simple texts. 袁进（Yuan Jin），《中国文学观念的近代变革》（*Zhongguo wenxue guannian de jindai biange*）[*The Modern Transformation of Chinese Literary Concepts*], p. 36. I obtained this information from Des Forges' book *Mediasphere Shanghai*, p. 9.

[2] See Des Forges, *Mediasphere Shanghai*, pp. 7-8, specifically note 18.

hierarchy of literacy was highly recognizable. In this novel the sister reading pictorials probably goes under the category of the illiterate "masses" of this historical period. The ability and probably the willingness to read, as manifested in this protagonist of Wu Jianren's novel, belonged to the elite gendered as male, while the visual was accessible by the mass, like this protagonist's sister. Another example of this is from Hu Shi, when he was in Anhui province 1891—1903 before he went to Shanghai:

> 至于学图画，更是不可能的事。我常常用竹纸蒙在小说书的石印绘像上，摹画书上的英雄美人。有一天，被先生看见了，挨了一顿大骂，抽屉里的图画都被搜出撕毁了。于是我又失掉了学做画家的机会。
>
> When it came to learn to paint, it became more unlikely. I often put bamboo paper onto lithographic pictorial pictures of fiction books, and learned to mimic beauties and heroes from the books. One day, this was found out by the master, and I was given a great lesson. The picture books hidden in drawers were all taken out and torn into pieces. Then, I lost my chance to become a painter[1].

The spectrality of crowds as primarily existent in visual media and mediation, and its historical loss, thus present a gendered history of visuality and textuality.

Coda

In 1902, the Enlightenment project was defined as the mission of literary print political fiction by Liang Qichao. Since 1912, the technology of photography began to be widely disseminated, which made news-photos in newspapers possible. At the same time, many newspapers chose to have columns with sketches or inserts. The pictorial newspapers of the *Dianshizhai* kind began to dwindle out of fashion. The 1920s pictorials like *The Good Companion* (*Liang you*), which was published in

---

[1] Hu Shi 胡适,《胡适文集》(*Hushi wenji*) [*Selected Works by Hu Shi*], vol. 1, p. 10.

Shanghai from 1926, had photos as its major content, and began to be significantly different from the *Dianshizhai*[1]. The literacy rate, after the New Culture Movement, rose much higher than in the 1890s. Thirty two of fifty-eight working class families studied by Olga Lang in Peiping in the 1930s included men who read newspapers[2].

In April 1919, Lu Xun (Lu Hsun), one of the first modern Chinese intellectuals, writes of crowds in modern vernacular Chinese when Xia Yu, a revolutionary character of the Republican China, is to be executed: Old Chuan looked in that direction too, but could only see people's backs. Craning their necks as far as they would go, they looked like so many ducks held and lifted by some invisible hand. For a moment all was still; then a sound was heard, and a stir swept through the on-lookers. There was a rumble as they pushed back, sweeping past Old Chuan and nearly knocking him down[3].

Here, the crowd becomes a ghost-like existence (like ducks), puppets without soul ("held and lifted by some invisible hand"). This literary specter occurs in one of the well-written modern Chinese stories titled "Medicine," which is supposed to cure Chinese spiritual disease in order to save the nation. The watching crowds are denigrated so that an enlightening literary subjectivity and interiority—such as that of Lu Xun—is well established. The once inter-media immersion of visual experience becomes one-dimensional and now needs some interiorized "invisible hand" to spiritualize, which is made possible through a modern Chinese literature. Visuality yields to textuality at the expense of a lost embryonic state of collective being taken as passive.

---

[1]See Xiong Yuezhi and Zhang Min,《上海通史・晚清文化》(*Shanghai tongshi Wanqing wenhua*) [*A Survey History of Shanghai: Late Qing Culture*], p. 481.

[2] See Lee and Nathan, "The Beginning of Mass Culture," p.373.

[3] See Lu Hsun, *Selected Stories of Lu Hsun*, p. 26.

Figure 1 奇园读画, Reading the Pictorial in the Qi Garden

Bibliography

Aarsleff, Hans. *From Locke to Saussure: Essays on the Study of Language and Intellectual History*. Minneapolis: The University of Minnesota Press, 1982.

Abrams, Meyer Howard. "The Correspondent Breeze: A Romantic Metaphor," in *English Romantic Poets: Modern Essays in Criticism*. New York: Oxford University Press, 1960: 37-54.

Abrams, Meyer Howard. "Structure and Style in the Greater Romantic Lyric," in *From Sensibility to Romanticism: Essays Presented to Frederic A. Pottle*. Ed. by Frederick W. Hilles and Harold Bloom. Oxford: Oxford University Press, 1965: 533-539.

Abrams, Meyer Howard. *Natural Supernaturalism*. New York: Norton, 1971.

Abu-Lughod, Lila. *Veiled Sentiments: Honor and Poetry in a Bedouin Society*. Berkeley: The University of California Press, 1986.

Agamben, Giorgio. *What Is an Apparatus and Other Essays*. Trans. by David Kishik and Stepan Pedatella. Stanford: Stanford University Press, 2009a.

Agamben, Giorgio. "What Is an Paradigm?" in *The Signature of All Things: On Method*. Trans. by Luca D'Isanto with Kevin Attell. New York: Zone Books, 2009b: 9-32.

Agnew, Jean-Christophe. *Worlds Apart: The Market and the Theatre in Anglo-American Thought, 1550—1750*. London: Cambridge University Press, 1986.

Althusser, Louis. *For Marx*. London: Verso, 1969.

Altieri, Charles. "Wordsworth's Poetics of Eloquence: A Challenge to Contemporary Theory," in *Romantic Revolutions: Criticism and Theory*. Ed. by Kenneth R. Johnson, et al. Indianapolis: Indiana University Press, 1990: 371-407.

Anderson, Benedict. *Imagined Communities: Reflections on the Origin and Spread of Nationalism*. London: Verso, 1991.

Anderson, Perry. *Lineages of the Absolutist State*. London: Verso, 1996.

Anzieu, Didier. *The Skin Ego*. Trans. by Chris Turner. New Haven: Yale University Press, 1989.

Arac, Jonathan. *Critical Genealogies: Historical Situations for Postmodern Literary Studies*. New York: Columbia University Press, 1987.

Arendt, Hannah. *The Human Condition*. 2nd ed. Chicago: The University of Chicago Press, 1958.

Aristotle. *De Anima* (*On the Soul*). Trans. by W. S. Hett. Cambridge, Mass.: Harvard University Press, 1936.

Aristotle. *On Rhetoric: A Theory of Civic Discourse*. Trans. and ed. by George A. Kennedy. New York: Oxford University Press, 1991.

Armstrong, Nancy. *Desire and Domestic Fiction: A Political History of the Novel*. New York: Oxford University Press, 1987.

Armstrong, Nancy. *Fiction in the Age of Photography: The Legacy of British Realism*. Cambridge, Mass.: Harvard University Press, 2002.

Asad, Talal. *Formations of the Secular: Christianity, Islam, Modernity*. Stanford: Stanford University Press, 2003.

Averill, James H. *Wordsworth and the Poetry of Human Suffering*. Ithaca: Cornell University Press, 1980.

Averill, James H. "Inner Feelings, Works of the Flesh, the Beast Within, Diseases of the Mind, Driving Force, and Putting On a Show: Six Metaphors of Emotion and Their Theoretical Extensions," in *Metaphors in the History of Psychology*. Ed. by David E. Leary. Cambridge: Cambridge University Press, 1990: 104-132.

A Ying 阿英 (Qian Xingcun, 钱杏邨).《晚清文艺报刊述略》(*Wanqing wenyi baokan shulue*) [*A Brief History of Newspapers and Periodicals in Late Qing*]. Beijing: Gudian wenxue chubanshe, 1958.

Bacon, Francis. *The New Organon*. Trans and eds. by Peter Urbach and John Gibson. Chicago and La Salle: Open Court, 1994.

Bao, Tianxiao 包天笑.《钏影楼回忆录》(*Chuanyinglou huiyilu*) [*Memoirs of Kushiro Studio*]. Beijing: Zhongguo dabaike quanshu chubanshe, 2008.

Bao, Weihong 包卫红. "A Panoramic Worldview: Probing the Visuality of *Dianshizhai Huabao*," in *Journal of Modern Chinese Literature*, 2005, 32 (March): 405-461.

Bao, Weihong 包卫红. "Biomechanics of Love: Reinventing the Avant-garde in Tsai Ming-liang's Wayward 'Pornographic Musical,'" in *Journal of Chinese*

Cinema, 2007, 1 (2): 139-160.

Barbauld, Anna Laetitia. *The Correspondence of Samuel Richardson*. London: Printed for R. Phillips [by] Lewis and Rodem, 1804.

Barish, Jonas. *The Antitheatrical Prejudice*. Berkeley: The University of California Press, 1981.

Barker, Paul. "Medium Rare: With Big Brother Bestriding the Global Village, a Chance to Read What McLuhan Really Wrote," in *Times Literary Supplement,* March 17, 2006.

Bate, W. J., J. M. Bullitt, and L. F. Powell. *Samuel Johnson: The Idler and Adventurer*. New Haven: Yale University Press, 1963.

Bathes, Roland. "The Death of the Author," in *Image-Music-Text*. Trans. by Stephen Heath. New York: Hill and Wang, 1978: 142-148.

Baudrillard, Jean. *Simulacra and Simulation*. Trans. by Sheila Faria Glaser. Ann Arbor: The University of Michigan Press, 1995.

Bauman, Richard, and Charles L. Briggs. *Voices of Modernity: Language Ideologies and the Politics of Inequality*. Cambridge: Cambridge University Press, 2003.

Bender, John B. *Spenser and Literary Pictorialism*. Princeton: Princeton University Press, 1972.

Bender, John B. *Imagining the Penitentiary: Fiction and the Architecture of Mind in Eighteenth-Century England*. Chicago: The University of Chicago Press, 1987.

Bender, John B. "Novel Knowledge: Judgment, Experience, Experiment," in *This Is Enlightenment*. Ed. by Clifford Siskin and William Warner. Chicago: The University of Chicago Press, 2010: 284-300.

Benjamin, Walter. *Illuminations*. Trans. by Harry Zohn. London: Fontana, 1973.

Berger, John. *Ways of Seeing*. London: BBC and Penguin, 1972.

Berlant, Lauren. "The Female Complaint," in *Social Text*, 1988, 19/20 (Autumn): 237-259.

Berlant, Lauren. *The Female Complaint: The Unfinished Business of Sentimentality in American Culture*. Durham: Duke University Press, 2008.

Bermingham, Anne, and John Brewer. *The Consumption of Culture 1600—1800: Image, Object, Text*. London: Routledge, 1995.

Bewell, Alan. *Wordsworth and the Enlightenment: Nature, Man, and Society in the Experimental Poetry*. New Haven: Yale University Press, 1989.

Biagioli, Mario. *Galileo's Instruments of Credit: Telescopes, Images, Secrecy*. Chicago: The University of Chicago Press, 2006.

Bialostosky, Don H. *Making Tales: The Poetics of Wordsworth's Narrative Experiments*. Chicago: The University of Chicago Press, 1984.

Blair, Hugh. *Lectures on Rhetoric and Belles Lettres*. 2 vols. London: W. Strahan and T. Cadell, 1783.

Bloom, Harold. *The Best Poems of the English Language: From Chaucer through Robert Frost*. New York: HarperCorllins Publishers, 2004.

Bolter, Jay David, and Richard Grusin. *Remediation: Understanding New Media*. Cambridge, Mass.: The MIT Press, 1999.

Boswell, James. *Life of Johnson*. Oxford: Clarendon, 1934.

Boulton, J. T. "Editor's Introduction," in Edmund Burke. *Philosophical Enquiry into the Origin of Our Ideas of the Sublime and Beautiful*. New York: Columbia University Press, 1958: xv-cxxxvii.

Bourdieu, Pierre. *Outline of a Theory of Practice*. Trans. by Richard Nice. Cambridge: Cambridge University Press, 1977.

Brewer, John. "Sentiment and Sensibility," in *The Cambridge History of English Romantic Literature*. Ed. by James Chandler. Cambridge: Cambridge University Press, 2008: 21-44.

Briggs, Asa, and Peter Burke. *A Social History of the Media: From Gutenberg to the Internet*. Cambridge: Polity, 2002.

Brissenden, R. F. *Virtue in Distress: Studies in the Novel of Sentiment from Richardson to Sade*. London: MacMillan, 1974.

Broadie, Alexander. "Sympathy and the Impartial Spectator," in *The Cambridge Companion to Adam Smith*. Ed. by Knud Haakonssen. Cambridge: Cambridge University Press, 2006: 158-188.

Brooks, Peter. *The Melodramatic Imagination: Balzac, Henry James, Melodrama, and the Mode of Excess*. New Haven: Yale University Press, 1976.

Brooks, Peter. "The Tale vs. the Novel," in *Why the Novel Matters: A Postmodern Perplex*. Ed. by Mark Spilka and Caroline McCracken-Flesher. Bloomington: Indiana University Press, 1990: 303-310.

Brown, Laura. *Fables of Modernity: Literature and Culture in the English Eighteenth Century*. Ithaca: Cornell University Press, 2003.

Bruhm, Steven. *Gothic Bodies: The Politics of Pain in Romantic Fiction*.

Philadelphia: The University of Pennsylvania Press, 1994.

Bryce, J. C. "Introduction." in *Lectures and Rhetoric and Belles Lettres*. Ed. by J. C. Bryce. Oxford: Clarendon Press, 1983: 1-37.

Buck-Morss, Susan. "Hegel and Haiti" in *Critical Inquiry*, 2000, 26 (4): 821-865.

Bunzl, Matti. "Foreword," in Johannes Fabian. *Time and the Other: How Anthropology Makes Its Object*. New York: Columbia University Press, 2003: ix-xxxiv.

Burchell, Graham. "Peculiar Interests: Civil Society and Governing 'The System of Natural Liberty,'" in *The Foucault Effect: Studies in Governmentality with Two Lecturers and an Interview with Michel Foucault*. Ed. by Graham Burchell, Colin Gordon, and Peter Miller. Chicago: The University of Chicago Press, 1991: 119-150.

Burke, Edmund. *Reflections on the Revolution in France*. London: MacMillan, 1890.

Burke, Edmund. *A Philosophical Enquiry into the Origin of Our Ideas of the Sublime and Beautiful*. Notre Dame: The University of Notre Dame Press, 1958.

Bush, Christopher. *Ideographic Modernism: China, Writing, Media*. Oxford: Oxford University Press, 2010.

Butler, Judith. *The Psychic Life of Power: Theories in Subjection*. Stanford: Stanford University Press, 1997.

Campbell, R. H. *Scotland since 1707: The Rise of an Industrial Society*. New York: Barnes & Noble, 1965.

Cao, Juren 曹聚仁. 《文坛五十年》(*Wentan wushinian*) [*Fifty Years of Literary Career*]. Beijing: Sanlian shudian, 2010.

Caruth, Cathy. *Empirical Truths and Critical Fictions: Locke, Wordsworth, Kant, Freud*. Baltimore: The Johns Hopkins University Press, 2009.

Caygill, Howard. *Art of Judgment*. Oxford: Blackwell, 1989.

Caygill, Howard. *A Kant Dictionary*. Oxford: Blackwell, 1995.

Chandler, James. *Wordsworth's Second Nature*. Chicago: The University of Chicago Press, 1984.

Chandler, James. "Sentiment and Sensibility," in *The New Cambridge History of English Literature*. Ed. by James Chandler. Cambridge: Cambridge University Press, 2009: 21-44.

Chang, Hao. *Liang Ch'i-ch'ao and Intellectual Tradition in China, 1890—1907.*

Cambridge, Mass.: Harvard University Press, 1971.

Chartier, Roger. *The Order of Books: Readers, Authors, and Libraries in Europe Between the 14th and 18th Centuries*. Trans. by Lydia G. Cochrane. Stanford: Stanford University Press, 1994.

Chen, Jianhua 陈建华.《从革命到共和：清末至民国时期文学、电影与文化的转型》(*Cong geming dao gonghe: qingmo zhi minguo shiqi wenxue dianying yu wenhua de zhuanxing*) [*From Revolution to Republicanism: Transformations in Literature, Cinema and Culture from Late Qing to Republican China*]. Guilin: Guangxi shifan daxue chubanshe, 2009.

Chen, Pingyuan 陈平原.《新闻与石印——〈点石斋画报〉之成立》("Xinwen yu shiyin—*Dianshizhai huabao* zhi chengli") ["News and Lithography: the Establishment of the *Dianshizhai Pictorial*"], in《开放时代》(*Kaifang shidai*) [*Opening Era*], 2000 (July).

Chen, Pingyuan 陈平原.《导论：以"图像"解说"晚清"》("Daolun: yi 'tuxiang' jieshuo 'wanqing'") ["Introduction: an Interpretation of 'Late Qing' from the Perspective of 'Pictures and Images'], in《图像晚清》(*Tuxiang wanqing*) [*Pictures and Images in Late Qing*]. Edited and Annotated by Chen Pingyuan and Xia Xiaohong, Tianjin: Baihua wenyi chubanshe, 2001.

Chen, Pingyuan 陈平原.《以图像为中心——关于点石斋画报》("Yi tuxiang wei zhongxin—guanyu *Dianshizhai huabao*") [Centering Picture—on the *Dianshizhai Pictorial*], in《二十一世纪》(*Ershiyi shiji*) [*Twenty-First Century*], 2002 (June): 59.

Chen, Pingyuan 陈平原.《左图右史与西学东渐》(*Zuotu Youshi Yu Xixue Dongjian*) [*Left Picture and Right History in the Introduction of Westen Learning to China*]. Hong Kong: Sanlian shudian youxian gongsi, 2008.

Cheng, Jihua 程季华.《中国电影发展史》(*Zhongguo dianying fazhan shi*) [*A History of the Development of Cinema in China*]. Beijing: Zhongguo dianying chubanshe, 1963.

Christensen, Jerome. *Coleridge's Blessed Machine of Language*. Ithaca: Cornell University Press, 1981.

Christensen, Jerome. "The Impropriety of Coleridge's Literary Life," in *Romanticism and Language*. Ed. by Arden Reed. Ithaca: Cornell University Press, 1984: 144-167.

Christensen, Jerome. *Practicing Enlightenment: Hume and the Formation of a Literary Career*. Madison: The University of Wisconsin Press, 1987.

Clery, E. J. "Introduction," in Horace Walpole. *The Castle of Otranto, a Gothic Story*. New York: Oxford University Press, 1996: xxxi-xxxii.

Clery, E. J. *The Feminization Debate in Eighteenth-Century England: Literature, Commerce and Luxury*. New York: Palgrave Macmillan, 2004.

Cohen, Ted, and Paul Guyer. "Introduction," in *Essays in Kant's Aesthetics*. Ed. by Ted Cohen and Paul Guyer. Chicago: The University of Chicago Press, 1982: 1-17.

Coleridge, Samuel T. *Specimens of the Table Talk of the Late Samuel Taylor Coleridge*. New York: Harper & Brothers, 1835.

Coleridge, Samuel T. *The Notebooks of Samuel Taylor Coleridge*. 3 vols. New York: Pantheon / Princeton: Princeton University Press, 1957.

Coleridge, Samuel T. *The Friend*. London: Routledge & Kegan Paul, 1969.

Coleridge, Samuel T. *Lay Sermons*. [S.l.]: Routledge & Kegan Paul, 1972.

Coleridge, Samuel T. *Biographia Literaria*. Princeton: Princeton University Press, 1983.

Colley, Linda. *Britons: Forging the Nation, 1707—1837*. New Haven: Yale University Press, 1992.

Condorcet, Antoine-Nicolas de. *Sketch for a Historical Picture of the Progress of* The Human Mind. Trans. by June Barraclough. London: Weidenfeld & Nicolson, 1955.

Crary, Jonathan. "Modernizing Vision," in *Vision and Visuality*. Ed. by Hal Foster. Seattle: Bay Press, 1988: 29-50.

Crary, Jonathan. *Techniques of the Observer: On Vision and Modernity in the 19th Century*. Cambridge, Mass.: The MIT Press, 1990.

Crary, Jonathan. *Suspensions of Perception: Attention, Spectacle, and Modern Culture*. Cambridge, Mass.: The MIT Press, 2001.

Darwin, Erasmus. *Zoonomia, or the Laws of Organic Life*. London: J. Johnson, 1796.

Davis, Lennard J. *Factual Fictions: The Origins of the English Novel*. New York: Columbia University Press, 1983.

De Certeau, Michel. *Practice of Everyday Life*. Trans. by Steeven F. Rendall. Berkeley: The University of California Press, 1984.

De Certeau, Michel. *Heterologies: Discourse on the Other*. Trans. by Brian Massumi. Minneapolis: The University of Minnesota Press, 1986.

Deleuze, Gilles, and Felix Guattari. *Anti-Oedipus: Capitalism and Schizophrenia.*

Trans. by Robert Hurley, Mark Seem, and Helen R. Lane. New York: Viking, 1977.

De Man, Paul. "Literary History and Literary Modernity," in *Daedalus*, 1970, 99 (2, Spring, Theory in Humanistic Studies): 384-404.

De Man, Paul. *The Rhetoric of Romanticism*. New York: Columbia University Press, 1984.

Denton, Kirk. *Modern Chinese Literary Thought: Writings on Literature, 1893—1945*. Stanford: Stanford University Press, 1996.

Derrida, Jacques. *Speech and Phenomena and other Essays on Husserl's Theory of Signs*. Trans. By David B. Allison. Evanston: Northwestern University Press, 1973.

Derrida, Jacques. "White Mythology: Metaphor in the Text of Philosophy," in *Margins of Philosophy*. Trans. by Alan Bass. Chicago: The University of Chicago Press, 1982: 207-272.

Derrida, Jacques. *Dissemination*. Trans. by Barbara Johnson. Chicago: The University of Chicago Press, 1983.

Derrida, Jacques. *Limited INC*. Trans. by Samuel Weber. Evanston: Northwestern University Press, 1988.

Derrida, Jacques. "Paper or Me, You Know ... (New Speculations on a Luxury of the Poor)," in *Paper Machine*. Ed. and trans. by Rachel Bowlby. Stanford: Stanford University Press, 2005: 41-65.

Des Forges, Alexander. *Mediasphere Shanghai: The Aesthetics of Cultural Production*. Honolulu: The University of Hawaii Press, 2007.

Dickey, Laurence. "Historicizing the 'Adam Smith Problem': Conceptual, Historiographical, and Textual Issues," in *Journal of Modern History*, 1986, 58: 579-609.

Dixon, Thomas. *From Passions to Emotions: The Creation of a Secular Psychological Category*. Cambridge: Cambridge University Press, 2003.

Eagleton, Terry. *The Rape of Clarissa*. Minneapolis: The University of Minnesota Press, 1982.

Eagleton, Terry. *The Ideology of the Aesthetic*. Cambridge, MA: Basil Blackwell, 1990.

Eagleton, Terry. *The Idea of Culture*. Oxford: Wiley-Blackwell, 2000.

Eco, Umberto. *The Search for the Perfect Language*. Oxford: Blackwell Publishers Ltd., 1994.

Egan, Ronald. "The Controversy over Music and 'Sadness' and Changing Conceptions of the *Qin* in Middle Period China," in *Harvard Journal of Asiatic Studies*, 1997, 57: 5-66.

Egginton, William. *How the World Became a Stage: Presence, Theatricality, and the Question of Modernity*. Albany: State University of New York Press, 2003.

Eisenstein, Elizabeth L. *The Printing Press as an Agent of Change: Communications and Cultural Transformations in Early Modern Europe*. 2 vols. Cambridge: Cambridge University Press, 1979.

Eisenstein, Elizabeth L. *Print Culture and Enlightenment Thought*. Chapel Hill: Hanes Foundation, Rare Book Collection, 1986.

Ellis, Markman. *The Politics of Sensibility*. New York: Cambridge University Press, 1996.

Ellison, Julie. *Cato's Tears and the Making of Anglo-American Emotion*. Chicago: The University of Chicago Press, 1999.

Ellison, Katherine E. *Fatal News: Reading and Information Overload in Early Eighteenth-Century Literature*. New York: Routledge, 2006.

Erickson, Lee. *The Economy of Literary Form: English Literature and the Industrialization of Publishing 1800—1850*. Baltimore: Johns Hopkins University Press, 1996.

Fara, Patricia. "Marginal Practices," in *The Cambridge History of Science: Eighteenth Century Science*. Ed. by Roy Porter. Cambridge: Cambridge University Press, 2003: 485-510.

Fastrup, Anne. "Mediating *le philosophe*: Diderot's Strategic Self-Representations," in *This Is Enlightenment*. Ed. by Clifford Siskin and William Warner. Chicago: The University of Chicago Press, 2010: 265-283.

Feather, John. *Publishing, Piracy and Politics: an Historical Study of Copyright in Britain*. London: Mansell, 1994.

Festa, Lynn. *Sentimental Figures of Empire in Eighteenth-Century Britain and France*. Baltimore: The Johns Hopkins University Press, 2006.

Fielding, Penny. *Writing and Orality: Nationality, Culture, and Nineteenth-Century Scottish Fiction*. Oxford: Clarendon Press, 1996.

Firth, Roderick. "Ethical Absolutism and the Ideal Observer," in *Philosophy and Phenomenological Research*, 1951—1952, 12: 317-345.

Foster, Hal. *Vision and Visuality*. Seattle: Bay Press, 1988.

Foucault, Michel. *Madness and Civilization: A History of Insanity in the Age of Reason*. Trans. by Richard Howard. New York: Random House, 1965.

Foucault, Michel. *The Order of Things: An Archaeology of the Human Sciences*. New York: Vintage, 1970.

Foucault, Michel. *Archaeology of Knowledge and the Discourse on Language*. Trans. by A. M. Sheridan Smith. New York: Pantheon, 1972.

Foucault, Michel. *Power / Knowledge: Selected Interviews and Other Writings 1972—1977*. Trans. by Colin Gordon, et al. New York: Pantheon, 1980.

Foucault, Michel. *The History of Sexuality: An Introduction*. Trans. by Robert Hurley. New York: Vintage, 1990.

Foucault, Michel. "What Is an Author?," in *Aesthetics, Methods, and Epistemology*. Ed. by James D. Faubion. New York: The New Press, 1998: 205-222.

Fox, Christopher. *Psychology and Literature in the Eighteenth Century*. New York: AMS Press, 1987.

Fox, Christopher. *Locke and the Scriblerians: Identity and Consciousness in Early Eighteenth-Century Britain*. Berkeley: The University of California Press, 1988.

Franta, Andrew. *Romanticism and the Rise of the Mass Public*. Cambridge: Cambridge University Press, 2009.

Freud, Sigmund. "A Case of Paranoia Running Counter to the Psycho-Analytic Theory of the Disease," in *The Standard Edition of the Complete Psychological Works*. Trans. and ed. by James Strachey. London: The Hogarth Press and the Institute of Psychoanalysis, 1966. 14: 261-272.

Fried, Michael. *Absorption and Theatricality: Painting and Beholder in the Age of Diderot*. Chicago: The University of Chicago Press, 1980.

Fried, Michael. *Art and Objecthood*. Chicago: The University of Chicago Press, 1998.

Frye, Northrop. "Towards Defining an Age of Sensibility," in *ELH*, 1956, 23 (2): 144-152.

Frye, Northrop. *Anatomy of Criticism: Four Essays*. Princeton: Princeton University Press, 1957.

Gage, John. "Synaesthesia," in *The Encyclopedia of Aesthetic: vol. 4*. Oxford: Oxford University Press, 1998: 348-351.

Gallagher, Catherine. *The Body Economic: Life, Death, and Sensation in*

Political Economy and the Victorian Novel. Princeton: Princeton University Press, 2008.

Gamer, Michael. *Romanticism and the Gothic: Genre, Reception, and Canon Formation*. Cambridge: Cambridge University Press, 2000.

Genette, Gerard. "The Frontiers of Narrative," in *Figures of Literary Discourse*. Trans. by Alan Sheridan. New York: Columbia University Press, 1982: 127-143.

Gibbon, Edward. *The Letters of Edward Gibbon*. London: Cassell, 1956.

Giddens, Anthony. *Modernity and Self-Identity: Self and Society in the Late Modern Age*. Stanford: Stanford University Press, 1991.

Gilroy, Paul. "Cultural Studies and Ethnic Absolutism," in *Cultural Studies*. Ed. by Lawrence Grossberg, Cary Nelson, Paula A. Treichler. London: Routledge, 1992: 187-198.

Ginzburg, Carlo. "Killing a Chinese Mandarin: The Moral Implications of Distance," in *Critical Inquiry*, 1994, 21 (1): 46-60.

Ginzburg, Carlo. *Wooden Eyes: Nine Reflections on Distance*. Trans. by Martin Ryle and Kate Soper. New York: Columbia University Press, 2001.

Gitelman, Lisa. *Always Already New: Media, History, and the Data of Culture*. Cambridge, Mass.: The MIT Press, 2006.

Goldstein, Joshua. *Drama Kings: Layers and Publics in the Re-creation of Peking Opera, 1870—1937*. Berkeley: The University of California Press, 2007.

Gombrich, E. H. *The Ideas of Progress and Their Impact on Art*. New York: Cooper Union School of Art and Architecture, 1971.

Goody, Jack and Ian Watt. "The Consequences of Literacy," in *Literacy in Traditional Societies*. Ed. by Jack Goody. Cambridge: Cambridge University Press, 1968: 27-84.

Gossman, Lionel. "Literary Education and Democracy," in *Modern Language Notes*, 1971, 86: 761-789.

Greenblatt, Stephen. *Renaissance Self-Fashioning: From More to Shakespeare*. Chicago: The University of Chicago Press, 1980.

Griffin, Andrew L. "Wordsworth and the Problem of Imaginative Story: The Case of 'Simon Lee,'" in *PMLA*, 1997, 92 (3): 392-409.

Griffin, Robert J. *Wordsworth's Pope: A Study in Literary Historiography*. Cambridge: Cambridge University Press, 1995.

Gross, Daniel M. *The Secret History of Emotion: From Aristotle's Rhetoric to Modern Brain Science*. Chicago: The University of Chicago Press, 2006.

Gross, Daniel M., and William M. Keith. *Rhetorical Hermeneutics: Invention and Interpretation in the Age of Science*. Albany, N.Y.: SUNY Press, 1996.

Guillory, John. *Cultural Capital: The Problem of Literary Canon Formation*. Chicago: The University of Chicago Press, 1995.

Guillory, John. "Genesis of the Media Concept," in *Critical Inquiry*, 2010, 36 (Winter): 321-346.

Gunning, Tom. "Tracing the Individual Body: Photography, Detectives, and Early Cinema," in *Cinema and the Invention of Modern Life*. Ed. by Vanessa R. Schwartz and Leo Charney. Berkeley: The University of California Press, 1995: 15-45.

Guo, Enci 郭恩慈, and Su Jue 苏珏.《中国现代设计的诞生》(*Zhongguo xiandai sheji de dansheng*) [*The Birth of Modern Chinese Design*]. Shanghai: Dongfang chuban zhongxin, 2008.

Habermas, Jürgen. *The Structural Transformation of the Public Sphere: An Inquiry into a Category of Bourgeois Society*. Trans. by Thomas Burger with the assistance of Frederick Lawrence. Cambridge, Mass.: The MIT Press, 1989.

Hacking, Ian. *Why Does Language Matter to Philosophy?*. Cambridge: Cambridge University Press, 1975.

Hansen, Miriam. *Babel in Babylon: Spectatorship in American Silent Film*. Cambridge, Mass.: Harvard University Press, 1991.

Harkness, Deborah E. *The Jewel House: Elizabethan London and the Scientific Revolution*. New Haven: Yale University Press, 2007.

Hartman, Geoffrey. *Wordsworth's Poetry, 1787—1814*. New Haven: Yale University Press, 1964.

Hartman, Geoffrey. *The Unmediated Vision: An Interpretation of Wordsworth, Hopkins, Rilke, and Valéry*. New York: Harcourt, Brace & World, 1966.

Hartman, Geoffrey. *Beyond Formalism: Literary Essays, 1958—1970*. New Haven: Yale University Press, 1970.

Hartman, Geoffrey. "The Use and Abuse of Structural Analysis: Riffaterre's Interpretation of Wordsworth's 'Yew-Trees,'" in *New Literary History*, 1975 (7): 165-189.

Havelock, Eric. *Preface to Plato*. Cambridge, Mass.: Harvard University Press,

1963.

Hay, Jonathan. "Painting and the Built Environment in Late Nineteenth-Century Shanghai," in *Chinese Art: Modern Expressions*. Ed. by Maxwell K. Hearn and Judith G. Smith. New York: The Metropolitan Museum of Art, 2001: 61-101.

Hayles, N. Katherine. *Writing Machine*. Cambridge, Mass.: The MIT Press, 2002.

Hayot, Eric. *The Hypothetical Mandarin: Sympathy, Modernity, and Chinese Pain*. Oxford: Oxford University Press, 2009.

Hazlitt, William. *Collected Works of William Hazlitt*. London: J. M. Dent, 1902—1904.

Headrick, Daniel R. *When Information Came of Age: Technologies of Knowledge in the Age of Reason and Revolution, 1700—1850*. Oxford: Oxford University Press, 2000.

Heffnan, James. *The Re-Creation of Landscape: A Study of Wordsworth, Coleridge, Constable, and Turner*. Hanover, N. H.: Dartmouth, 1985.

Heffnan, James. "Ekphrasis and Representation," in *New Literary History*, 1991, 22 (2): 297-316.

Heffnan, James. *The Museum of Words: The Poetics of Ekphrasis from Homer to Ashbery*. Chicago: The University of Chicago Press, 1994.

Heidegger, Martin. *The Question Concerning Technology and Other Essays*. Trans. and with an Introduction by William Lovitt. New York: Harper & Row Publishers Inc., 1977.

Heidegger, Martin. *Off the Beaten Track*. Ed. and trans. by Julian Young and Kenneth Haynes. Cambridge: Cambridge University Press, 2002.

Hirschman, Albert O. *The Passions and the Interests: Political Arguments for Capitalism before Its Triumph*. Princeton: Princeton University Press, 1997.

Hirsch, E. D. *Wordsworth and Schelling: A Typological Study of Romanticism*. New Haven: Yale University Press, 1960.

Hitchcock, Tim. *English Sexualities, 1700—1800*. New York: St. Martin's Press, 1997.

Hobbes, Thomas. *English Works of Thomas Hobbes*. Ed. by Sir William Molesworth. London: Bohn, 1839—1845; rpt. Aalen, Germany: Scientia Verlag Aalen, 1966.

Holstun, James Ross. *A Rational Millennium: Puritan Utopias of Seventeenth-Century England and America*. Oxford: Oxford University Press, 1987.

Homans, Margaret. "Eliot, Wordsworth, and the Scenes of the Sister's Instruction," in *Writing and Sexual Difference*. Ed. by Elizabeth Abel. Chicago: The University of Chicago Press, 1982.

Home, Henry. *Essays on the Principles of Morality and Natural Religion*. 3rd ed. Edinburgh: Bell and Murray, 1779.

Home, Henry. *Sketches of the History of Man: considerably enlarged by the last additions and corrections of the author*. 3 vols. Edinburgh: Printed for W. Creech, and Bell & Bradfute, 1813.

Home, Henry. *Characteristics of Men, Manners, Opinions, Times*. 3 vols. Indianapolis: Liberty Fund, 2001.

Home, Henry. *Elements of Criticism: Vol 1*. 6th ed. Indianapolis: Liberty Fund, 2005.

Home, R. W. "Mechanics and Experimental Physics," in *The Cambridge History of Science vol. 4: Eighteenth-Century Science*. Ed. by Roy Porter. Cambridge: Cambridge University Press, 2003: 354-374.

Horkheimer, Max, and Theodor W. Adorno. *Dialectic of Enlightenment*. Trans. by John Cumming. New York: Seabury, 1972.

Howe, Kathleen Stewart. *Intersections: Lithography, Photography, and the Traditions of Printmaking*. Albuquerque: The University of New Mexico Press, 1998a.

Howe, Kathleen Stewart. "Introduction and Acknowledgments," in *Intersections: Lithography, Photography, and the Traditions of Printmaking*. Albuquerque: The University of New Mexico Press, 1998b: vii-x.

Howell, Wilbur Samuel. *Eighteenth-Century British Logic and Rhetoric*. Princeton: Princeton University Press, 1971.

Hu, Shi 胡适. 《胡适文集》 (*Hushi wenji*) [*Selected Works by Hu Shi*]. Beijing: Beijing daxue chubanshe, 2013.

Hume, David. *The Letters of David Hume*. 2 vols. Oxford: Clarendon, 1932.

Hume, David. *The Philosophical Works of David Hume*. 4 vols. Edinburgh: Adam Black and William Tait, 1826; rpt. Darmstadt: Scientia Verlag Aalen, 1964.

Hume, David. *A Treatise of Human Nature*. 2nd ed. Oxford: Oxford University Press, 1978.

Hume, David. *Essays, Moral, Political, and Literary*. rev. ed. Indianapolis: Liberty Classics, 1985.

Husserl, Edmund. *The Crisis of European Science and Transcendental Phenomenology*. Trans. by David Carr. Evanston: Northwestern University Press, 1970.

Huters, Theodore. *Bringing the World Home: Appropriating the West in Late Qing and Early Republican China*. Honolulu: The University of Hawaii Press, 2005.

James, William. *The Principles of Psychology*. New York: Holt, 1890.

Jameson, Fredric. *Postmodernism, or, the Logic of Late Capitalism*. Durham: Duke University Press, 1991.

Jay, Martin. "Scopic Regimes of Modernity," in *Vision and Visuality*. Ed. by Hal Foster. Seattle: Bay Press, 1988: 3-23.

Jay, Martin. *Downcast Eyes: The Denigration of Vision in Twentieth-Century French Thought*. Berkeley: The University of California Press, 1994.

Jiang, Tao 姜涛.《公寓里的塔：1920 年代的文学与青年》(*Gongyu li de ta: 1920 niandai de wenxue yu qingnian*) [*The Ivory Tower in Apartments: Literature and Youth in the 1920s*]. Beijing: Beijing daxue chubanshe, 2015.

Johns, Adrian. *The Nature of the Book: Print and Knowledge in the Making*. Chicago: The University of Chicago Press, 2000.

Johnson, Samuel. *A Dictionary of the English Language on CD-ROM*. Cambridge: Cambridge University Press, 1996.

Jones, Caroline. "Senses," in *Critical Terms for Media Studies*. Ed. by W. J. T. Mitchell and Mark B. N. Hansen. Chicago: The University of Chicago Press, 2010: 88-100.

Jones, R. F. "Science and Language in England of the Mid-Seventeenth Century," in *J. E. G. P.,* 1932, XXXI: 315-331.

Jorden, Edward. *A Disease Called the Suffocation of the Mother*. London: [s.n.], 1603; rpt. New York: Walter J. Johnson Incorporated, 1971.

Kahn, Madeleine. *Narrative Transvestism: Rhetoric and Gender in the Eighteenth-Century English Novel*. Ithaca: Cornell University Press, 1991.

Keats, John. *The Letters of John Keats, 1814—1821*. 2 vols. Cambridge, Mass.: Harvard University Press, 1958.

Keen, Paul. *Revolutions in Romantic Literature: An Anthology of Print Culture, 1780—1832*. Toronto: Broadview Press, 2004.

Keller, Evelyn Fox. *Reflections on Gender and Science*. New Haven: Yale University Press, 1985.

Kernan, Alvin. *Samuel Johnson and the Impact of Print*. Princeton: Princeton University Press, 1987.

Kittler, Friedrich A. *Discourse Networks, 1800/1900*. Trans. by Michael Metteer, with Chris Cullens. Forward by David E. Wellbery. Stanford: Stanford University Press, 1992.

Kittler, Friedrich A. *Literature, Media, Information Systems*. Amsterdam: G+B Arts International, 1997.

Kittler, Friedrich A. *Gramophone, Film, Typewriter*. Trans. by Geoffrey Winthrop-Young and Michael Wutz. Stanford: Stanford University Press, 1999.

Klancher, Jon P. *The Making of English Reading Audiences, 1790—1832*. Madison: The University of Wisconsin Press, 1987.

Krishnan, Sanjay. *Reading the Global: Troubling Perspectives on Britain's Empire in Asia*. New York: Columbia University Press, 2007.

Lacan, Jacques. *The Four Fundamental Concepts of Psycho-Analysis*. Trans. by Alan Sheridan. New York: W. W. Norton & Company, 1978.

Lacqueur, Thomas. *Making Sex: Body and Gender from the Greeks to Freud*. Cambridge, Mass.: Harvard University Press, 1990.

Langan, Celeste. "Understanding Media in 1805: Audiovisual Hallucination in the Lay of the Last Minstrel," in *Studies in Romanticism*, 2001, 40 (1): 49-70.

Langan, Celeste, and Maureen N. McLane. "The Medium of Romantic Poetry," in *The Cambridge Companion to British Romantic Poetry*. Ed. by James Chandler and Maureen N. McLane. Cambridge University Press, 2008: 239-262.

Langbaum, Robert. *The Poetry of Experience*. New York: Random House, 1957.

Latour, Bruno. *We Have Never Been Modern*. Trans. by Cathererine Porter. Cambridge, Mass.: Harvard University Press, 1993.

Law, Alma, and Mei Gordon. *Meyerhold, Eisenstein and Biomechanics: Actor Training in Revolutionary Russia*. London: McFarland & Company, 1996.

Lee, Leo Ou-fan. *Shanghai Modern: The Flowering of a New Urban Culture in China, 1930—1945*. Cambridge, Mass.: Harvard University Press, 1999.

Lee, Leo Ou-fan., and Andrew J. Nathan. "The Beginning of Mass Culture: Journalism and Fiction in the Late Ch'ing and Beyond," in *Popular Culture in Late Imperial China*. Ed. by David Johnson, Andrew J. Nathan, Evelyn S.

Rawski. Berkeley: The University of California Press, 1985: 360-395.

Lessing, Gotthold Ephraim. *Laocoon: an Essay on the Limits of Painting and Poetry*. Trans. by Edward Allen McCormick. Indianapolis, Bobbs-Merrill, 1962.

Levinson, Marjorie. *Wordsworth's Great Period Poems: Four Essays*. Cambridge: Cambridge University Press, 1986.

Li, Hsiao-t'i 李孝悌.《恋恋红尘：中国的城市、欲望和生活》(*Lianlian hongchen: zhongguo de chengshi, yuwang he shenghuo*) [*Ashes of Time: China's City, Desire and Life*]. Shanghai: Shanghai renmin chubanshe, 2007.

Liang, Qichao 梁启超.《论小说与群治之关系》("Lun xiaoshuo yu qunzhi zhi guanxi") ["On the Relation between Fiction and the Government of the People"], in 《二十世纪中国小说理论资料》(*Ershi shiji zhongguo xiaoshuo lilun ziliao*) [*Theoretical Materials of Chinese Novels in the Twentieth Century*]. Ed. by Chen Pingyuan 陈平原 and Xia Xiaohong 夏晓虹. vol. 1. Beijing: Beijing daxue chubanshe, 1989a: 33-37.

Liang, Qichao 梁启超.《译印政治小说序》("Yiyin zhengzhi xiaoshuo xu") ["Preface to the Published Series of Translations of Political Fiction"], in 《二十世纪中国小说理论资料》(*Ershi shiji zhongguo xiaoshuo lilun ziliao*) [*Theoretical Materials of Chinese Novels in the Twentieth Century*]. Ed. by Chen Pingyuan 陈平原 and Xia Xiaohong 夏晓虹. vol. 1. Beijing: Beijing daxue chubanshe, 1989b: 21-22.

Liang, Qichao 梁启超.《清代学术概论》(*Qingdai xueshu gailun*) [*A General Survey of Qing Dynasty Scholarship*]. Shanghai: Shanghai guji chubanshe, 1998.

Lindenberger, Herbert. *On Wordsworth's "Prelude."* Princeton: Princeton University Press, 1963.

Liu, E. *The Travels of Lao Ts'an*. Trans. by Harold Shadick. Ithaca: Cornell University Press, 1952.

Liu, Lydia H. *Translingual Practice: Literature, National Culture, and Translated Modernity-China, 1900—1937*. Stanford: Stanford University Press, 1995.

Liu, Lydia H. *The Freudian Robot: Digital Media and the Future of the Unconscious*. Chicago: The University of Chicago Press, 2010.

Livingston, Ira. *Arrow of Chaos: Romanticism and Postmodernity*. Minneapolis: The University of Minnesota Press, 1997.

Locke, John. *An Essay Concerning Human Understanding*. Ed. with a Foreword by Peter H. Nidditch. New York: Oxford University Press, 1975.

Lovejoy, Arthur O. "On the Discrimination of Romanticisms," in *PMLA*, 1924, 39 (2): 229-253.

Lovejoy, Arthur O. *The Great Chain of Being: A Study of the History of an Idea*. Cambridge, Mass.: Harvard University Press, 1936.

Lowe, Donald M. *History of Bourgeois Perception*. Chicago: The University of Chicago Press, 1982.

Lu Xun (Lu Hsun) 鲁迅 (Zhou Shuren 周树人). 《鲁迅全集》(*Lu Xun quanji*) [*Complete Works of Lu Xun*]. Beijing: Renmin wenxue chubanshe, 1981.

Lu Xun (Lu Hsun) 鲁迅 (Zhou Shuren 周树人). *Selected Stories of Lu Hsun*. Trans. by Yang Hsien-yi and Gladys Yang. New York: W. W. Norton & Company, 2003.

Luhmann, Niklas. "The Individuality of the Individual: Historical Meanings and Contemporary Problems," in *Reconstructing Individualism: Autonomy, Individuality, and the Self in Western Thought*. Eds. by Thomas C. Heller, Martin Sosna, and David E. Wellbery. Stanford: Stanford University Press, 1986: 313-328.

Luhmann, Niklas. *Art as a Social System*. Trans. by Eva Knodt. Stanford: Stanford University Press, 2000.

Lutz, Catherine A. *Unnatural Emotions: Everyday Sentiments on a Micronesian Atoll and Their Challenge to Western Theory*. Chicago: The University of Chicago Press, 1988.

Ma, Guangren 马光仁. 《上海新闻史 1850—1949》(*Shanghai xinwen shi 1850—1949*) [*History of Journalism in Shanghai, 1850—1949*]. Shanghai: Fudan daxue chubanshe, 1996.

Mack, Mary P. *Jeremy Bentham: An Odyssey of Ideas, 1748—1792*. London: Heinemann, 1962.

Mackie, Erin. *The Commerce of Everyday Life: Selections from The Tatler and The Spectator*. Boston and New York: Bedford/St. Martin's, 1998.

MacKenzie, Henry. *Letter to Elizabeth Rose of Kilravock on Literature, Events, and People, 1768—1815*. Edinburgh: Oliver and Boyd, 1967.

Macpherson, C. B. *The Political Theory of Possessive Individualism*. Oxford: Oxford University Press, 1962.

Manning, Peter. *Reading Romantics: Texts and Contexts*. Oxford: Oxford

University Press, 1990.

Manning, Susan. "Antiquarianism, Balladry and the Rehabilitation of Romance," in *The Cambridge History of English Romantic Literature*. Ed. by James Chandler. Cambridge: Cambridge University Press, 2009: 45-70.

Marshall, David. "Adam Smith and the Theatricality of Moral Sentiments," in *Critical Inquiry*, 1984, 10 (June): 562-613.

Marshall, David. *The Surprising Effects of Sympathy: Marivaux, Diderot, Rousseau, and Mary Shelley*. Chicago: The University of Chicago Press, 1988.

Marshall, P. J. "Introduction." *The Oxford History of the British Empire: The Eighteenth Century*. Ed. by P. J. Marshall. New York: Oxford University Press, 2001: 1-27.

Mayo, Robert. "The Contemporaneity of the Lyrical Ballads," in *PMLA* 1954, 69: 486-522.

McDowell, Paula. "Defoe and the Contagion of the Oral: Modeling Media Shift in *A Journal of the Plague Year*," *Publications of the Modern Language Association*, 2006, 121 (Special Issue: "Book History and the Idea of Literature"): 87-106.

McDowell, Paula. "Mediating Media Past and Present: Toward a Genealogy of 'Print Culture' and 'Oral Tradition,'" in *This Is Enlightenment*. Ed. by Clifford Siskin and William Warner. Chicago: The University of Chicago Press, 2010: 229-246.

McGann, Jerome. *The Romantic Ideology: A Critical Investigation*. Chicago: The University of Chicago Press, 1983.

McGann, Jerome. *The Poetics of Sensibility: A Revolution in Literary Style*. Oxford: Oxford University Press, 1996.

McKenzie, Alan T. *Certain Lively Episodes: The Articulation of Passion in Eighteenth-Century Prose*. Athens: The University of Georgia Press, 1990.

McKeon, Michael. "Historicizing Patriarchy: the Emergence of Gender Difference in England, 1660—1760," in *Eighteenth-Century Studies*, 1995, 28 (3): 295-322.

McLane, Maureen N. "Ballads and Bards: British Romantic Orality," in *Modern Philology* , 2001, 98 (3): 423-443.

McLane, Maureen N. *Balladeering, Minstrelsy, and the Making of British Romantic Poetry*. Cambridge: Cambridge University Press, 2008.

McLuhan, Marshall. *The Gutenberg Galaxy: The Making of Typographic Man*. Toronto: The University of Toronto Press, 1962.

McLuhan, Marshall. *Understanding Media: The Extensions of Man*. New York: McGraw-Hill, 1964.

McLuhan, Marshall, and Bruce R. Powers. *The Global Village: Transformations in World Life and Media in the 21st Century*. New York: Oxford University Press, 1989.

McLuhan, Marshall, and Bruce R. Powers. *Essential McLuhan*. [S.l.]: Basic Books, 1995.

Meng, Yue. *Shanghai and the Edges of Empires*. Minneapolis: The University of Minnesota Press, 2006.

Merchant, Carolyn. *The Death of Nature*. San Francisco: Harper & Row, 1980.

Miles, Robert. "Romanticism, Enlightenment, and Mediation: The Case of the Inner Stranger," in *This Is Enlightenment*. Ed. by Clifford Siskin and William Warner. Chicago: The University of Chicago Press, 2010: 173-188.

Mill, J. S. "What Is Poetry?" in *Mill's Essays on Literature and Society*. Ed. by J. B. Schneewind. New York: Collier, 1965.

Miller, J. H. "Narrative," in *Critical Terms of Literary Study*. Ed. by Frank Lentricchia and Thomas McLaughlin. Chicago: The University of Chicago Press, 1995: 66-79.

Mitchell, W. J. T. *Blake's Composite Art: A Study of the Illuminated Poetry*. Princeton: Princeton University Press, 1978.

Mitchell, W. J. T. *Iconology: Image, Text, Ideology*. Chicago: The University of Chicago Press, 1986.

Mitchell, W. J. T. *Picture Theory: Essays on Verbal and Visual Representation*. Chicago: The University of Chicago Press, 1994.

Mitchell, W. J. T. "Word and Image," in *Critical Terms for Art History*. Ed. by Robert S. Nelson and Richard Shiff. Chicago: The University of Chicago Press, 1996a.

Mitchell, W. J. T. "What Do Pictures 'Really' Want?" in *October*, 1996b, 77 (summer): 71-82.

Mitchell, W. J. T. "Romanticism and the Life of Things," in *Critical Inquiry*, 2001, 28 (1): 167-184.

Mitchell, W. J. T. *What Do Pictures Want?: The Lives and Loves of Images*. Chicago: The University of Chicago Press, 2006.

Mitchell, W. J. T., and Mark B. N. Hansen. "Introduction." in *Critical Terms for Media Studies*. Ed. by W. J. T. Mitchell and Mark B. N. Hansen. Chicago: The University of Chicago Press, 2010: vii-xxii.

Monk, Samuel H. *The Sublime: A Study of Critical Theories in XVIII-Century England*. Ann Arbor: The University of Michigan Press, 1960.

Monk, Samuel H. "The Sublime: Burke's *Enquiry*," in *Romanticism and Consciousness*. Ed. by Harold Bloom. New York: W. W. Norton, 1970: 24-41.

Morison, Stanley. *The English Newspaper, 1622—1932: An Account of the Physical Development of Journals Printed in London*. Cambridge: Cambridge University Press, 2009.

Morton, Timothy. *Radical Food: The Culture and Politics of Eating and Drinking 1790—1820*. 3 vols. London: Routledge, 2000.

Mullan, John. *Sentiment and Sociality: The Language of Feeling in the Eighteenth Century*. New York: Oxford University Press, 1988.

Murphy, Peter T. *Poetry as an Occupation and an Art in Britain, 1760—1830*. Cambridge: Cambridge University Press, 1993.

Nancy, Jean-Luc, and Philippe Lacoue-Labarthe. *The Title of the Letter: A Reading of Lacan*. Albany, NY: SUNY Press, 1992.

Nelson, Benjamin. *The Idea of Usury: From Tribal Brotherhood to Universal Otherhood*. Chicago: The University of Chicago Press, 1969.

Neu, Jerome. *Emotion, Thought, Therapy: A Study of Hume and Spinoza and the Relationship of Philosophical Theories of the Emotions to Psychological Theories of Therapy*. Berkeley: The University of California Press, 1977.

Newman, Gerald. *The Rise of English Nationalism: A Cultural History 1740—1830*. New York: St. Martin's Press, 1997.

Nicholson, Colin. *Writing and the Rise of Finance: Capital Satires of the Early Eighteenth Century*. Cambridge: Cambridge University Press, 1994.

Nietzsche, Friedrich. *The Will to Power*. Trans. by Walter Kaufmann and R. J. Hollingdale. New York: Random House, 1968.

Nussbaum, Martha. *Upheavals of Thought: The Intelligence of Emotions*. Cambridge: Cambridge University Press, 2001.

Ong, Walter J. *The Presence of the Word: Some Prolegomena for Cultural and Religious History*. New Haven: Yale University Press, 1967.

Ong, Walter J. *Orality and Literacy: The Technologizing of the Word*. London:

Routledge, 1982.

Ong, Walter J. "The Shifting Sensorium," in *The Varieties of Sensory Experience: A Sourcebook in the Anthropology of the Senses*. Ed. by David Howes. Toronto: The University of Toronto Press, 1991: 25-30.

Ong, Walter J. *Ramus, Method, and the Decay of Dialogue: From the Art of Discourse to the Art of Reason*. Chicago: The University of Chicago Press, 2005.

Paine, Thomas. *Rights of Man*. Harmondsworth: Penguin, 1984.

Pang, Laikwan. "The Pictorial Turn: Realism, Modernity and China's Print Culture in the Late Nineteenth Century," in *Visual Studies*, 2005, 20 (1): 19-21.

Pang, Laikwan. *The Distorting Mirror: Visual Modernity in China.* Honolulu: The University of Hawaii Press, 2007.

Park, Roy. "*Ut Pictura Poesis*: The Nineteenth Century Aftermath," in *Journal of Aesthetic and Art Criticism*, 1969, 28: 155-164.

Parrish, Stephen Maxfield. *The Art of the "Lyrical Ballads."* Cambridge, Mass.: Harvard University Press, 1973.

Pascal, Roy. *Design and Truth in Autobiography*. Cambridge, Mass.: Harvard University Press, 1960.

Paulson, Ronald. *Representations of Revolution*. New Haven: Yale University Press, 1983.

Paulson, Ronald. *The Beautiful, Novel, and Strange: Aesthetics and Heterodoxy*. Baltimore: The Johns Hopkins University Press, 1996.

Percy, Thomas. *Reliques of Ancient English Poetry, Consisting of Old Heroic Ballads, Songs, and Other Pieces of Our Earlier Poets, Together with Some Few of Later Date* (3 vols., 1765). Ed. by Henry B. Wheatley, 1886; reprint, New York: Dover, 1996.

Pinch, Adela. *Strange Fits of Passion: Epistemologies of Emotion, Hume to Austen*. Stanford: Stanford University Press, 1996.

Piper, H. W. *The Active Universe*. London: Athlone, 1962.

Pittock, Murray. *Celtic Identity and the British Image*. Manchester: Manchester University Press, 2000.

Plumb, John H., Neil McKendrick, and John Brewer. *The Birth of a Consumer Society: The Commercialization of Eighteenth-Century England*. Bloomington: Indiana University Press, 1982.

Pocock, J. G. A. *Virtue, Commerce, and History: Essays on Political Thought and History, Chiefly in the Eighteenth Century*. Cambridge: Cambridge University Press, 1985.

Pocock, J. G. A. "Adam Smith and History," in *The Cambridge Companion to Adam Smith*. Ed. by Knud Haakonssen. Cambridge: Cambridge University Press, 2006: 270-287.

Pollock, Sheldon. "Indian in the Vernacular Millennium: Literary Culture and Polity, 1000—1500," in *Daedalus*, 1998a, 127 (3): 41-74.

Pollock, Sheldon. "The Cosmopolitan Vernacular" in *Journal of Asian Studies*, 1998b, 57 (1): 6-37.

Poovey, Mary. *A History of the Modern Fact*. Chicago: The University of Chicago Press, 1998.

Porter, David L. "A Peculiar but Uninteresting Nation: China and the Discourse of Commerce in Eighteenth-Century England," in *Eighteenth-Century Studies*, 2000, 33 (22): 181-199.

Porter, David L. *Ideographia: The Chinese Cipher in Early Modern Europe*. Stanford: Stanford University Press, 2001.

Porter, Roy. *Flesh in the Age of Reason*. London: Penguin Books, 2005.

Pratt, Mary Louise. *Imperial Eyes: Travel Writing and Transculturation*. New York: Routledge, 1992.

Rai, Amit S. *Rule of Sympathy: Sentiment, Race, and Power, 1750—1850*. New York: Palgrave, 2002.

Rancière, Jacques. *The Politics of Aesthetic: The Distribution of the Sensible*. Trans. with an Introduction by Gabriel Rockhill. London: Continuum, 2004.

Raphael, D. D., and A. L. Macfie. "Introduction." in *The Theory of Moral Sentiments*. Ed. by D. D. Raphael and A. L. Macfie. Indianapolis: Liberty Fund, 1984: 1-52.

Raven, James. "The Book Trades," in *Books and Their Readers in Eighteenth Century England: New Essays*. Ed. by Isabel Rivers. London: Leicester University Press, 2001: 1-34.

Rawski, Evelyn. *Education and Popular Literacy in Ch'ing China*. Ann Arbor: The University of Michigan Press, 1979.

Redfield, Marc. *Phantom Formations: Aesthetic Ideology and the Bildungsroman*. Ithaca: Cornell University Press, 1996.

Reiss, Timothy J. *The Discourse of Modernism*. Ithaca: Cornell University Press,

1982.

Richardson, Samuel. *Pamela, or Virtue Rewarded.* New York: W. W. Norton, 1958.

Richards, Thomas. *Imperial Archive: Knowledge and the Fantasy of Empire*. London: Verso, 1993.

Rogers, Nicholas. "Policing the Poor in Eighteenth-Century London: The Vagrancy Laws and Their Administration," in *Histoire sociale / Social History*, 1991, 24: 127-147.

Rorty, Richard. *Philosophy and the Mirror of Nature*. 30th anniversary ed. Princeton: Princeton University Press, 2009.

Rose, Mark. *Authors and Owners: The Invention of Copyright*. Cambridge, Mass.: Harvard University Press, 1993.

Ross, Marlon. *The Contours of Masculine Desire: Romanticism and the Rise of Women's Poetry*. New York: Oxford University Press, 1989.

Rousseau, G. S. "Nerves, Spirits, and Fibres: Towards Defining the Origins of Sensibility," in *Studies in the Eighteenth Century III: Papers Presented at the Third David Nichol Smith Memorial Seminar, Canberra 1973*. Ed. by R.F. Brissenden and J.C. Eade. Canberra: Australian National University Press, 1996.

Royce, Josiah. "Psychological Reasons for Lessing's Attitude toward Descriptive Poetry," in *PMLA*, 1911, xxvi: 593-603.

Schaffer, Simon, and Steven Shapin. *Leviathan and the Air-Pump*. Princeton: Princeton University Press, 1989.

Schor, Esther. *Bearing the Dead: The British Culture of Mourning from the Enlightenment to Victoria*. Princeton: Princeton University Press, 1994.

Scott, Walter. *The Lay of the Last Minstrel*. London: Harles Daly, 1835.

Scott, Walter. *Lives of the Novelists*. London: Everyman, 1910.

Shaftesbury, Anthony Ashley Cooper, Third Earl of. *Characteristics of Men, Manners, Opinions, Times*. Ed. by Lawrence E. Klein. Cambridge: Cambridge University Press, 1999.

Shang, Wei. "The Making of the Everyday World: *Jin Ping Mei Cihua* and Encyclopedias for Daily Use," in *Dynastic Crisis and Cultural Innovation from the Late Ming to the Late Qing and Beyond*. Ed. by David Der-wei Wang. Cambridge, Mass.: Harvard University Press, 2006: 63-92.

Shearer, Edna Aston. "Wordsworth and Coleridge Marginalia in a Copy of

Richard Payne Knight's *Analytical Inquiry into the Principles of Taste*," in *Huntington Library Quarterly*, 1937 (1): 73.

Shih, Shu-mei. *Visuality and Identity: Sinophone Articulations Across the Pacific*. Berkeley: The University of California Press, 2007.

Silverstein, Michael. "Metapragmatic Discourse and Metapragmatic Function," in *Reflexive Language: Reported Speech and Metapragmatics*. Ed. by John A. Lucy. Cambridge: Cambridge University Press, 1993: 33-58.

Simpson, David. *Romanticism, Nationalism, and the Revolt against Theory*. Chicago: The University of Chicago Press, 1993.

Siskin, Clifford. *The Historicity of Romantic Discourse*. Oxford: Oxford University Press, 1988.

Siskin, Clifford. *The Work of Writing: Literature and Social Change in Britain, 1700—1830*. Baltimore: The Johns Hopkins University Press, 1999.

Siskin, Clifford, and William Warner. *This Is Enlightenment*. Chicago: The University of Chicago Press, 2010.

Smith, Adam. *Essays on Philosophical Subjects*. Oxford: Oxford University Press, 1980.

Smith, Adam. *Lectures on Rhetoric and Belles Lettres*. Oxford: Clarendon Press, 1983.

Smith, Adam. *The Theory of Moral Sentiments*. Indianapolis: Liberty Fund, 1984.

Smith, Adam. *The Wealth of Nations*. Intro. by Robert Reich. New York: The Modern Library, 2000.

Smith, Elsie. *An Estimate of William Wordsworth by His Contemporaries 1793—1822*. Oxford: Blackwell, 1932.

Smith, Olivia. *Politics of Language, 1790—1819*. Oxford: Oxford University Press, 1986.

Smollett, Tobias. *The Adventures of Ferdinand Count Fathom*. Ed. with an Introduction and Notes by Paul-Gabriel Boucé. Harmondsworth, UK: Penguin Classics, 1990.

St Clair, William. *The Reading Nation in the Romantic Period*. Cambridge: Cambridge University Press, 2007.

Stein, Gertrude. *Everybody's Autobiography*. New York: Cooper Square Publishers, 1971.

Stephens, Mitchell. *A History of News*. 3rd ed. New York: Oxford University Press, 2007.

Sterne, Laurence. *The Life and Opinions of Tristram Shandy (1759—1767)*. Ed. by Melvyn New and Joan New. Vols. 1-2 in the Florida Edition of the Works of Laurence Sterne. Gainesville: University Press of Florida, 1978.

Stewart, Dugald. *Elements of the Philosophy of the Human Mind*, Part I [1792], reprinted in *The Collected Works of Dugald Stewart*. Ed. by William Hamilton. 11 vols. Edinburgh: T. Constable and Co., 1854—1860.

Stewart, Susan. "Notes on Distressed Genres," in *The Journal of American Folklore*, 1991, 104 (41): 5-31.

Stewart-Robertson, J. C., and David F. Norton, "Thomas Reid on Adam Smith's Theory of Morals," in *Journal of the History of Ideas*, 1980, 41: 381-398, and 1984, 45: 309-321.

Stillman, Robert E. *The New Philosophy and Universal Language in Seventeenth-Century England: Bacon, Hobbes and Wilkins*. Cranbury: Associated University Press, 1995.

Stolnitz, Jerome. "On the Origins of 'Aesthetic Disinterestedness,'" in *The Journal of Aesthetics and Art Criticism*, 1961, 20 (2): 131-143.

Suter, J. F. "Burke, Hegel, and the French Revolution," in *Hegel's Political Philosophy—Problems and Perspectives*. Ed. by Z. A. Pelczynski. Cambridge: Cambridge University Press, 1971: 52-72.

Swann, Karen. "Public Transport: Adventuring on Wordsworth's Salisbury Plain," in *ELH*, 1988, 55 (4): 533-553.

Taylor, Charles. "Inwardness and the Culture of Modernity," in *Philosophical Interventions in the Unfinished Project of Enlightenment*. Ed. by Axel Honneth, Thomas McCarthy, Claus Offe, et al. Trans. by William Rehg. Cambridge, Mass.: The MIT Press, 1992: 88-112.

Taylor, Charles. "Conditions of an Unforced Consensus on Human Rights," in *The East Asian Challenge for Human Rights*. Eds. by Joanne R. Bauer and Daniel A. Bell. Cambridge: Cambridge University Press, 1999: 124-146.

Taylor, Charles. *A Secular Age*. Cambridge, Mass.: Belknap Press, 2007.

Terada, Rei. *Feeling in Theory: Emotion after the "Death of the Subject."* Cambridge, Mass.: Harvard University Press, 2001.

Tiffany, Daniel. *Toy Medium: Materialism and Modern Lyric*. Berkeley: The University of California Press, 2000.

Todd, Janet. *Sensibility: An Introduction*. London: Routledge, 1986.

Toulmin, Stephen. "The Inwardness of Mental Life," in *Critical Inquiry*, 1979, 6

(1): 1-16.

Trilling, Lionel. *Sincerity and Authenticity*. Cambridge, Mass.: Harvard University Press, 1972.

Trotter, Thomas. "A View of the Nervous Temperament: Being a Practical Enquiry into the Increasing Prevalence, Prevention and Treatment of Those Diseases, 2nd ed. (Newcastle, 1807)," in *Radical Food: The Culture and Politics of Eating and Drinking 1790–1820*. 3 vols. Ed. by Timothy Morton. London: Routledge, 2000.

Veblen, Thorstein. *The Theory of the Leisure Class*. New York: McMillan, 1899.

Vinograd, Richard. *Boundaries of the Self: Chinese Portraits, 1600—1900*, Cambridge: Cambridge University Press, 1992.

Voltaire. *Philosophical Dictionary*. Ed. and trans. by Theodore Besterman. New York: Penguin, 1972.

Von Mücke, Dorothea. *Virtue and the Veil of Illusion: Generic Innovation and the Pedagogical Project in the Eighteenth-Century Literature*. Stanford: Stanford University Press, 1991.

Wagner, Rudolf G.《进入全球想象图景：上海的〈点石斋画报〉》("Jinru quanqiu xiangxiang tujing: Shanghai de *Dianshizhai huabao*) ["Joining the Global Imaginary: the *Dianshizhai Pictorial* in Shanghai"], in《中国学术》(*Zhongguo xueshu*) [*Chinese Scholarship*], 2001, 2 (4): 1-96.

Walpole, Horace. *The Castle of Otranto, a Gothic Story*. New York: Oxford University Press, 1996.

Wang, David Der-wei. *Fin-de-Siècle Splendor: Repressed Modernities of Late Qing Fiction, 1849—1911*. Stanford: Stanford University Press, 1997.

Wang, Ermin 王尔敏.《近代文化生态及其变迁》(*Jindai wenhua shengtai jiqi bianqian*) [*Cultural Ecology of Modern Times and Its Changes*]. Nanchang: Baihuazhou wenyi chubanshe, 2002.

Wang, Eugene Y. "Sketch Conceptualism as Modernism Contingency," in *Chinese Art: Modern Expression*. Ed. by Maxwell K. Hearn and Judith G. Smith. New York: The Metropolitan Museum of Art, 2001: 60-101.

Warner, William. *Licensing Entertainment: The Elevation of Novel Reading in Britain, 1684—1750*. Berkeley: The University of California Press, 1998.

Wasserman, Earl R. "The Pleasures of Tragedy," in *ELH*, 1947, 14: 283-307.

Watt, Ian, and Jack Goody. "The Consequences of Literacy," in *Literacy in Traditional Societies*. Ed. by Jack Goody. Cambridge: Cambridge University

Press, 1968: 27-68.

Weber, Samuel. *Mass Mediauras: Form, Technics, Media*. Stanford: Stanford University Press, 1996.

Weber, Samuel. "The Virtuality of the Media," in *Contemporary French and Francophone Studies*, 2000, 4 (2): 297-317.

Weber, Samuel. *Theatricality as Medium*. New York: Fordham University Press, 2004.

Wecter, Dixon. "The Missing Years in Burke's Biography" in *PMLA*, 1938, 53 (4): 1102-1205.

Wecter, Dixon. "Burke's Theory concerning Words, Images, and Emotion," in *PMLA*, 1940, 55 (1): 167-181.

Wellbery, David E. *Lessing's "Laocoon": Semiotics and Aesthetic in the Age of Reason*. London: Cambridge University Press, 1984.

Wellbery, David E. "Forward," in Friedrich A. Kittler. *Discourse Networks, 1800/1900*. Trans. by Micheal Metteer, with Chris Cullens. Stanford: Stanford University Press, 1990: vii-xxxiii.

Whytt, Robert. *Observations on the Nature, Causes, and Cure of those Disorders which have been commonly call'd Nervous, Hypochondriac, or Hysteric*. Edinburgh: J. Balfour, 1765.

Wilde, Oscar. *The Soul of Man Under Socialism and Selected Critical Prose*. Harmondsworth: Penguin, 2001.

Williams, Raymond. *Culture and Society*. New York: Columbia University Press, 1958.

Williams, Raymond. *Keywords: A Vocabulary of Culture and Society*. Rev. ed. New York: Oxford University Press, 1976.

Williams, Raymond. *Marxism and Literature*. New York: Oxford University Press, 1977.

Williams, Raymond. "Means of Communication as Means of Production," in *Problems in Materialism and Culture: Selected Essays*. London: NLB, 1980: 50-63.

Williams, Raymond. *Writing in Society*. Verso, 1983.

Wilson, Kathleen. *The Sense of the People: Politics, Culture and Imperialism in England, 1715—1785*. Cambridge: Cambridge University Press, 1998.

Wlecke, Albert O. *Wordsworth and the Sublime*. Berkeley: The University of California Press, 1973.

Wollstonecraft, Mary. *A Vindication of the Rights of Men*. London: Printed for J. Johnson, 1790.

Wood, Gillen D'Arcy. *The Shock of the Real: Romanticism and Visual Culture, 1760—1860*. New York: Palgrave Macmillan, 2001.

Woodmansee, Martha. *Author, Art and the Market: Rereading the History of Aesthetics*. New York: Columbia University Press, 1996.

Wordsworth, Jonathan. *The Music of Humanity: A Critical Study of Wordsworth's "Ruined Cottage"; Incorporating Texts from a Manuscript of 1799—1800*. New York: Harper & Row, 1969.

Wordsworth, William. *The Poetical Works of William Wordsworth*. 5 vols. Oxford: Clarendon Press, 1952—1959.

Wordsworth, William. *The Prose Works of William Wordsworth*. 3 vols. Oxford: Clarendon Press, 1974.

Wordsworth, William. *"The Ruined Cottage" and "The Pedlar."* Ithaca: Cornell University Press, 1979a.

Wordsworth, William. *The Prelude: 1799, 1805, 1850*. New York: Norton, 1979b.

Wordsworth, William. *Poems, in Two Volumes, and Other Poems, 1800—1807*. Ithaca: Cornell University Press, 1983.

Wordsworth, William. *Early Poems and Fragments, 1785—1797*. Ithaca: Cornell University Press, 1997.

Wordsworth, William, and Samuel T. Coleridge. *Lyrical Ballads*. London: Oxford University Press, 2006.

Wordsworth, William, and Dorothy Wordsworth. *The Letters of William and Dorothy Wordsworth*. 3 vols. 2d ed. Oxford: Clarendon, 1970.

Worringer, Wilhelm. *Abstraction and Empathy: A Contribution to the Psychology of Style*. Trans. by Michael Bullock. New York: International Universities Press, Inc., 1953.

Wu, Duncan. *Romanticism: An Anthology*. 3rd ed. Oxford: Blackwell Publishing, 1994.

Wu, Jianren 吴趼人.《二十年目睹之怪现状》(*Ershinian mudu zhi guaixianzhuang*) [*The Strange State of the World Witnessed over Twenty Years*]. Beijing: Renmin wenxue chubanshe, 2000.

Wu, Meifeng 吴美凤.《从〈点石斋画报〉看晚清时期的民间信仰意识》("Cong *Dianshizhai huabao* kan wanqing de minjian xinyang yishi") ["Folk

Belief and Mentality in Late Qing through an Analysis of the *Dianshizhai*"], in《台湾历史博物馆馆刊》(*Taiwan lishi bowuguan guankan*) [*Proceedings of the Taiwan Historical Museum*]. 2000 (2): 1-10.

Xia, Xiaohong 夏晓虹.《觉世与传世——梁启超的文学道路》(*Jueshi yu chuanshi: Liang Qichao's wenxue daolu*) [*To Enlighten the World and to Be Valuable for Posterity: Liang Qichao's Literary Career*]. Beijing: Zhonghua shuju, 2006.

Xiong, Yuezhi 熊月之, and Zhang Min 张敏.《上海通史・晚清文化》(*Shanghai tongshi Wanqing wenhua*) [*A Survey History of Shanghai: Late Qing Culture*]. Shanghai: Shanghai renmin chubanshe, 1999.

Xu, Jilin 许纪霖.《中国知识分子十论》(*Zhongguo zhishi fenzi shilun*) [*Ten Essays on Chinese Intellectuals*]. Shanghai: Fudan daxue chubanshe, 2004.

Yates, F. "Bacon and the Menace of English Lit.," in *New York Review of Books*, 27 March 1969.

Ye, Kaidi 叶凯蒂.《哪里是上海》("Nali shi Shanghai?") ["Where was Shanghai?"], in《二十一世纪》(*Ershiyishiji*) [*Twenty-first Century*], 1998, 48 (June): 72-88.

Ye, Xiaoqing. *The Dianshizhai Pictorial: Shanghai Urban Life, 1884—1898*. Ann Arbor: Center for Chinese Studies, 2003.

Yeh, Catherine Vance. "Creating the Urban Beauty: The Shanghai Courtesan in Late Qing Illustrations," in *Writing and Materiality in China: Essays in Honor of Patrick Hanan*. Ed. by Judith T. Zeitlin and Lydia H. Liu. Cambridge, Mass.: Harvard University Asia Center, 2003.

Yeh, Catherine Vance. *Shanghai Love: Courtesans, Intellectuals, and Entertainment Culture, 1850—1910*. Seattle: The University of Washington Press, 2006

Yeo, Richard. "Classifying the Sciences." in *The Cambridge History of Science: Eighteenth Century Science*. Ed. by Roy Porter. Cambridge: Cambridge University Press, 2003: 241-266.

Zhang, Zhen. *An Amorous History of the Silver Screen: Shanghai Cinema, 1896—1937*. Chicago: The University of Chicago Press, 2005.

Zheng, Yimei 郑逸梅.《上海的画报潮》("Shanghai de huabaochao") ["Waves of Pictorials in Shanghai"], in《书报旧话》(*Shubao jiuhua*) [*Stories of Old Times Regarding Books and Newspapers*]. Shanghai: Xuelin chubanshe, 1983.

Zheng, Zhenduo 郑振铎.《郑振铎艺术考古文集》(*Zheng Zhenduo yishu kaogu wenji*) [*Collected Essays on Art and Archaeology by Zheng Zhenduo*]. Beijing: Wenwu chubanshe, 1988.

Index

H

L

M

N

O

P

后　记

这本书是在我博士论文的基础上修改而成的，其中论述了现代文学素养机制的形成。这涉及现代意义上个体感觉感官和意识的形成、整个书写体制的建立、现代知识生产体制的产生，以及帝国和全球化的问题。我将这些放到英国漫长的 18 世纪的背景中进行讨论，同时在最后一章试图进行一项初步的具有比较视野的研究。这整个的问题谱系来自非常个人化的因素。长期以来，我一直对“自我反思”“剧场性”与现代情感形式的起源着迷，也一直关心普遍与地方之间的张力转换中个体的变化形式。在本书中，这些问题是与现代“印刷文化”的形成并置在一起进行讨论的。其他更个人化的缘起，这里就不再赘述了。

论文的写作是在美国纽约州进行的，记录了我生命之中一段离散（diasporic）的岁月。因此，我很珍惜它。自然，现在想来，生活在晚期资本主义时代的我们，离散何尝不是一种常态？我们的学术工作能帮助我们寻回曾经的家园吗？我常常很困惑，也很彷徨。也许，这种状态是朝向未来的一种看起来并不那么明朗的方式发展。

书稿付梓之际，我依然坚持原论文中的诸多观点，并会在将来的学术工作中继续其中某些方向的研究。与此同时，随着生活地点等的变化，我也会开始以新的方式，思考新的问题。

本书原来的标题是《情感与书写》（*Emotion and the Work of Writing*），在其将要完成时，我遇到了刘璐，我的爱人。书写的工作以爱的形式绽放，没有比这更有意义的了！

图书在版编目(CIP)数据

情感美学与近代文本文化的兴起：英国漫长的18世纪文学文化研究 / 姜文涛著. —杭州：浙江大学出版社，2018.9(2019.9重印)
ISBN 978-7-308-18352-9

Ⅰ.①情… Ⅱ.①姜… Ⅲ.①英国文学-文学研究-1689-1850 Ⅳ.①I561.094

中国版本图书馆CIP数据核字(2018)第128809号

情感美学与近代文本文化的兴起
英国漫长的18世纪文学文化研究
姜文涛 著

责任编辑 诸葛勤
责任校对 於国娟 袁菁鸿
封面设计 周 灵
出版发行 浙江大学出版社
(杭州市天目山路148号 邮政编码310007)
(网址：http://www.zjupress.com)
排　　版 杭州时代出版服务有限公司
印　　刷 虎彩印艺股份有限公司
开　　本 880 mm×1230 mm 1/32
印　　张 10.25
字　　数 445千
版 印 次 2018年9月第1版 2019年9月第2次印刷
书　　号 ISBN 978-7-308-18352-9
定　　价 48.00元

浙江大学出版社市场运营中心联系方式 (0571)88925591；http://zjdxcbs.tmall.com